LET THE
DEAD
BURY THEIR
DEAD

Also by Randall Kenan:

A VISITATION OF SPIRITS (1989)

Randall Kenan

LET THE DEAD BURY THEIR DEAD

AND OTHER STORIES

Harcourt Brace Jovanovich, Publishers

New York   San Diego   London

Excerpt from *Pale Horse, Pale Rider* copyright 1937 and renewed 1965 by Katherine Anne Porter, reprinted by permission of Harcourt Brace Jovanovich, Inc.

"The Archaic Torso" from *The Selected Poetry of Rainer Maria Rilke* by Rainer
Maria Rilke, translated by Stephen Mitchell, copyright 1982 by Stephen Mitchell.
Reprinted by permission of Random House, Inc.

"Let's Stay Together" words and music by Al Green, Al Jackson, Jr., and Willie
Mitchell copyright © 1971 Irving Music, Inc. (BMI). All rights reserved.
International copyright secured.

For "This Far; or, A Body in Motion," the author makes grateful acknowledg-
ment to Louis R. Harlan's *Booker T. Washington: The Making of a Black Leader,
1856–1901* and *Booker T. Washington: The Wizard of Tuskegee, 1901–1915* (Oxford);
and to Washington's own *Up from Slavery*.

Library of Congress Cataloging-in-Publication Data
Kenan, Randall.
Let the dead bury their dead and other stories/Randall Kenan.—
1st ed.
p.   cm.
Contents: Clarence *and* The dead—Things of this world; or, Angels unawares—
The foundations of the earth—The origin of whales—Cornsilk—The strange
and tragic ballad of Mabel Pearsall—This far; or, A body in motion—Run,
mourner, run—What are days?—Ragnarök! The day the gods die—Tell me,
tell me—Let the dead bury their dead.
ISBN 0-15-149886-5
1. North Carolina—Fiction. I. Title.
PS3561.E4228L48   1992
813'.54—dc20   91-36179

Designed by Trina Stahl
Printed in the United States of America
First edition
A B C D E

ACKNOWLEDGMENTS

For financial and artistic support:
The MacDowell Colony, Inc;
the New York Foundation for the Arts;
and Columbia's Center for Cultural Studies.

Overflowing gratitude to Eric Ashworth
for having faith.
And to Alane Salierno Mason
for her surpassing editorial skill,
saintlike patience,
and the tenacious cajoling
of a boxing trainer.

CONTENTS

Granite walls, whirlpools, stars are things. None of them is death, nor the image of it. Death is death, said Miranda, and for the dead it has no attributes. Silenced she sank easily through deeps under deeps of darkness until she lay like a stone at the farthest bottom of life, knowing herself to be blind, deaf, speechless, no longer aware of the members of her own body, entirely withdrawn from all human concerns, yet alive with a peculiar lucidity and coherence; all notions of the mind, the reasonable inquiries of doubt, all ties of blood and the desires of the heart, dissolved and fell away from her, and there remained of her only a minute fiercely burning particle of being that knew itself alone, that relied upon nothing beyond itself for its strength; not susceptible to any appeal or inducement, being itself composed entirely of one single motive, the stubborn will to live. This fiery motionless particle set itself unaided to resist destruction, to survive and to be its own madness of being, motiveless and planless beyond that one essential end. Trust me, the hard unwinking angry point of light said. Trust me. I stay.

Pale Horse, Pale Rider
KATHERINE ANNE PORTER

LET THE
DEAD
BURY THEIR
DEAD

CLARENCE AND THE DEAD

(AND WHAT DO
THEY TELL YOU, CLARENCE?
AND THE DEAD
SPEAK TO CLARENCE)

ON THE DAY CLARENCE Pickett died, Wilma Jones's hog Francis stopped talking. Now of course no one else had ever heard the swine utter word the first, but Wilma swore up and down that the creature had first said to her "Jesus wept" on a sunny day in June. But the peculiar thing was that Wilma had not known of Clarence's death when she declared the hog's final hushing up; and oddly enough it was on the exact day of Clarence's birth, five years before, that Wilma had commenced preaching that the hog could talk.

They say that day the sun shone while the rain poured—the old folk say that's when the devil beats his wife—the day Estelle Pickett died giving birth to Clarence. Her mama was out in the cucumber patch when Estelle went into labor and we came to get her—Miss

I

Eunice, not being an excitable woman, asked if the midwife had been sent for and when we said yeah, she insisted on topping off her bushel before heading home. Estelle's papa, Mr. George Edward, was away in Wilmington that day looking for a new tractor since he was sick and tired of his old Farmall breaking down every other row and needing more oil than gasoline.

We never knew if Miss Eunice blamed herself, cause she never admitted to it, one, and two we never saw much sign that she did. We all arrived at the Pickett place at the same time as the midwife. We walked in on one of the most hideous sights we can remember seeing or hearing tell of: there lay Estelle on the bed, her legs apart, her eyes rolled back in her head, her body kind of twisted to the side in a pool so deep red it could have been a maroon sheet she was sitting on instead of white; and on the floor squalling like a stuck pig was Clarence, a twitching, pitiful little thing, in a soup of blood and purple mess and shit. There wont no caul to worry about being over his face as people came to gossip. Just not so. The caul seemed to be everywhere else though, on his head, on his hands, on his belly like a raw liver, quivery and oozy, him coated in a mucky white paste like snot. A nasty enough mess to make you lose your breakfast. Miss Eunice went to fix him up straightaway and the midwife looked to Estelle.

"She's gone, child. Poor thing," she said.

"Well . . ." Miss Eunice didn't say anything else, but that "Well . . ." seemed to say everything and nothing. She handed the baby to the midwife to cut and tuck his stem. (Folk who said he didn't have a belly button just don't know what they're talking about, cause we saw it knotted.)

That summer turned out to be a mild one—only a few days over a hundred. And ever since that day back in June folk had been wondering if we should take it upon ourselves to have Wilma committed and her talking hog butchered proper, seeing as she didn't have any children to see after her. But we left her alone, saying that all that meanness she had had all her life and all that insurance money she'd collected from two husbands and all that land they left her had come back to visit her in the form of a hallucination about a talking hog which she'd collar folk to come hear, only to be met by an occasional grunt or squeal, them scratching their noggins and casting sideways glances at Wilma, feeling a little sorry for her but not daring to say a word since she may well of kicked them out of their houses or called in mortgages they owed her. So when she took the damn thing into her house, making it a canopy bed with frills and ruffles, feeding it topshelf Purina Hog Chow, along with Spanish omelettes and tuna casserole (she forbore to give it pork cause that would be cannibalism, of course), we didn't say a thing other than "Oh that's nice, Wilma," and rolled our eyes.

Nothing much happened to point out that Clarence was different, not until that summer three years later when he began to talk, the day Ed Phelps found him out in his cow pasture surrounded by buzzards and talking in complete sentences. Of course folk said they knew of strange thises and thats to have occurred in hindsight, but we didn't believe none of it cause we hadn't heard tell of any of it at the time; we didn't believe anything except what happened after he turned three and commenced to talk, which we did believe cause we were witness to most of it—unlikely though it seems.

But Ed Phelps found him that day—some claim it was the exact same day of Clarence's third birthday, but we couldn't seem to come to an agreement after the fact, seeing as nobody had thought to note it down—after Miss Eunice and Mr. George Edward had like to gone crazy looking for the boy. They were already perturbed, understandably, over the child since, at near on three years, he hadn't yet said a blessed word, and neither Miss Eunice, nor Mr. George Edward for that matter, was too keen on having a retarded heir, seeing as Estelle had been their last living child—Henry, the oldest, died in Korea, and Frederick, who called himself Long John, had died in a shoot-out in Detroit. So when the child disappeared, its leave-taking allowed them to give vent to a whole slew of emotions these normally buttoned-down folk kept under their hats. About six hours after they'd searched and called and hollered, having the whole town in a fit to find the child, Ed drove up into Miss Eunice and Mr. George Edward's yard with Clarence in his arms. The toddler ran to Miss Eunice and hollered, "Miss Eunice, Miss Eunice." She just looked at the boy, her eyes big as Mr. George Edward's, who asked Ed where he found the boy. Ed said he'd come out on his porch after his after-dinner catnap and heard this awful fuss coming from the side of the house. He went to investigate, he said, and came to see seven or eight buzzards playing—that was the word he used—playing with little Clarence Pickett. All the cows were at the other end of the pasture avoiding the birds. Said he went and got his shotgun and fired but the scavengers didn't pay him no notice, so he shot one of them through the neck—had to shoot the damn thing again to kill it—and the others took off hopping and tripping and stumbling into the air.

When they asked Clarence what he was doing in the cow pasture and how he got there and a whole other passel of questions, he just smiled and grinned possumlike. And just as Ed Phelps was about to leave, Clarence turned to Miss Eunice with all the innocence and seriousness you're apt to see on the face of a three-year-old and asked: "Why'd he kill it, Miss Eunice?" Of course she didn't answer him; of course she didn't know how to answer him. The look on her face seemed only to ask for peace.

Yet it seemed the end of peace in that house. Even though Clarence still sucked on his bottle he could and would talk to Miss Eunice and Mr. George Edward like an adult. We had to admire the two of them cause where it would of spooked some into their graves they took it all in stride. But people will accept some pretty outrageous behavior from their own blood, and after all it was just talking. But it wont the talking itself that caused the problem: it was what he said.

One time Emma Chaney stopped by to say hey to Miss Eunice and Mr. George Edward and just before she left Clarence walked into the room and said: "Your mama says Joe Hattan is stepping out on you with that strumpet Viola Stokes." Well, everybody was shocked and embarrassed and Mr. George Edward took a switch to Clarence telling him he shouldn't say such things to grownfolks, and all the while Clarence yelled through his tears: "But Miss Ruella told me to tell her." "Boy, quit your lying," Mr. George Edward said through his teeth. "Miss Ruella been dead." Mr. George Edward gave Clarence a few extra licks for lying, all the while wondering how on earth the boy'd come to know about a woman long dead before Clarence was even thought about.

Well, come to find out—seems Emma's curiosity was piqued and she followed Hattan on the sly—that her husband *was* cheating on her with that low-down Viola Stokes. Emma had a bullwhip of her daddy's and went into the house right on the spot and lashed the both of them good-fashioned. Viola got out her pistol and—not being a good shot—got Hattan in the hind parts.

Emma went straight back to Mr. George Edward and Miss Eunice wanting to know how the boy knew, and when he said Miss Ruella told him Mr. George Edward took the switch to him again.

Of course it didn't stop there. Clarence would tell people who happened by the Pickett place that this or that person was out to get them; that this woman was going to have twins; that that man had prostate cancer; that that woman's husband intended to give her a cruise for their wedding anniversary. He was good for getting up in the morning and announcing: "Such and such a person's going to die today," or "Such and such a person died last night." He told one person where they put an old insurance policy they'd lost, another where they mislaid their keys. Most folk came to avoid going by Miss Eunice and Mr. George Edward's house if they could, and prayed they wouldn't bring along Clarence when they came a-calling.

One green May day Mabel Pearsall stopped by to give Miss Eunice a mess of mustard greens. As they sat gossiping over a glass of lemonade in the kitchen, Clarence walked in clutching his soldier-doll. "Mr. Joe Allen wants a apple pie tonight," he said to Mabel the way an old woman coaches a new bride. "He been wanting one for months. You ought to make it for him."

Mabel laughed nervous-like and looked to Miss Eunice for help, who shooed Clarence away with a broom, presently turning to admit to Mabel: "I just don't know what to do with that boy." Mabel left not long after that.

On the way home Mabel stopped by McTarr's Grocery Store and got fixings for a pie—she said she wont paying any mind to that crazy boy, just had a craving for one, she said; but who could believe her? She baked the pie and her husband Joe Allen ate it without a word; and Mabel *harrumphed* and washed the dishes and went to bed laughing at herself and that strange boy, thinking she should tell Miss Eunice to be harder on him in the future. But that night, she said, she had a dream, and in the dream she dreamt that Joe Allen had come home and she hadn't baked the pie and in the middle of supper they had an argument and Joe Allen up and left her that very night. Mabel said she woke up from that dream in the wee hours of the morning powerfully afeared since the dream had the taste and feel of real life. She went back to sleep, to be waked up not by the rooster but by Joe Allen rocking on top of her, singing in her ear. (She admitted to some of us that he hadn't touched her in a year; though we suspect it had been closer to five, considering Mabel.)

Soon the boy seemed to get more outlandish in his testaments—as if what he'd said before wont outlandish enough. He told Sarah Phillips to stop fretting, that her husband forgave her for the time she tried to stab him with that hunting knife; he told Cleavon Simpson his mama despised him for tricking her to sign all of her property over to him and for putting her in a nursing home; he told Sealey Richards her daddy apologized for the times he tried to have his way with her. Clarence told people things a four-year-old boy ain't had no business knowing the language for, let alone the circumstances around them. All from people dead five, six, ten, twenty, and more years. Secrets people had shared with no living person, much less a boy who could do well to stand and walk at the same time and who refused to give up his bottle. Miss Eunice and Mr. George Edward tried as hard as they could to ignore the boy, to shrug off his testimonials from the grave, but you could see that it preyed on their minds heavily, and it's a wonder they could get to sleep at night in the same house with him. God only knows what all went on in the dark in that old house.

Wilma soon started throwing parties for the Holy Hog Francis (as she'd taken to calling him in mixed company "My Holy Hog"). She'd invite all the little children (except Clarence) and they had ice cream and cake and orange and grape and strawberry soda and little hats, and Francis sat at the head of the table with a hat on, making a mess of his German chocolate cake, and the parties were a great success, and one boy, Perry

Mitchell, came away and somebody asked if he heard
the pig talk, and everybody was amazed cause he said
yes, kind of offhanded-like and unimpressed, and they
asked what did the pig say, and the boy said: "Oink,
oink."

When Clarence was four and a half, folk started
seeing things. Ben Stokes was driving down the road
and saw a white shepherd come up to Clarence in Miss
Eunice and Mr. George Edward's yard—and he said he
didn't think much of it at first but he backed up and
looked again and he said he could swear it was Rickie
Jones's ole dog Sweetpea that got hit by a truck a year
back, and he said the dog had the same ole red collar
on. Ab Batts said he drove by one day and saw Clarence
sitting up in a walnut tree with crows all on the limbs
like black fruit, caw-cawing to beat the band. Hettie
Mae Carr said she saw him swinging in a porch swing
with a woman she swore had to be Mr. George Edward's mother, Miss Maybelle, dead now on twenty-
seven years. G. W. Gillespie said he came to visit one
day and as he knocked at the door he heard a whole
bunch of menfolk talking. He knocked again and Mr.
George Edward came from the side of the house. "You
having a party inside, Mr. George Edward?" "No," said
Mr. George Edward. "Ain't nobody in there but Clarence." When they opened the door, he said, they both
could hear men's voices in the kitchen. Mr. George Edward called out and the voices stopped. They went into
the kitchen and saw six hands of cards set in midgame
of poker, with Clarence sitting at the head of the table
holding a hand. A flush. Mr. George Edward didn't ask
for explanation, just fussed about Clarence knowing

better than to mess with his playing cards and collected them and put them on a high shelf out of the boy's reach. G. W. left right soon after that.

But it was around the time Wilma decided Francis needed to attend regular church services, and argued down the Reverend Barden that the hog should and could attend First Baptist. That's when all hell—or whatever you've a mind to call it—really broke loose.

Seems one day things just didn't want to go right at the Pickett place: Miss Eunice couldn't seem to find her car keys; the refrigerator broke down; the hens didn't lay egg one; the water pump lost pressure; the fuse box blew; plates fell out of the cabinet and broke. But the most curious thing had to do with Clarence. He acted like he was scared to death, Miss Eunice said. He'd cling to Mr. George Edward's leg like he might to be gobbled up any minute. Mr. George Edward and Miss Eunice were so distracted and annoyed by all those other fixes that they were just more bothered by the boy and just didn't think to put two and two together.

Mr. George Edward took Clarence with him to disk the old field over the branch, and riding on the dusty tractor Clarence kept looking back like they were being followed; but when Mr. George Edward would ask what the matter was the boy'd just look at him, not saying a word.

Now after Mr. George Edward had disked up one piece of land—he recollected later that the five-year-new tractor was suddenly giving him the devil with stalling and the hydraulic lifts just wouldn't lift without coaxing—he got tired of Clarence sitting in his lap and put him down at the end of a row and told him to sit out a couple of turns.

The boy pitched a fit, but Mr. George Edward had no intention of giving in, and as he headed back to the tractor Clarence started talking.

"He says he's gone get you, Granddaddy. He says you's a dead man!"

Mr. George Edward turned around, a little spooked. "Who, boy? Who you talking bout?"

"Fitzhugh Oxendine. Fitzhugh Oxendine! He say he gone fix you good, Granddaddy!"

Mr. George Edward was doubly spooked now. Specially seeing as how the five-year-old boy had no way heard tell of ole Fitzhugh Oxendine. Seems when he was a young turk, Mr. George Edward worked laying new track for the railroad all along the southeast of the state. Now among the boys he worked with there was a fellow by the name of Fitzhugh Oxendine from Lumberton, who was just plain bad news. Well, the long and the short of it is that one payday while enjoying the end of the week them boys got themselves into a piece of trouble with a bunch of white sailors in Wilmington. A white boy got bad-off hurt, and Fitzhugh went on the lam. The law was giving them colored boys hell to find Fitzhugh and finally Mr. George Edward broke down and told them where they'd find him. Fitzhugh went to jail and from then on went in and out of the state penitentiary like it had a revolving door. Mr. George Edward said he always did regret doing what he done.

But that day Mr. George Edward just shook his head

and tried to put that hollering boy and his queer knowledge out of his mind and looked onto the lower back
field, which he wanted to finish before dinnertime. He
climbed up on the tractor and put it in gear.

Now a ole John Deere tractor—which is the kind
Mr. George Edward had—if you play the clutch and
the gas and the brake just right, will rear up its front
part just like a horse. Boys round Tims Creek use to do
it all the time to impress folk, pretending they were in
the wild wild west. It's not too likely it'll rear up like
that with a cultivator attached to the back; but it happens. Well, that's what Mr. George Edward's tractor
done that day, he said, and it went higher than he could
ever recollect one going without flipping over—which
happens too—and he fell slam off his seat, onto the
ground, and the tractor kept going and the cultivator
went right over his hand. It didn't slice clean off, but
seeing how he'd just got the cultivator new it was sharp
as the devil and cut into the bone deep. What done the
true damage was the dragging since he couldn't well get
aloose.

The most curious thing happened next. Mr. George
Edward said amidst his agony and yelling for help he
saw through all the tears and dust in his eyes a woman
hop up on the tractor and jerk it to a stop. Wilma Jones
leapt down and pulled Mr. George Edward free. He said
he could hear the bone crack as she got him loose. He
said he couldn't verify for true as he was so overcome
by the pain and the sight of his blood-muddy mangled
hand, but he heard what he thought was Clarence
screaming, and as Wilma got him to his feet and begun
walking him to her station wagon he could tell it wasn't

Clarence at all: it was Francis, caterwauling and squeal-
ing and rolling about and biting in the dirt, like it was
fighting with something or somebody. Mr. George Edward said this brought to his mind the scene from the
Good Book when our Lord cast the demon from the
man and sent it into the swine. Soon the dust was so
thick you couldn't see the hog, only hear it; and after a
while the thing came trotting out with a look like con-
tentment about its face.

"How . . . ?" was about all Mr. George Edward
could utter. Wilma had tied off the hand with her apron
to keep him from bleeding to death.

"Just rest easy now, Mr. George Edward. You gone
be all right. You'll be at York General before you know
it. I can drive this ole Bessie when I got to. Francis took
care of everything else."

Mr. George Edward said he passed out then with
the hog staring at him with them beady eyes, its great
big head stuck over the front seat staring at him, its
frothy slobber drooling on his overalls. When he come
to he found Miss Eunice humming "At the Cross" and
saw that them know-nothing doctors had left him with
a stump instead of a left hand. But all he could think
about was them gray eyes. "Eunice, that hog got eyes
like a human person's."

"Go on back to sleep, George Edward. All hogs do."

We found out a few weeks later that the day before
all this happened Fitzhugh Oxendine had died in Central
Prison.

Well, after that episode if you think folk avoided
Miss Eunice and Mr. George Edward and their grandbaby before, you should of seen how they stayed away

now. From Wilma too, for that matter. And her sacred hog. When she told them the pig had told her Fitzhugh Oxendine was after Mr. George Edward and up to evil business, people whispered a little louder about calling the folks at Dorothea Dix. But after all, she did save Mr. George Edward from his tractor. How did she know? Probably just happened by, we said. Paying no mind to the fact that you didn't "just happen by" a field a mile off a secondary road.

Of course we all hear and all have heard tell about children born with a sixth sense or clairvoyance or ESP or some such, out of the mouths of babes and all that, but, we being good, commonsensical, level-headed, churchgoing folk, we didn't have no truck with such nonsense and third-hand tales. But the evidence kept accumulating and accumulating till you'd have to be deaf, dumb, blind, and stupid to whistle, nod your head, and turn away. But that's exactly what most of us did anyhow. Ain't it strange how people behave?

Some folk didn't ignore it though. Those full of the Holy Ghost preached against the boy, and at a Pentecostal revival meeting one preacher, after a round of prayers for the souls of Mr. George Edward and Miss Eunice, said the boy ought to be bound to a stake and burnt or left on a dry riverbed for the devil to claim his own. (Oddly, he didn't mention the hog Francis, who was at that moment attending prayer meeting at First Baptist.) Dead chickens and blood on the doorpost became regular morning greetings at the Pickett place.

Now there were a few who saw opportunity in the boy; just as there'll always be scheming rascals who see opportunity in other folks' misery. But they soon learned their lesson. One woman came to see if she had a prosperous future. Clarence told her she'd die at forty-nine of heartbreak and sugar diabetes. One man came to get in touch with his dead grandmother—we later found out rumor had it that she'd buried gold somewhere on her property. Clarence just told him: "Wont no gold, Jimmy, you damn fool. Why don't you quit looking for get-rich-quick and learn to work for what you want in life?" The man stormed out after cussing Mr. George Edward good-fashioned. In two weeks the man and his family just went, left everything, without a word. Finally come back that the man had moved to Oregon to get as far away from Tims Creek as he could. Said, according to what we heard, strange things commenced to happening in the house, which was his grandma's in the first place: doors slamming, lights coming on and going off, footsteps, you know, the usual. We just laughed and said, some people . . .

Nobody looking for profit much bothered Clarence after that.

The summer before Clarence was about to begin school—Wilma had set out to start a church for Francis, seems the Deacon Board and the Board of Trustees at First Baptist finally put their foot down about cleaning up hog droppings after service—well, Clarence met Ellsworth Batts. Miss Eunice had taken Clarence with her to do the Saturday shopping at McTarr's, and Ellsworth had just been dropped off there after helping Ab Batts clean out his turkey house. Ellsworth didn't show his face much in Tims Creek but he was a good and hard worker who did an odd job now and again for beer money. Miss Eunice said they passed Ellsworth on the way to the car, him not smelling or looking too pretty after a hot morning of shoveling turkey manure. She gave her most courteous hey, not being one to discourage hard and decent work, and kept going, but Clarence stopped and went back to Ellsworth.

"Clarence, come back here."

She said Clarence reached out for the man's hand but didn't touch it and said: "She says she grieves for your pain, but you were wrong to give it all up for her . . ."

"What? Who?" Miss Eunice said Ellsworth's eyes looked madder than she'd ever seen them look and he commenced to quake and tremble.

"Mildred. She says she wants you to return to the living folk. She says you have eternity to be dead. You love too much, she says. There's more to life than love."

"Mildred? Mildred. Mildred!"

Well, Miss Eunice said she grabbed Clarence by the hand and ran to the car cause Ellsworth put the fear of God in her and after she had thrown the groceries in the backseat and rolled the windows up and locked the door, Ellsworth kept calling: "Mildred, Mildred," crying and pounding on the door. She said he had the look of a wild bear on his face with all his beard and hair. Fearing for herself and the boy, Miss Eunice slowly pulled the car out and started down the road, leaving Ellsworth running behind in the dust hollering: "Mildred, Mildred, Mildred."

Mildred had been his childhood sweetheart, a fresh cocoa-brown gal with the biggest, brightest eyes and the prettiest smile. Even before they were married Ellsworth was crazy with love for her, once almost beating a boy to death who he claimed looked too long at her. Sweethearts since childhood, they'd agreed to marry after he got out of the army. He'd see Mildred as often as he could, writing her once a day, sometimes more, and dreaming of that little house and children and nice supper after a hard day's work and all the foolishness young boys have in their heads that marriage is all about and ain't.

Well, when he got out they got married at First Baptist Church and set up a home so nice and pretty it'd make you sick—in a house owned by Wilma Jones's first husband, by the way. Nobody's sure exactly what caused the fire; Ellsworth always blamed Wilma's husband for faulty wiring—but three months after their honeymoon at Myrtle Beach, the house caught afire. They couldn't even show Mildred's body at her funeral.

They say Ellsworth cried every day for a month and after that just seemed to give up. Seems he didn't have any other dreams than that one with Mildred and didn't see the use in conjuring up any more to replace it the way folk have to do sometime. When his mama died and the house started to fall apart from plain ole neglect, Ellsworth took to living in a broken-down bus shell one of his brothers bought for him at a junkyard.

He let his hair grow wild, his teeth go bad, his clothes get ragged and tattered. His brothers tried to help, but he refused more than an occasional meal and pocket change now and again, and made it clear he wanted to be left alone. We just shrugged and accepted his crazy behavior as one of those things that happen. And the memory of why he'd come to live like he did just faded in our minds the way colors in a hand-me-down quilt wash out after time.

Clarence had set off something deep in Ellsworth. The next day, first thing in the morning, he presented himself at the Pickett place and asked Mr. George Edward if he could talk to the boy.

"I don't want no trouble now, Ellsworth. You hear me? You like to scared Miss Eunice clear to death. You shoulda heard—"

"I beg you and Miss Eunice's pardon, Mr. George Edward. But if I . . ."

Clarence came out and he and Ellsworth talked for about half an hour, sitting in the swing on the front porch. Mr. George Edward said he couldn't remember what all was said, but he could testify to a change coming over Ellsworth. First he cried and the boy admonished him stern-like, Mr. George Edward said, saying the time for tears had long passed. They talked and talked and directly Ellsworth and the boy laughed and giggled and after a while Mr. George Edward, who said he was coming to feel a touch uneasy, said he figured it was time for Ellsworth to be on his way. Ellsworth stood to go, Mr. George Edward said, and the look on his face made Mr. George Edward worried. Tweren't the sort of look a grown man shows to a five-year-old boy.

The next day Ellsworth came at dusk dark, and lo and behold, said Miss Eunice, he'd fixed himself up, washed and trimmed his hair, and had on a nice clean set of clothes—God knows where he got them from— looking in a spirit she hadn't seen him in since he went

off to the army. Not knowing what to do, after a spell
she invited Ellsworth in to supper and they all ate listening to the boy talk to Ellsworth about what Mildred
had said. At one point, forgetting himself, Ellsworth
grasped the boy's hand. Mr. George Edward had to clear
his throat to reacquaint Ellsworth with the impropriety
of doing what he was doing. Right then and there, Miss
Eunice said, she knew this was going to be nothing but
trouble but could see no way to put a peaceable end to
it.

Every day for a week Ellsworth showed up to see
Clarence and every day Miss Eunice and Mr. George
Edward would exchange weary glances and shrugs,
while one would stand guard over what begun to look
more and more like courting and sparking. Ellsworth
brought candy and then flowers, which Miss Eunice
took from Clarence straightaway and finally said to Mr.
George Edward: "This has just got to stop." And
Mr. George Edward said: "I know. I know. I'll talk
to him."

Nothing like talk of crimes against nature gets people
all riled up and speculating and conjecturing and pos-
tulating the way they did when word got out about
Ellsworth Batts's "unnatural affection" for Clarence
Pickett. The likelihood of him conversing with his dead
Mildred through the boy paled next to the idea of him
fermenting depraved intentions for young and tender
boys. Imaginations sparked like lightning in a dry August wood, and folk took to shunning poor Ellsworth
and keeping an extra eye on their womenfolk and children and locking doors after dark.

Thrice Ellsworth tried to get to Clarence, who seemed about as indifferent to his grandparents' commands as he was to Ellsworth's advances. Once Ellsworth motioned to him from under a sweetgum tree and embraced and kissed him in the shade; Clarence didn't say a mumbling word. When Mr. George Edward saw it he hollered and ran to get his gun but lost Ellsworth after chasing him and missing him—Mr. George Edward had been a good shot but the lack of a hand hindered him something awful—after missing him four times in the thick of the woods.

The second time, Ellsworth snuck into the house after twelve midnight and had the nerve to slip under the covers with the boy. Miss Eunice heard noises and woke Mr. George Edward. He had the gun this time when he found him, but he missed again and Ellsworth was covered by the night. He left his shoes.

By this time folk were on the lookout for Ellsworth Batts, figuring he was a true menace. They staked out his bus and had his brothers come to town to take charge of him but they found no Ellsworth.

About a week later—and we still can't believe that he did—Ellsworth snuck into the house again and tried to take the boy away. It was soon in the morning and everybody had just got out of bed. Mr. George Edward had only his long drawers on and Miss Eunice was out in the chicken coop collecting eggs. Ellsworth had the boy up in his arms when Mr. George Edward came out of the bathroom.

"You can't keep us apart. We were meant to be together."

"You one crazy son of a bitch is what you is, Ellsworth Batts."

Miss Eunice saw him running out the back door and tackled him, breaking all her eggs. Mr. George Edward had his gun by now, and having learned how to aim the gun with his stump finally shot Ellsworth in the foot. Running as best he could Ellsworth got a lead in the woods, but by now Mr. George Edward was joined by seven men who'd heard the shotgun and were ready.

They chased Ellsworth Batts for a good hour, figuring this time they had him. Cleavon Simpson and G. W. Gillespie had their bloodhounds on the trail now. They finally spotted him on the Chinquapin River bridge and he tried to double back but they had him trapped on both sides. Ellsworth Batts didn't look, they said, he just jumped. The Chinquapin was at its lowest, so it was pretty easy to find the body with the broken neck.

We were all mostly relieved seeing what we considered a threat to our peace and loved ones done away with; a few of us—the ones who dared put one iota of stock in believing in Clarence and his talking dead folk—figured it to be a kind of happy ending, seeing as Ellsworth would now be reunited with his beloved beyond the pale. But the most of us thought such talk a load of horse hockey, reckoning if that was the answer why didn't he just kill himself in the first place and leave us off from the trouble?

Some of us entertained fancies about the type of stories we'd begin hearing when Clarence got to school. But we never got to hear any such tales. Just before he was to start kindergarten, he took sick and died. Doctors say it was a bad case of the flu on top of a weak heart we'd never heard tell of. We figured there was more to it than that, something our imaginations were too timid to draw up, something to do with living and dying that we, so wound up in harvesting corn, cleaning house, minding chickenpox, building houses, getting our hair done, getting our cars fixed, getting good loving, fishing, drinking, sleeping, and minding other people's business, really didn't care about or have time or space to know. Why mess in such matters?—matters we didn't really believe in in the first place, and of which the memory grows dimmer and dimmer every time the sun sets.

At his funeral Miss Eunice and Mr. George Edward looked neither relieved nor sad. Just worn out; like two old people who did what their Lord had asked of them, and who, like Job, bore the tiresome effort unhappily but faithfully. Robins and sparrows perched on the tombstones near the grave as the dust-to-dust was said and the dirt began to rain down on the too-short coffin, and as we walked away from the Pickett cemetery we noted a herd of deer congregating at the edge of the wood. Of course we put this all out of our minds, eager to forget. And life in Tims Creek went on as normal after he died: folk went on propagating, copulating, and castigating, folk loved, folk hated, folk debauched, got lonely and died. No one talks about Clarence, and God only knows what lies they'd tell if they did.

As for Francis, oddly enough Wilma Jones stopped proclaiming the hog's oracular powers and eventually butchered him. But at the last minute, with the poor

thing roasting over a pit, Wilma had a crisis of con-
science and couldn't eat it; so she gave it a semi-Christian
burial with a graveside choir and a minister and pallbearers, all made hungry by the scent of barbecue. Finally Wilma stopped raising hogs altogether. She opened
a shoe store with her cousin Joceline in Crosstown.

THINGS OF
THIS WORLD

; OR , ANGELS UNAWARES

ON THE SIXTH OF June of that year a man of
decidedly Asian aspect appeared in Mr. John Edgar Stokes's front yard, near the crepe myrtle bush he
had planted in the southwest corner back in 1967, which
now had ornery drooping limbs that Mr. John Edgar
had to prune each year. The man lay face down and
motionless in the grass, his legs in the gully, feet pointing toward the road. He wore dusty jeans and a bright
red-and-blue flannel shirt. His shoes, brogans.

Not until the dog, Shep, continued to make such a
ruckus after he had yelled at him for a score of minutes
to hush up, figuring it was just somebody passing in
the road, did Mr. John Edgar come out of his kitchen
where he had just lingered over his eggs, bacon, and

coffee, and then washed the dishes, to investigate what the matter could be.

When he first saw the man Mr. John Edgar gave a barely audible *Huh*, almost a sigh as if he had been pushed in the chest by some invisible hand. He stood there staring, contemplating whether or not he did indeed see a Chinaman, or what looked to him to be a Chinaman, from the back, face down in the southwest corner of his yard. Glory be, he thought, might be one of them migrant workers. Mexican. Dead drunk.

As he approached the prone figure it occurred to him—and he was annoyed that it hadn't occurred to him on the first go-round—that the man might well be dead.

He called to the corpse: "Hey. Hey there. What you doing?"

But the figure did not move.

"I say, you there. Feller. Is you quick or dead?"

Mr. John Edgar looked around and scratched his head, wanting to have a witness before proceeding. Not particularly eager to flip the thing over and say "Morning" to the Grim Reaper. He felt a creepy sort of sensation in the back of his neck.

But as he neared the man he heard what amounted to a groan and, sure enough, saw a slight twitching in the shoulder region of the body, and a kind of spasm in the leg.

Mr. John Edgar crouched down and nudged the man. "Scuse me, boy. You ain't sleep, is you?"

The body roused a bit more, now moaning louder, the sound making a little more sense, seemed he was saying: "Fall" or "Fell" or "Falling."

"Son? You all right?" Mr. John Edgar poked him again, and as if in reward the man, with some effort and a great sigh, raised his head.

"Jesus, son." Though the man's eyes were closed, Mr. John Edgar could tell the man was not Mexican. A Chinaman. Just like he had seen on TV. Look at them eyes, he thought. Just as slanted as a cat's. The man had a gash on his forehead and the fresh blood trickled down his face, over some already dried. Blood oozed from his mouth. "Jesus."

Mr. John Edgar lifted the man before he even considered the act, reacting perhaps to the blood, his heart beating now a little faster. He didn't appear to have stumbled down drunk, Mr. John Edgar reasoned. Somebody must have beaten him. He felt a twinge of pity. Poor fool.

Mr. John Edgar lifted him and began toward the house. The man didn't seem to weigh more than a hundred pounds. If that. No more than two feed sacks. Still, carrying him wasn't too bad for an eighty-six-year-old man. Mr. John Edgar carried his groaning load into the kitchen and set him down on a cot he kept in the corner. He wet a rag and wiped the blood from the man's head and mouth. Didn't seem to be serious. But I ain't no doctor, he reminded himself. Might better call Doc Streeter.

At that very second the man's eyes blinked wide open with a start, but his voice was quite calm and soft: "No." His face held a look of such bewilderment and confusion and fear that Mr. John Edgar felt a tug in his belly.

"Boy, who messed you up like this?" Mr. John Edgar's voice came out firm and solid, tinged with a little anger, not at the Chinaman but at the fact that someone had perhaps taken advantage of him.

"Messed? . . . messed me? . . . mess? . . ."

"I say, did some of them white bastards jump you?"

"Jump? White? No. I . . . I fell . . ."

"You *fell?* What the hell you talking bout, boy? How you going to hurt yourself like that just falling down in my yard?"

The man looked around, taking in the kitchen, the oilcloth-covered table, the blue porcelain plates on the wall, the wrought-iron spider on the stove, the worn-through linoleum, the string of brilliant red peppers hanging over the door, Mr. John Edgar Stokes himself. He began to shiver.

"You all right, boy?"

Mr. John Edgar went to get him a blanket. As he put it over him, the man said, "Thank you," seeming less frightened but still confused. "Thank you. You are kind."

"How did you get into this condition, son?"

"I'm fine, really. I'm fine. I just need to . . . to . . . a little. Yes. A little . . ."

Mr. John Edgar watched him, expecting him to say more, but the man had closed his eyes. Now Mr. John Edgar felt confident he was just sleeping.

He sat down on the other side of the room, ran his hand over his face. What the *hell?* Should he call Doc Streeter? He'd wait. Figure out what the problem was.

He put on some soup. By the time the kitchen was smelling of chicken and tomato and parsley and salt, the man had roused himself. He seemed rested but still a bit weak.

Mr. John Edgar brought a cup of the soup to the man. "Bet you're hungry. It's going on eleven o'clock."

"Thank you. You're very kind."

He handed the man a cup of soup and a spoon, but the stranger began to tremble from the effort and the soup to slosh a bit.

"Here. Here." Mr. John Edgar took it and commenced to feed the man, spoonful by spoonful, carefully, grasping at this rare opportunity to nurture, and in some inexpressible way felt pleased each time the Chinaman swallowed and smiled. He finished the whole cup, burped, excused himself, and wiped his mouth with the back of his hand.

"That was good. I was hungry."

Mr. John Edgar walked to the sink. "So. You one of them migrant workers or something, is you? You don't look Mexican at all. How you come to be in Tims Creek? What's your . . . ?" Mr. John Edgar turned around to see the man had dozed off again into—if his face told no lies—what had to be a healing sleep.

"Well, go on and sleep then," Mr. John Edgar muttered under his breath, and went outside to finish propping up his tomato bushes in the garden, heavy laden with plump green tomatoes promising many platefuls of eating, stewed and raw-sliced, in just a few weeks.

Shep sat at the edge of the garden, watchfully, his tongue out, panting in the midmorning sun. Shep, Mr. John Edgar reasoned, was getting old, though he still gallivanted about like a wet-behind-the-ears puppy. His sire, Yoke, had lived to be eighteen. And Yoke's dame, Sam, had lived to the grand old age of twenty, not faltering one step till the day she died. Maybe the same would be true for Shep.

Already the temperature had reached the high eighties and the humidity was thick as moss. Sweat beaded on the tonsure of Mr. John Edgar's head as he stooped and poked and tied, inhaling the sharp odor of the plants.

He had almost forgotten about the man when he heard the toilet flush. Mr. John Edgar figured he had better go and look in on him.

The man sat on the cot, his head in his hands.

"You ain't crying there, is you, feller?"

The man looked up, a smidgen stronger, with a faint smile. "No. Not at all. I'm just still a bit tired." The man had no accent as Mr. John Edgar could place, which puzzled him a bit. But then he had seen Chinamen on TV who spoke English better than the whiteman.

"You from round here?"

"No. Just passing through."

"Where you headed?"

"To see a friend."

"Round here?"

"Yes."

"Would I know—?"

"Oh, how rude of me. My name is—" The man stood as if to shake Mr. John Edgar's hand but crumpled over.

"Now now, why don't you just lay back now?" Mr. John Edgar helped him stretch out.

His head back on the pillow, cocked to one side, he said: "Chi. My name is Chi."

"Pleased to meet you, Mr. Chi. Now I should call Doc Streeter. He's the town doctor, you know. I spect you may need a look-see."

"No." The Chinaman said it with a firmness that took Mr. John Edgar by surprise.

"No? What you mean, 'No'?"

"No. I'll be fine. It's not serious. I just fell. I know. I've done it before. No need for a doctor. I just need to rest. Trust me."

"Trust you? I don't know a damn thing about you."

"Please. I won't stay long."

Mr. John Edgar furrowed his brow and frowned. He narrowed his eyes like an owl about to say "Who."

"Ain't nobody chasing you, is they?"

"No. Nobody's chasing me."

"You wouldn't lie to me, would you?"

"No, Mr. Stokes. I do not lie."

"Well." Mr. John Edgar scratched his head. "All right. For a little while. But if you get worser, I'm calling Doc Streeter. Okay?"

"I won't get worse. I promise."

He walked out of the room and then it struck him: "*Mr. Stokes*"? But when he went back into the kitchen the man was deep in slumber. How did he know my name? But the man might have seen it on the mailbox or on something in the house when he went to the bathroom, Mr. John Edgar reasoned while walking to the porch.

That night Mr. John Edgar made them liver and onions, and cabbage and carrots, with some cornbread and bitter lemonade to drink. Chi seemed to enjoy the food though he didn't say much. Mr. John Edgar, after a while of silence, went off telling tales: about laying tracks for the railroads in his youth, about the biggest snake he had killed, about the price of corn and how he now leased all his land to the biggest landowner in town, Percy Terrell, the son of old evil Malcolm Terrell, against his better judgment. He talked long after they had finished eating. Chi said very little, and by and by Mr. John Edgar came round to the idea of what Chi was going to do.

"Well, you can stay on here tonight if you want. Ain't nobody but me." He said it without a second thought, for he trusted this strange Chinese man for some reason, though he couldn't quite put a finger on why he did.

Chi accepted with a gracious thank-you and Mr. John Edgar showed him the second bedroom and told him he could take a bath if he wanted, and laid out clean towels and some fresh clothes he thought might fit him.

In bed, his false teeth out, rubbing his bare gums together pleasurably, enjoying the wet friction, Mr. John Edgar considered the foolishness of what he had done by inviting a complete stranger into his house: He could sassinate me this very night, cut my head clean off in the middle of the night. But I've lived my life. What would it matter?

He turned on his side, oddly confident in his instinct, and glided off into sweet slumber.

The next morning he found Chi at the table looking somewhat better, a tad more dignified, upright, though he could tell the small Chinaman had not regained his full mettle. Mr. John Edgar scrambled up some eggs and fried up some bacon, and Chi munched with delight, saying Mr. John Edgar was a good cook.

Chi followed Mr. John Edgar around all that day: in the garden he helped him pick peas, chop collards and cabbage, and pull some of the last sweet corn; he rode with him into town in Mr. John Edgar's 1965 Ford pickup truck to buy some wire and nails and light bulbs; he helped him fix the roof of the pump house; all the while saying little, and Mr. John Edgar, perhaps induced by the Asian man's silence, talked on of his days of courting and sparking and of this gal Cindy and that gal Emma Jo and of that ole Callie Mae Harris's mama, Cleona, who was evil as a wet hen. Or he'd simply sit in silence enjoying the good company of his guest.

That night he roasted a hen, fried some mustard greens, and boiled some of the sweet corn they'd pulled that day and some rice. Again Chi complimented Mr. John Edgar's cooking, asking him where he'd learned to cook so well.

"A man living by himself'll pick up what he needs to, I reckon's all there is to it."

"You never married." Chi put it more as a statement than a question.

"No. Never got round to it."

They sat on the porch afterward, mostly in silence. Mr. John Edgar was now yarned out. After a spell of rocking he asked: "What it like in China?"

"I'm not from China."

"You ain't a Chinaman, then?"

"No."

"Oh." Mr. John Edgar wanted to ask where the hell

he *was* from then, but felt somewhat embarrassed, figuring he should know. So they rocked, saying nothing, listening to the twilight noises leavened by the sound of trucks and cars on the highway in the far distance.

The next morning Mr. John Edgar rose at about five and decided to clean his gun. As he moved to put it back in the closet off the parlor, outside the window something caught his eye. Mr. John Edgar stood perplexed: There in the backyard was Chi. Seemed at first to be doing some queer dance. No. No. Fighting some invisible somebody. No. Dancing. But no, the way he's a-moving . . .

As he watched Chi, with his arms moving like a puppet's, Mr. John Edgar wanted to think him crazy, but something about the look on his face, the reverence with which he moved, with grace, yes, that's what it was, the grace of his movements, like a cat, made him think better of it. Looked like a ritual of some kind. Was he casting a spell? Praying? Maybe this was how they prayed where this feller was from. Clutching the gun, Mr. John Edgar stood at the window watching, and presently Chi sat down in the dew-misted grass. Motionless, his legs folded up before him, his head straight ahead toward the sun, his eyes closed.

Well, I'll be damned, Mr. John Edgar thought, half expecting the man to float; and at length, when he didn't, Mr. John Edgar Stokes took his gun back to the parlor.

By the time he got back to the kitchen, there sat Chi at the table, looking pert. He had regained all his dignity. The scar on his forehead was a mere red shadow, his black eyes glistened.

"Good morning, Mr. Stokes."

"Morning there, feller. Like some eggs and ham?"

"Thank you. Please."

Mr. John Edgar went about preparing the meal as he had done for scores of years, humming. He truly wanted to ask what the man had been doing in his back-yard facing the morning sun, but felt by turns embar-rassed and guilty and prying, as if he had witnessed something private between this foreigner and his Lord. Best not to be nosy. Mind your own business.

They lingered over coffee, Mr. John Edgar ticking off those things he had to do for the day, waiting pa-tiently to hear the man say it was time to go, thinking his hospitality had reached its limit and the polite thing would be for the man to move on, seeing as he was hale and hearty. But at the same time he did enjoy the strange man's company. There was something comforting about it. So he got up to cut the grass, and as he stood at the shed door he heard a truck drive up.

Joe Allen Pearsall got out of his truck and Mr. John Edgar could tell he had bad news by the way he was slumped over in the shoulders, looking at the ground.

"Well, morning to you, Joe Allen. How you been?"

"All right, Mr. John Edgar. How you?"

Mr. John Edgar searched his own mind, trying to beat Joe Allen to the news. He hated surprises. Maybe something had happened to that crazy wife of his. Maybe somebody had died. Who? Zeke Cross? Carl Fletcher? Maggie Williams? Ada Mae . . .

"Mr. John Edgar. Something bad happened."

The old man wanted to say: "Well, I know that." But he said nothing, waiting for Joe Allen to complete his thought. Instead of letting more words drop out of his mouth—must be mighty bad or he woulda just said it—Joe Allen backed to the end of his truck, motioning for Mr. John Edgar to follow. He let the tailgate down.

They stood there for a good minute. Mr. John Edgar just stared, no saliva in his mouth. Not looking at Joe Allen, he asked: "Who done it?"

"Them Terrell boys. Say that he been shitting in their yard and that this morning he was in their cow pasture chasing a heifer. So . . . so . . . I was at the store when they done it."

By the time Chi had come around to the truck, Mr. John Edgar had the dog, Shep, already stiffening, up in his arms, the tongue hanging pendulously; drool, an admixture of blood and froth, leaving a gelatinous pool on the bed of the truck; the head a horrid confusion of tattered bone, flesh, white fluid, and what was left of a grey brain. Blood stained the tan coat.

As Mr. John Edgar carried Shep to the backyard, to where the yard met the garden, Joe Allen turned with questions in his eyes to the strange man at his side standing as perplexed and sad as he.

"Who . . . ?"

"I am Chi."

They stood, and it was obvious that Joe Allen wanted to ask Chi what he was doing there. But they were both distracted by the somber goings-on.

Mr. John Edgar laid Shep down and went into the shed to retrieve a shovel and an old quilt, faded yet still Joseph's coat–like in its patchwork colors.

"Let me do it, Mr. John Edgar." But he seemed neither to hear nor to see Joe Allen as he went about the task of digging a hole wide enough, long enough, deep enough. Chi and Joe Allen, useless pallbearers, watched Mr. John Edgar, who seemed neither to sweat a drop nor strain a muscle, as he went about the duty with a skill that would have made anybody who didn't know better think it his occupation.

Tenderly he swaddled the cooling pup in the quilt and lowered him to his forever bed. When the last shovelful of earth had been patted down, Mr. John Edgar picked up two large stones from a pile at the other end of the garden, stones swallowed by moss, and placed one at Shep's feet and one at his nose. He took a long pause, his breath miraculously even, a barely seen dew of sweat on his brown head, but he didn't seem to grieve or meditate or tremble in anger: he seemed only to wait, peering at the shallow grave, as if expecting the dog to claw out of the earth, brain intact, healed, panting, resurrected.

Presently he said under his breath: "Damn," turned and walked back to the shed, put the shovel down, and went into the house.

Chi and Joe Allen followed him with their eyes. Joe Allen shuffled awkwardly, clearly having no words or actions he felt would suffice. He regarded Chi with only slightly less suspicion than before.

"You from round here?"

"No."

"I didn't think so. Never seen you before. Helping Mr. John Edgar out, is you?"

"Yes. I've been staying with him for a few days."

"Have? Wh—?"

The door slammed with a loud crack and they both

pivoted to see Mr. John Edgar, gun in hand, marching toward his truck.

"Oh, Jesus. We got to stop him." Joe Allen ran toward the truck, Chi close behind.

"Mr. John Edgar. Mr. John Edgar! Now you can't just . . . You can't . . ."

But the old man paid Joe Allen no heed, cranking up the truck and backing out, running over a few marigolds to avoid hitting Joe Allen's truck. He shot down the road, pushing the old truck as fast as she would go.

Come on, Joe Allen motioned to Chi. They took off after him. Joe Allen, in his haste, ran over more marigolds.

The Terrell General Store was no more than five miles from Mr. John Edgar Stokes's house, barely within the town limits. He pulled up, the truck lurching to a stop. All three Terrell boys congregated on the front porch of the large warehouse of a store. One called out: "Well, if it ain't John Edgar Stokes. To what do we owe the pleasure." They all laughed.

Their jocular tone changed when Mr. John Edgar got out of his automobile and they could see he was carrying a Smith & Wesson. One Terrell boy whispered to another: "Better get Daddy," and the boy zipped off like a housefly.

Mr. John Edgar, his head held high, barely gave the boys a glance, but it was clear that the half-look equated them in his mind with hog slop. Choking his gun by the neck, he stomped along the side of the store.

By the time the boys ran up to Mr. John Edgar, Joe Allen and Chi had arrived and were among the boys who hollered at him.

The Terrell boys jumped in front of Mr. John Edgar but he did not stop; merely leveled his gun, cocked it, and kept walking. The boys got out of the way. "Crazy old nigger. What's he doing?"

Percy Terrell came bursting out the back door: "John Edgar Stokes. What you doing back here? What you aiming to do with that gun? Deer season is over. Now, John Edgar—"

Mr. John Edgar stopped in front of a hutch of hound dogs. Five dogs in all. Percy's prize coon dogs. Yapping in the confusion.

Joe Allen ran up to him from behind and whispered: "You oughtn't to do this, Mr. John Edgar."

"Nigger, I will kill you," one of the Terrell boys said, fist clenched, trembling, face all red. He took a step forward and Mr. John Edgar raised the gun to the level of the boy's heart.

"John Edgar!" Percy Terrell howled. The boy's eyes twitched with fear, given two seconds to contemplate his mortality. Another Terrell stepped forward and Mr. John Edgar, implacable, pointed the gun toward him; after the boy froze, toward the third; and finally toward Percy Terrell himself. They stood stock-still, less from the reality of the gun than from the look in Mr. John Edgar Stokes's eyes, a curse of loathing and damnation as if from God's own Counsel on Earth.

In a motion approaching nonchalance, Mr. John Edgar reeled to the hound dogs and aimed at the one on the end, the one Percy called Billy.

"Hell, no!"

The bullet went through the chicken wire, pretty and neat, not breaking a strand. The dog didn't make sound the first. He just fell over on his side like a spent toy. Mr. John Edgar got him square in the head. The blood came dripping down.

The youngest Terrell lunged toward him, but Mr. John Edgar just cocked his gun again, shot the ground, cocked it again, and pointed it at the boy. Mr. John Edgar began backing away, shaking his head *no*; but now the look on his face said that any more killing he had to do would be incidental and painless. Another Terrell boy babbled loudly and incoherently, his rage making him the color of raw beef, his arms flailing, yammering a high-pitched patois of hate: "Paw we gotta kill him nigger sombitch killing cocksucker nigger Paw Paw do something."

Terrell shook his head gravely. "You done it now, you ole fart. John Edgar, you a dead man. You'll pay for this, you goddamn fool."

Mr. John Edgar got into his truck unaccosted and drove away, this time obeying the speed limit, followed by a shaken Joe Allen and Chi.

By the time Joe Allen and Chi got out of the truck, Mr. John Edgar had set himself down in his rocker on the front porch and was rocking.

"Now, Mr. John Edgar, you shouldn'ta done that, now. You reckon ole Terrell gone let you get away with that?"

Mr. John Edgar said not a word, answering Joe Allen with the creak of the chair on the floorboards, his gun in his lap.

Joe Allen tried to talk more but it became clear that Mr. John Edgar intended to keep silent. Flustered, Joe Allen went into the house and made a few phone calls.

Chi sat with Mr. John Edgar in silence. Joe Allen came back, visibly worried, and just looked at the two of them. "Jesus H. Christ."

Dr. Streeter arrived first. The Reverend Barden came with Ed Phelps. Joe Allen recapped the entire incident, showing himself to be more than a little proud of what ole Mr. John Edgar had done, and smiled broadly at the end. The men all laughed and congratulated Mr. John Edgar in whoops and guffaws and slaps on the shoulder.

"Dog's dead, though." Mr. John Edgar continued to rock in the same rhythm, staring steelily into the front yard.

The men all became grave in countenance, heads bowed. It was Dr. Streeter who finally voiced everyone's unspoken curiosity. Turning to Chi, he scratched his white beard and fidgeted with his glasses in a lordly manner. "And who are you?"

Chi, who was standing now, looked as though he felt at home among this gathering. "My name is Chi. I am a friend."

"I see. You're not from around here, are you? Migrant worker or something?"

"No. Just passing through."

"We ought to hide him," Ed Phelps broke in. "Mr. John Edgar, you ought to hide. Ain't no telling what they'll do."

"Might not be a bad idea." Joe Allen looked worried.

Mr. John Edgar Stokes kept on rocking.

In the distance a siren came screaming. They could all see the sheriff's car zipping toward the house, followed by two other cars.

"Oh, Lord, my Lord." The Right Reverend Hezekiah Barden's face was wet with sweat. "What we gone do now? Terrell don't play, you know."

"You aren't afraid, are you, Reverend?" Dr. Streeter winked at Barden.

"Maybe we should pray?"

"Well,"—Dr. Streeter straightened his tie—"you better pray fast, Hez. Better pray fast."

Sheriff Roy Brinkley parked his car beside the road in front of the yard, the light still blinking on the top. Brinkley, a man of brood-sow girth and a small and jowly head, came rolling across the lawn with Percy Terrell at his right hand. The boys behind.

"Well, well, well." Dr. Streeter stood at the foot of the steps. "To what do we owe this visit from the county's finest?"

"Out of my way, Streeter. I ain't got time for your Yankee foolishness. You know why I'm here."

"Why?" Barden had composed himself, wiped away all the sweat with his Panama hankie. "Looks to me like the two things you're lacking is some white sheets and a cross."

"Now you know it ain't like that, Reverend." Brinkley himself was sweating now; the walk across the lawn had surely been an overexertion.

"Stop all this bullshit." Terrell pointed to Mr. John Edgar. "You all know good and well why we come here. To get him."

"To string him up?" Ed Phelps came down to ground level with Dr. Streeter.

"Yeah." Joe Allen stepped forward too. "Your boys killed his dog, you know. I don't see no sheriff coming for you."

"That was different and you know it." Brinkley wiped his red and sweating face with his bare hand.

"How come?" Ed Phelps shrugged.

"Cause John's dog was trespassing on Terrell's property. They was within their rights to shoot him. John was trespassing and maliciously destroyed property. He shoulda filed a complaint if he felt there was wrongdoing."

"Well, who do I file a complaint with now, you?"

"Shut up, Streeter." Terrell pointed. "This don't concern you."

"I'm not one of your employees, like the sheriff here. I can speak when and where I please."

"Well, talk all you want to. Roy, arrest that nigger and let's go so I don't have to listen to this fancy boy shoot off at the mouth. I got better things to do."

Rankled by what sounded like an order, Sheriff Brinkley advanced between Ed Phelps and Dr. Streeter and put his foot on the first step to the porch.

"Get the hell off my porch." Mr. John Edgar had stopped rocking.

"Now, John. You—" Brinkley took another step and Mr. John Edgar picked up his gun.

"I said get off my porch."

"You can't do this."

"I can and I am. I said get off my porch." He cocked the gun and took aim at Brinkley's belly.

Roy Brinkley trembled with anger, his belly quivering despite the tight brown uniform. "You broke the law, John Edgar Stokes. The law says you got to come with me."

"Well, the Bible say 'an eye for an eye,' don't it,

Reverend? An Eye for an Eye and a Tooth for a Tooth. That's the onliest Law I'm studying about. Now get the hell off my porch or they'll have to scrape you off."

Sheriff Brinkley took one step back and almost fell into the Right Reverend Hezekiah Barden. He swung his great girth around and walked back to his squad car.

"Where the hell you going, Roy?" Terrell chased after him. "Arrest him. *Arrest* him, goddamn it. What do I pay . . . what were you elected to do? Goddamn it, arrest him, I say."

The men on the porch all laughed and slapped Mr. John Edgar's back. Mr. John Edgar again commenced to rocking, not smiling with the men.

Voices from the squad car carried to the porch.

"You fat fairy. You a goddamn coward is what you is. Scared of one old nigger with a buncha coons and a shotgun. He ain't gon—"

"Be quiet, Percy. Just hush."

"Scared is all you is. Scared. I gone take my boys and—"

"Hush, Percy." From the porch they heard static. "Luella? This is Sheriff Brinkley. I'm requesting assistance."

"Assistance, my left titty. You just scared. Afeared of a ole nigger."

"Hush, Percy, please! Yeah, at the residence of John Edgar Stokes in Tims Creek . . ."

On the porch the men became silent, looking to one another in puzzlement, looking to Chi in even greater puzzlement, each finding himself questioning the extent of his own courage on what had seemed earlier to have been a routine June day. The white men stood about the sheriff's car in the road; the black men on the porch, a strange Asian man in their midst. Chi said nothing, just looked from one group to another, seeming to drink it all into his Dead Sea–calm black eyes.

"Maybe." The Reverend Barden's face shone once again with sweat. "Maybe you ought to go on with them, John Edgar. Maybe . . ."

Two state patrol cars came down the road, one from each direction. Three tall troopers got out and conferred with Brinkley and Terrell. Two troopers were white, one black. They each had rifles in their hands. After a time they approached the house: the two white patrollers on either side, guns at the ready, the black one in the middle with Brinkley, Terrell, and his boys behind.

Before the steps Brinkley called out in a voice too loud: "In the name of the People of York County, the Governor of the Great State of North Carolina, and the Constitution of these United States of America, John Edgar Stokes, you are under arrest for willful and malicious destruction of property, resisting arrest, and threatening the life of an officer of the law. Now you come on down here and let me take you to the courthouse, why don't you?"

Mr. John Edgar just kept on rocking and rocking, as if the sights and sounds before him were no more than hoot owls and mist in the dark, unworthy of heed. All the men eyed one another tremulously, expecting everything, daring nothing.

"Go get him, son," Brinkley said to the black trooper.

As the black man, his eyes veiled behind smoky sunglasses, walked up the steps, Mr. John Edgar did nothing, outnumbered by two guns trained on his head and heart. The officer of the law took the gun from the old man without a struggle and pulled him forward, and Malcolm Streeter, M.D., was heard to say: "Pernicious infamy. O foul and black traitor of fate." But the man placed handcuffs on Mr. John Edgar Stokes just the same, and Brinkley, rocking on his heels in his new-found self-confidence and delight, commenced to recite: "You have the right to remain silent . . ."

"What difference does it make in Terrell County?"

"Now you stay out of this, Streeter. This is the law talking."

"The law? Law? Jim Crow law if you ask me."

"Streeter, if you don't hush up I'll arrest you too."

"Go ahead, and you'll see more lawyers swarming over your precious courthouse than you're already going to see in about an hour. Come on, arrest me."

"Brinkley!" Terrell stepped forward. "Come on. We don't have to stand here and take this shit. Come on." They began to walk away.

"His master's voice," Streeter said through clenched teeth.

Brinkley looked back but Terrell beckoned *come on* from the squad car's open door.

"If you harm one hair on that saintly man's head, I'll have your badge, your career, and your life. You pusillanimous hippopotamus!"

Dr. Streeter's words rang out to no avail as they stuffed Mr. John Edgar Stokes into the back of the sheriff's car. Terrell gloated and waved at the men as he got into the front seat, and began laughing as they drove off.

Word got out in the community in a hurry, and scores of people from all around Tims Creek followed the car containing Mr. John Edgar to Crosstown, and watched, yelling and screaming, as he was processed and spirited away behind steel doors. Though Brinkley's people were besieged by black and white telling them they had committed a heinous sin by putting an eighty-six-year-old man behind bars, the clerks and officers remained tight-mouthed as ordered and would not speak of release. Dr. Streeter and the Right Reverend Barden thundered about human rights and the travesty of justice, and placed phone calls to the state capitol and beyond well into the early morning. Early the next day Mr. John Edgar was released on five hundred dollars' bail, which Dr. Streeter promptly posted. Reporters from the York County *Cryer* and the Raleigh *News and Observer* and the Wilmington *Star* asked him questions; photographers snapped his picture; women hugged his neck and men shook his hand. He said little. Getting into the backseat of Dr. Streeter's car, he looked up to see Chi. He asked him how he was doing.

"Fine, sir. I'm just fine. How are you holding up?"

"I do all right. For a old man."

Back home he sat in his parlor, contemplating the room, looking for pictures of family, knowing there were only a few: his mother, his father, both born slaves, dead for decades; his old sweetheart Lena Thompson, who he felt he would have married had he not waited so damn long; his nephew Joshua in Philadelphia; Joshua's two children. A daguerreotype, a large print, some snapshots, a few Polaroids, elementary-school pictures.

Not much. Not enough to fill one of those good-size albums they sell at the department stores. All else was dull: mementos of affectless happenings he could barely remember; gifts bearing little significance. Mr. John Edgar Stokes sat in his parlor on the day after his release from the county jail, troubled yet transformed, studying not just the present but the eighty-six years that had led him there. Amazed to now be awaiting a hearing, a trial. It had come up all of a sudden like a summer storm, but unlike a thundercloud this wouldn't leave things pretty much the way it found them.

Folk came by to talk, but he had very little to say to them. They left feeling a vague unease, not able to articulate their disquiet. Thinking, in the end, that that fine old gentleman, who had lived so long alone with his good dog, cooking, working in his garden, who had stopped farming some ten-odd years ago, had finally come upon the penultimate trouble of his life in the form of senility. Poor old gent.

He didn't have to cook, seeing as so many womenfolk in the community had brought over pies, collard greens, spareribs, fried chicken, potato salad. He and Chi ate in unperturbed quiet, and afterward they returned to the dimly lit parlor and sat in quietude.

By and by Mr. John Edgar looked up to Chi and said: "You know, I hated to kill that dog. I surely did. But I had to. Just had to." He paused, looking out into the June-warm blackness of evening. "Seems like up to now I been sitting right here in this chair waiting, waiting. But you know what?"

"No, sir."

"It sho was worth it. Worth it to see the look on that ole Terrell's face. I stood up to that cocksucker. Yes sir."

He smiled. Chi inclined his head thoughtfully and nodded with a strange look of understanding, complicity, and warmth.

"You know what else?"

"No. What, Mr. Stokes?"

"I wisht I could die. Die right now to spite his sorry ass. Yes sir. To show he ain't got no power over death. Yes sir. I could die right now—content."

"Could you?" Chi's black eyes seemed to shimmer in the lamp's faint light.

"Sho nuff could. With pleasure." He grinned.

When they found Mr. John Edgar Stokes he was sitting upright in a chair by his kitchen sink, his back straight as a swamp reed, not slouching one whit, clutching a large wooden spoon; his eyes stretched wide with astonishment, his mouth a gaping O—though his false teeth had held admirably to the gums—as if his last sight had been something more than truly remarkable, something wonderful and awesome to behold.

They found no sign of the man called Chi.

THE FOUNDATIONS
OF THE EARTH

I

OF COURSE THEY DIDN'T pay it any mind at first: just a tractor—one of the most natural things in the world to see in a field—kicking dust up into the afternoon sky and slowly toddling off the road into a soybean field. And fields surrounded Mrs. Maggie MacGowan Williams's house, giving the impression that her lawn stretched on and on until it dropped off into the woods far by the way. Sometimes she was certain she could actually see the earth's curve—not merely the bend of the small hill on which her house sat but the great slope of the sphere, the way scientists explained it in books, a monstrous globe floating in a cold nothingness. She would sometimes sit by herself on the patio late of an evening, in the same chair she was sitting in

now, sip from her Coca-Cola, and think about how big
the earth must be to seem flat to the eye.

She wished she were alone now. It was Sunday.

"Now I wonder what that man is doing with a tractor out there today?"

They sat on Maggie's patio, reclined in that after-
Sunday-dinner way—Maggie; the Right Reverend Hezekiah Barden, round and pompous as ever; Henrietta
Fuchee, the prim and priggish music teacher and president of the First Baptist Church Auxiliary Council;
Emma Lewis, Maggie's sometimes housekeeper; and
Gabriel, Mrs. Maggie Williams's young, white, special
guest—all looking out lazily into the early summer,
watching the sun begin its slow downward arc, feeling
the baked ham and the candied sweet potatoes and the
fried chicken with the collard greens and green beans
and beets settle in their bellies, talking shallow and pleasant talk, and sipping their Coca-Colas and bitter
lemonade.

"Don't they realize it's Sunday?" Reverend Barden
leaned back in his chair and tugged at his suspenders
thoughtfully, eyeing the tractor as it turned into another
row. He reached for a sweating glass of lemonade, his
red bow tie afire in the penultimate beams of the day.

"I . . . I don't understand. What's wrong?" Maggie
could see her other guests watching Gabriel intently,
trying to discern why on earth he was present at Maggie
MacGowan Williams's table.

"What you mean, what's wrong?" The Reverend
Barden leaned forward and narrowed his eyes at the
young man. "What's wrong is: it's Sunday."

"So? I don't . . ." Gabriel himself now looked embarrassed, glancing to Maggie, who wanted to save him but could not.

" 'So?' 'So?' " Leaning toward Gabriel and narrowing his eyes, Barden asked: "You're not from a church-going family, are you?"

"Well, no. Today was my first time in . . . Oh, probably ten years."

"Uh-huh." Barden corrected his posture, as if to say he pitied Gabriel's being an infidel but had the patience to instruct him. "Now you see, the Lord has declared Sunday as His day. It's holy. 'Six days shalt thou labor and do all thy work: but the seventh day is the sabbath of the Lord thy God: in it thou shalt not do any work, thou, nor thy son, nor thy daughter, thy manservant, nor thy maidservant, nor thy cattle, nor thy stranger that is within thy gates: for in six days the Lord made heaven and earth, the sea, and all that in them is, and rested the seventh day: wherefore, the Lord blessed the sabbath day, and hallowed it.' Exodus. Chapter twenty, verses nine and ten."

"Amen." Henrietta closed her eyes and rocked.

"Hez." Maggie inclined her head a bit to entreat the good Reverend to desist. He gave her an understanding smile, which made her cringe slightly, fearing her gesture might have been mistaken for a sign of intimacy.

"But, Miss Henrietta—" Emma Lewis tapped the tabletop, like a judge in court, changing the subject. "Like I was saying, I believe that Rick on *The Winds of Hope* is going to marry that gal before she gets too big with child, don't you?" Though Emma kept house for

Maggie Williams, to Maggie she seemed more like a sister who came three days a week, more to visit than to clean.

"Now go on away from here, Emma." Henrietta did not look up from her empty cake plate, her glasses hanging on top of her sagging breasts from a silver chain. "Talking about that worldly foolishness on TV. You know I don't pay that mess any attention." She did not want the Reverend to know that she secretly watched afternoon soap operas, just like Emma and all the other women in the congregation. Usually she gossiped to beat the band about this rich heifer and that handsome hunk whenever she found a fellow TV-gazer. Buck-toothed hypocrite, Maggie thought. She knew the truth: Henrietta, herself a widow now on ten years, was sweet on the widower minister, who in turn, alas, had his eye on Maggie.

"Now, Miss Henrietta, we was talking about it t'other day. Don't you think he's apt to marry her soon?" Emma's tone was insistent.

"I *don't know*, Emma." Visibly agitated, Henrietta donned her glasses and looked into the fields. "I wonder who that is anyhow?"

Annoyed by Henrietta's rebuff, Emma stood and began to collect the few remaining dishes. Her purple-and-yellow floral print dress hugged her ample hips. "It's that ole Morton Henry that Miss Maggie leases that piece of land to." She walked toward the door, into the house. "He ain't no God-fearing man."

"Well, that's plain to see." The Reverend glanced over to Maggie. She shrugged.

They are ignoring Gabriel, Maggie thought. She had

invited them to dinner after church services thinking it
would be pleasant for Gabriel to meet other people in
Tims Creek. But generally they chose not to see him,
and when they did it was with ill-concealed scorn or
petty curiosity or annoyance. At first the conversation
seemed civil enough. But the ice was never truly broken,
questions still buzzed around the talk like horseflies,
Maggie could tell. "Where you from?" Henrietta had
asked. "What's your line of work?" Barden had asked.
While Gabriel sat there with a look on his face somewhere between peace and pain. But Maggie refused to
believe she had made a mistake. At this stage of her life
she depended on no one for anything, and she was certainly not dependent on the approval of these self-
important fools.

She had been steeled by anxiety when she picked
Gabriel up at the airport that Friday night. But as she
caught sight of him stepping from the jet and greeted
him, asking about the weather in Boston; and after she
had ushered him to her car and watched him slide in,
seeming quite at home; though it still felt awkward, she
thought: I'm doing the right thing.

II

"WELL, THANK YOU FOR inviting me, Mrs. Williams. But I don't understand . . . Is something wrong?"

"*Wrong?* No, nothing's wrong, Gabriel. I just
thought it'd be good to see you. Sit and talk to you.
We didn't have much time at the funeral."

"Gee . . . I—"

"You don't want to make an old woman sad, now
do you?"

"Well, Mrs. Williams, if you put it like that, how can I refuse?"

"Weekend after next then?"

There was a pause in which she heard muted voices in the wire.

"Okay."

After she hung up the phone and sat down in her favorite chair in the den, she heaved a momentous sigh. Well, she had done it. At last. The weight of uncertainty would be lifted. She could confront him face to face. She wanted to know about her grandboy, and Gabriel was the only one who could tell her what she wanted to know. It was that simple. Surely, he realized what this invitation meant. She leaned back looking out the big picture window onto the tops of the brilliantly blooming crepe myrtle trees in the yard, listening to the grandfather clock mark the time.

III

HER GRANDSON'S FUNERAL HAD been six months ago, but it seemed much longer. Perhaps the fact that Edward had been gone away from home so long without seeing her, combined with the weeks and days and hours and minutes she had spent trying not to think about him and all the craziness that had surrounded his death, somehow lengthened the time.

At first she chose to ignore it, the strange and bitter sadness that seemed to have overtaken her every waking moment. She went about her daily life as she had done for thirty-odd years, overseeing her stores, her land, her money; buying groceries, paying bills, shopping, shopping; going to church and talking to her few good living friends and the few silly fools she was obliged to suffer. But all day, dusk to dawn, and especially at night, she had what the field-workers called "a monkey on your back," when the sun beats down so hot it makes you delirious; but her monkey chilled and angered her, born not of the sun but of a profound loneliness, an oppressive emptiness, a stabbing guilt. Sometimes she even wished she were a drinking woman.

The depression had come with the death of Edward, though its roots reached farther back, to the time he seemed to have vanished. There had been so many years of asking other members of the family: Have you heard from him? Have you seen him? So many years of only a Christmas card or birthday card a few days early, or a cryptic, taciturn phone call on Sunday mornings, and then no calls at all. At some point she realized she had no idea where he was or how to get in touch with him. Mysteriously, he would drop a line to his half-sister, Clarissa, or drop a card without a return address. He was gone. Inevitably, she had to ask: Had she done something evil to the boy to drive him away? Had she tried too hard to make sure he became nothing like his father and grandfather? I was as good a mother as a woman can claim to be, she thought: from the cradle on he had all the material things he needed, and he certainly didn't want for attention, for care; and I trained him proper, he was a well-mannered and upright young fellow when he left here for college. Oh, I was proud of that boy, winning a scholarship to Boston University. Tall, handsome like his granddad. He'd make somebody a good . . .

So she continued picking out culprits: school, the

cold North, strange people, strange ideas. But now in her crystalline hindsight she could lay no blame on anyone but Edward. And the more she remembered battles with the mumps and the measles and long division and taunts from his schoolmates, the more she became aware of her true anger. *He owes me respect, damn it. The least he can do is keep in touch. Is that so much to ask?*

But before she could make up her mind to find him and confront him with her fury, before she could cuss him out good and call him an ungrateful, no-account bastard just like his father, a truck would have the heartless audacity to skid into her grandchild's car one rainy night in Springfield and end his life at twenty-seven, taking that opportunity away from her forever. When they told her of his death she cursed her weakness. Begging God for another chance. But instead He gave her something she had never imagined.

Clarissa was the one to finally tell her. "Grandma," she had said, "Edward's been living with another man all these years."

"So?"

"No, Grandma. Like man and wife."

Maggie had never before been so paralyzed by news. One question answered, only to be replaced by a multitude. Gabriel had come with the body, like an interpreter for the dead. They had been living together in Boston, where Edward worked in a bookstore. He came, head bowed, rheumy-eyed, exhausted. He gave her no explanation; nor had she asked him for any, for he displayed the truth in his vacant and humble glare and had nothing to offer but the penurious tribute of his trembling hands. Which was more than she wanted.

In her world she had been expected to be tearless, patient, comforting to other members of the family; folk were meant to sit back and say, "Lord, ain't she taking it well. I don't think I could be so calm if my grandboy had've died so young." Magisterially she had done her duty; she had taken it all in stride. But her world began to hopelessly unravel that summer night at the wake in the Raymond Brown Funeral Home, among the many somber-bright flower arrangements, the fluorescent lights, and the gleaming bronze casket, when Gabriel tried to tell her how sorry he was . . . How dare he? This pathetic, stumbling, poor trashy white boy, to throw his sinful lust for her grandbaby in her face, as if to bury a grandchild weren't bad enough. Now this abomination had to be flaunted. —Sorry, indeed! The nerve! Who the hell did he think he was to parade their shame about?

Her anger was burning so intensely that she knew if she didn't get out she would tear his heart from his chest, his eyes from their sockets, his testicles from their sac. With great haste she took her leave, brushing off the funeral director and her brother's wives and husband's brothers—they all probably thinking her overcome with grief rather than anger—and had Clarissa drive her home. When she got to the house she filled a tub with water as hot as she could stand it and a handful of bath oil beads, and slipped in, praying her hatred would mingle with the mist and evaporate, leaving her at least sane.

Next, sleep. Healing sleep, soothing sleep, sleep to make the world go away, sleep like death. Her mama had told her that sleep was the best medicine God ever made. When things get too rough—go to bed. Her family had been known as the family that retreated to bed. Ruined crop? No money? Get some shut-eye. Maybe it'll be better in the morning. Can't be worse. Maggie didn't give a damn where Gabriel was to sleep that night; someone else would deal with it. She didn't care about all the people who would come to the house after the wake to the Sitting Up, talking, eating, drinking, watching over the still body till sunrise; they could take care of themselves. The people came; but Maggie slept. From deeps under deeps of slumber she sensed her granddaughter stick her head in the door and whisper, asking Maggie if she wanted something to eat. Maggie didn't stir. She slept. And in her sleep she dreamed.

She dreamed she was Job sitting on his dung heap, dressed in sackcloth and ashes, her body covered with boils, scratching with a stick, sending away Eliphaz and Bildad and Zophar and Elihu, who came to counsel her, and above her the sky boiled and churned and the air roared, and she matched it, railing against God, against her life—*Why? Why? Why did you kill him, you heartless old fiend? Why make me live to see him die? What earthly purpose could you have in such a wicked deed? You are God, but you are not good. Speak to me, damn it. Why? Why? Why?* Hurricanes whipped and thunder ripped through a sky streaked by lightning, and she was lifted up, spinning, spinning, and Edward floated before her in the rushing air and quickly turned around into the comforting arms of Gabriel, winged, who clutched her grandboy to his bosom and soared away, out of the storm. Maggie screamed and the winds grew stronger, and a voice, gentle and sweet, not thunderous as she expected, spoke to her from the whirlwind: *Who is this that darkeneth counsel by words without knowledge? Gird up now thy loins like a man; for I will demand of thee, and answer thou me. Where wast thou when I laid the foundations of the earth? Declare if thou hast understanding . . .* The voice spoke of the myriad creations of the universe, the stupendous glory of the Earth and its inhabitants. But Maggie was not deterred in the face of the maelstrom, saying: *Answer me, damn you: Why?*, and the winds began to taper off and finally halted, and Maggie was alone, standing on water. A fish, what appeared to be a mackerel, stuck its head through the surface and said: *Kind woman, be not aggrieved and put your anger away. Your arrogance has clouded your good mind. Who asked you to love? Who asked you to hate?* The fish dipped down with a plip and gradually Maggie too began to slip down into the water, down, down, down, sinking, below depths of reason and love, down into the dark unknown of her own mind, down, down, down.

Maggie MacGowan Williams woke the next morning to the harsh chatter of a bluejay chasing a mockingbird just outside her window, a racket that caused her to open her eyes quickly to blinding sunlight. Squinting, she looked about the room, seeing the chest of drawers that had once belonged to her mother and her mother's mother before that, the chairs, the photographs on the wall, the television, the rug thickly soft, the closet door slightly ajar, the bureau, the mirror atop the bureau, and herself in the mirror, all of it bright in the crisp morning light. She saw herself looking, if not refreshed, calmed, and within her the rage had gone, replaced by a numb humility and a plethora of questions. Questions. Questions. Questions.

Inwardly she had felt beatific that day of the funeral, ashamed at her anger of the day before. She greeted folk gently, softly, with a smile, her tones honey-flavored but solemn, and she reassumed the mantle of one-who-comforts-more-than-needing-comfort.

The immediate family had gathered at Maggie's house—Edward's father, Tom, Jr.; Tom, Jr.'s wife, Lucille; the grandbaby, Paul (Edward's brother); Clarissa. Raymond Brown's long black limousine took them from the front door of Maggie's house to the church, where the yard was crammed with people in their greys and navy blues, dark browns, and deep, deep burgundies. In her new humility she mused: When, oh when will we learn that death is not so somber, not something to mourn so much as celebrate? We should wear fire reds, sun oranges, hello greens, ocean-deep blues, and dazzling, welcome-home whites. She herself wore a bright dress of saffron and a blue scarf. She thought Edward would have liked it.

The family lined up and Gabriel approached her. As he stood before her—raven-haired, pink-skinned, abject, eyes bloodshot—she experienced a bevy of conflicting emotions: disgust, grief, anger, tenderness, fear, weariness, pity. Nevertheless she *had* to be civil, *had* to make a leap of faith and of understanding. Somehow she felt it had been asked of her. And though there were still so many questions, so much to sort out, for now she would mime patience, pretend to be accepting, feign peace. Time would unravel the rest.

She reached out, taking both his hands into her own, and said, the way she would to an old friend: "How have you been?"

I V

"BUT NOW, MISS MAGGIE . . ."

She sometimes imagined the good Reverend Barden as a toad-frog or an impotent bull. His rantings and ravings bored her, and his clumsy advances repelled her; and when he tried to impress her with his holiness and his goodness, well . . .

". . . that man should know better than to be plowing on a Sunday. Sunday! Why, the Lord said . . ."

"Reverend, I know what the Lord said. And I'm sure Morton Henry knows what the Lord said. But I am not the Lord, Reverend, and if Morton Henry wants to plow the west field on Sunday afternoon, well, it's his soul, not mine."

"But, Maggie. Miss Maggie. It's—"

"Well,"—Henrietta Fuchee sat perched to interject her five cents into the debate—"but, Maggie. It's your land! Now, Reverend, doesn't it say somewhere in Exodus that a man, or a woman in this case, a woman is responsible for the deeds or misdeeds of someone in his or her employ, especially on her property?"

"But he's not an emplo—"

"Well,"—Barden scratched his head—"I think I know what you're talking about, Henrietta. It may be in Deuteronomy . . . or Leviticus . . . part of the Mosaic Law, which . . ."

Maggie cast a quick glance at Gabriel. He seemed to be interested in and entertained by this contest of moral superiority. There was certainly something about his face . . . but she could not stare. He looked so *normal . . .*

"Well, I don't think you should stand for it, Maggie."

"Henrietta? What do you . . . ? Look, if you want him to stop, *you* go tell him what the Lord said. I—"

The Right Reverend Hezekiah Barden stood, hiking his pants up to his belly. "Well, *I* will. A man's soul is a valuable thing. And I can't risk your own soul being tainted by the actions of one of your sharecroppers."

"My soul? Sharecropper—he's not a sharecropper. He leases that land. I—wait! . . . Hezekiah! . . . This doesn't . . ."

But Barden had stepped off the patio onto the lawn and was headed toward the field, marching forth like old Nathan on his way to confront King David.

"Wait, Reverend." Henrietta hopped up, slinging her black pocketbook over her left shoulder. "Well, Maggie?" She peered at Maggie defiantly, as if to ask: *Where do you stand?*

"Now, Henrietta, I—"

Henrietta pivoted, her moral righteousness jagged and sharp as a shard of glass. "Somebody has to stand up for right!" She tromped off after Barden.

Giggling, Emma picked up the empty glasses. "I don't think ole Morton Henry gone be too happy to be preached at this afternoon."

Maggie looked from Emma to Gabriel in bewilderment, at once annoyed and amused. All three began to laugh out loud. As Emma got to the door she turned to Maggie. "Hon, you better go see that they don't get into no fistfight, don't you think? You know that Reverend don't know when to be quiet." She looked to Gabriel and nodded knowingly. "You better go with her, son," and was gone into the house; her molasses-thick laughter sweetening the air.

Reluctantly Maggie stood, looking at the two figures—Henrietta had caught up with Barden—a tiny cloud of dust rising from their feet. "Come on, Gabe. Looks like we have to go referee."

Gabriel walked beside her, a broad smile on his face. Maggie thought of her grandson being attracted to this tall white man. She tried to see them together and couldn't. At that moment she understood that she was being called on to realign her thinking about men and women, and men and men, and even women and women. Together . . . the way Adam and Eve were meant to be together.

v

INITIALLY SHE FOUND IT difficult to ask the questions she wanted to ask. Almost impossible.

They got along well on Saturday. She took him out to dinner; they went shopping. All the while she tried with all her might to convince herself that she felt comfortable with this white man, with this homosexual, with this man who had slept with her grandboy. Yet he managed to impress her with his easygoing manner and openness and humor.

"Mrs. W." He had given her a *nickname*, of all things.

No one had given her a nickname since . . . "Mrs. W.,
you sure you don't want to try on some swimsuits?"

She laughed at his kind-hearted jokes, seeing, oddly
enough, something about him very like Edward; but
then that thought would make her sad and confused.

Finally that night over coffee at the kitchen table she
began to ask what they had both gingerly avoided.

"Why didn't he just tell me?"

"He was afraid, Mrs. W. It's just that simple."

"Of what?"

"That you might disown him. That you might stop
. . . well, you know, loving him, I guess."

"Does your family know?"

"Yes."

"How do they take it?"

"My mom's fine. She's great. Really. She and Edward got along swell. My dad. Well, he'll be okay for
a while, but every now and again we'll have these talks,
you know, about cures and stuff and sometimes it just
gets heated. I guess it'll just take a little more time with
him."

"But don't you *want* to be normal?"

"Mrs. W., I *am*. Normal."

"I see."

They went to bed at one-thirty that morning. As
Maggie buttoned up her nightgown, Gabriel's answers
whizzed about her brain; but they brought along more
damnable questions and Maggie went to bed feeling
betrayal and disbelief and revulsion and anger.

In church that next morning with Gabriel, she began
to doubt the wisdom of having asked him to come. As

he sat beside her in the pew, as the Reverend Barden sermonized on Jezebel and Ahab, as the congregation unsuccessfully tried to disguise their curiosity—("What is that white boy doing here with Maggie Williams? Who is he? Where he come from?")—she wanted Gabriel to go ahead and tell her what to think: *We're perverts* or *You're wrong-headed, your church has poisoned your mind against your own grandson; if he had come out to you, you would have rejected him. Wouldn't you?* Would she have?

Barden's sermon droned on and on that morning; the choir sang; after the service people politely and gently shook Gabriel and Maggie's hands and then stood off to the side, whispering, clearly perplexed.

On the drive back home, as if out of the blue, she asked him: "Is it hard?"

"Ma'am?"

"Being who you are? What you are?"

He looked over at her, and she could not meet his gaze with the same intensity that had gone into her question. "Being gay?"

"Yes."

"Well, I have no choice."

"So I understand. But is it hard?"

"Edward and I used to get into arguments about that, Mrs. W." His tone altered a bit. He spoke more softly, gently, the way a widow speaks of her dead husband. Or, indeed, the way a widower speaks of his dead husband. "He used to say it was harder being black in this country than gay. Gays can always pass for straight; but blacks can't always pass for white. And most can never pass."

"And what do you think now?

"Mrs. W., I think *life* is hard, you know?"

"Yes. I know."

VI

DEATH HAD FIRST INTRODUCED itself to Maggie
when she was a child. Her grandfather and grandmother
both died before she was five; her father died when she
was nine; her mother when she was twenty-five; over
the years all her brothers except one. Her husband ten
years ago. Her first memories of death: watching the
women wash a cold body: the look of brown skin dark-
ening, hardening: the corpse laid out on a cooling board,
wrapped in a winding-cloth, before interment: fear of
ghosts, bodyless souls: troubled sleep. So much had
changed in seventy years; now there were embalming,
funeral homes, morticians, insurance policies, bronze
caskets, a bureaucratic wall between deceased and be-
reaved. Among the many things she regretted about
Edward's death was not being able to touch his body.
It made his death less real. But so much about the world
seemed unreal to her these dark, dismal, and gloomy
days. Now the flat earth was said to be round and bum-
blebees were not supposed to fly.

What was supposed to be and what truly was. Maggie
learned these things from magazines and television and
books; she loved to read. From her first week in that
small schoolhouse with Miss Clara Oxendine, she had
wanted to be a teacher. School: the scratchy chalkboard,
the dusty-smelling textbooks, labyrinthine grammar
and spelling and arithmetic, geography, reading out
loud, giving confidence to the boy who would never

learn to read well, correcting addition and subtraction problems, the taste and the scent of the schoolroom, the heat of the potbellied stove in January. She liked that small world; for her it was large. Yet how could she pay for enough education to become a teacher? Her mother would smile, encouragingly, when young Maggie would ask her, not looking up from her sewing, and merely say: "We'll find a way."

However, when she was fourteen she met a man named Thomas Williams, he sixteen going on thirty-nine. Infatuation replaced her dreams and murmured to her in languages she had never heard before, whispered to her another tale: *You will be a merchant's wife.*

Thomas Williams would come a-courting on Sunday evenings for two years, come driving his father's red Ford truck, stepping out with his biscuit-shined shoes, his one good Sunday suit, his hat cocked at an impertinent angle, and a smile that would make cold butter drip. But his true power lay in his tongue. He would spin yarns and tell tales that would make the oldest storyteller slap his knee and declare: "Hot damn! Can't that boy lie!" He could talk a possum out of a tree. He spoke to Maggie about his dream of opening his own store, a dry-goods store, and then maybe two or three or four. An audacious dream for a seventeen-year-old black boy, son of a farmer in 1936—and he promised, oh, how he promised, to keep Maggie by his side through it all.

Thinking back, on the other side of time and dreams, where fantasies and wishing had been realized, where she sat rich and alone, Maggie wondered what Thomas Williams could possibly have seen in that plain brown girl. Himself the son of a farmer with his own land, ten sons and two daughters, all married and doing well. There she was, poorer than a skinned rabbit, and not that pretty. Was he looking for a woman who would not flinch at hard work?

Somehow, borrowing from his father, from his brothers, working two, three jobs at the shipyards, in the fields, with Maggie taking in sewing and laundry, cleaning houses, saving, saving, saving, they opened their store; and were married. Days, weeks, years of days, weeks of days, weeks of inventory and cleaning and waiting on people and watching over the dry-goods store, which became a hardware store in the sixties while the one store became two. They were prosperous; they were respected; they owned property. At seventy she now wanted for nothing. Long gone was the dream of a schoolhouse and little children who skinned their knees and the teaching of the ABCs. Some days she imagined she had two lives and she preferred the original dream to the flesh-and-blood reality.

Now, at least, she no longer had to fight bitterly with her pompous, self-satisfied, driven, blaspheming husband, who worked seven days a week, sixteen hours a day, money-grubbing and mean though—outwardly— flamboyantly generous; a man who lost interest in her bed after her first and only son, Thomas, Jr., arrived broken in heart, spirit, and brain upon delivery; a son whose only true achievement in life was to illegitimately produce Edward by some equally brainless waif of a girl, now long vanished; a son who practically thrust the few-week-old infant into Maggie's arms, then flew off to a life of waste, sloth, petty crime, and finally a menial job in one of her stores and an ignoble marriage to a woman who could not conceal her greedy wish for Maggie to die.

Her life now was life that no longer had bite or spit or fire. She no longer worked. She no longer had to worry about Thomas's philandering and what pretty young thing he was messing with now. She no longer had the little boy whom Providence seemed to have sent her to maintain her sanity, to moor her to the Earth, and to give her vast energies focus.

In a world not real, is there truly guilt in willing reality to cohere through the life of another? Is that such a great sin? Maggie had turned to the boy—young, brown, handsome—to hold on to the world itself. She now saw that clearly. How did it happen? The mental slipping and sliding that allowed her to meld and mess and confuse her life with his, his rights with her wants, his life with her wish? He would not be like his father or his grandfather; he would rise up, go to school, be strong, be honest, upright. He would be; she would be . . . a feat of legerdemain; a sorcery of vicariousness in which his victory was her victory. He was her champion. Her hope.

Now he was gone. And now she had to come to terms with this news of his being "gay," as the world called what she had been taught was an unholy abomination. Slowly it all came together in her mind's eye: Edward.

He should have known better. I should have known better. I must learn better.

VII

THEY STOOD THERE AT the end of the row, all of them waiting for the tractor to arrive and for the Reverend Hezekiah Barden to save the soul of Morton Henry.

Morton saw them standing there from his mount atop the green John Deere as it bounced across the broken soil. Maggie could make out the expression on his face: confusion. Three blacks and a white man out in the fields to see him. Did his house burn down? His wife die? The President declare war on Russia?

A big, red-haired, red-faced man, his face had so many freckles he appeared splotched. He had a big chew of tobacco in his left jaw and he spat out the brown juice as he came up the edge of the row and put the clutch in neutral.

"How you all today? Miss Maggie?"

"Hey, Morton."

Barden started right up, thumbs in his suspenders, and reared back on his heels. "Now I spect you're a God-fearing man?"

"Beg pardon?"

"I even spect you go to church from time to time?"

"Church? Miss Maggie, I—"

The Reverend held up his hand. "And I warrant you that your preacher—where *do* you go to church, son?"

"I go to—wait a minute. What's going on here? Miss Maggie—"

Henrietta piped up. "It's Sunday! You ain't supposed to be working and plowing fields on a Sunday!"

Morton Henry looked over to Maggie, who stood there in the bright sun, then to Gabriel, as if to beg him

to speak, make some sense of this curious event. He
scratched his head. "You mean to tell me you all come
out here to tell me I ain't suppose to plow this here
field?"

"Not on Sunday you ain't. It's the Lord's Day."

" 'The Lord's Day'?" Morton Henry was visibly
amused. He tongued at the wad of tobacco in his jaw.
"The Lord's Day." He chuckled out loud.

"Now it ain't no laughing matter, young man." The
Reverend's voice took on a dark tone.

Morton seemed to be trying to figure out who Gabriel was. He spat. "Well, I tell you, Reverend. If the
Lord wants to come plow these fields I'd be happy to
let him."

"You . . ." Henrietta stomped her foot, causing dust
to rise. "You can't talk about the Lord like that. You're
using His name in vain."

"I'll talk about Him any way I please to." Morton
Henry's face became redder by the minute. "I got two
jobs, five head of children, and a sick wife, and the Lord
don't seem too worried about that. I spect I ain't gone
worry too much about plowing this here field on His
day none neither."

"Young man, you can't—"

Morton Henry looked to Maggie. "Now, Miss
Maggie, this is your land, and if you don't want me to
plow it, I'll give you back your lease and you can pay
me my money and find somebody else to tend this here
field!"

Everybody looked at Maggie. How does this look,
she couldn't help thinking, a black woman defending a
white man against a black minister? Why the *hell* am I

here having to do this? she fumed. Childish, hypocritical idiots and fools. Time is just slipping, slipping away and all they have to do is fuss and bother about other folk's business while their own houses are burning down. God save their souls. She wanted to yell this, to cuss them out and stomp away and leave them to their ignorance. But in the end, what good would it do?

She took a deep breath. "Morton Henry. You do what you got to do. Just like the rest of us."

Morton Henry bowed his head to Maggie, "Ma'am," turned to the others with a gloating grin, "Scuse me," put his gear in first, and turned down the next row.

"Well—"

Barden began to speak but Maggie just turned, not listening, not wanting to hear, thinking: When, Lord, oh when will we learn? Will we ever? *Respect*, she thought. Oh how complicated.

They followed Maggie, heading back to the house, Gabriel beside her, tall and silent, the afternoon sunrays romping in his black hair. How curious the world had become that she would be asking a white man to exonerate her in the eyes of her own grandson; how strange that at seventy, when she had all the laws and rules down pat, she would have to begin again, to learn. But all this stuff and bother would have to come later, for now she felt so, so tired, what with the weekend's activities weighing on her three-score-and-ten-year-old bones and joints; and she wished it were sunset, and she alone on her patio, contemplating the roundness and flatness of the earth, and slipping softly and safely into sleep.

THE ORIGIN
OF WHALES

THE WOMAN SAT. SHE sat on a porch under the roof of an old white house, with a massive oak before her, apple trees and plum trees and peach trees to the right and left, a grape arbor at the edge of the backyard, and an abandoned chicken coop at the other end near an empty smokehouse. She sat in a wicker-bottomed rocking chair like some grim guardian, peering into the late-September air as if searching for the place where the air gives way.

A car approached from the distance, creating a mean and dusty cloud that rose up and vanished. The car stopped in front of the house. The woman who drove the car stepped out and a boy jumped out from the other side: the boy clad in ripped and sporty clothes, his shoes unlaced; the woman nicely coiffured, smartly dressed.

"How you doing today, Aunt Essie?"

"Fine, child, just fine." The old woman's voice trembled like ripples across a pond. "Can't complain. Things sho could be whole lot worser. How you doing, gal? You and Thad ready to go?"

"Yes, ma'am. Soon as I get Little Thad straightened away with you, we'll be ready to go." Her voice was small but sharp, like a bird's. She absently watched the boy over by the ditch at the edge of the yard poking at something with a branch.

"Well, I knows y'all is looking forward to it."

"Yes, ma'am, we are. And I want to thank you for looking after Thad for us."

"Tain't no trouble atall. Where his things at?"

"In the car. He'll get them." The woman turned on the porch, her high heels clicking on the wood, and called to the boy, telling him to get his suitcase and tote bag out of the car, Mama's got to go, and did he have his books to study?, and to be good.

Through all this the boy continued to kick at clods of dirt around the ditch, his hands in his pockets, his head down.

"Thad, did you hear me?"

"Yeah," said the boy, without looking up.

"Come on, Thad. I've got to get on the road."

"You do it then." He did not look at her.

Closing her eyes as if in pain, she started toward the car.

"Wait." Essie stopped rocking. "Boy," her voice rolled forth. "You get your little black butt to that car and get your mess out. This very minute. Do you hear me?"

The boy stood still and stared at the older woman. After a while he did as she'd told him, without saying a word.

The mother sighed. "Seems I just can't do anything with him these days. I really do appreciate your keeping him, Aunt Essie. I hope he doesn't give you too much trouble."

Essie commenced to rock. "Now don't you worry about a thing, child. You all enjoy the convention and we'll be fine."

"Thank you, Aunt Essie." The woman gave a little girl's prim smile. "Oh, and Aunt Essie, how is Cousin Ruth? I heard she wasn't doing too well."

The old woman fixed her with a peculiar narrowing of the eyes. "Well, I don't know, girl. I just don't know. Saw her yestidy. Reverend Greene took me. Didn't look good. Had another stroke, you know." She shrugged. "But the Lord do know best, don't he?" Her voice trailed off into the blue. "You know." Essie's face lightened. "You know, me and her was born on the same day."

"Yes, Thad told me."

"Did?"

The woman smoothed the pleats in her dress with the palms of her hands. She glanced at her watch. "Oops! I better head on out."

The boy climbed the steps carrying his bags and looking stern. His mother smiled sweetly. "Now you be a good boy and do what your Aunt Essie says. Okay?"

He groaned.

She tried to kiss him, but he stepped back. "Aw, come on, Ma."

"Give your mama a good-bye kiss, boy, or I'll put this here walking stick upside your head. Go on now. Do it."

He gave the old woman a who-the-hell-do-you-think-you-are? glare but kissed his mother, grudgingly.

The mother thanked Essie again and walked to her car.

The old woman watched the car slide down the dirt road. She turned to the boy, who peered at her. She rolled her eyes. Presently the boy made his way over to the opposite side of the porch, walking its edge like a tightrope.

Essie turned her gaze toward the sky again. She told him where to put his bags and where he would be sleeping. She asked him if he was hungry. He said no. She told him they would eat in about half an hour.

"I'm going to look around."

"What?"

"I said I'm going out to take a look-see around in the yard. Okay?"

"You are?"

"Yeah."

"Is that a fact?" Essie bent over her cane, the gray wig on her head a little askew. She cocked her head to the side the way a listening fawn would.

The boy crossed his arms and tapped his feet. She began to tap her cane in counterpoint. They went on, ta-tap-tap, ta-tap-tap, like a couple of retired vaudevillian hoofers, their eyes locked in determination.

Finally the boy said, "*May* I go scout around?"

" 'Scout around'?"

"Ah, come on. Give me a break."

"Beg your pardon?" Her expression did not change nor did she stop tapping her stick.

He dropped his hands to his side. "Miss Aunt Essie, ma'am, may I *please* go out in the yard to play, Miss Aunt Essie, ma'am, thank you, may I, please, ma'am?" He bugged his eyes and stretched his mouth sorrowfully.

"Well, I reckon if you got the sense to ask somebody, you can go." The boy dashed down the steps, only touching one with his foot. "You stay out of them ditches!" she yelled after him. "And don't go no further than the yard."

Essie slowly made her way inside and down the hall, past the heavily framed sepia photographs of stern-looking men and women and past vases of dried flowers on doily-covered tabletops to the kitchen. She lifted a pot and filled it with water. Measured out cornmeal. Dipped out lard. Washed and drained a silvery-steel pan full of green-hued collard and mustard leaves. Stuffed them in a pot. Measured out a cup of rice. Put more water on to boil. Her hands moved about the cups and spoons and jars with an exaggerated deliberateness.

"Pssst! Pssst! Aunt Essie. Aunt Essie."

She peered out the window over the sink. "What you want now, boy?"

"Want to play hide-and-go-seek?"

Her expression did not change. She wiped her hand with a cloth. "Okay. Be right out." She checked the

pots and the water and walked out the back door, paus-
ing to look at a clock.

At the foot of the back door steps he met her.

"All right. Who's gone be It?"

"You."

"Uh-uh. You always hide. I'm gone hide this time,
feller."

The boy heaved an impatient sigh, shifted his
weight, and rolled his eyes. "Okay. Okay. I'll be It.
Ready?"

The woman started to walk away. "Well? Turn
around now. And start counting, why don't you? And
don't count too fast neither. To a hundred."

"A hundred!"

"Yeah, a hundred. And don't peep neither. Turn
round, I say."

"Good enough?" The boy had his back to her, his
hands over his face. "One hundred, ninety-nine, ninety-
eight . . ."

Essie crept away as best she could, tip-tip-tippy-
toed. She walked over to the old chicken coop, the door
off its hinges. She peeked in, paused, and shook her head
no. She turned to the grape arbor.

". . . seventy-six, seventy-five, seventy-four . . ."

She crouched slightly behind the big mother-stalk at
its center, which was twice as wide as she.

". . . twenty-four, twenty-three, twenty-two . . ."

She hunched there grinning, her back to the stalk,
leaning on her cane. She glanced into the net of green-
dark leaves above her head, saw a cluster of grapes, and
plucked one off.

". . . nine, eight, seven . . ."

With a grimace and a pucker she spat out the unripe grape, then quietly spat out more of the hull.

"Ready or not, here I come!"

She tilted her head to the right and listened. She tiptoed to a post at the edge of the arbor and peeked out. Little Thad was tiptoeing, just as she had, toward the front of the house. When he had vanished from sight, Essie snuck out from the arbor toward the steps. She began to smile, for she had almost arrived at home base. Something grabbed her elbows—

"Got you!" Thad had come up from behind her.

Essie jumped with a start. "Whooooweeee! You scared the devil out of me, you little—" Playfully, laughing, she swung her cane at him. He ducked like a gazelle.

"Your turn. Your turn." His face betrayed glee.

Essie advanced to the steps.

"Turn your back and close your eyes now."

"I know, boy. I know. I was playing this before your daddy was a itch in his daddy's breeches. Now go on and let me count. One hundred, ninety-nine, ninety-eight, ninety-seven . . ." Essie stopped counting out loud.

"Aunt Essie. Keep counting. Come on now, play fair."

"I am playing fair." She grinned. ". . . eighty-eight, eighty-seven, eighty-six, eighty-five . . ."

She looked through her hands through the screen door into the house, straight to the front door and out, across the fields in the front, out and out.

". . . thirty-five, thirty-four, thirty-three . . ."

Above her head she noted a spiderweb, and in it a

spider making a living mummy out of freshly caught prey. A wooden thud sounded in the distance not far behind her. A smirk spread across her face.

"... four, three, two, one. Ready or not, I'm gone get you." She turned and with a mockingly purposeful walk made her way toward the chicken coop. At its door she paused and inspected the ground around it.

"Now, Thad. I know you're in there and ain't but one way out. So come on, I got you."

No sound came from the henhouse.

"Come on, boy."

She bent over and peered in.

Suddenly Thad jumped up, yelling: "You got to get me fore I get to base." He tried to make a run for it, but Essie quickly stuck out her cane, tripping him to the ground.

Tears welled up in the corners of her eyes and slipped down her cheeks, and she could hardly catch her breath for laughing.

"Teach you. Teach you to mess with ole Essie. Teach you."

The boy sat stunned in disbelief and soon began to laugh along with her. They giggled and snickered outside the henhouse, pointing and poking at one another.

Essie suddenly stood up straight and gasped.

"Aunt Essie? What? What is it?"

"My collards, boy. I bet they's burnt." With that she made her way as quickly as she could to the house.

In the kitchen, over the pot, she sighed with relief when she found a smidgen of water left. Her breathing came short and she awkwardly sat in a chair. "Getting old. Getting old. Can't keep doing this foolishness. Gone kill me sho," she murmured as she tried to catch her breath and calm her breast. After a spell she rose, with more effort than before, and finished preparing the meal.

"Boy, come on in here and wash your face and hands and get ready for some supper. Hear?"

"Okay. What's for grub, Granny?"

"Watch your lip, son. Your grandma's dead. I'm your Aunt Essie. Remember that." She kept her eyes on the iron skillet as she tended the frying cornbread with a spatula.

The boy came back from the bathroom and sat at the table. The woman served his plate.

"Now you eat."

"What's this?"

"What you mean, 'What's this?' " She looked as perplexed as if someone had asked her why the sun burned in the sky. "It's collards, with some mustard greens mixed in. A little bit a fatback, rice, and cornbread. What you been eating all your life. What you think it is?"

"Collards!" The boy squinched his face up into an awful frown. "I can't eat no collards or no fatback neither." He stared at the plate as though it held a pile of dung.

"Boy, you eat that somethingtoeat. I ain't slaved all this time in this here kitchen to put up with your mouthing bout what you is and ain't gone eat. Eat." She looked at him hard, and he lifted his fork and ate. He mumbled something to himself.

"Your maw ate this here food when she was coming up. Your paw ate this here food when he was coming up. I ate it. My maw and paw ate it, and if it were good enough for them I reckons it'll suit you." She served her plate and slowly sank into her chair across the table from the boy, who picked at his food as though stirring leaves.

"Boy, stop picking in that food and start eating. Y'all chilren don't know what good eating is. Get you some nice smothered collard greens, some fatback, a nice piece of cornbread. Uh-uh. Now, boy, that's eating. Y'all young folks don't know. You just don't know." She stuffed some more collards into her mouth. The boy's eyes were fixed on his plate.

"You say you don't love no collards. You ever hear talk of my brother Hugh?"

"No, ma'am."

"Well, I don't know why. You should. He was my brother. Now, Hugh—he loved him some collard greens. You hear me? Sho did. I remember one time. Round August. Maw had cooked a great big ole pot of collards. Now ole Hugh—he couldn't a been more than your age—well, he knew them collards was about done. We was all out in the fields. So Hugh, he slips back to the house, you know, cause Maw left the pot on. And he ate that whole pot of collards."

"A whole pot! How? He couldn't have. He—"

"If I'm lying, I'm flying. Ate the whole blessed pot. Well, we come home for supper and there ain't no collards. Paw's furious. Say he's sho that Hugh done and ate them collards. 'No, no, Paw,' Hugh say. 'Twon't me. I seen a bear, Paw. I bet hit was a bear.'

"Now Paw wont no stupid man. He knew Hugh ate them collards. But he was a slick one, Paw was. So he just scratched his head a mite and say: 'Now, boy, if twas a bear they ought to be tracks, now oughten they?'

"Well, Hugh agreed, cause there wont nothing else to do but say he ate them collards, and he sho didn't want Paw to lay into him. So Paw and Hugh went out and I figured they was going to the woodpile so Paw could whup Hugh good. But guess what?"

"What?" Thad spoke from behind wide eyes and through a mouth full of greens.

"See, there had been a rainstorm the night before and the ground was soft. Hugh and Paw come back and say he be damned if there wont some tracks out yonder. Now I could see that ole Hugh didn't know what to think, cause he knowed he was lying. But Paw didn't give him a whupping, since he seen them tracks sho enough.

"But that night Hugh couldn't get to sleep. He twisted. He turned. He paced the floor."

"What was wrong with him?"

"He had the runs."

"The runs?"

"Diarrhea. The squirts. You know what I'm talking bout, boy."

"Oh. Well, why didn't he just go to the bathroom?"

"Cause,"—Essie threw her head back and chuckled—"son, in them days we didn't have no bathrooms in the house. No, Lord, we had a outhouse."

"Why didn't he go there?"

"Cause! He was scared the bear was gone get him."

"What happened?"

Essie took a swig from her lemonade. "Well, ole Hugh lasted till about eleven-thirty—in them days we went to bed at about nine or ten o'clock—and he just had to get out of there to make a stink real bad. So he went out the door. Bout two minutes later we heard yelling and screaming and in come Hugh, yelling: 'Paw, Paw, get your gun, get your gun, I seen a bear,' and he had messed all over himself. Paw whupped him good too."

"What about the bear?"

"Tsk." Essie rolled her eyes and picked up her fork. "Wont no bear, fool." Her eyes lit with the chewing of the greens and she nodded and rocked as she ate to show how good the food tasted to her. She winked at the boy. After a time of silence she began to hum. A low, rich tune. A hymn.

After supper Thad helped Essie clear the table, put away food, and wash dishes.

"Help me with my homework?" Thad rubbed a dishtowel across a plate until it squeaked.

"Don't I always?"

On the cleared kitchen table, atop the green-and-white oilcloth, Thad piled up his books: modern mathematics, spelling, social studies, science. Essie went to her black purse in the hall for her eyeglasses, which had round lenses and silver frames.

Thad and Essie sat at the table. By and by the brilliant horizon could be seen through the window; the sun was just setting; blues mingled with reds mingled with yellows as if the air were ablaze.

"Science first. We're doing biology now. Evolution. This says that all animals began as lower animals and adapted into what they are now. Do you believe that, Aunt Essie?"

"Not particularly." She frowned over her spectacles at the color-bright picture of dinosaurs and shaggy elephants in the book.

"Whales even were supposed to walk on the earth with legs and stuff once upon a time. Cause they're mammals like us and not fishes like goldfishes and sharks. Do you believe that?"

"No, I—"

The phone rang.

She jumped as if someone had come into her house uninvited.

"Boy, get that for me." She struggled to get to her feet, reaching for her walking stick. The boy ran to the phone in the front hall.

"Hello," he said. "Yes. Yes, ma'am . . . This is Thad . . . Thad Williams . . . Yes, ma'am . . . Aunt Essie is . . . Yes, ma'am . . . No, ma'am, I'm Thad Williams, the dentist's son . . . Yes, ma'am, Leota's boy . . . No, ma'am, my mama's Denise . . ."

"Who that, boy?" Essie looked almost angry with worry. The boy, confused, handed the phone to her. She took it while still asking him who it was.

"Hello!" She yelled into the receiver as though she had to push her voice through the wire. "Whasay? . . . Uh-huh, yeah . . . This *is* Essie. Hattie, that you? . . . Oh, girl, how you doing? . . . Uh-huh. Uh-huh. Yeah.

What? Lordchildyouknowitaintso . . ." She became silent for a time, nodding occasionally. The boy went
back to the kitchen table, flipping through his book.

"Which hospital is she in?"

The boy looked out the window into the newly har-
vested soybean field, into the ever-darkening sky.

"Who there with her?"

Through the window in the door before which she
stood, Essie watched a squirrel scamper up the oak tree
in the front yard. It had an acorn in its mouth and its
movements were quick and sharp.

"Well, I wisht I could go see bout her, but I'm keeping this boy of Thad's . . . Uh-huh . . . And, well, I
might bring him with me in the morning. Uh-huh.
Well, the Lord's time ain't man's time. Yes, Lord."

Essie hung up the phone.

"Who in the hospital?"

"Don't vex me, boy."

Essie took off her eyeglasses and gently placed them
by the phone. Haltingly, visibly tired, she walked out
the front door to the porch and her rocking chair. The
sky gathering velvet. Evening tangible. The squirrel
darted up and about tree limbs like some devilish der-
vish. Essie sat in the chair and began to hum. After a
few bars she stopped; but her rocking continued.

Thad stood in the doorway, behind the screen door,
watching Essie. She rocked. Finally he opened the door,
carefully so as to keep it from creaking, and sat down
on the floor next to the metronome figure rocking back
and forth. He reached up for her hand, but as his neared
hers he stopped. He stared at her hand on the arm of

the chair: pecan-colored, large-veined, the nails clipped short, wrinkles like stitching. He balled his fist up tight, looked at it, drew it to his chest.

"Gone help me with my homework?"

"Directly."

CORNSILK

for Amy

1. I SIT HERE. I sit here thinking hard about the smell of blood. It's been so long since that first time; I can barely remember its true color, its smell—like iron, perhaps? slightly funky?—its taste, thick, salty, again iron and iron. I sit here sniffing my fingers like some nasty boy, which I am, and all I can smell is the faint residue of soy sauce and MSG; not blood; not iron. What I would give to smell it again. To taste it. Hers. Her blood.

I've started smoking again. I did it at first because she did it; I didn't much like it then. But she looked so sexy when she did it, leaning up against the headboard, her hair in her eyes, her legs gapped open, a pillow between them. She could French-inhale. I can do it now.

I couldn't then. Back then I would damn near choke. Now I smoke two packs a day.

So much is said of that one good cigarette after a heavy, good meal. For me it's that one good cigarette after orgasm. They aren't the same now, the orgasms. I need the blood, the slickery sensation, the mess, the horror, the grossness, the danger. These days blood is a dangerous thing, even more so than in those days. It makes cigarettes seem harmless.

I smoke too much.

2. SHE LIFTS HER BREAST up for me to suck. She likes that. The nipple darkly brown, its areola too broad for a twenty-four-year-old woman; the small bumps pebble-hard, prickly. I bite it: she sucks in air through her nose. I suck her titty, my sugar-tit, my teat, my pacifier. In my mouth it hardens, opens, a cactus blossom in my mouth. I want it to ooze bitter milk. Her breath comes short, as if she were sprinting, her legs begin to tread water on either side of me, she calls my name urgently: *Aaron, Aaron*, as if I am to save her, as if she's about to expire. Her legs spread wider. I smell her. I feel her. Wet, hot, her pelvis speaks to me in Babylonian tongues, wild and insane, singing an ancient tune, dulcimer and zither and cymbal, vibrating, humming; I am flute, cornet, bow: we sing. We make a joyful noise unto the Lord, a raucous noise, an unholy song of heat and lust to an unholy Lord.

Lord, Lord, Lord.

3. DAYS OF DUST AND debris and desolation. Dry days. Deathly dull days. Days of dim doom, dawn to

dusk. My days. But that's what I wanted, isn't it? Se-
curity. Safety. That's why I got my English degree at
Duke, my MBA at Georgetown, and my JD at Vanderbilt. Right? Why I chose tax law, for Christsakes.
Blessed be the name of bankruptcy, depreciation,
amortization.

A glorified accountant. That's what I truly am, regardless of the prestige of the firm, or how brightly the
receptionist grins in the morning when I step off the
elevator; or how the paralegals and the very junior as-
sociates seem to tremble in my presence. Who cares?
Who will remember me, fifty years after my death, even
if I become the first black partner at Henson, Spitzer,
Klein, et al.? A rich old nigger who climbed up the
money heap of junk bonds and golden parachutes and
mergers and estate management. Big deal. Washington
is full of bright, rich, bland, myopic black people. I'm
just another one.

But how many change at night? I wonder. I can't be
the only one. Out of my suit, into my jeans or naked
on the floor. Jekyll to Hyde (or is it Hyde to Jekyll?).
My mind a blight of wrongdoing and wickedness. Is
she corrupted by so much iniquity? Does she, in her
husband's arms, dream of me? Does she faint trying to
remember the taste of sweat on my neck? I doubt it. I
very seriously doubt it. So I'm alone.

Some days I can't wait to get home, can't wait for
the sun to go down, to fling off my clothes, get in bed,
pick up the phone and dial 1-900-555-GIRL or 1-900-
555-PSSY or 1-900-555-SEXX. It doesn't matter, now
does it? Sometimes I try the party lines. Regardless, I
am unsatisfied. So little poetry to their descriptions, their

talk pedestrian, crude, nigh-illiterate, sad, depressing.
Sometimes I begin to cry. Sometimes I just ask: Tell me
about your nipples. While hammering myself violently.
I come too quickly. In my sleep—I know it's a bad
cliché—I dream of her.

You see, I've tried videos; I own over a hundred
now. I look for likenesses, resemblances, but few have
my sister's mulatto hue, or her particular features, like
my father's nose or my father's lips.

So I don't watch the videos anymore. They only
frustrate me.

4. AN OLD MAN ONCE told me that to plant corn
properly you must put at least three seeds in a hole at a
time. This way, when the plants grow up tall and begin
to ovulate there will be another plant close enough to
fertilize the next. Their pollen is heavy. Not like the
pollen of azaleas or apple blossoms or peach blooms.
They need to be close to insure the infection that leads
to fat ears of corn. Isn't that something else? Must be
nice.

5. I DON'T HATE MY father, though I suspect you
suspect I do. No, he engenders fear in me, perhaps the
way Yahweh inspired fear in Abraham's bosom.

He's a big man, both literally and figuratively. He's
a doctor, the only doctor in a small town in North
Carolina called Tims Creek. Where my mother is from.
He's six-one, darkly handsome, sports a full white beard
at fifty-five. A striking figure. He grew up in New
York, went to Morehouse and Howard Medical School.
He was the sort of man who studied Arabic while

interning at Columbia-Presbyterian. Very radical in the
sixties. He met Mom in Atlanta. In the seventies, dis-
illusioned with "the Movement" by the time I was about
ready for high school, he decided the most effective use
of his skills would be to practice in the rural South,
where good medical care was hard to come by. Fateful
decision.

But not as fateful as his decision—characteristic of
Dad, morally upright, constantly challenging himself—
to take in the one Big Mistake he had made in his life:
the nineteen-year-old daughter he had conceived before
college. His father, a doctor too, in Harlem, had done
right by the girl, but Pop felt the need—why, I still can't
quite understand—to readopt her. You see, he didn't
approve of the life her mother, poor, living in Spanish
Harlem, was providing for his firstborn. He had plans
for his progeny. Great Yahweh, Malcolm Aaron Streeter, *and his Covenant will go unbroken throughout the ages,
for time immemorial, for your children and your children's
children's children. Amen.*

What would ole grey-beard say if he knew what he
had set in motion? He'd probably quote the Bhagavad
Gita or the Koran or some obscure Aztec text.

I really don't hate my father. I'm just scared to death
of him. This is the honest truth.

6. TRUST ME. (THOUGH YOU should never trust
a lawyer who actually says: Trust me.) I know it sounds
Freudian; but it is not Freudian, not Freudian in its intent, though perhaps in its execution; Freudian in its
caresses, Freudian in its French kisses and sucking, its

licking and gasps and funk. Not Freudian in its uncon-
scious meaning. No. I beseech you, as Cromwell said,
"in the bowels of Christ, to think it that you might be
wrong." Not Freud, okay? Not in his symbolism or his
interpretation. Jung perhaps. An archetypal fuck-up, a
consciousness of sin. But Freud, much as I respect him,
has nothing to do with it. So please put away your *Totem
and Taboo* and your *Interpretation of Dreams* and your
Psychopathology of Everyday Life and your copy of *Three
Contributions to the Theory of Sex*. Okay? I've read them,
you see. I've read them all. And trust me. Freud and his
ideas don't figure into this little drama.

7. I HATED TIMS CREEK at first, but not as much
as she did, and not as long. She still hates it, she tells
me. Even though she's never truly left the state since
she came to live there, keeps going back to see her father
and stepmother in Tims Creek, and lives in a town very
like Tims Creek. But she insists she hates it.

I can't hate it now. It's become a part of me. A part
of my internal landscape. The forests, the pastures, the
hog pens, the barns and chicken coops, the tobacco
fields, the soybean fields, and of course the cornfields.
Not to make too much of them. They're there, certainly,
and I can't avoid them.

I remember my first look into them, at the edge as
if I were staring into a Conradian jungle, a North American Congo. I expected Indians to come dashing out,
not real Indians but the Indians of a twelve-year-old's
imagination: tomahawk-toting, befeathered, howling.
A racist notion, yes, but innocent in its intent. Some-

times I imagined drums, like the beat of copulation, though I had no idea at the time that that was the rhythm of sex, the rhythm I imagined, felt in my soul. Though in truth it's also the thud of the heart, the motion of the lungs, the same harmless, infectious rhythm.

But there was nothing sinister about those first years before she came, before I lost interest in imaginary games with imaginary playmates, spaceships, super-heroes, sorcerers. The fields, the woods, gave me such freedom, more than a kid growing up on West 135th Street could have dreamed of.

At first we lived with my grandmother, Miss Jesse. Thin, deceptively delicate, Victorian, Wilmington-bred; daughter of a realtor, widow of an insurance man with land that became hers. Imperious, hard as brass knuckles, Miss Jesse, cloaked in cigarette smoke, issued hoarse commands obeyed without question; her eyes saw levers and switches instead of people. She could fell a man with one well-placed word, disintegrate a woman with an accurately calibrated glance.

Her relationship with Jamonica was contentious at best. This urban girl of 116th Street and Third Avenue, now ordered to mop floors, cut grass, wash windows and porches. Jamonica fussed. Miss Jesse glared back regally, conceding nothing. My mother sat in the wings embroidering, knitting, reading, choosing not to get involved. Ole Malcolm was much too busy working out the salvation of his Chosen People to be bothered, or to care. So Miss Jesse and Jamonica finally worked out a truce of sorts. Though I believe, secretly, Miss Jesse enjoyed the spirited young girl's protests and the domestic warfare.

How would she, now, from her grave, comment upon our forbidden coupling?

8. I'VE TRIED THE ESCORT services. Pathetic. These women, I mean. Sad. I like to think of myself as a feminist, or at least one who does more than pay lip service. But don't all men harbor secret romantic visions about prostitutes, about carefree, totally free, uninhibited human toys? I must be honest here.

But these poor women. Some bitten by the Horatio Alger bug of saving and working to get through college, maybe to become bank tellers or flight attendants or pizza joint managers. Even they seem sad, in the end, lost to their hard-to-realize dreams. I rarely talk to them about their lives anymore. Not that I see them that often. The services don't take MasterCard.

I describe what I want sent over and they're generally all wrong. Nothing like Jamonica. Some come as stereotypical harlots: gum-chewing, lipsticked in vivid red, fluffy-haired, ill-spoken—a vision of delight, to be sure, for some fat, impotent beer distributor. Or they come young, bewildered, innocent still, though in the very maw of the monster; pure yet defiled. Or they'll send me hardened, practical women, good at their trade— for it is a trade to them, serving up fantasy. I never tell them they are to be my sister. Though they're probably used to much kinkier.

One girl—sorry: woman—called herself Rose. She came the closest of any I've seen so far. But I heard no Assyrian music, felt no ancient demons howl; I ended up holding her, eyes closed, limp as yarn, calling, calling softly.

"Who's Jamonica?" Rose asked me.

"An old lover."

She kissed me coyly, a kiss reeking of sentimentality and audacious pity. I told her to leave.

Perhaps it's true then, what I've thought all along. What's that old platitude—I know it's tacky as hell to mention, but why not? you'll think of it anyway—how does it go? The closer kin, the deeper in?

Exactly.

9. I SIT HERE AND wonder if I'm truly crazy. Am I? Crazy?

I've tried shrinks. They think the problem is with my family. No shit.

Am I sitting here amid boxes of chicken and snow-peas, beef and broccoli, gooey rice and the remnants of an eggroll dabbled in mustard and duck sauce, scribbling the thoughts of a madman? Or am I merely depraved? Are these the thoughts of a neurotic? A psychopath? Or am I just more honest than most? Smarter? Am I daring greatly? Or have I been cursed for violating a sacred trust older than Yoruba legend and Nippon lore? Am I the victim of the gods' own jealous wrath? Eat of any tree in the garden, but you are damned if you eat of the fruit of the One Tree. Double-damned if you enjoy it. Triple-damned if you can't get enough.

Damn.

10. LET ME TELL YOU about my sister. I already have, you'll say. But no. I've told you of my infatuation and my obsession. Of lovemaking. But Jamonica herself is something else again.

She visited two summers in a row before she came to live with us. I hated her at first, resenting the intrusion in our lives, this illegitimate half-breed distracting my father, who already had problems focusing on me. Selfish little bastard, wasn't I?

Jamonica despised the country, she said. Claiming allergies to everything—grass, dogs, air—she carried the city around with her in her makeup, her clothing, her perfume, her sneering at the dull country folk, saying: "Oh, you're so *country!*," impatient in conversation. Everything, everything moved too slow for her. She was surrounded by bumpkins as far as she was concerned and kept dreaming aloud of Manhattan and subways and sidewalks. I thought she was crazy.

She wanted to smoke. She did smoke. Miss Jesse and Dad said: No. She persisted, sneaking a smoke in her room, in the backyard. My mom said: Hell no, and Jamonica went even farther out of her way to defy them. I would tattle on her whenever I had hard evidence, hoping maybe they'd get rid of her.

But all this changed that second summer, perhaps the harbinger of my ordeal, my fixation, the bad habit to come. Let's be portentous.

At first the boys would hang around the barn, loudly laughing at us laboring country folks. The boys? Phil, Terry, and Vaughn. Three nephews of the man who leased Miss Jesse's land. Bad boys from the Bronx. Visiting for the summer. Nineteen, seventeen, sixteen. Walking bombs of testosterone, adrenaline, semen, hot blood, and bad attitude. The barn? The tobacco barn, where my little sister, Miss Jesse, I, and groaning, moaning, protesting, fussing Jamonica backhanded the bright-green leaves to be tied and sent into the barn for firing. Miss Jesse insisted we work in tobacco. It built character. Tobacco. *Nicotiana tabacum.* It's a member of the nightshade family, you know? Belladonna and all that. Now there's a symbol for you.

I loved the work; it was more like play to me. Playing with doodlebugs in the sand around the barn, listening to the women gossip. Sweat and toil were new and thrilling to me. But Jamonica never stopped bitching. Hated the black tar the leaves left caked on her hand. Hated the talk of soap operas and boyfriends and unfaithful husbands. I think at one point she even threatened to kill Miss Jesse.

Like wolves the boys came. Maybe they heard Jamonica was from Harlem. Maybe they were bored. Maybe they smelled her, her especially, caught her scent in the wind.

"Hey, you. Yeah, you. Where you from?"

"Why? Where you from?"

"A Hundred and Seventy-first and Grand Concourse. Okay? Where're you from?"

"Around a Hundred and Sixteenth."

"Got a boyfriend?"

"Yeah."

"And he let you come down here in these woods all by yourself?"

They snorted and chortled and heh-heh-hehed. I wanted to stuff tobacco leaves down their throats.

"Why don't you boys start working?" Miss Jesse gave the oldest a stare that I'm sure would have turned me into lead. "If you plan to hang around bothering us."

"Aaaah. No, thank you. We on vacation."

"Well, then. In that case I suggest you vacate these premises."

"But we like it here."

I had never seen boys look at other people like that. Or perhaps I had just not noticed it. A look like hunger, but where hunger involves the head and belly, this involved the entire body, the legs, the arms, the hips, the backbone. They leered. But the most disturbing thing, to GI Joe-toting, *Batman*-reading, electric-train-set-operating me, was the way Jamonica flirtatiously, coquettishly, seemed to be egging them on, with her eyes, with her lips. Could she be enjoying this? Of course not. These boys were dogs.

"I said"—Miss Jesse stepped back from work and began walking toward the boys—"you boys had better find another place to amuse yourselves. We are working here!" She stood before the oldest boy, Phil.

Obviously, he intended to hang tough at first, but apparently Miss Jesse's psychic bullwhip lashed out and snap-crackled his brain. He stumbled backward and swallowed. "Okay, Miss. We hear you, all right? All right."

They left, looking back purposefully, their rowdy talk trailing off behind them, jackals slinking into the distance.

"Those boys are no good." Miss Jesse shook her head, going back to work. "No good."

No good, but not gone. They made their presence known to Jamonica, and I picked up on it as though I had a shortwave attached to her, eavesdropping. Here, there, around Tims Creek, they lurked. I kept my watergun full.

One day—perhaps, being portentous, I should say: One Fateful Day—Jamonica and I were walking back home from working at the barn. The boys approached us from the other direction. I remember the feeling I fought against. The fear of being bested in a fight, the anger of intrusion, the newborn desire to protect my sister. Maybe even jealousy, inchoate, innocent, impossible.

"Where you heading, little lady?"

"Nowhere you going or been."

They guffawed too loudly, stroking their chins, eyeing her as if she were a new car.

"You sure about that?"

My cue. I leapt forward. "Leave her alone, you—"

"What the fuck is this?" Phil barely gave me a full look. "Tell it to go away fore I squash it."

"He's my brother. And I suggest you keep your hands to yourself." She grabbed me from behind and my diastolic blood pressure surely jumped ten points from humiliation.

"With my feet, babe. Not my hands. The hands is for you."

They had us encircled, or, more accurately, entriangled.

"You full of talk, Phil."

"*Talk?* Course I got a rap. But, sweet thang, I got something else."

"Like what?"

"Come on, I'll show you."

He stood in front of me, facing her, me squished

between the two of them like so much baloney. I punched him between the legs.

What happened next I remember only impression-istically, due mostly to the whir of activity but also to not wanting to remember: Phil furiously pushes me to his brothers: they jostle me about, making rude comments about my size, manhood, and intelligence: I try to watch what peculiar negotiations Phil is making with my sister: she apparently negotiates back: I see him nod toward the cornfield off the road: I'm on the ground crying: the three boys and Jamonica go into the field.

Sobbing, I stood at the edge of the cornfield, part of me scared to death, part of me confused, and part of me, the part familiar with comic-book heroes, ready to slip into my costume and fly into the field and deliver my sister from harm. I had no cape, no ray gun, no smoke bombs. Batman never cried. I ran in. The tall corn swatting me in the face, the uneven earth making it hard to keep my footing, I knocked over stalks to find them. After a time I did, peering through the stalks as through leafy prison bars.

He seemed to be hurting her. Her pants were open at the top, revealing panties, pubic hair; his hand was between her legs; he held her closely, violently, his mouth all over hers; his pants were down about his knees; his penis a small, black dragon. The other two boys looked on lewdly, rubbing their pants. I heard Jamonica giggle. I lunged toward them but something stopped me.

Even now my eyes tear a bit. Not for what they did to my sister but because that slap hurt. No one has ever hit me quite so hard. I sat between two cornrows, rocking like a spinning top about to fall, the breath knocked out of me. I looked on. Saw the dragon disappear. Saw that she enjoyed it and clutched him, hard, as if he were saving her.

I did not stop running until I got to the house, looking over my shoulder most of the way thinking the boys would catch me and perhaps do the same wicked thing to me. I suspected I would not enjoy it.

Miss Jesse sat on the porch with Mrs. Pearsall. Out of breath, face covered with dirt and sweat, weeds and corn tassels about my hair, tears in my eyes, I yelled at the top of my voice: "Grandma, Phil is doing it to Jamonica in the cornfield!"

She did not blink. She reached for a cigarette smoldering there in a nearby ashtray. I can still hear her, how she formed her words, the sound of the words as they whipped through me: clear, measured, firm, piercing:

"Young man, you will learn there are things you do not tell your elders. A tattletale is not an admirable thing to be. Now go wash your face and hands—you look a sight."

For once I did not obey her. I sat on the stoop and stared at the cornfield, unbraided, picking at my confusion like a new sore.

Finally she hollered for me to do as she said, and I did.

At length Jamonica returned, calm, a look I now know is called afterglow on her face, a few strands of hair askew, a piece of tassel here and there.

"Sister,"—Miss Jesse always called younger women Sister, even my mother—"Sister, supper's about done. Go wash up."

No one said a word about it. Not even I. Nor has she said a word to me, to this day. I often replay the scene in my mind. Tell you a deep secret: in my replay I am Phil. Jamonica is Jamonica is Jamonica. Wicked, no?

11. CORN. *ZORN MAZE* OR *Zea Mays*. A very peculiar plant, as much vegetable as grain. An ingenious invention of nature. Its seeds can be eaten either young or aged, ground into a powder, turned into a paste, and cooked. The Native Americans, as we all know from TV commercials, called it *maize*. But it's indigenous, in certain varieties, to Australia and Africa as well. The Egyptians grew it. The word we use comes from the Anglo-Saxon *coren* or *korn(e)* or *corne* or *coorn*, borrowing from the Middle Teutonic *korno*, meaning grain, finally coming to mean "a worn-down particle." In that way it was applied to any grain at first, wheat, rye, barley, etc.; or to small seeds such as apple or grape seeds; or to mean a bit of gunpowder or salt. The first known use as applied to *maize* was in 1679 and it stuck.

You've seen cornfields. You've seen how they move in the breeze. You've known the feeling I've spoken of, the dread and excitement. Expectation. Fear. As if something were lurking there. Imagine that feeling applied to a woman.

12. I WANTED TO BECOME a doctor, but that would have made him too happy. Couldn't do that. (You think it's because I hate him; but I don't, as I've told you; I don't. If I had become a doctor, I'd have failed him in the end. So his happiness would have been

short-lived. And I'd have been humiliated. See?) So I chose botany first. He was lukewarm about that. He finally came around by the time I said ethnobotany, in my freshman year. This made him a wee bit happier. Christmas of my junior year I changed my mind. I told him before I went back to school that January that I had chosen to declare pre-law. You should have seen the look on his face. Later he changed his tune; I suspect he could envision me a judge. When I got to law school he fully expected me to specialize in civil rights law. (At Vanderbilt? He just wasn't thinking.) When I broke the news over dinner that it would be tax law, I could see that he had pretty much given up on me. Not that I wouldn't do well; well was a given. But not exceptionally. Not gloriously. There is no glory in tax law.

13. SHE STARTED IT. I know how petulant and boy-like such a statement sounds. *She started it.* But it's true. She did.

Does the math confuse you? It's confusing. Dr. Streeter reached down into the miry clay when he was nineteen, just before he went off to Morehouse, and made Jamonica of a comely Puerto Rican woman. He begat me upon my mother in holy matrimony while in residency, when he was twenty-seven. Actually, chronologically speaking, six years, not seven, separate us. My younger sister came along three years later. Okay? I was nineteen—we Streeter men have a thing for the number nineteen and carnality—when it started. She was twenty-five. Not so daunting an idea. Well, the math at least.

Before that moment, before we entered the door

with the hidden No Exit sign, where you couldn't get
a refund on your ticket, before I truly knew her like
David knew Bathsheba, we were just big sis and little
bro. She was someone to annoy me, reprove me, get
in the bathroom before me, to drive me around before
I got my license, to tattle on, to play practical jokes on
and make fun of. There were other girls and nasty sex
before her—I never claimed to be an angel. But she was
the milestone, the dividing line between BC and AD.

How? Don't be silly. Why? Don't be naïve. What?
Now there's an intelligent question. I don't know, *what?*
What made us do it. Alone in the house. She had finally
graduated from NC Central after taking a few semesters
off here and there. Papa proud. Mama relieved. Other
mother happy. Grandma dead. I was about to go off to
Duke. Summer. Summer of possibilities. Did we both
sense it? All the possibilities? There on the couch, everybody gone? Did we both think, He/she's only my *half-*
sister/brother? I think not. I don't think we thought.

You must understand there was a general excitement
in the atmosphere. You know, the flip side of teenage
angst for me—the freedom to come; for her the horizon
of life, career, *possibilities* . . .

Oh, but this is too abstract. I can't get you to understand me, if not to empathize then to sympathize,
through cold and vague language. Let me be romantic,
people respond to that. Let me be dramatic. Let me
conjure.

Okay. It's June. Early June. Dr. and Mrs. Streeter
and little sister Streeter are away, not for a day or a
weekend but for two whole weeks. Jamonica and Aaron
are home with nothing to occupy them for the duration.

They talk, now both young adults, about this and that. They become close. It's as if they were new people to each other. Aaron has had those pernicious growth spurts since Jamonica has been away; he is handsome, strapping; his voice has deepened; his chest and arms and legs are hard from tennis and track and basketball. At twenty-five Jamonica is—well, I'm being romantic, right?—a flower, a Tahitian nymph out of Gauguin, her lips plump and rich; her eyes, blackly, oilily, sinisterly, smokily, with magic in them, remind him of reptiles, not in repulsion but in cold heat . . . This isn't doing it, is it? I could play with words all night, but they would only start to get at how the sight of her on a stool, sitting carelessly, or lounging on the sofa smoking, made my pulse flitter, my penis roll over and sigh . . . I give up . . .

They sit before the television watching *Sanford and Son* (I even remember the episode but I won't bore you). They have become more and more lewd in their innuendo and joking. Aaron grabs her now and then, at first brotherly, jocularly, but the grasp lingers a bit long and Aaron senses that she does not mind, that she is even solicitous. That day while watching TV, Aaron, erect as a stalk of corn, notices her skirt hitched up to her thigh. That moment changes things. Irrevocably. A circuit fuses in his mind. *Psssst.*

He gets on his knees as if to pray. He spreads her legs, his hands trembling on her knees. He begins to kiss the tender insides of her thighs. She coos and grabs his head, urging him on. He inches up to her panties, pulls them down. She gives a giggle. He sees it there.

Humble little thing. He pauses only for a moment: already defying propriety, holy law, why stop? Against her half-uttered protests, he pulls it out: smelly, clotted, horrid. Her skirt is ruined, a spot will be left on the couch, a deep-maroon Rorschach, which his mother will never mention. The cushion will remain forever turned over.

Okay. So I lied. I started it then.

We practically lived in bed after that. I expected to hear Dad's car drive up at the most inopportune moments. But miraculously, we were left to our iniquity. Precious, sinful freedom. Wild positions. I learned much that week. I long to be able to forget it all and return to ignorance. What bliss I'd know.

14. TRUTH IS, I WOULD have made a terrible botanist. A terrible scientist. I flunked chemistry and my interest in the field is very limited. At best.

15. SOME NIGHTS I LEAVE my house and wander the streets of Washington, visiting those places where love is for sale, or at least for barter. While walking I question my sanity again, wonder if any mother's daughter is safe with me on the prowl. Might I see my sister's likeness and thrust myself upon her, poor cherub? Unsuspecting victim of incest, innocent yet spoiled? But I'm not capable. You see, I have to be invited in, as she invited me. Legs spread, eyes rolled back St. Sebastian–like, trilling: Come. So I look for the willing.

I've tried everything. Trust me. You name it, as

kinky and as raunchy as they make it. Leather, spanking, drugs, domination, water sports—hoping to find a replacement for my addiction. I even tried bestiality once but broke out laughing too hard to go through with it; I fear I traumatized the pitiful creature.

I don't walk the streets as much as I used to. Too many people searching for too many things. Confusion is my enemy. My focus is clear.

16. I SIT HERE WRITING, scribble, scribble, scribble. What do I think I'm accomplishing? All else has failed, do I think writing will exorcise the demon in me? Am I possessed? Is Merrim, Prince of the Air, whispering over my shoulder? Claptrap. I have one of the best educations money can buy and all I can do is confide to paper. What's wrong with this picture?

I've done my reading. All my homework. Should I tell you what I've found? Shall I quote Whitman or Auden or Pound? Shall I give you a Canto or a Quartet? Hughes or Baraka or Hayden? Lincoln or Du Bois? Eliot's "No! I am not Prince Hamlet, nor was meant to be"? Stevens's "If her horny feet protrude, they come / To show how cold she is, and dumb"? Brooks's "Where you have thrown me, scraped me with your kiss"? Moore's "Arise, for it is day!"? From Dr. Miller, Dr. Sacks, Dr. Bettelheim, Dr. Gruen? Anything. Read to you from my commonplace book, tease you with the profane, the sacred phrases that strike me, struck me? De Sade, Miller, Lawrence? I have them all. Words. Babble. They give me no answers, so I choke on them, give them back, spit them up and out. I sniff them but I smell no blood. Alas.

17. I MUST BE FAIR. She's struggling now. Not about me. Not with the memory of what's been done. No. She has no time for that luxury. Seems Dr. Streeter's scheme didn't quite work for her. She's trapped, you see. She fell in love. She married. But it's not a happy tale. (Do I gloat?) He's a trucker. Big, crude, sentimental. Name's Fred. Can you believe it? Fred. Jesus. It seems after all those years in college and all that talk about the Big City she opted to remain in North Carolina, manage a Dairy Queen, and make babies with Fred. Yes, Fred. The third is on the way. I don't know what kind of magic that hairy, beer-guzzling, australopithecine cretin has in his pants or wherever he hides it, but she stays in a trailer outside Whiteville of all places, like a slave, a mere shadow of the racy, witty, intelligent Jamonica I knew.

I visited her last month but I didn't see her. Not the woman I smuggled into my dorm room, the woman I made laugh at horror movies and baked banana-walnut bread with, the sister I've known better than any brother should. Her body now misshapen from multiple births, now sullen-eyed, smoking even more, a sepia and hollering baby in her arms, another in the high chair. She smiles, she looks, but her eyes never truly focus on anything, not on TV, not on her babies, not on her dingy trailer, not on Fred, certainly not on me.

Tell me. Who am I searching for now? Where is she?

He beats her, you know. Now there's a fucking cliché for you. "Oh, yeah, my sister, the pretty one, she's a battered wife now." He beats my sister and she refuses to let anyone do anything about it. She goes home for a day, two; she goes back to him.

"You don't have to put up with this shit," I tell her.

She just looks at me, through me really. Her eyes are dry. Not reptilian but pathetically mammalian. "You don't get it, do you? Of course you don't. How can you?"

She looks away. Not even staring into the wall, just looking.

I want to say: Teach me. Teach me.

18. MADNESS? OBSESSION? DEPRAVITY? ALL I can think of is the smell of pubic hair, its look; the upper thigh, you know, where it connects to the center, that crevice there where the nerves cluster; the foot, you've licked a foot before, nibbled a heel? The sight, just the sight, of the clitoris, that red, wonderful proboscis. Anatomy, anatomized, particles of a person. Hers, all hers. Just so much flesh otherwise. Not her. Not her. Her.

19. TWO YEARS. FRESHMAN AND sophomore years. Truly wicked. You see, nobody knew. Nobody knew she was my sister. She'd come for a weekend. A week, twice or thrice, staying in my room. All the guys thought me such a stud. I guess I was. More than even I knew. This *older* woman at my service, slipped past

the RA, gasping in my room; my roommate, if not in bed with his own joy-toy, envious beyond expression. Hellacious fantasy. We did all the things college sweet-kins do, the football games, the basketball games, the rock concerts, the pizza parlors, the movies. We were defying someone to blow our cover. I was too stupid, I guess *we* were too stupid, to think beyond the moment. They never found out. They never knew. If they had looked, and looked closely, they would have seen; if they had looked beyond her light skin, my dark skin, her thick, long, mermaid's hair, my tightly curled, closely cropped hair, they could have seen, if they had truly looked, that our mouths, our eyes, our chins cried: Brother, sister, sister, brother! But who would dare think such a thing? Who would dare *do* such a thing?

Two years of iniquitous bliss. And when it ended, I ended. How's that for melodramatic?

20. THAT YEAR, THE END of the second year, I had a major fight with Dr. Streeter. You know, the one I don't hate.

My grades were not up to snuff. I wonder why? I had been placed on something very like probation. Academic watch, they called it.

"My son? A son of mine?"

"Dad—"

"No. I don't know what you're doing up in Durham but it's got to stop. It—"

We hurtled words for hours, and somehow it managed to go beyond grade point and "discipline." It got to father-and-son bullshit and at the top of my voice I remembered yelling: "But I don't want to be *you*. Can't you get it through your fucking skull? Don't you know I hate your black ass?"

He did not move, aside from a twitching of his jaw. He left the room. He left the room and did not speak to me for two days. When he did it was to take me back to school. Making clear my fate was in my own hands. He had washed his.

I said I hated him. That day. Even then I didn't. I don't. I didn't have the words to express what I felt, so I said the opposite of what I meant. Does this make sense? Even now, my prolixity notwithstanding, I don't know if I could tell him, face to face. I don't even know if I can tell myself.

21. IF SHE DIDN'T START IT she certainly did end it. Of course I was prepared, but how can you prepare to end something you had no business starting in the first place?

I noticed the change when she came to Duke that Friday. The way she seemed uncomfortable, not able to look me in the face. Our lovemaking became quick, mercilessly violent, yet elegiac in a telltale way, our bodies saying: No more. End it.

I took her to the airport that Sunday. She was going to visit her mother in New York. In the terminal she said she had to talk to me. We had a cup of coffee at the hot dog stand, fifteen minutes before she had to board.

"We've got to stop this, Aaron."

"Why? We've been doing it for years now."

I'd seen her livid, but not like this. Not angry, but betraying a mixture of anger, fear, and what I'd like to flatter myself was the anticipation of lack of love. Pain.

" 'Why?' Think, son. Stop and think. Stop being Horny Joe College and think. Will you do that, please? Think."

I held my breath, fearing what I might say, knowing nothing.

"Are we going to get married, huh? Huh? Tell me, you idiot. Are we going to slip up and have a little abortion on our hands? Huh? Oh, God. Shit, Aaron. It's wrong. Okay? Just wrong."

"But—"; but that "but" hung there in the air between us, it did a somersault, that word, a conjunction, a connection. It broke. Shattered. I saw it. A busted word.

"Oh, Jesus. You're beautiful. You're smart. But you're such a shit. A beautiful shit. A selfish, beautiful son of a bitch. God save us both, you little shit."

"I'll miss . . . I'll . . . I'll—"

"Save it for Thanksgiving."

She rolled her eyes and reached for her bags. "We've both got some growing up to do."

I watched her plane gaining altitude, and I know I sound like the violins at the end of the movie, but there it was, there it went. There she went. Up, up, and away. Lights out. Show's over. The dancing bear is done. The fat lady has quit singing. The freak show is over, buddy. Go home.

Here I sit, waiting for the Second Coming. But she ain't coming a second time. I know that. But I wait, I write, I screw. My faith is the size of a kernel of corn. *Ave Jamonica.*

That Christmas I switched my major from botany to pre-law.

I think it's obvious why.

22. THERE'S A DREAM. THERE'S always a dream. You want to hear corny? No, it's not in a cornfield. And I don't marry her. No, in my dream we're home: in my mother and father's bed: we're at the height: we're outside our skins: and they walk in: Dad, Mom, and Miss Jesse too: and get this: they're happy. They approve. They throw a party. They tell everyone. *Everyone.* There's a celebration. I tell my dad I love him. I tell him I want to be just like him.

Talk about depravity. Talk about signs and symbols and shit. Talk about wish fulfillment.

23. YOU KNOW, SIN IS like an American Express card. You grin with delight when you use it, you're the Aga Khan; but you cry like hell when the bill comes.

I sit here. I sit here beyond pity and love and hope, a vomitous bone-house of shit and spit and semen and shame. I sit here regurgitating the past as if to heal myself with confession, knowing I can't, I won't. I sit here, thinking of a woman who does not exist, will never exist. Some Faulknerian heroine, some clichéd tragic mulatto from antebellum trash, some Greek daughter of the gods come down to taunt, to tease, to test my mettle. I failed. Miserably. My hubris has poisoned me; my sin has undone me. I am a pathetic, weak, fart-filled clod of earth, earth to which I shall surely return, soon and very soon, unworthy of pity, wretched in my groveling, pitiful in my remorse: I am the blind beggar who does not deserve to see—and if I were so blessed, guess whom I'd look for?

THE STRANGE
AND TRAGIC
BALLAD OF
MABEL
PEARSALL

ABEL GOING DOWN THE road. Mabel in her
car. Mabel's mind a flurry. Mabel's mind like
Mabel's car. Racing. Down the road. Down, down,
down. Mabel. Mabel. Mabel thinks:

Peculiar. That was the word he had used. *Peculiar.*
She could not believe that that man. That man had
actually sat her down just to call her—peculiar! Not
troubled. Or strict. Or tired. Which she was really.
Tired. All those bad children running around the class-
room. All day long. Five days a week. Then back home
to cook. Wash clothes. Clean up after everybody. Fuss
at them for not cleaning up after themselves. And then
to run to church to help out with one group or the other.
The choir. The Women's Club. The Usher Board. The
4-H Club. The Finance Committee. Every night. Some

group. Some organization. No. Not tired. That ugly old white man. Sitting not a yard from her. *Peculiar.* To her face. Oh, he tried to be compassionate. Puffing that cigarette. Always puffing that damn cigarette. Trying to be kind. Still she couldn't believe the sheer gall. That he.

A deer leaps in front of Mabel's car. Magical. Graceful. Lithe. From the woods. From the blue. Like a sign from God. Mabel gasps. So hard she thinks she might pass out. In front of her with its hind legs in the air. Its tail up. Then gone. She jerks the wheel hard to the left. She stomps on the brakes. The car lurches. Screeches. Her head barely misses the wheel. The car slides roughly into the opposite lane. The front left tire bites into the grassy shoulder. Followed by the rear left tire. The long blue car halts only inches from the gully. A jerky stop.

Mabel doesn't linger over what would have happened. What could have happened. If a car had been in the other lane. She stops to say a word of thanks. To her Lord Jesus. Her mind's eye fixates on the tail. It all happened so fast. All she had clearly seen was the snowy tail. That sparkling white tail. Like a star. Mabel cannot think. Only see. See the tail. Searing into her mind. A brand. Charring the center of her brain. Hotter. Brighter. Until it becomes a pain. At the base of her skull. Thud-thudding with the force of a hammer.

A few cars whiz past. No one she knows. No one stops to see if anything is wrong. Why is she like this on the side of the road? Slowly she begins to remember. To feel her heart beating like a frantic bird. To realize that her car is partially off the road. Stopped. Facing the wrong direction. She tells herself she must right the car.

Continue on home. About her neck are gathered all the
aches and sorrows of the day. The pressures. The tiny
scars. The minute wounds. Pains. They all rise to the
center of her head. A balloon expanding up and behind
her eyes. She refuses to let it push through. Mabel is
afraid. So she sits. Trying hard to push back the throbbing. To keep that hoard of hurts behind her face. One
slips through. Hot. Another. And another. Until like a
broken dam. A cracked dike. She weeps. Sobs. So relieved. Mabel is finally crying. Mabel collapses in the
seat. Closes her eyes. Mabel has wanted to cry for so
long.

Mabel in homeroom. Earlier that day. Mabel taking
the roll of her seventh-grade class. Phillip Pickett taunted
Felicia Jones, who sat across from him. An impish white
girl with longish blond hair. Phillip picked at her and
pulled her hair. Felicia constantly whining: "Mrs. Pearsall! Mrs. Pearsall! Make Phillip leave me alone! I'm
gonna hit him!"

"You ain't gone hit nobody, gal." Phillip looked
round to his running mates. Mabel's stomach churned.
These boys giving so much attention. To this silly girl.

"Phillip, leave that girl alone. This minute. You had
better be studying for that test this—"

The intercom cut her off. It snapped and crackled on
so sharply. It made her start. Embarrassed to jump before the children.

"Mrs. Pearsall?"

"Yes, Mr. Todd?"

"I need to see you this afternoon after the buses
leave."

"Okay."

"Thank—" The old speaker gave the same electric fire-snap-crackle.

What could he want with me? Perhaps it's something about one of the students. But which one? Or maybe it's about the girl they found lice on the other day. Or one of the three children flunking? Or that little girl whose father regularly beats her and her mother? Or . . .

So much. Mabel could not bear waiting six hours to find out. She was sure it was some little thing. Something about one of her students. But his tone. He usually had an impatience in his slow drawl. But there had been something else in his voice this time. Something too nice. Too.

All day she kept her ears and eyes open. What could Mr. Todd want? She scattered hints like bread crumbs when she talked to the librarian. She dangled bait before the cafeteria people. She coaxed her fellow teachers as if sprinkling birdseed to sparrows. No one bit or nibbled at any of her hints. No one volunteered anything. No one dispelled her not knowing. They all smiled. Nodded. As if they didn't know.

Lies. They knew. She knew they knew. All the "Good morning, Mabel"s. All the "How you feeling today—how's Allen?"s. All the "Sure is a pretty day, isn't it?"s. All said behind normal smiling everyday faces. Behind eyes reflecting placid routine. Behind cups of stale instant coffee. They knew. And behind their raisin buns and chicken salad sandwiches they talked. Snickering. Laughing. At her.

Wasn't it about her? Of course. It had to be. She had seen it coming. She had felt the change in people.

Whispering behind her back. Like wind in the grass. Concealing. Conjecturing. Condemning. Her.

The day went on. The tension grew worse and worse. A headache threatened but never fully came. The children rowdy as hell. Throwing paper airplanes. Getting into fights. Talking when she was lecturing. Shooting spitballs. Throwing books. She sent five boys into the hall. Reprimanded ten girls for talking.

Finally the last bell rang. Children scampered out to the lines of yellow buses. Like rodents into blocks of cheese. She sat in her room. Absorbing all the festive colors all about. The puppets. The posters. The maps. Bright. Intended to entice children to learn. She inhaled. Smelling the chalk and the dust. She wondered who she had been at twelve years old. She watched the afternoon sun through the tall oak trees. Beyond the high windows that lined the wall. Thick with a milky and distorted film. She sat waiting. For the proper moment to get up. To go down the hall with the dark wood floors. Down the creaky, ancient stairway. Down the hall to Mr. Todd. Mabel felt dread. Noxious as black coffee in her belly.

"You can go on in, Mrs. Pearsall." The overweight secretary grinned. She knew. The thing Mr. Todd concealed. Mabel always felt better when in the same room with that cow. She made the few pounds Mabel could not lose seem light.

Smoke in the hot room attacked Mabel. Rushing up her nostrils. Forcing her to cough. Mr. Todd sat at his desk as though a part of it. Motioned to a seat in front of his desk. He did not rise as a gentleman should. He

did not ask her about her health. Her family. Her state
of mind. Or what she thought about the weather. He
did not look at her. As if talking to a child. Staring out
the window. Onto the schoolyard. Now showing signs
of spring. He was puffing his cigarette.

"Mrs. Pearsall. I've been receiving a few complaints." He paused. Puffed on his cigarette. Stubbed it
out.

"Complaints?"

"You see, some of the parents have called in. Said
their children have been . . . have been saying . . . *things*
about you."

"Things?"

"Yes. And I wouldn't have said anything if there
hadn't been . . . so many."

"I don't—"

"And then, you see, some of your colleagues . . .
well, they have added to that and have suggested that
you . . . that you might not be . . ."

"Mr. Todd . . ."

"That you weren't quite yourself."

"I don't understand what you're talking about."

He cast an impatient look at Mabel. She had always
considered him an ugly man. Now he was more so.

"Do you feel okay, Mrs. Pearsall? Is there anything
we can help you with? Some problems you've not told
us about?"

"Mr. Todd. Exactly what are you talking about?
. . . I don't . . . there's nothing wrong with me—"

"Well, why are you behaving so . . . so peculiar?
You seem to be . . . well, a bit . . . preoccupied, shall

we say? Perhaps you should consider . . . Well, to be frank. You're beginning to frighten the children. And I've noticed it myself. I'll tell you—"

"Mr. Todd, I—"

"Now please don't get angry or anything. Do you need some time off? Is that it? I can understand that, Mabel." He actually called her Mabel. The first time he had ever been so familiar. She found herself resenting it. "You've been here for twenty years. I've been here for eleven of those twenty. And I've noticed a significant change in—"

"Mr. Todd, like I said, I didn't realize that I was behaving . . . abnormally. I—"

"Well, you have . . . downright peculiar, to be honest . . . peculiar . . . and . . ."

Mabel. Mabel. Mabel. Mabel down the road. In her car. Stalled on the road. Now salt water bathes Mabel's nutmeg cheeks. The image of the deer's tail still burns in the back of Mabel's mind. Mabel comes to see what has befallen her. She is powerless. She cannot understand it. Cannot help it. But she feels it. In the morning when she rises to cook breakfast. She looks out the back window into the rising sun. But she feels no joy. Her heart feels hollow. Numb. A fear and a longing have taken up residence in her soul. She prays to the sweet Lord Jesus. Please lift me up. Praying does not help. She prays. And prays. And prays. Like the old people. Rising only to fall to her knees in the morning. Bending her knees before she sleeps at night. She remembers everyone she can think of in her prayers. But for all her supplication she has been ignored. Nothing has changed.

She knows the sun shines for free. She knows she has food to eat. A fine place to live. Good clothes to wear. Why does she feel so forsaken then? So wrong?

Mabel wipes away her tears. Retouches her makeup. Using the mirror behind the sun visor. She notes her face. Sagging. No longer taut and ripe. Not wrinkling. Just sagging. Her eyes now red. She turns the car back onto the highway. Feeling not better. But less sad. Numb. Again. The bright tail still flashes in her head.

The late-afternoon sun paints an abstract color. Across the sky. Explodes. Ambers and coppers and violets and infinity. Over corn and soybeans. Vivid. Alive. Fire and water. Mabel wants to be there. Where the fire is. Mabel's numb is like the sky. Mabel. Mabel. Mabel.

Mabel turns into the lonesome road leading home. An old red car ambling to meet her. Down the road. Patricia. Mabel does not understand why the Good Lord had chosen this day. To test Mabel so. Patricia. The last person she needs. Wants. To see.

Patricia stops her car. Rolls down the window. Smiling that sweet lemon-juice-and-marigold smile.

"Miss Mabel! How are you?"

"How you doing, Pat?"

"Just fine. Just fine." The flash at the base of Mabel's skull grows. Brighter and brighter. Mabel lets her smile grow with the pain. An opening blossom.

"You think you'll be able to keep Alexander tomorrow night, again?" Patricia has rich skin. Like good earth. Mabel just knows it yields soft. Goosedown-soft.

"Of course, Pat."

"How's Allen?"

Mabel does not flinch. Mabel's eyes do not quiver. Her smile blossoms more. "Oh, he's fine. Working hard. But he loves hard work, you know."

"Well, I better go on. Tend to the baby."

Mabel continues to smile. As she heads toward home. The blossom-smile finally drops off. Petal by petal.

She turns into the yard and sees the lawn mower. Sitting abandoned. No grass cut. That boy, that boy. She gathers her book bag and her purse. Hurriedly. She marches into the house.

"Perry! Perry!"

No answer. She walks into the family room. There they both sit. Before the television. Stuffing their mouths with chocolate bars. Perry fifteen. Now weighing two hundred pounds. No taller than five feet ten. Anne, his sister, there too. She a plump one hundred and sixty. Shorter than Perry.

"Boy, didn't I tell you to mow the lawn? You were supposed to do it yesterday."

Perry does not move his eyes. "*G-Man*'s on now. I'll do it a little later."

"*G-Man* was on yesterday." The pain in Mabel's head gives a strong throb. She winces. "*G-Man* will be on tomorrow, and the next day. And after *G-Man*, *Sanford and Son* and then *The People's Court*, and then it'll be too dark. Get up *now*."

She walks over to the television. Switches it off.

"Ma." Perry frowns. Mabel puts her hands on her hips. Akimbo. He gets up and switches the television back on. "In a minute."

Mabel runs her hand over her face. "Anne? Did you do the laundry like I asked you?"

"No."

"Why?"

"In a minute."

Mabel stands there staring. Afloat in her pain. Rage. Humiliation. She can only fume. Finally she asks: "Where's your father?"

"Shed."

They can't even speak in full sentences. Me a teacher. And they can't speak in full sentences. She flees the room. Why can't I get them to cooperate? To stop eating? It's Allen's fault. He.

"Allen, why didn't you make Perry cut the grass?"

Allen. Tall. Slender. A bit of a paunch forming. Just a little. He bends over the open hood of an old Buick. The innards of the car stare at her. Angry metal monsters. Mabel knows they hate her. "He'll get to it, honey."

"It took him two weeks last time."

"You want me to talk to him?"

"Yes."

"Okay."

"When?"

"Christ, Mabel. Does everybody have to drop every damn thing the minute you say? I'll talk to him, I said."

Mabel goes back to the house. Into the kitchen. Of course Anne has not started supper. Mabel checks the beef she left out to thaw. She thinks of everything that has happened today. Of the Simpson boy calling her a witch. Of the look Frances Miller gave her in the cafeteria. Of the way Mr. Todd spoke to her. Of the way Patricia flounced before her. Of the way her own issue are ignoring her. Of the tone in Allen's voice. Of the deer. Of the car's wrenching. Of the light in the back of her mind. Mabel. Mabel. Mabel.

Mabel sits down. Mabel wrings her hands. A child. She feels exactly like a child on a ride. A high scary ride. She wants to get off so desperately. Whom does she tell? She starts to pray. Then stops. No one is listening. Why? Is she so bad? Peculiar and evil like everyone is saying? She closes her eyes. Just closes her eyes. Calm yourself, woman. Won't do any good to get all worked up. No good. No good at all. The light begins to shrink. Slowly. Like a plane into the distance. Smaller. Into a tiny pinprick of light. A morning star in the north of her brain.

> *Ain't no reason to sit and cry.*
> *You'll be an angel, by and by.*

"Ma, what's for supper?"

Part of her wants to throw a chair at him. Yet she remains motionless. Her eyes closed.

"Roast beef and rutabaga."

"Ugh."

Mabel ignores him. Gets up and starts the laundry. Seeing Anne has no such intention. She thinks about cutting the grass. No. Allen. Maybe later.

Mabel goes about fixing dinner. The peas. The mashed potatoes. The rutabagas. The iced tea. She calls them in at a quarter after six. Again at six-thirty. At twenty minutes to seven she huffs into the family room.

"I told you twenty-five minutes ago that supper was ready, didn't I? Didn't I? I work hard all blessed day. Come home. Nobody's done anything. Nobody *will* do anything. I have to wash the clothes, clean the house. I cook and you don't have the respect to come eat before it gets cold. I swear you'll all drive me crazy. I—"

"What's the matter, honey?" Allen walks in behind her. Wiping his wet hands on a clean white towel. Smearing it with engine grease. Mabel almost bites through her cheek. To stop herself from yelling at him. She has told him before.

"Supper's ready and they just sit here. I told them—"

"Perry. Turn that TV off and go eat your supper. You too, Anne."

Sluggishly the two rise. First Anne. Then Perry. Perry mutters: "Always fussing."

"Boy, don't you talk back to me. And don't talk ill about your mama."

A graveyard gloom hangs over the table. Perry complains about the rutabagas. Declares he will not eat them. Mabel demands he eat them. Allen grunts. Perry doesn't eat them. Mabel tries to tell Allen about the deer. About Mr. Todd. About. But though he grunts he doesn't hear a word. He never does. He doesn't have time to listen to her. She knows. He thinks Mabel's peculiar too. He hates her. His mind on that damn car. Some blessed carburetor. And that woman.

Perry and Anne fight over who is to do the dishes just as they do every night. Mabel hangs out the clothes. In early twilight. The pain no longer pounds at the back of her skull. The light twinkles on the horizon of her mind. The hanging of clothes soothes her. It always soothes her. The smell of the fabric softener. April-fresh. What an odd way to describe it. The feel of moist terry and cotton and nylon. The sight of a stretched sheet rolling in a slight breeze.

Mabel has no papers to grade tonight. No church meetings. No community meetings. No choir rehearsals. Nothing to run off to. She sits with the family in the family room and watches television. Sipping iced tea. Allen falls asleep after the game shows. He snores bearishly. Mabel can never understand how he can sleep there. In such an uncomfortable position. A tender relief comes to her at nine o'clock. Her favorite show commences. Wealthy women in smart clothes. Tall, sinfully handsome men. Elegantly appointed rooms. Swimming pools. Expensive cars. Children who don't talk back. Sex. Romance. Mabel knows it's only fantasy. But such fun. The good are clearly good. The bad baldly bad. Both good and bad always nice to look at. Secretly, it is more than fun and fantasy to Mabel. Deep down. She truly longs to step out of her life. Into the television world. But so secretly even she doesn't know.

Tonight: the evil rich woman is attempting to sabotage the catering business of the good, hard-working, nice-looking heroine. Mabel is that heroine. Patricia the evil saboteur. Though in age and position it is clearly the other way round. That doesn't matter to Mabel. Mabel's heart goes out to the heroine. Mabel roots for her. Mabel alone with her family. Mabel silently cheering. Mabel left hanging. Mabel waiting for next week. Mabel dreaming of caviar and diamonds. Mabel. Mabel. Mabel.

Mabel lies awake many a night. Waiting for Allen to come to bed. After he has dozed on the recliner. As late as one or two in the morning. Finally she drifts off. To awaken at five-thirty. Untouched. Allen thick with slumber. On his side of the bed. A quarantine box. It has been over a year since they last did it. Before that maybe six months. This is the dead giveaway. How she knows something is seriously wrong. The way she knows that Patricia has stolen her man. At first she reprimanded herself. Thinking: It's crazy, Mabel. He hasn't been sleeping with that no-good tart. She had pushed it from her mind.

But things would happen. Here a clue. There a hint. She noticed more and more the strange way Patricia regarded her when Mabel spoke. If not Patricia then who? She noted how Allen would react when she questioned him. When he was inexplicably absent or late. With anger. Unwarranted anger if he had done nothing. A wife has a right to ask. Allen, I just asked. Don't start yelling at me just because you take an hour to go pick up something that should take only fifteen minutes.

Then the baby. Of course the baby. Yes, the baby. He had Allen's eyes and Allen's smile. And if you put Patricia's and Allen's tones together you'd get that damn baby's color and why did she have to go and name it Alexander if it wasn't Allen's? Nobody in her family named Alexander and.

Mabel in bed. Mabel at night. Mabel can't sleep. Mabel's mind slips away from her. So many rabbits out of a broken hutch door. Mabel can't catch them. They scamper. They hop. They flee. Mabel in the dark. Mabel in an empty bed. Mabel watching the star in her mind. Mabel. Mabel. Mabel. Thinking:

I almost left college because of him. He was the first one. He was the last one. Mama told me I didn't have to marry him. Daddy said I didn't have a choice. If I wanted to live. I wouldn't know how to be with another man. Wouldn't know how to feel. Allen taught me everything I know about being with a man. I knew it was a sin then. But I wanted to please Allen. Allen. Allen. When I came home the summer before my senior year. To work in tobacco. He paid attention to me. Nobody else ever really did. He looked so good. All sweaty. So good even with dirt all over him and his hands caked with tar. Allen would take me out on Saturday nights that summer. Allen gave me my first drink of beer. And Allen—I knew it was a sin, Lord, but I was a little drunk and after we did it once I didn't see any harm in it and it made Allen so happy. He needed me to make him happy. It didn't make any difference to me and, Allen, why don't you come to bed? Allen, why Patricia? It was that Christmas. It had to have been then. That night. Christmas Eve. It was cold in that car. It was in the backseat. An old Ford Fairlane. His hands smelled of grease. But good. He was already working as a mechanic down at the base. I didn't know for sure until February. I was showing at graduation. We were married right after. Allen. You ain't got to marry him. But I can't teach, Mama, if I don't. I love him. My voice cracked when I said that. I don't know if I loved him or not. But I wanted him. I wanted him. And the baby died. After all that. Can you believe that? Is that why, Allen? Cause the baby died? Cause Perry came along two years later and he turned out sorry? And Anne came along three years later and she turned out sorry? Allen? Is that why? Cause I can't have another, or so that doctor keeps saying? Is that why? Allen? Mabel finally falls asleep. Looking at the light on the television screen of her mind.

Mabel at church. Mabel in a white dress. Mabel smiling for all the world. Mabel good. Mabel true. Mabel washed in the Blood of the Lamb. But the Lamb won't save Mabel. Yet Mabel won't give up on the Lamb. So Mabel smiles. Mabel prays. Mabel pays her dues. Mabel. Mabel. Mabel.

Look who's here. Mabel cranes her neck. Mabel sees the bright and the good of Tims Creek. Dr. Streeter. Such a good catch for Clarissa. Mrs. Maggie Williams. Looking so fine and well-to-do. All good, upstanding Christian people. Not like Patricia. An unwed mother. Seducer of other people's husbands. Oh hello, Reverend. How are you? Just fine. Of course I'll chair the committee. My pleasure.

After the service Mabel moves through the crowd on the church lawn. She's well respected. A model Christian. A faithful servant. A good and faithful servant.

She talks to Gloria Brown about new robes for the choir. She notes Allen talking with Patricia Jones. Over by the sycamore tree.

". . . ton blend will be easier to clean . . . Mabel? Mabel? What's wrong, honey? You don't look so good. You look kinda faint."

"No, Gloria. I'm fine. I'm fine. Just fine. What were you saying?"

"That the cotton and nylon blend would look better
but the rayon is just more practical and . . ."

The nerve, Mabel thinks. The gall. To talk to him
here. In public. In my presence. Among good *Christian*
folk. To flaunt her sin. With my own husband. How
dare the little strumpet. How dare the.

"Mabel, honey? You sure you're all right?"

"Oh. Oh, yes, Gloria. Yes. I'm sorry. You know
the preacher is coming to the house for dinner and I'm
just a little distracted, you know. Why don't we talk
later. I'm going to collect Allen and the children and get
on home."

Mabel walks over to Allen. Now talking to Fred
Jordan.

"Allen, honey, we better get on to the house. I got
to finish dinner for Reverend Barden."

"Oh, okay now. Talk to you later, Fred."

Mabel in the car. Mabel thinking. Mabel wishing.
Mabel hoping.

"What did Patricia Jones want with you?"

"Hgh?"

Mabel interprets his shock—is it really shock,
Mabel?—as confirmation of guilt.

"Patricia Jones."

"Oh, that Jones girl. Her car. She needs a tuneup.
Wants me to do it. Wanted to know when she can bring
it around."

"Oh really?"

"Really. Why?"

Why. Why. Why. Why. Why? *Why?*

"Why you want to know?"

"Just curious."

Mabel at the dinner table. Mabel in the kitchen. Mabel talking to the Reverend. Mabel reminding the children to mind their manners. Mabel serving greens and beets. Mabel serving ham and rice. Mabel trying not to think about Patricia. Mabel trying to stay calm. To not be peculiar. Mabel so blue beneath her smile. Mabel. Mabel. Mabel.

They wave good-bye to the pastor. As he backs out of the driveway. The phone rings. Anne answers: "Ma, it's for you."

Who could it be? Gloria I bet. "Hello. Yes, honey. How are you? Good sermon today, wasn't it. Pastor just left. What can I do for you? Uh-huh. Why of course I will, Patricia. No problem at all. What time you leaving? Okay, fine. Don't think nothing of it, child. My pleasure."

Mabel wants to slam the receiver down. But she replaces it gently. Like a living thing. Not wanting to harm it. The hussy. The brazen little whore. The gall. To ask me to babysit my husband's baby. The hateful little bitch. I should have told her to.

"Who was that, Mabel?"

"Patricia Jones."

"What she want?"

"Me to babysit. Again."

"Oh."

Oh. Oh. Oh. Oh. The star in Mabel's mind gives a little flicker. Just a little flare. Allen didn't even—couldn't even—say a word. Of course he couldn't. I'm sure he gets a kick out of me babysitting his own child.

"Ma, can I go play with Timmy Phillips?"

"No!"

Everyone just stops. Everyone. Allen. Perry. Anne. All stop what they are doing. And stare at Mabel. Eyes wide with dismay. Mouths open in astonishment. She feels her hands clenched into tight balls. Her shoulders trembling.

"Honey, you okay?"

"I'm fine. Just fine." Mabel leaves the room. Goes into the bathroom. She wishes she could do the laundry. But it is Sunday. No work on the Lord's Day. Mabel the good Christian. Mabel obedient to the Law. Mabel faithful. Mabel forlorn. Mabel on a Sunday. Mabel. Mabel. Mabel.

Mabel at three o'clock. Mabel at Patricia's door. Mabel with a magazine in one hand. A purse on her shoulder. Mabel knocking on the door. Mabel ignoring the light. In her head. Mabel thinking how good she is to have come. How Christian of Mabel. Washed in the Blood of the Lamb.

"Miss Mabel. Thank you so much for keeping Alex. You know where everything is. I should be back before nine."

"No problem. Don't worry now. Everything will be fine. Just fine."

The mobile home smells of fish and onions. Doesn't the little homewrecker know to heat a little vinegar? In a dish. To take the scent away. And look at the furniture. Naugahyde. Peeling. Disgusting. Dust an inch thick behind the chair. Hasn't swept under the sofa.

Mabel looks in on Alex. Such a little cute thing. Sleeping quietly. With Allen's eyes. But are they Allen's eyes, Mabel, really? Of course they're Allen's eyes. Just look. Just look. If you've got eyes to see you'll see they're Allen's eyes.

Mabel paces. Mabel looks at her magazine. Mabel looks out the window. The baby cries. Mabel feeds him. Mabel thinks how good she must be to feed her husband's bastard child. How many women are as good as Mabel? How many? Mabel is good. Mabel is strong. Mabel rocks the child to sleep. Mabel sings:

> *Go to sleepy, little baby,*
> *Go to sleepy, little baby,*
> *Mama and Papa both gone away,*
> *Left nobody but the baaabeee.*

Mabel thinks: Mama. Papa. Who is your papa, little bastard child? Will you ever know? Will you ever know it's my husband? The star in Mabel's mind begins to *krrkkt* like a match being lit. The baby sleeps. Mabel puts it back in its bassinet. Mabel is a good woman. Mabel is strong.

Mabel turns on the television. A good TV movie is on. Mabel has seen it before. A nice family. A nice husband. A nice wife. A nice home. Nice car. Nice children. Nice. Nice. Mabel sees nice and nice sees Mabel and Mabel begins to wonder when she will be nice. Nice like the people on the screen. Oh just stop it, Mabel. It's just television. No one anywhere lives like this. No one. Maybe some. Maybe Miss Maggie. Certainly Gloria Brown and Clarissa Streeter. Their husbands are nice. Their hands are always clean. Not caked eternally with grease.

The baby begins to cry. Mabel picks it up. A bit annoyed. She wants to watch her program. She paces the floor. The baby stops. Mabel places it down. Gently.

Mabel tries to calm herself. To watch the television movie. The light now the size of a quarter. It pulses. She feels a slight thud in the back of her head. She watches television. The nice man has an affair with a good friend of the nice wife. A nice affair. No babies. Not like real life, Mabel thinks. Not like. The baby begins to cry. The pain. In her skull. Mabel's right eye twitches.

Mabel checks the diaper. Nothing. Mabel rocks the cradle. Coos. Looks on the baby's quiet. Envies the baby's innocence. Was I ever so innocent? Mabel thinks of her childhood. Of her mother. Fussing. Complaining. Talking about her. In front of others. As though Mabel were not there. Saying: "She's gonna be a big one. Fat I spect. Just hope she marries off before she runs to fat. Don't eat so much, girl. Put that cake right back." No innocence for Mabel.

Mabel goes back to her show. The climax. The nice wife confronts the nice-though-philandering husband and the nice-but-wicked friend is in peril and the nice man must help and the nice wife must choose. The baby cries.

Mabel tries to ignore the baby. Sits. But the wail the wail. Mabel goes to the cradle and looks down on the baby. The baby with Allen's lips. But are they Allen's lips, Mabel? Of course they are. And she rocks the cradle. Yet the baby only yells more. Loud. What's the matter, child? So loud. Demanding. Just like all of them. Demanding. Hush hush hush. But the baby just cries. The light in Mabel's head like on the first day. Brighter. Harsher. And Mabel cannot see. Cannot see for the light. Bright bright bright. Mabel frantic. The baby's wail high-pitched. Piercing. Piercing her head. Or is it the light? She tries to pick up the baby. But cannot see cannot see cannot see. The light stabs the back of her eyes. Courses through her limbs. Shoots through her fingers. She finds the child. Good. But the wailing the wailing. It slices to the quick of her. She flinches and drops the babe. It hits the ground. Gives a breathy *uummph*. Begins to scream afresh. Mabel manages to pick it up but the blaze in her head and the baby's cries hurt. Oh blessed Lord blessed Lord it hurts so much why so much? Too much. In Mabel's head the wail becomes a choir of voices. Images. The deer. Mr. Todd. Patricia. Anne. Perry. Allen. Allen. Allen. Screeches of hate. Accusation. She wants to go away. Into the television forever. She wants to be nice forever. Oh shut up, Mabel yells. Shut up shut up shut up all of you just leave me alone.

Mabel puts the baby back in the bassinet. Mabel trembles. Mabel thinks: Calm yourself. Mabel steels herself against the wall of sound. Mabel picks up the baby. Baby baby screaming baby. *Sssshuuusssh. Sssshusssh. Ssshusssh.* But the baby keeps screaming. Oh it hurts. It hurts so much.

Mabel throws Alexander. She does not think. She does not see. Her eyes are closed. She throws Alex hard. As though he were a wild creature. Tearing at her brain. Up. Away. Go. She hears the sound. The thud. She hears silence. She smiles. At last. And Mabel's whole mind is flooded with God's Holy Light. Just as in the

Garden. Him treading the Earth in the First Morning Dew. Silently. Such peace. She can see. So clearly. The light makes no sound. Mabel walks over to the baby. He makes no sound. He is still. His black eyes gaze heavenward. Mouth agape. Sweet little baby. Allen's little baby. Allen's and my little baby. I'll adopt it. Yes. I'll make everything all right. All right. Yes. I can. I will. We will name it Elroy. After my father. Yes.

Mabel picks up the baby. Gently now. Mabel sits before the television. Seeing only the Holy Light. Bathed in the electric-blue glow. Rocking rocking rocking. Singing:

Hush, little baby, don't you cry,
Papa's gonna buy

Mabel in an ambulance. Mabel in handcuffs. Mabel calling for her baby. Calling for the Lamb. The ambulance flashes red. The patrol car flashes blue. Quietly. Like the light in Mabel's mind. People stand all around. Staring. An inky sky above them. The stars wink down upon them. But can they hear the chorus below them? Singing:

Get sixteen pretty maidens to carry my coffin.
Sixteen pretty maidens to sing me a song.
Put branches of roses over my coffin,
So I'll look pretty as I ride along.

Mabel's mind a field of lilies. Not a sound in Mabel's mind. Only sweet light in Mabel's mind. Sing a song for Mabel. Washed in the Light of the Lamb. Sing a song for Mabel. Mabel. Mabel. Mabel.

THIS FAR

A man who wishes to make a profession of goodness in everything must necessarily come to grief among so many who are not good. Therefore it is necessary for a prince, who wishes to maintain himself, to learn how not to be good, and to use this knowledge and not use it, according to the necessity of the case.

—Chapter XV, "Of the
Things of Which Men,
Especially Princes, Are
Praised or Blamed,"
THE PRINCE,
Niccolò Machiavelli

OCTOBER 20, 1915. YOU will be dead in less than a month, and though you do not know it you sense It, this crouching, mystery-shrouded doom. It has been your constant companion, a shadow-cloaked marvel, since 1867 when you first stepped inside General Ruffner's house to be a houseboy—a post-Emancipation slave is more accurate; but a life better than life in the salt mines or the coal mines, better than the streets of Malden, West Virginia; better than the smell of urine and rotting garbage and the sounds of drunken men raising hell. People like to think the sweet smell of success drove you, drives you. You know better, don't you?

You know who has been at your side all these years.

You are tired and sick and fatigued with fighting, with moving. You have been in constant motion since 1856, *fifty-nine years*, as if from the first day you understood the Newtonian axiom: A body in motion tends to stay in motion. Yet you can't seem to slacken the pace. And why bother?

Your traveling secretary, Nathan Hunt, a Tuskegee product, tells you you are nearing Tims Creek. You wonder: Why? Why did you come? After all these years, why did you make this special trip, out of the way, to see these two, Elihu & Tabitha McElwaine? It has been thirty-three years. Eighteen and seventy-two. Fall. Hampton Normal and Agricultural Institute. You have come so far since then it seems someone else's history, but you have told the tale so many times, so many ways, made the story of the unwashed little peasant boy from the coal mines of West Virginia such a powerful weapon in the battle to become Emperor de facto of the Negro race—the truth, full of duplicity and sin, is of little use to you now. Does it sting to remember?

So ignorant and pitiful you were then, the shame of it still lingers like the smell of shit on the fingers, just like the hunger which still gnaws beneath your wool suit, tailor-made for you in London, beneath the solid-gold watch and chain that dangles from your vest pouch, a gift from E. Julia Emery, one of your many wealthy white patrons—but it gnaws and bites and growls just the same. You cannot rid yourself of it, can you?

You feel the train slow its *chu-chug-chug*, and from the window you note how different the North Carolina forests are from those in Alabama, how like Virginia's, the pines lusher, the undergrowth more sparse. Nathan begins to pack up the papers at which you have stared absently since leaving D.C., your mind wandering, wondering what the two of them will look like after so many years; and how you will look in their eyes.

"Dr. Washington, sir. We've arrived."

I was completely out of money when I graduated. In company with other Hampton students, I secured a place as a table waiter in a summer hotel in Connecticut, and managed to borrow enough money with which to get there. I had not been in this hotel long before I found out that I knew practically nothing about waiting on a hotel table. The head waiter, however, supposed that I was an accomplished waiter. He soon gave me charge of a table at which there sat four or five wealthy and rather aristocratic people. My ignorance of how to wait upon them was so apparent that they scolded me in such a severe manner that I became frightened and left their table, leaving them sitting there without food. As a result of this I was reduced from the position of waiter to that of a dish-carrier.

—*Chapter IV,*
"Helping Others,"
UP FROM SLAVERY

TIMS CREEK IS LIKE so many of the other towns you have stepped into from a train. In 1909 you had fulfilled a commitment to the Standard Oil magnate Henry H. Rogers, touring small Virginia towns from Norfolk to

Charleston. Certainly, you hated every minute of it: the poverty, the stench of unclean bodies, the overcooked food, the humidity, the messiah-expectant look of black faces—boys and girls and rheumy-eyed old men—who regarded you as something of a king, a wizard. Wizard, indeed. Did they have any idea how much sacrifice it took to . . . ?

"Dr. Washington. Booker, if I can presume to call you that after so many years. You can't know how glad I am you could come. I knew you would."

"My *good* Tabitha. If you didn't call me Booker, I would be offended. And how on earth could I possibly not come? I'm honored that you asked me."

How do you see her? Thirty-three years is a long time. Perhaps you want to preserve an image of her unaffected by the years: the dark molasses of her slender and dimpled face unsullied by time; her figure still shapely. But you have too keen an eye. You must see time in her face, the comfortable weight of small-town inertia in her hips, the curve of her jaw obscured by gravity. No, at sixty she is not the same; you are not the same. Yet do you sense the same spirit, in her eyes? They absorb you. Yes.

You doff your hat and take her hand and kiss it, and her smile—as you take note, or are you merely beginning to create an illusion?—still quickens you and promises to haunt you late in the evening.

"Booker, old man. It's good to see you again. At last."

The grip of Elihu McElwaine has to be one of the stronger ones you have encountered in years—and you have shaken an incalculable multitude of hands, from

Buffalo to Biloxi. His hands are not rough, but they have known tremendous work. Perhaps you see that time has affected him even more deeply than Tabitha. Where once his face had an impish glow, it seems now solidly grave, not unhandsome, in fact very handsome, dark as his sister, with broad features like those masks from the Dark Continent; and unmistakably there lurks behind those jet eyes—you can sense it straightaway— a regal competence and pride. You have always feared Elihu McElwaine, haven't you? And now, your large beige hand vised in his massive midnight fist, despite your titles, your wealth, your influence, your power . . . surely you must flinch inwardly?

"Come, Booker." Tabitha grasps your hand as she did when you were a freshman, walking very near you. Her voice drops to a whisper as if conspiring, and you are engulfed within a calm. "You'll be staying with us, in my father's house. The ceremony is this evening."

That voice. You have had three wives. Fanny, who died in '84; Olivia, who died in '89; and Margaret, sweet, good, witty, clever, eminently competent Margaret, who lectured you severely when she discovered you were making this trip, after the doctors had prescribed rest: rest rest rest rest. Three wives you have had, and none of them with a voice like Tabitha's. You have carried it around with you for thirty-three years; a voice you wish your mother, Janie—that sad, coarse woman, mumbling and swallowing words—had possessed; a husky, night-fluted sound, rimmed by a faint North Carolina curve on the vowels and *g*'s; slow, deliberate, schooled yet soft:

"Again, I want you to know how much this means

to the people of Tims Creek. And to me, of course. It's not much of a town, no more than a thousand people. But it's home to some good souls. I know how busy you are, Booker, your schedule has to be an—"

"Yes, Booker." The interjection of Elihu's voice makes you start. "From what I hear, you're practically everywhere at once. Even now you're in New York and London and Paris and Cleveland *and* Tuskegee. Probably even Japan. Quite a feat." Over the years his voice has roughened, no doubt peppered by whiskey and tobacco.

You see him smile, but you know there is an innuendo in his *bon geste*. He has always been a subtle one. In fact, you learned to be subtle from Elihu McElwaine. And from reports you have gotten through "the Machine"—God! how you hate that epithet, but it's so useful, so accurate—he is even more subtle now, more dangerous.

You step into the buggy, Nathan next to you, Tabitha facing you, Elihu driving the team, and you all start down the bumpy road, and perhaps for a moment you have lost sight of It, now that you are spellbound—not by the present but by the steady re-creation of the past you are conjuring; and as you whiff the dray horse odor, you feel that once again you are that frightened boy shunned by the other students, more so even than your fellow Indian students, the same boy shown mysterious kindnesses by these dark and strange twins, benefiting immeasurably from their patience and their plenty—and you feel a twinge of sublimated anger.

Perhaps now, thirty-three years later, you think you will truly discover who they are.

I shall always remember a bit of advice given me by Mr. George W. Campbell, the white man to whom I have referred as the one who induced General Armstrong to send me to Tuskegee. Soon after I entered upon the work Mr. Campbell said to me, in his fatherly way: "Washington, always remember that credit is capital."

—*Chapter IX, "Anxious Days and Sleepless Nights,"*
UP FROM SLAVERY

"BUT, DR. WASHINGTON, REALLY I must protest."

Emmett's voice has always annoyed you, that thinly disguised Texas drawl. But Emmett J. Scott is damned efficient and as smart as a needle and his memory is infallible and in the end he works even harder than you, *than even you*, which is in itself phenomenal.

For this reason alone you made him your chief lieutenant. But if you had known that he would not be the Board of Trustees' choice for your successor after your death; that he would merely step aside and allow "the Machine" to grind to a halt and allow Tuskegee to become slowly a sad relic of your once-power; that he would betray you, repeatedly, even now as he speaks . . . would you have chosen him? Was the idea of crowning an heir apparent too much of an invitation to that ever-crouching Shadow? Or were you just too busy being busy?

"Mr. Scott. *I'm going to North Carolina,* and that's final."

"But, sir, begging your pardon, there is no particular *reason*. There will be no real publicity as I see it; you will have to cut your meeting in Washington short; you will have to come all the way back here for the board meeting—you know Mr. Carnegie is expected—and then you will have to race back up to Connect—"

"I am fully aware of my obligations, Mr. Scott, and I'm going."

"We will have to arrange guards—"

"No guards."

"But—"

"That will be all, Mr. Scott."

"Yes, sir."

After Emmett left your office that day, did you take out Tabitha's letter? Admire her handwriting—elegant, spidery, precise—which reminded you of how she helped you with your own penmanship, now impeccable? You reread it for probably the fiftieth time, and it thrills you like the first:

Dear Dr. Washington,

I know it has been some time since our last communication, but I want you to know that you are often in my thoughts. I fondly recall our days at Hampton, and though I know I sound as if I am flattering myself and my brother, I remember our predicting that you would go far in accomplishing great and excellent things, and am happy to see that prediction come to fruition.

As you may remember I am mistress of the colored school here in my hometown and praise God we have almost completed a new three-room structure so that we will no longer need to use the church. I know this is short notice for one so highly sought after, but I was wondering if you might consider coming for the inauguration in October. Indeed, if you could come I am certain I could with great ease persuade other dignitaries in the state to attend which will in the end insure a bright future for the Tims Creek Colored School.

I in no way intend to compare my modest establishment with your grand institution, but I'm very certain you of all people will appreciate the dire need of support, in all its guises for such endeavors, and that it is of consummate importance for our people.

Please do not look upon this invitation as a nepotistic attempt from those dimly remembered acquaintances of your youth to capitalize on your fame and good fortune; rather envision it as an opportunity to raise up yet another handful of dark good minds into the enlightenment of learning as you and I and others have been so providentially met.

I remain,

most truly

and sincerely

yours,

Tabitha

McElwaine

Surely, your first impulse was to think: McElwaine? She never married! And to wonder: Why? You imagined her voice and her effect on you in those early years, the first woman who made you feel worthy of attention, who made time for you and cleared out a space for you

among the minutiae of her life . . . Did it never occur
to you that you might have, at one time, courted or
even considered *marrying* her? The very thought now
seems ludicrous, somehow striking you as profane.

You have received five letters from her in thirty-
three years. Once after the Atlanta speech made headlines; once after your dinner at the White House with
Theodore Roosevelt made even more headlines; once
after Fanny's death; once after Olivia's death; and this
one now.

You said *yes* instantly, not caring about the date or
any possible conflicts it might cause—they could be
worked out; and when she answered she also informed
you that her brother, Elihu, who had been working and
traveling all about, would be home, and perhaps you
felt a strange rejoicing and loathing, as if you knew this
was a summing up, as if you had been sent out from
them three decades thence and now had to make an
accounting of your deeds.

An accounting. That day in Tuskegee, behind your
baronial desk in your baronial office, surrounded by
students and workers, a scene in some ways reminis-
cent of an old-time planter's farm—who had called
it "Tuskegee Plantation"?—you sat, absolute master
of so many men's fates, covert appointer of judges,
deliverer of votes, invisible dispenser of funds. Did
you nonetheless struggle with the sensation that you
might not measure up? But you have always had
that sensation, that you might fail at any given
moment, that It might collect you and sweep you away.
Haven't you?

This sensation has kept you in motion.

If my life in the past has meant anything in the lifting up of my people and the bringing about of better relations between your race and mine, I assure you from this day it will mean doubly more. In the economy of God there is but one standard by which an individual can succeed—there is but one for a race. . . . We are to be tested in our patience, our forbearance, our power to endure wrong, to withstand temptations, to economize, to acquire and use skill; in our ability to compete, to succeed in commerce, to disregard the superficial for the real, the appearance for the substance, to be great and yet small, learned and yet simple, high and yet the servant of all.

> —*Speech upon receiving honorary degree of Master of Arts from Harvard University, 1896*

THE LITTLE SCHOOL IS packed to overflowing: they spill out the doors, people sit in the windows. As they glare at you in awe perhaps you think of that night in New York, just four years ago, when without provocation or logic a white man burst from his building on West 66th Street and began beating you. All your education and friends and good manners did not stop it, could not spare you the humiliation of arrest by the authorities . . . for why, even in New York City, would they believe a black man's word over the word of a white man? Certainly, this thought makes the presence of these wide-eyed gazers even the more bewildering.

The Governor could not make it, alas, but the Secretary of State of North Carolina brings his greetings along with those of the Speaker of the House, who wanted to attend but couldn't . . . the North Carolina Superintendent of Schools is present, as is a local white Presbyterian minister who said you had been a great inspiration in his ministry—how many white ministers have told you this to date?—and who asked you to sign a copy of *Up from Slavery* . . . there are a number of other whites whose names you have instantly forgotten and who peer at you as if you were John the Baptist himself; they sit in the front row. While behind them seethes the ubiquitous, overwhelming sea of black: coal black, nut black, yellowish black, black black. The faces. Always the same, aren't they, always the look of slavish wonder?

Your act is a magic show. Mesmerizing. Spellbinding. You start out somewhat folksy, down-home—without, of course, losing your magisterial air, without allowing them to forget who you are; you rise in grand oratorical fashion to the heights of Cicero and Seneca, to cadenced, rounded phrases, remembering the lines about the separate fingers and the unified fist, which made you famous, and the nugget about "Cast down your buckets where you are," which made you notorious. In truth you end not too far from where you began, as it is so damnably hot and stuffy in this pathetic little room—closing on the cavalry cry of hope, self-help, self-esteem, work work work work work, the only salvation of the poor, of the race.

As you step down to the cheers and palpitating applause and seek your chair, do you think of your critics and question how far work work work work work will really take these people? Work worked for you because you were ruthless, conniving, unscrupulous, untiring, and always brilliant. Without a doubt you know this. How many Negro men and women did you trample just to hold on? Just to hold on? It seems the more powerful the Machine becomes, the harder it is to remember your original goals. Why have a Machine which requires more and more time and effort to keep oiled and running when it seems to do so little good for the swarthy faces that always confront you?

Perhaps you never ask yourself these questions. You are always so busy going going going going going . . .

Tabitha thanks you and the audience, and now the real work commences: the shaking of the hands, the answering of asinine questions, the kissing of smelly babies. Emmett and Margaret have been trying—in their magical, invisible, effective way—to eliminate this grueling task, to have you whisked away in a twinkling of an eye; but how Du Bois and Trotter would love that! *The imperial Mr. Washington does not even deign to shake the hands of those he has so self-importantly condemned to sharecropping and blacksmithing.* No. You will clasp and grab till your hands are raw and aching, the man of the hour.

But today, as you pump and grin royally, does your mind drift back to Elihu & Tabitha in 1872? They had been a year ahead of you at college, twins of means, dressed always grandly, who cast an aura of mystery and wonder everywhere they went—or so it seemed to you. Whereas you had to work as a janitor and at untold other stinky, sweaty, smelly tasks to earn your keep—

it had taken you *two years* to accumulate the money to journey home to Malden—these two went home sometimes twice a semester; leisurely they prom-enaded about like landed gentlefolk . . . which they were. They clung together like dark trees, never apart. They seemed to read each other's thoughts and to accomplish everything they set out to do. They enchanted you, amazed and bewitched you, you down among your fellow ex-slaves and sons and daughters of ex-slaves and the few penniless Indians who also matriculated at Hampton in a grand "experiment"; but you didn't even have the cachet of being unusual in the eyes of the white missionaries who condescended so prettily to you, *Poor little waif, bright little nigger . . .*

Tabitha & Elihu. They changed your view of the possibilities for Negroes. You had dreamt of it, read of it, of Negroes who had something other than hunger and poverty and debts. But here before your bedazzled eyes were coloreds with a father who could keep *two* children in school, well provided for, and probably not even feel it. What amazing world did they come from? Yet what truly astonished you was the way they treated you: as an equal. You, the poorest among the poor, the first shunned, the last called, were taken under their wing, asked to accompany them at supper, on picnics . . . when you could steal away from work. Nor did they look down from their good fortune onto your nothing. Was it because you were a mulatto and they so dark? But they never once showed signs of being colorstruck; in fact they seemed unaccountably proud of their darkness.

"What do you want to do, Booker"—her voice haunting, mossy—"when you grow up?"

"I'm going to be a preacher. So people'll feed me and I can dress like General Armstrong and people'll look up to me."

The day, Virginia spring-green, just before the twins were to graduate. The new grass smelled of earth, and gnats and bees and beetles buzzed in the ear.

"Now, Booker"—Elihu always seemed to be correcting you, pushing you, and you welcomed it—"do you think you need a Bible and a suit to get people's respect?"

"Well, no. I reckon not. But I ain't gone work at sweating and such."

" '*I'm not*,' not 'I ain't.' Think, Booker, before you speak. Remember what Miss Lord taught us about enunciating."

At times you did resent them as much as you envied them—resented them so hard you would cry in your hard bed—but their way won you over, over and over; as ideals or models they held you transfixed; you would be them: you would be better than they . . . or did you even realize how envy motivated and poisoned what you took to be love and devotion?

Hatred is a form of fear. And eventually we come to love that which we fear most. For we have allowed the object of our fear to define us, to have supreme power over us; and the absence of that object would be more than we could bear. We need the fear to create us. Without this fear we are nothing. Often death itself is preferable to the excruciating process of re-creating ourselves against nothing, without our ineffable totem of fear.

> —*BTW from an unpublished diary (courtesy DeNabone Archives)*

WHEN WE LOOK AT a certain photograph of you, taken by Frances Benjamin Johnston in 1906: those light eyes, the arched eyebrow, the full nose, the prominent elfin ears, the Indian lips—the word "handsome" is impeached by "integrity." A solid dignity. The grey suit, finely cut, the dark tie, the pristine shirt, all collude and tell us: This is a man of profound seriousness and authority. Look at the dark flesh under the eyes—here's a man who's spent many a sleepless night poring over documents and papers to make men free!

Indeed, we see a solid Victorian Citizen in dark relief. But the longer we gaze, and are gazed at by those dark-rimmed eyes—particularly the way the right eye seems to squint oh so slightly—we cannot fight the impression of concentration; and as we gaze it dawns on us how you neither smile nor frown but appear to be considering, to be figuring. Yes, you seem to be calculating. The Calculating Citizen. And though we cannot call the photograph sinister, there is certainly a gravity which goes beyond statuesque solemnity; there exudes, unmistakably, a sense of readiness, a sure understanding of your own power, a sense that if you raised your hand and waved—voilà!—we would disappear.

But do we see the photograph as it was seen in 1906, when we all saw so differently?

How do you look upon the picture now?

I helped them to a place of safety and paid the money out of my own pocket for the comfort and treatment of the man while he was sick. Today I have no warmer friends than the man and his son. They have nothing but the warmest feelings of gratitude for me and are continually in one way or another expressing this feeling. I do not care to publish to the world what I do and should not mention this except for this false representation. I simply chose to help and relieve this man in my own way rather than in the way some man a thousand miles away would have had me do it.

> —*BTW to the Reverend Francis J. Grimké, November 27, 1895, regarding a wounded man in need of assistance turned away from the gates of Tuskegee by BTW.*

"A RIGHT FINE SPEECH, Mr. Washington."

The old man does not speak much and you are relieved, for his silence is unnerving enough. In all your years, all your travels, you have rarely come across anyone with more presence and bearing than this rod-straight old man with the missing eye, the twins' father.

He said little upon your arrival other than "Welcome." Not "It's an honor to host the great Dr. Booker

T. Washington." Not "I am so glad I've finally gotten
to meet you." Just "Welcome."

While in truth it was you who felt honored, you
who were glad, after all these years, to meet the Negro
man who had somehow made a fortune *before* the war;
who could hold his head high even in Ku Klux Klan–
and bigot-infested waters, in this white two-tiered farmhouse with spacious porches, situated amid acres and
acres of corn and tobacco and peanuts and hogs and
cows and mules and woods and woods and woods—of
course the reality is less opulent than you had imagined
as a young boy, fancying Elihu the elder to surely have
footmen and servants, and to ride around, country
squire–fashion, in a carriage like Catherine the Great's.

Now you are more deeply impressed: you have some
inkling of how difficult it is for a black man to acquire
any property, let alone a small county. There were other
men like Elihu McElwaine, dotted across the continent—and you knew and destroyed some of them. But
this one somehow had cast the original spell upon you,
and you want to sit at his feet and query him endlessly
about his escape from slavery, his profiteering, his resolve to bow to no white man, while you, the mighty
Principal of Tuskegee, *must* bow, and bow deeply and
often, for your very survival.

"Yes, Booker." Elihu the younger, surely the very
image of his father at an earlier age, passes you a plate
of mashed potatoes. "You have a lot of confidence in
the intention of the prevailing order to accord us a fair
stake in due time. But why must we wait?" He peers
at you across the table. It is as though he has slapped
you in the face with a pair of gloves.

"Well, Elihu." You knew it would happen eventually, you knew he was biding his time. Your sources have told you of Elihu McElwaine's troubling acquaintance with Du Bois, have told you that he was present at that accursed Niagara Conference and that he was there doing . . . whatever the hell it is he does, when they established the National Association for the Advancement of Colored Folk. "You see, time is the key, Elihu. We must build. Nothing substantial is achieved overnight. Our economic well-being and our relationship with the white man must *evolve* over time."

"Even if it means losing the vote?"

"The vote is not truly lost, Elihu. In time—"

"Time alone won't solve our problems, Booker. Surely, you realize that. Given an eternity, some things will never be simply granted. *Plessy v. Ferguson* will not be remedied by *time*. And Woodrow Wilson isn't at all like your Rough-Riding Teddy. And—"

"Elihu." You raise your hand and smile in that diplomatic way which you must feel you yourself invented. "I assure you that I have put an inordinate amount of time and energy—more than seems humanly possible —into resecuring our electorate."

"The electorate which will remain as separate as the fingers on a white hand but as equal as a black fist. Really, Booker, this is not just about the vote. It's about *full* participation from the highest to the lowest. Not just trade jobs. Not just farm work."

"Do you have something against farming, Elihu? Your father seems to have done quite well in the field."

The old man does not look at you. You are perhaps feeling a bit embattled now, surrounded, but you relish the challenge . . . or at least you once did. You are tired.

"Elihu." Tabitha wears an expression of mirth. Does she enjoy watching you fence? "Booker's methods may seem at odds with your own, but surely, you cannot imagine that Booker has anything but the betterment of our people at heart."

Do the words "methods" and "heart" confound you? Jab at you?

"Indeed, sister, but sometimes methods designed to save the heart can crush it."

"Booker, I hope you find the beef fitting." Are you astounded at how easily she defuses a bomb? "I know you've become accustomed to some mighty fancy dishes in your travels, considering the company you keep."

"No, no, Tabitha. This is indeed delicious. Trust me, the well-to-do white man may eat expensively, but he does not eat joyously."

You see that the mention of "well-to-do white man" rankles Elihu and you move to gain control while you have the floor: "So, Elihu, tell me what you have been doing with yourself these thirty-three years. Can you believe it, *thirty-three years* since Hampton?"

Elihu finishes chewing; the expression on his face suggests that nostalgia is beneath him. You shrink at the idea of showing yourself to be sentimental.

"Well, I had a touch of wanderlust for a bit there. I worked on a whaler for a year. Saw more of the world than I even wanted to see. After a year teaching in Texas, I went back to school and got a master's in theology— say, did I hear you started to—?"

"Yes, I started, but decided Education held more for me."

"Appears you were right. I helped start a couple of newspapers. One in Texas. Closed in six months. One in Buffalo. It had a good chance, but seems we offended some of the right people. But I'm sure you know all about that. How *is* Mr. T. T. Fortune these days?"

You now regret having asked Tabitha for a dinner with just the family and Nathan, realizing that the presence of others might have tempered Elihu's crackling verbal lashes. Elihu's gaze is absent of affection, and you know it is an accusation and you know it is true: you had his paper shut down with help from *The New York Age*.

"Well, I'm sorry to hear that."

"I'm sure you are. But don't worry, Booker. Du Bois asked me to come work for the *Crisis*, but I declined."

"Probably for the better."

"How do you mean that, exactly? Better to become an accommodationist?"

Nathan's eyes dart back and forth. Tabitha's expression seems indecipherable: Is she laughing at you? Does she think this is mere sport? Did she have this in mind from the beginning with that sly letter?

"Mr. McElwaine"—you daringly select the father as your weapon, you think you understand him, he will be an ally—"do you feel as your son does with regard to my position?"

At first he seems not to have heard you, but before you make a fool of yourself by repeating, he stirs.

"Well, sir." He wipes his mouth. "As ole Freddy Douglass was always fond of saying to me: 'Power concedes nothing without a demand; you may not get what you pay for in this world; but you will certainly pay for what you get.' There's truth in what both you and Dr. Du Bois have to say."

"You knew Mr. Douglass, sir?"

The old man's one eye fixes you. "Knew him? Hell, I saved his life once."

Involuntarily your jaw drops ever so slightly, and you are a young boy again, amazed by the possibilities of the world, and as you stare at that one eye, at that wizened and dark face, do you entertain the concept that you got it all wrong, that you took a wrong turn somewhere back in '79 or '89 or '01, before or after, sooner or later, there somewhere? . . .

Elihu the elder looks at you, and you feel unaccountably small.

At length the old man begins to chuckle—a wry, dry, mirthful, mocking sound, full of shadows—and his son begins to laugh, and Tabitha, behind her napkin, laughs, and soon Nathan, casting a cautious glance toward you as if praying for relief, giggles tentatively, and finally, after a moment of perplexed uncertainty, you join them and sense the tiresome debate is over.

"So, Booker, tell me about your family."

But who won? Do you care anymore? A chill envelops you, and you know not if it comes from your illness or from an irresistible craving for sleep.

Nathan begins to nod, and you know it is time to say good-night.

"I am sorry we have to leave so early, but I must attend to important business back in Tuskegee."

Tabitha takes your hand as she leads you to the stairs, just as she always has, her voice quiet, just for you—

but does your illusion hold? Do you listen for words beneath the words? "You will never know what good you have done by coming here, Booker. Do not give a second thought to leaving so soon. We are honored that you came at all."

As you ascend the stairs in the solid farmhouse, perhaps you imagine that you have passed the test, that the test was in coming, that the question had been: Were you willing to put your ministry truly at the service of the people? You see the twins like God and Satan wagering over Job, you, and believe that just by coming you have proven yourself worthy. But have you?

No, curiosity brought you here, you tell yourself.

You will die on November 15 of this year, at a quarter to five in the morning. You will become more tired, sicker; you will try to rest, but It will continue to spur you on, to cajole you to move. Even now in the darkness you hear Its voice—river-deep, soft, soothing. Soon, It says, soon and very soon. And you will keep moving moving moving moving moving to finish to finish to finish—what? Do you know?

So be still, your heart, as you blow out your candle. Be quiet walking dreams of once and future. Silence. Draw up the bridge. Close the gate. Quiet.

The Wizard of the Negro peoples sleeps.

RUN, MOURNER, RUN

. . . for there is no place that does not see you.
You must change your life.
—RILKE

DEAN WILLIAMS SITS IN the tire. The tire hangs
from a high and fat sycamore branch. He swings
back and forth, back and forth, so that the air tickles his
ears. His legs, now lanky and mannish, drag the ground.
Not like the day his father first hung the tire and hoisted
a five-year-old Dean up by the waist and pushed him
and pushed him and pushed him, higher and higher—
"Daddy, don't push so hard!"—until Dean, a little
scared, could see beyond the old truck and out over the
field, his heart pounding, his eyes wide; and his daddy
walked off that day and left Dean swinging and went
back to the red truck and continued to tinker under the
hood, fixing . . . Dean never knew what.

Eighteen years later Dean sits in the tire. Swinging. Watching the last fingers of the late-October sun scratch at the horizon. Waiting. Looking at an early migration of geese heading south. Swinging. Waiting for his mama to call him to supper—canned peas, rice, Salisbury steak, maybe. His daddy always use to say Ernestine wont no good cook, but ah, she's got.

Dean Williams stares off at the wood in the distance, over the soybean fields to the pines' green-bright, the oaks and the sycamores and the maples all burnt and brittle-colored. Looking at the sky, he remembers a rhyme:

> *A red sky at night is a shepherd's delight*
> *A red sky in the morning is a shepherd's warning.*

Once upon a time—what now seems decades ago rather than ten or fifteen years—Dean had real dreams. In first grade he wanted to be a doctor; in second, a lawyer; in third, an Indian chief. He read the fairy stories and nursery rhymes, those slick shiny oversized books, over and over, and Mother Goose became a Bible of sorts. If pigs could fly and foxes could talk and dragons were for real, then surely he could be anything he wanted to be. Not many years after that he dropped out and learned to dream more mundane dreams. Yet those nuggets from grade school stayed with him.

Dean Williams sits in the tire his daddy made for him. Thinking: For what?

See, there's somebody I want you to . . . to . . . Well, I want you to get him for me. So to speak.

Percy Terrell had picked him up that day, back in

March. Percy Terrell, driving his big Dodge truck, his Deere cap perched on his head, his grey hair peeking out, his eyes full of mischief and lies and greed and hate and.

Son, I think I got a job for you.

Sitting in the cab of that truck, groceries in his lap (his Ford Torino had been in need of a carburetor that day), he wondered what Percy was up to.

Now of course this is something strictly between me and you.

On that cemetery-calm day in March, staring into the soybean field and his mama's house, the truck stopped on the dirt road between the highway, he wondered whether Percy wanted to make a sexual proposition. It wouldn't have been the first time a grey-haired granddaddy had stopped his truck and invited Dean in. Dean had something of a reputation. Maybe Percy had found out that Dean had been sleeping with burly Joe Johnson, the trucker. Maybe somebody had seen him coming out of a bar in Raleigh or in Wilmington or in.

. . . if you dare tell a soul, it'll be your word against mine, boy. And well . . . you'd just be fucking yourself up then.

How could he have known what he'd be getting himself into? If some fortune-teller had sat him down and explained it to him, detail by detail; if he'd had some warning from a crow or a woodchuck; if he'd had a bad dream the night before that would.

Land.

Land?

They own a parcel of land I want. Over by Chitaqua Pond. In fact they own the land under Chitaqua Pond.

I got them surrounded a hundred acres on one side, two hundred acres on one side, one fifty on the other.

How much land is it?

It ain't how much that matters, son. They're blocking me. See? I want—I need that land. Niggers shouldn't own something as pretty as Chitaqua Pond. Got a house on it they call their homeplace. Don't nobody live in it. Say they ain't got no price. We'll see.

When he was only a tow-headed twenty-four-year-old with a taste for hunting deer and redheads, Percy Terrell had inherited from his daddy, Malcolm Terrell, about three thousand acres and a general store to which damn-near everyone in Tims Creek was indebted. Yet somehow fun-loving Percy became Percy the determined; hell-raising Percy became Percy the cunning, Percy the sly, Percy the conniving, and had manipulated and multiplied his inheritance into a thousand acres more land, two textile mills, a chicken plant, part ownership in a Kentucky Fried Chicken franchise in Crosstown, and God only knew what else. The day he picked Dean up he had been in the middle of negotiating with a big corporation for his third textile mill. Before that day Percy had never said so much as "piss" to Dean. In Percy's eyes Dean was nothing more than poor white trash: a sweet-faced, dark-haired faggot with a broken-down Ford Torino, living with his chain-smoking mama in a damn-near condemned house they didn't even own. So it was like an audience with the king for Dean to be picked up by ole Percy on the side of the road, for him to stop the car, to turn to Dean and say: I want you to get to know him. Real good. You get my meaning?

Sir?

You know what I mean. He likes white boys. He'll just drool all over you. Who knows. He probably already does.

That day in March Dean hardly knew who Raymond Brown was. Only that he was the one colored undertaker in town. How could he have known he was something of a prince, something of a child, something of a little brown boy in a man's grey worsted-wool suit, with skin underneath smooth like silk? So he sat there thinking: This one of them dreams like on TV? Surely, he wasn't actually sitting in a truck with the richest white man in Tims Creek being asked to betray the richest black man in Tims Creek . . . Shoot! Sure as hell must be a dream.

Sex with a black man. His first one—his only one till Ray—had been Marshall Hinton in the ninth grade just before Dean dropped out of high school. It had been nothing much: nasty, sweaty, heartbeat-quick—but Dean still remembered the touch of that boy's skin, petal-soft and hard at the same time—and the sensation lingered on his fingertips. With that on his mind, part of the same evil dream, with the shadow of Percy Terrell sitting there next to him in his shadow-truck, Dean had asked: Let's say I decide to go along with this. Let's just say. What do I get out of it?

What do I get?

Had he actually said that? He could easily have said at that point: No a thank you, Mr. Imaginary Percy Terrell. I know this is a test from the Lord and I ain't fool enough to go through with it. I ain't stupid enough. I ain't drunk enough. I ain't.

What do I get?

You know that factory I'm trying to buy from International Spinning Corporation? You work at that plant, don't you?

Yeah.

Well, how would you like a promotion to foreman? And a six-thousand-dollar raise?

More a dream or less a dream? Dean couldn't tell. But the idea—six thousand dollars—how much is that a month?—a promotion. How long does it take most people to get to foreman? John Hyde? Fred Lanier? Rick Batts? Ten, fifteen, seventeen years. And they're still on line. Foremen come in as foremen. That simple. People like Dean never get to be foremen . . . and six thousand dollars.

I don't understand, Mr. Terrell, how—?

You just get him in bed. That's all. I'll worry about the rest.

But how do I—?

Ever heard of a bar called The Jack Rabbit in Raleigh?

Yeah. A colored bar.

He goes there every second Saturday of every month, I'm told.

Dean stared at the dashboard. He admired the electronic displays and the tape deck with a Willie Nelson tape sticking out—What kind of guarantee I get?

Percy chuckled. A flat, good-ole-boy chuckle, with a snort and a wheeze. For the first time Dean was a little scared. Son, you do my bidding you don't need no guarantee. This—he stuck out his hand—this is your guarantee.

Dean had walked into the kitchen that day and

looked down at his mama, who sat at the kitchen table reading the *National Enquirer*, a cigarette hanging out of her mouth, ashes on her tangerine knit blouse, ashes on the table. Water boiling on the stove. The faucet they could never fix, dripping. Dripping. The linoleum floor needing mopping—it all seemed like a dream. Terrell.
Just get him in bed.

What Percy Terrell want with you?—She watched him closely as he put the grocery bags on the counter.
Nothing.

She harrumphed as she got up to take the cans out of the brown paper bag and finish supper. He stopped and took a good long look at her; he noticed how thin his mama was getting. How her hair and her skin seemed washed out, all a pale, whitish-yellow color. Is that when he decided to do it? When he took in how the worry about money, worry about her doctor bills, the worry about her job—when she had a job—worry about her health, worry about Dean, had fretted away at her? Piece by piece, gnawing at her, so manless, so perpetually sad.

He remembered how she had been when his daddy was alive. Her hair black. Her eyes child-like and playful. Her body full and supple and eager to please a man. She did her nails a bright red then. Went to the beauty parlor. Now she bit her nails, and her head was a mess of split ends.

Dean sits in a tire. A tire hung off the great limb of a sycamore tree. Swinging. Watching smoke rising off in the distance a ways. Someone burning a field maybe. But it's the wrong time of year. People are still harvesting corn.

No, it wasn't for his mama that he did it. He hated the line. Hated the noise and the dust and the smell. But he hated the monotony and the din even more, those millions of damn millions of fucking strands of thread churning and turning and going on and on and on. What did he have to lose? What else did he have to trade on but his looks? A man once told him: Boy, you got eyes that could give a bull a hard-on. Why not use them?

> *Oh, Mother, I shall be married to*
> *Mr. Punchinello*
> *Mr. Punch*
> *Mr. Joe*
> *Mr. Nell*
> *Mr. Lo*
> *To Mr. Punch. Mr. Joe.*
> *To Mr. Punchinello.*

That very next day in March at McTarr's Grocery Store he saw him. Dean's mama had asked him to stop on the way back home and pick up a jar of mayonnaise. Phil Jones gave him a lift from the plant, and as he got out and was walking into the store Raymond Brown drove up in his big beige Cadillac.

He'd seen Ray Brown all his life, known who he was by sight and such, but he had never really paid him any mind. Over six foot and in a dark-navy suit. A fire-red tie. A mustache like a pencil line. Skin the color of something whipped, blended, and rich. A deep color. Ray walked with a minister's majesty. Upright. Solemn. His head held up. Almost looking down on folk.

Scuse me, Mr. Brown.

Had he ever really looked into a black man's eyes before then? Dean stood there, fully intending to find some way to seduce this man, and yet the odd mixture of things he sensed coming out of him—a rock solidness, an animal tenderness, a cool wariness—made Dean step back.

Yeah? What can I do for you?—Ray spoke in a slow, round baritone. Very proper. (Does he like me?) He kept his too-small-for-a-black-man's nose in the air. (Does he know I'm interested?) Raised an eyebrow. (He just thinks I'm white trash.)—Can I help you, young man?—Ray started to step away.

W . . . what year is your car?

My? Oh, an '88.

Fleetwood?

No, Eldorado.

Drive good?

Exceedingly.

Huh?

Very.

Dean tried to think of something more to say without being too obvious to the folk going into the store. (What if Percy was tricking me? What if Ray Brown don't go in for men? What if—?)

That it?

Ah . . . yeah, I—

Well, please excuse me. I'm in something of a hurry. Ray nodded and started to walk off.

Mr. Ray—

When Raymond Brown turned around, the puzzled look on his face softened its sternness: Dean saw a boy wanting to play. Ray smiled faintly, as if taking Dean in for the first time. His eyes drifted.—Well, what is it?

Nothing. See you later.—Dean smiled and looked down a bit, feigning shyness.

A grin of recognition passed over Ray's face. His eyes narrowed. At once he was all business again; he turned without a word or a gesture and walked into the store.

> *Lavender blue and rosemary green,*
> *When I am king you shall be queen;*
> *Call up my maids at four o'clock,*
> *Some to the wheel and some to the rock;*
> *Some to make hay and some to shear corn,*
> *And you and I will keep the bed warm.*

Dean Williams gazes down now at the trough in the earth in which his feet have been sliding. For eighteen years. Sliding. The red clay hard and baked after years of sun and rain and little-boy feet. Exposed. His blue canvas hightops beaten and dirty and frayed but comfortable. His mother says time and again he should get rid of them. A crow *caw-caw-ca-caws* as it glides over his head, as he swings in the old tire. As he thinks. As he wonders what Raymond Brown is doing. Thinking. At this moment.

Some things you just let happen, Ray had said that night. Dean never quite understood what he meant by that. Ray gestured grandly with his hands as he went on and on. He was a little pompous—is that the word? A little stuck-up. A little big on himself and his education. With his poetry and his books and his reading and his plays. But he had such large hands.

Well-manicured. So clean. And a gold ring with a shiny black stone he called onyx. He said his great-granddaddy took it off the hand of his slavemaster after killing him. Dean had thought an undertaker's hands would be cold as ice; Ray's hands were always warm.

A few days after McTarr's, Dean finally made his play at The Jack Rabbit. A rusty, run-down, dank, dark, sleazy, sticky-floored sort of place, with a smudged, wall-length mirror behind the bar, a small dance floor crowded with men and boys, mostly black, jerking or gyrating to this guitar riff, to that satiny saxophone, to this syrupy siren's voice, gritty, nasty, hips, heads, eyes, grinding. Dean found Ray right off, standing at the edge of the bar, slurping a scotch and soda, jabbering to some straggly-looking, candy-assed blond boy with frog-big blue eyes, who looked on as if Ray were speaking in Japanese or in some number-filled computer language.

Scuse me, Mr. Ray.

Ray Brown's eyes narrowed again the way they had in front of McTarr's. This time Dean did not have to wonder if Ray was interested. The straggly-looking boy drifted away.

You're that Williams boy, aren't you?

Yeah.

Buy you a drink?

Some smoky voice began to sing, some bitter crooning, some heart-tugging melody, some lonely piano. They were playing the game now, old and familiar to Dean, like checkers, like Old Maid; they were dancing cheek to cheek, hip to thigh. Dean knew he could win. Would win.

Ray talked. Ray talked about things Dean had no notion or knowledge of. Ray talked of school (Morehouse—the best years of my life. I should have become an academic. I did a year in Comp Lit at BU. Then my father died and my Aunt Helen insisted I go to mortuary school); Ray talked of his family (You know, my mother actually forbade me to marry Gloria. Said she was too poor, backward, and good-for-nothing. Wanted me to marry a Hampton or a Spellman girl); Ray talked of the funeral business (It was actually founded by my great-grandfather, Frederick Brown. What a man. Built it out of nothing. What a man. Loved to hunt. He did); Ray talked of undertaking (I despise formaldehyde; I loathe dead people; I abhor funerals); Ray talked on the President and the Governor and the General Assembly (Crooks! Liars! Godless men!); Ray talked. In soft tones. In icy tones. In preacher-like tones. This moment loud and thundering, his baritone making heads turn; the next moment quiet, head tilted, a little boy in need of a shoulder to lean on. Dean had never heard, except maybe on the radio and on TV, someone who knew so damn much, who carried himself just so, who.

But my wife—Ray would somehow smile and look despairing at the same time—I love her, you know. She could have figured it out by now. She's not a dumb woman, really.

Why hasn't she?

Blinded. Blinded by the Holy Ghost. She's full of the Holy Ghost, see.—Ray went off on a mocking rendition of a sermon, pounding his fists on the bar for emphasis (cause we're all food for worms, we know not the way to salvation, we must seek—yes, seek

—*Him*). He broke off.—Of course there's the money too.

The money?

Yeah, my money.

Oh.

Ray became silent. He stared at Dean. The bartender stood at the opposite end of the bar wiping glasses with a towel; the smoky air had cleared somewhat but still appeared blue-grey, alight with neon; one lone couple ground their bodies into each other on the dance floor to a smoldering Tina Turner number.

How about you?

What about me?

Whom do you love?

Dean laughed.—Who loves me is the real question. Don't nobody give a shit about me. My mama, maybe.

Ray put his large hand over Dean's: Ray's full and strong, Dean's dry and brittle and rough and small. —Well, I wouldn't put it exactly like that. He kissed Dean's hand as though it were a small and frightened bird.

As simple as breaking bones. Had he thought of Percy and how he was to betray this mesmerizing man? Did he believe he could? Would?

I want to show you something.

Yeah, I'll bet.—Dean smirked.

No, really. A place. Tonight. Come on.

They drove back to Tims Creek, down narrow back roads, through winding paths, alongside fields, into woods, into a meadow Dean had never seen before, near Chitaqua Pond. They arrived at the homeplace around midnight.

Is this where you take your boys?

Where did you think? To the mortuary?

So the house actually exists, Dean thought. This is for real. Part of him genuinely wanted to warn Ray, to protect him. But as Ray gave him a brief tour of the house where he had grown up (Can you believe this place is nearly ninety years old?): the kitchen with the deep enamel sink and the wood stove, the pantry with the neat rows of God-only-knows-how-old preserves and cans and boxes, the living room with the gaping fireplace where Christmas stockings had hung, the sur- prisingly functional bathroom; as they entered the bed- room where measles had been tended and babies created; as Ray rambled on absently about his Aunt Helen and Uncle Max (Aunt Helen is my great-granddaddy's youngest sister. She insists nothing change about this house. Nothing. If we sold it, it'd kill her); as he un- dressed Dean (No, please, allow me); as Dean, naked, stood with his back to Ray, those tender fingers ex- ploring the joints and the hinges of his body; as a wet, warm tongue outlined, ever so lightly, the shape of his gooseflesh-cold body, Ray mumbling trance-like (All flesh is grass, my love, sweet, sweet grass) between bites, between pinches; as they slid into the plump feather bed that *scree-eee-creeked* as they lay there, underneath a quilt made by Ray's great-grandmother, multicolored, heavy; as they joined at the mouth; as Dean trembled and tingled and clutched—all the while in his ears he heard a noise: faint at first, then loud, louder, then deaf- ening: and he was not sure if the quickening *thu-thump- thump, thu-thump-thump* of his heartbeat came from Ray's bites on his nipples or from fear. Dean felt certain he heard the voices of old black men and old black women screaming for his death, his blood, for him to be strung up on a Judas tree, to die and breathe no more.

> *Far from home across the sea*
> *To foreign parts I go;*
> *When I am gone, O think of me*
> *And I'll remember you.*
> *Remember me when far away,*
> *Whether asleep or awake.*
> *Remember me on your wedding day*
> *And send me a piece of your cake.*

Dean!—His mother calls to him from the door to the house where she stands.—Dean! Did you get me some Bisquick?

Noum, he yells back, not stopping his back-and-forth, the rope on the limb creaking like the door to a coffin opening and closing.

How could you forget? I asked you this morning.

I just did.

You 'just did.' Shit. Well, we ain't got no bread neither so you'll just eat with no bread. Boy, where is your mind these days?

Dean says nothing. He just rocks. Remembering. Noting the sky richening and deepening in color. Remembering. Seeing what he thinks might be a deer, way, way out. Remembering.

Remembering how it went on for a month, the meetings at the homeplace. Remembering how good being with Ray felt as spring crept closer and closer. Remembering the daffodils and the crocuses and the blessed jonquils and eating chocolate ice cream from the carton in bed afterward and mockingly calling each other honey and listening to the radio and singing, and Ray quoting some damn poet ('There we are two, content, happy in beauty together, speaking little, / perhaps not a word,' as Mr. Whitman would say), and would nibble at his neck and breathe deeply and let out a little sigh and say: I've got to get home. Gloria—yeah, yeah, I know. I know—remembering how he would tell himself: I ain't jealous of no black woman and of no black man. I don't care how much money he got. remembering how he would drive home and climb into his cold and empty bed with the bad mattress and reach up and pull the metal chain on the light bulb that swung in the middle of the room. Remembering how he would huddle underneath the stiff sheets, thinking of Ray's voice, the feel of his skin, the smell of his aftershave, imagining Ray pulling into the driveway of his ranch-style brick house, dashing through rooms filled with nice things, wall-to-wall-carpeted floors, into the shower, complaining of the dealers and their boring conversations (I'm really sorry, honey, John Simon insisted we go to this barbecue joint in Goldsboro after the meeting and told me all this tedious foolishness about his mother-in-law and)—how he would probably kiss her while drying himself with a thick white towel as she sat reading a Bible commentary, and she would smile and say, Oh, I understand, Ray, and he would ooze his large mahogany body into a king-sized bed with her under soft damask sheets, fresh and clean and warm, and say, Night, honey, and melt away into dreams, perhaps not even of Dean.—Hell, I don't give a shit, Dean would think, staring into his bare, night-filled room. So what if he doesn't. So what if he does. Don't make no nevermind to me, do it? I'm in it for the money. Right?

Yet Dean had no earthly idea what Percy had in mind for Ray and, after a few weeks, thought it might have already happened or maybe never would.

But one morning, one Sunday morning in April, when Gloria and the girls had gone to Philadelphia for a weekend to see a sick sister and Ray had decided to spend the night with Dean at the homeplace, the first and only time Dean was to see morning there (through the window that sunrise he could see a mist about the meadow and the pond), while they lolled, intertwined in dreams and limbs, he heard the barking of dogs. Almost imperceptible at first. They came closer. Louder. He heard men's voices. As he turned to jog Ray awake he heard someone kick in the front door. The sound of heavy feet trampling. Hooting. Jeering.

Where is they? Where they at? I know they're here.

The order and the rhyme of what happened next ricocheted in a cacophony in Dean's head even now: Ray blinks awake: Percy: his three sons: the sound *snap-click-whurrr, snap-click-whurrr, snap-click-whurrr*: dogs yapping: tugging at their leashes: Well, well, well, look-a-here, boys, salt-n-pepper: a dog growls: the boys grin and grimace: Dean jumping up, naked, to run: Get back in that bed, boy: No I—: I said, get back in that bed: *snap-click-whurrr, snap-click-whurrr*: a Polaroid camera, the prints sliding out like playing cards from a deck: the sound of dogs panting: claws on wooden floors: the boys mumbling under their breath: fucking queers, fucking faggots: damn, out of film.

Like a voice out of the chaos Ray spoke, steely, calm, almost amused.—You know, you *are* trespassing, Terrell.

Land as good as mine now, son. I done caught you in what them college boys call *flagrante delecto,* ain't that what you'd call it, Ray? You one of them college boys. In the goddamn flesh. You got to damn-near give me this here piece of property now, boy.

How do you figure that, Percy?

You a smart boy, Ray. I expect you can figure it.

Ray reached toward the nightstand. (A gun?)

A Terrell boy slammed a big stick down on the table in warning. A dog snapped.

Ray shrugged sarcastically.—A cigarette, maybe?

Bewildered, the boy glanced to his father, who warily nodded okay. Ray pulled out a pack of Lucky Strikes—though Dean had never known him to smoke—and deftly thumped out a single one, popped it into his mouth, reached for his matches, lit it, inhaled deeply, and blew smoke into the dog's face. The hound whined.

You got to be kidding, Terrell. You come in here with your boys and your dogs and pull this bullshit TV-movie camera stunt and expect me to whimper like some snot-nosed pickaninny, 'Yassuh, Mr. Terrell, suh, I'll give you anything, suh. Take my house. Take my land. Take my wife. I sho is scared of you, suh.' Come off it.—He drew on his cigarette.

Percy's face turned a strawberry color. He stood motionless. Dean expected him to go berserk. Slowly he began to nod his head up and down, and to smile. He put his hands on his hips and took two steps back.

—Now, boys, I want you to look-a-here. I respect this
man. I do. I really do. How many men do you know,
black or white, could bluff, cool as a cucumber, caught
butt-naked in bed with a damn whore? A white boy
whore at that. Wheee-hooo, boy! you almost had me
fooled. Shonuff did.—Percy curled his lip like one of
his dogs.—But you fucked up, boy. May as well admit it.

Ray narrowed his eyes and puffed.

You a big man in this county, Ray. You know it
and I know it. Think about it. Think about your ole
Aunt Helen. Think about what that ole Reverend Barden'll say. A deacon and a trustee of his church. Can't
have that. Think of your business. Who'll want you to
handle their loved ones, Ray? Think of your *wife. Your
girls.* I got me some eyewitnesses here, boy. Let somebody get one whiff of this . . . He turned with self-
congratulatory delight to his boys. They all guffawed
in unison, a sawing, inhuman sound.

Think on it, Ray. Think on it hard. Like I said, you're
a smart boy. I'll enjoy finally doing some business with
you. And it won't be on a cool slab, I guarantee.

Percy walked, head down, feet clomping, over to
Dean. He reached over and mussed Dean's hair as
though he were some obedient animal. —You did a fine
job, son. A mighty fine job. I'll take real good care of
you. Just like I promised.

Dean had never seen Ray's face in such a configuration of anger, loathing, coldness, disdain, recognition,
as though he suddenly realized he had been in bed with
a cottonmouth moccasin or a stinking dog. It made the
very air in the room change color. He stubbed out his

cigarette and stared out the window.—Get out of my
house, Terrell.—He said it quietly but firmly.

Oh, come on, Ray. Don't be sore. How else did you
think you could get your hands on such a *fine* piece of
white ass? I'm your pimp, boy. I'll send the bill directly.

Get out.

Percy patted Dean's head again.—I'll settle up with
you later. Come on, boys. We's done here.—He tipped
his hat to Ray, turned, and was gone, out the door, the
boys and the dogs and the smell of mud and canine
breath and yelping and stomping trailing out behind him
like the cloak of some wicked king of darkness. Dean
sat numb and naked, curled up in a tight ball like a cat.
As if someone had snatched the covers from him and
said: Wake up. Stop dreaming.

You get the hell out too.—Ray sat up, swinging his
feet to the floor. He reached for another cigarette.

Dean began to shiver; more than anything else he
could imagine at that moment, he wanted Ray to hold
him, more than six thousand dollars, more than a new
car. He felt like crying. He reached out and saw his pale
hand against the broad bronze back and sensed the
enormity of what he had done, that his hand could never
again touch that back, never glide over its ridges and
bends and curves, never linger over that mole, pause at
this patch of hair, that scar. He looked about the room
for some sign of change; but it remained the same: the
oil lamp: the warped mirror: the walnut bureau: the
cracked windowsill. But it would soon be gone. Percy
would see to that.

Ray, I'm s—

I don't want to hear you. Okay? I don't want to see

you. I don't want to know you. Or that you even existed. Ever. Get out. Now.

As Dean stood and pulled his clothes on, he wanted
desperately to hate Ray, to dredge up every nigger, jun-
glebunny, cocksucking, motherfucking, sambo insult he
could muster; he wanted to relearn hate, fiery, blunt,
brutal; he wanted to unlearn what he had learned in the
very bed on which he was turning his back, to erase it
from his memory, to blot it out, scratch over it. Forget.
Walking out the door he paused, listening for the voices
of those dark ancestors who had accosted him upon his
first entering. They were still. Perhaps appeased.

Little Miss Tuckett
Sat on a bucket,
Eating some peaches and cream.
There came a grasshopper
And tried hard to stop her,
But she said, "Go away, or I'll scream."

Dean looks over at his Ford Torino and worries that
it may never run again. It has been in need of so many
things, a distributor cap, spark plugs. The wiring about
shot. Radiator leaks. He just doesn't have the money.
Will he ever? He stands up with the tire around him and
walks back, back, back, and jumps up in the air, the
limb popping but holding. He swings high. He pushes
a little with his legs on the way back. He goes higher.
Higher.

Who said money is the root of all evil? Or was it the
love of money? Love.

Six thousand dollars. This is my guarantee.

Dean waited six months. Twenty-four weeks. April. May. June. July. August. September. He watched the spring mature into summer and summer begin to ripen into autumn. He waited as his mother went into the hospital twice. First for an ovarian cyst. Next for a hysterectomy. He waited as the bills the insurance company would not take care of piled high. He waited as his mother was laid off again. He waited as the news blared across the York County *Cryer* and the Crosstown papers and the Raleigh papers: TERRELL FAMILY BUYS TEXTILE MILL, INTERNATIONAL SPINNING SOLD TO TERRELL INTERESTS, INTERNATIONAL SPINNING TO BECOME YORK EAST MILL. He waited through work, through the noise and the dust, through the gossip about daughters who ran off with young boys wanting to be country music stars, grandmothers going to the old folks' home, adulterous husbands and unwed mothers. He waited through some one-night stands with nameless truckers in nameless truckstops and bored workers at boring shopping malls. He waited. He waited through the times he ran into Ray, who ignored him. He waited through the times he had only a nickel and a dime in his pocket and had to borrow for a third time from his cousin Jimmy or his uncle Fred, and his mama would have to search and search in the cabinets for something to scare up supper with. He waited. He waited through news of Terrell making a deal with the Brown family for a tiny piece of property over by Chitaqua Pond, and of Raymond Frederick Brown's great-aunt Helen making a big stink, and taking to her bed ill. They said she was close to dead. But Dean waited. And waited. One hundred sixty and eight days. Waiting.

I'm going to Terrell, he finally decided on the last day of September. A late-summer thundercloud lasted all that day. Terrell still worked out of the general store his father had built, in an office at the back of the huge, warehouse-like structure. His boys ran the store. What if he says he ain't gone do nothing? What do I do then? Dean stood outside the store peering inside, wind and rain pelting his face.

Terrell kept the store old-fashioned: a potbellied stove that blazed red-hot in winter: a glass counter filled with bright candies: a clanging granddaddy National Cash Register. The cabinets and the benches and the dirt all old and dark. Deer heads looked down from the walls. Spiderwebs formed an eerie tent under the ceiling. As Dean entered, he looked back to the antique office door with TERRELL painted on the glass; it seemed a mile from the front door.

What you want? The oldest Terrell boy held a broom.

Come to see your daddy.

What for?

Business.

What kind of business?

Between him and me.

The youngest Terrell walked up to Dean.—Like hell.

Dean saw Percy through the glass, preparing to leave. He jumped between the boys and ran.

Hey, where the hell you going?

Dean's feet pumped against the pine floor. He could hear six feet in pursuit. Terrell tapped on his hat as Dean slid into the wall like a runner into home plate, out of breath.—Mr. Terrell, Mr. Terrell, I got to talk to you. I got—

What you want, son?

Panting, Dean began to speak, the multitude of days piling up in the back of his throat crowding to get out all at once.—You promised. My mama been in the hospital twice since March. My car's broke down. I just need to know when. When I—

When what, son?

All he had wished to tell Percy seemed to dry up in his head like spit on a hot July sidewalk. His mouth hung open. No words fell out.—You . . . you guaranteed . . .

'Guaranteed'? Boy, what *are* you talking about?— Terrell turned the key in the office door.

Ray Brown. Ray. You know. You promised. You . . .

Son—Terrell picked up his briefcase and turned to go—I don't know what in the Sam Hill you talking about.

Dean grabbed Percy's sleeve. The boys tensed.— Please, Mr. Terrell. Please. I did everything you asked. I . . .

Percy stared at Dean's hand on his sleeve for an uncomfortably long period. He reached down with his free hand and knocked Dean's away as though it were a dead fly.—Don't you ever lay a hand on me again, faggot.

He began to walk away, calling behind him: Don't be too long closing up, boys. You know how your mama gets when you're late.

Dean stood in the shadows watching Percy walk

away.—I'll tell, goddamn it. I'll tell.—Dean growled, not recognizing his own voice.

Percy stopped stock-still. With his back to them all, he raised his chin a slight bit.—Tell? Who, pray tell, will you tell?—He pivoted around, a look of disgust smearing his face.—And who the *fuck* would believe you?

Dean felt his breathing come more labored, heavy. He could not keep his mouth closed, though he could force out no words. He felt saliva drooling down his chin.

Look at you—Percy's head jerked back—Look-at-you! A pathetic white-trash faggot whore. Who would think any accusation you brought against me, specially one as far-fetched as what you got in mind to tell, would have ary one bit of truth to it. Shit.—Percy said under his breath. He walked to the door.—Show him the way out, boys. And don't be late now, you hear?—The wind *wa-banged* the door shut.

They beat him. They taunted him with limp wrists and effeminate whimpers and lisps. They kicked him. Finally they threw him out into the rain and mud. Through it all he said not a mumbling word. He did not weep. He sat in a puddle. In the rain. One eye closed. His bruises stinging. The taste of blood in his mouth. He sat in some strange limbo, some odd place of ghosts and shadows, knowing he must rise, knowing he had been badly beaten, knowing that the boys had stopped on their way out and, snickering, dropped a twenty-dollar bill in front of him (We decided we felt sorry for you. Here's a little something for you. Price of a blowjob), knowing he could use the money, knowing he would be late for supper, knowing he could never really explain, never really tell anyone what had happened, knowing he would surely die one day, hoping it would be now. He could not move.

After a while, though he had no idea how long a while, something stopped the rain from falling on him. An old man's voice spoke to him: You all right, son? You lose something?

Is that you, Lord? he thought. Have you come to take me? With all the energy he could gather he lifted his head and looked through his one good eye.

An umbrella. An old grey-haired, trampy-looking man Dean did not know. Not the Lord. Dean opened his mouth and the cut in his lip spurted fresh blood into his mouth. He moaned. No I'll be all right yes yes yes I will be all right yes.

Yes, sir. I did lose something. Something right fine.

Moses supposes his toeses are roses,
But Moses supposes erroneously;
For nobody's toeses are posies of roses
As Moses supposes his toeses to be.

Dean!—His mother calls to him.—Dean! Supper's ready. Better come on.

Dark has gobbled up the world. He can see the light from a house here and there. People are sitting down to suppers of peas and chicken. A bat's *ratta-tatta-tatta* wings dip by. He continues to swing. He continues to wait. He continues to wonder.

Wondering about how two weeks after going to Terrell's office—two weeks after, the wounds and bruises had mostly healed—two weeks after knowing he would not get a raise or a promotion, two weeks of wondering if he should tell someone something, how he was walking down the road toward home with two bags of groceries. How the bag split and how rice, beans, canned tuna, garbage bags, white bread, and all came tumbling to the ground (though the milk carton didn't burst, he was happy to see), and how as he knelt down to pick everything up a beige Cadillac drove up, and how he heard the electric *whur* of the power windows going down, and how he heard a soft female voice say—Can I help you out?

He had never actually met Gloria Brown. She sat behind the wheel, her honey skin lightly powdered and smooth, her lips covered in some muted red like pink but not pink, her eyes intelligent and brown. In the backseat perched her two daughters, Ray's two daughters, their hair as shiny black as their patent-leather shoes. Their dresses white and green and neat.

It's all right, ma'am. I'm just down the road a piece.

But it's on my way. And you do seem to be having a little trouble. Hop on in. No trouble.

Dean collected the food and got into the front seat. I've never been in this car, he thought, feeling somehow entitled while knowing he had no right.

An a cappella gospel song in six-part harmony rang out from the stereo. Awful fine car, Dean wanted to say. But didn't.

We're heading to a revival meeting over at the Holiness Church.—She held the wheel gingerly, as if intimidated by the big purring machine. Her fingernails flashed an earthy orange color. Dean could smell her sweet and subtle perfume.

What church do you belong to?

Me? I don't, ma'am.

That's a shame. Well, you know Jesus loves you anyway. Are you saved?

Saved? From what?

Why, from Hell and Damnation, of course.

I guess not.

Well, keep your heart open. He'll speak to you. 'For all have sinned and fallen short of the will of God.'

Dean felt slightly offended but could think of nothing to say. He groped for words. Finally he said: Some things you just let happen.

Gloria turned to him the way one would turn upon hearing the voice of someone long dead; at first puzzled, then intrigued.—My husband always says that. Now ain't that funny.

Dean forced a chuckle.—Yes, ma'am. I reckon it is.

Gloria dropped him off at his house, her voice lilting after him with concern (Can you get to the house all right? Want the girls to help you?). He thanked her, no, he could manage. The Cadillac drove off into the early evening. This a road of ghosts, he thought. Spooks just don't like for a soul to know peace. Keep on coming to haunt.

> *If all the world was apple pie*
> *And all the sea was ink,*
> *And all the trees were bread and cheese,*
> *What would we have to drink?*

Dean! Boy, you better bring your butt on in here, now. Food's getting cold.

He doesn't feel hungry. He doesn't feel like sitting at the table with his mama. He doesn't feel like listening to her talk and complain or to the TV or to the radio. He doesn't feel like telling her that he was notified today that as of next Friday he will be laid off "indefinitely." He feels like sitting in the tire. Like swinging. Like waiting.

Waiting for the world to come to an end. Waiting for this cruel dream world to pass away. Waiting for the leopard to lie down with the kid and the goats with the sheep. Waiting for everything to be made all right—cause I know it will be all right, it has to be all right—and he will sit like Little Jack Horner in a corner with his Christmas pie and put in a thumb and pull out a plum and say: What a good, what a good, O what a good boy am I.

WHAT ARE DAYS?

for Z

LENA ROSE EARLY THAT Monday morning. She drew a large tub of soapy water and eased herself into it, listening to the music that now matched her mood, Al Green, the slow night music, love music, sex music, that had played over and over all night. *Let me say since . . . Since we been together . . . loving you forever . . . Is all I neeeeeed . . .*

After a time she stood, and while powder-puffing her body and face she looked over at him lost in slumber. He had not roused, had not even turned over. A rough sleeper: his lean brown legs tangled among the sheets; his plump, bowl-round buttocks exposed; his head beneath a pillow. For a moment she thought he might be dead. But staring at him from the mirror, she saw that he was quick, for his back rose and fell, rose and fell, like a boat on a calm sea. A tawny arm extended to where she had lain. So young.

Let me be the one you come running toooo . . .
I'll never be untrue . . .

She turned back to her mirror and saw herself. A mature woman of experience. A ripened woman. Unmistakably. Perhaps she had thought that a baby-man's love might transfigure her, magically remake her into one of the lovely young things in fairy stories. Lovely. She began to brush her hair. Black with solid streaks of white. She squinted and felt a slight tinge of panic: she began to notice bags—there, little puffs—and wrinkles—here, deep creases where graceful lines had been and—Am I really a good-looking woman? Was I ever?—she took a very deep breath and sighed loudly.

Lena stood, tying her robe about her, and walked over to the boy. A brooch rested on the table, the pin open. Swinging the pin all the way up like a hypodermic, she held the brooch over one of his sweet, sweet buttocks, paused momentarily to take in its rotund charm, its faint dusting of hair, and, ever so gently, stabbed it.

"Good morning."

THAT FRIDAY, THE SAME day the boy came to her door like a lost and fallen angel, Lena had gone to visit Cannonball's grave.

At first she felt strange having her husband buried up north, rather than back down south, in Tims Creek, where they had both come from. But he had been an orphan and the woman who raised him died when he was young.

Lena herself had been an only child and both her parents were dead by the time she turned thirty. True, there were some cousins, maiden aunts, and protective uncles still living in Tims Creek, but the ones she had known well were long gone. The others she hardly knew. She rarely went home now. So she decided to have Cannonball buried here in Newark. They had come to know each other here; they had fallen in love here; they had been married here; and here they would both lie buried. She had seen to that.

To think of him made her tingle. From an early age Cannon had been built like a bull. He had spent ten years in the Marine Corps. He stood no taller than five-foot-ten but weighed well over two hundred pounds. Precious little of it fat.

Thurman "Cannonball" Walker, the men had nicknamed him. Over in Germany, over in Korea, over in Okinawa, he had made a legend of himself. Hell-raising. Heavy-drinking. Womanizing. The men loved him better than the women. Even after he had been honorably discharged he seemed to be always surrounded by men and boys and cigar smoke and uproarious laughter. He had driven a truck all over the country. His own truck. A shiny blue Peterbilt he had sweated and toiled for years to buy. So he could be his own man, he said.

She wanted desperately to be angry with him for leaving her a forty-seven-year-old childless widow. She had tried to tell him: Cannonball, stop your drinking, Cannonball, stop your smoking, Cannon, honey, Doctor says you got to cut out the pork, Cannon, you know your blood pressure is high, baby. But how on earth could she bring herself to say no when he would pull in from Miami at two o'clock in the morning with a gigantic cured ham and beg her to fry some up? Cannonball just wouldn't have been Cannonball if he had lived any differently. How could she be mad at him for departing ahead of schedule?

He never raised a hand to her. Oh, they fought. She threw him out of the house three times. But he never struck her. He cussed like a son of a bitch but never hit her. She remembered him for that and for other kindnesses and wickednesses—forever peeing on the toilet seat; remembering their anniversary with roses and a steak dinner; forgetting to help with the utility bills and getting mad as hell when she asked; making love to her as if she were some bandy-legged virgin, something good to get into.

So that Friday she stood at the graveyard with a potted white chrysanthemum. She knew it was queer to come to Cannonball's grave on her own birthday, but turning fifty-one conjured up a harsh and heated longing. She looked about her, at the charcoal-grey New Jersey sky and the desolate sameness of the cemetery, row after row of stone and beige-colored grass. Damn your black ass, Cannonball. Just like a nigger. Unreliable as hell.

She had originally intended to stop by the mall on the way home to pick up a coat she had on layaway at Woody's, a gift to herself. But now she simply didn't feel up to it. Maneuvering her car through the Parkway traffic, she thought how she might spend her Friday night: pop some popcorn: watch some soap operas: take a long bath: alone.

Parking the car, she remembered she needed milk and decided to walk down to the corner bodega. As she walked down the street it occurred to her to wonder how long the mums could last, how long before the curved petals would begin to droop, then spill onto her husband's grave. This thought saddened her more than anything else that day, and she steeled her jaw and quickened her step.

On the corner stood six boys. Giraffe-tall, earth-dark, shamelessly young; dressed in their loud running suits and kangol caps and gold chains and red sneakers. Their talk had the quality of a prayer meeting, full of *uh-huh*s, *yeah*s, and nodding heads. Up to no good, she reckoned. Mostly boys she had known all their lives, Sadie Philips's boy, and Craig Rogers's boy, and—that one, the one called Shang. The one with the mouth. The one who kept. His family had just moved into the neighborhood, apparently. From somewhere. She kept seeing him around.

"How you doing, Miss Walker?" Sadie Philips's boy always did have good manners. Too bad he didn't have the good sense to stay in school.

"Just fine."

"Dreary day, ain't it?"

"Yeah. And on my birthday."

"It's your *birthday*?" Three of the boys spoke in unison. They all wished her a happy day.

Lena smiled in spite of herself, her sadness lightened. Shang stood behind the rest of the boys. What was it about that boy? Good Lord: the darkest, most liquid eyes she could remember seeing: eternally puckered lips, so very dark, as if rubbed with berry juice . . . she found herself staring.

"Happy birthday." His wish came at the end, and he winked at her.

"Why thank you, boys. Thank you all. You make a old woman feel good."

"You ain't old, Miss Walker." That Philips boy was so polite.

"No, ma'am." Now Shang narrowed his eyes the way a card shark does just before he says: Hit me. "*Old* ain't the word I'd use at all." She knew the rest of the boys could not see Shang's face as he spoke. Yet she was unsettled just the same. He made her feel naked. Indecent. He looked her up and down, slowly, smiling in a way that made her suspect he saw it all, every crevice and cranny; and then looked directly into her eyes and winked, puckering his lips. Lena looked away, grinning despite herself, and went into the store.

She lingered over the old cooler, her hand on a milk carton. Face throbbing, temples fluttering, she could not remember the last time she had actually felt her blood, heard it swirl in her ears. In the brief time she had known him, Shang had showed more interest in her than seemed proper; but nothing like this: playing some Don Juan role from a B movie. Child, she thought, it feels good. She checked herself: What if the boy were up to something? What if his flirting were part of a scam, a fleecing, a con game? After all I am old enough to be his grandma. Probably, he ain't even eighteen yet. How—?

"Miss Walker?"

Startled out of her deep pondering, Lena flinched involuntarily and the milk carton slipped from her hands. Shang caught it with an exaggerated dip and a flourish of his other hand. Show-off. He handed it back to her.

"I wanted to say Happy Birthday. Again. Doing anything special?" He raised an eyebrow devilishly.

"Why?"

Shang moved closer to her. Too close. She couldn't step left nor right. He smelled of cocoa butter.

"Can I bring you over a birthday present?"

Lena felt the cool milk carton pressed against her palm, heard the buzz of the fluorescent light bulbs over-head, and heard Señor Rivera on the phone at the front counter gossiping in Spanish. What the hell did this kid want? What game was he running? Could he, would he harm—?

"Please." Suddenly the Casanova before her turned into a Boy Scout, on his face a look of wonderment and anticipation. "Let me come over, please. I'll be a nice boy." This was much too strange, she thought, relaxing just a bit, wondering why she had thought this barely weaned child, with whom she had talked on only a few occasions, had approached her too boldly.

"Well, of course. I don't see why not, Shang. I'm—"

"About eight, okay?" He had utterly changed from devil to cherub, a brown boy doing a good deed. She stood amazed. Had she simply imagined the provocative leer?

"Fine. Fine." She started to giggle though she wished

she wouldn't, being a grown woman, but couldn't stop—giggling from nervousness, from relief, from bemusement, from the sensation between her legs where stirred a fresher longing than her memory could place. Devilish, pretty, sweet boy. Damn, these black men certainly can put you through some changes.

"See you then." He backed away, and without taking his eyes off her face he blew a kiss: not a boyhood "I love you, Mom" kiss, no; nor a "You nice *older* woman, let me be polite and gallant" kiss, uh-uh; not a kiss of insincerity and lies, which she felt confident she could divine; oh, no. This was one of those young-boy kisses that spoke of tongues and hot juices and getting naked and . . . He went out the door and she could tell he was slightly bowlegged. Lord, did she like bow-legged men.

Lena stood motionless—if anyone had come upon her she could not even have pretended to be doing anything—for a long moment, her skull aswim in confusion. Presently she looked about nervously; and she sighed in relief to see no one else in the store but Señor Rivera. She righted herself. Just because a fine young man is playing *serious* games with me does not mean . . .

She paid for the milk. Señor Rivera showed no sign of having overheard or seen. He rang up her milk without interrupting his conversation on the phone, fussing in tropical inflections. When she emerged the boys were gone. She looked from side to side, down one uneven avenue, up another littered street. Mrs. Clay ambled by ("Hello, how you?"), but not sign the first of the boys.

She went on home, laughing to herself. I'm a fifty-one-year-old woman today. Fifty-one. Can't be silly now.

"YOU KNOW," FREDERICA PERRY had said to her, "last week a new family moved in down at number eighty-seven."

"Yeah. How many?"

"Well, Helen said a mama and five youngins. She's Spanish, but apparently her husband was black."

"Was?"

"Apparently, he left her. Don't know the full story."

"Another no-account Negro? Please."

"You know how it is as good as I do, Lena."

Another new family in the neighborhood. Could be good; could be bad.

She saw Shang two days later, on the number twenty-seven bus going downtown. She knew he was new to the neighborhood; she noticed his apple-butter skin and gently wavy hair and figured he must be from the family Frederica had told her about. He had smiled at her that day, with those berry-black lips, but she had thought nothing of it. Just being friendly.

She saw him at the Pathmark Supermarket and at the chicken place and at the bus stop again. You must be from that new family. Number eighty-seven? I'm Lena Walker. —They call me Shang. —Nice to meet you. —He shook her hand.

He certainly seemed to be a nice boy. But something was amiss. The way he looked at her? The way he smiled? Could he actually be interested in a widow on the brink of fifty-one? At first she was annoyed. She felt disrespected. How dare—? But then, very quickly, she was overcome by a deep sense of flattery. The next Sunday, while she was walking home from church, he appeared as if from nowhere.

"Mind if I walk with you?"

"Course not."

She really couldn't remember what they had said. For even then his glance, his particular hesitancy, his arm movements bespoke courtship. How peculiar. Playfully, absently, without even giving thought to repercussions, she spoke right back to him. A conversation above the spoken words, beyond their meanings. Some folk call it chemistry; some call it lust; some call it honesty. She enjoyed this boy Shang's company. She liked him. But she fully expected that to be the extent of it. Sweet. Doleful. He seemed at once older and younger than his age. She could use a young friend, she rationalized. Especially one so pleasing to look at. Someone to help move furniture, or fix a pipe, maybe; paint. Lena had been prepared to settle for a helpful, platonic relationship. Yes, indeed.

LENA WORKED AS A registered nurse at an institution for the mentally incompetent called Bramgate Hills in Perth Amboy. She rode in a van each morning with five other workers, two men and three women. Most of the patients suffered from Down's syndrome, some had severe emotional disorders, some were autistic, a few had received head injuries. Most days were uneventful, punctuated by the occasional nastiness of misplaced feces or urine; the ruminator who had to be kept from eating his own vomit; the chronic masturbator's shameless discharge. She rarely had to clean up these smelly and pitiful messes, having generally to distribute pills, give shots, and try to create order out of God-made chaos. Yet at the end of each day her feet hurt, her back ached, her hands were slightly puffy from so much standing, and she invariably had a headache.

On the van back to Newark everyone would be too tired to chat, except for Angeline, a young, twig-haired girl who fancied herself a militant. Annoying Angeline.

"Why is it that men think women need them?" she would say, constantly having man trouble.

"Maybe because we do—"

"How could you say such a thing, Lena? I mean, a woman can be independent just like a man. Why should it be different? I say it's a double standard."

"Did you ever think that maybe men need women, just like women need men?"

Angeline made Lena tired and her headaches worse.

At home she would climb the stairs to the top of the two-family house Cannonball bought three years after he got his truck. The insurance money from his death finished paying for it. Mr. Clifford, a bachelor high-school teacher, rented out the ground floor.

Three bedrooms. A long living room. A dining room. Eat-in kitchen. Full of bric-a-brac and furniture she no longer liked.

She would switch on the television. Soak her feet. Munch popcorn. Read the gossip magazines. Talk on the phone to one of her three or four girlfriends. But they all had husbands.

On weekends she would go shopping at one of the big malls outside Elizabeth or Woodlawn. Sometimes with a girlfriend; sometimes alone.

She would clean house. Each room: dust, mop, vacuum, scrub. Never allowing herself to pause or question, for fear she might ask: Why? For whom did she keep going going going? If she allowed herself to stop and wonder she would surely be overwhelmed by the emptiness. Better to fool herself into thinking her days were so full, full of errands and tasks and chores. A multitude of little things. But of course her eye would happen to run across some token, some memento, some worn photograph fallen between a cushion, behind a dresser, of Cannonball. How could she not remember? Not question chasing after dust motes and bargain prices? Not click off the television in disgust after seeing one too many happy families or romantic encounters, and swaddle herself in sheets, in bed alone, and wonder about the myriad ways everything could have been, should have been, might have been, instead of the way everything was?

LENA TOLD HERSELF THE roast beef was for her—it had been in the freezer, so easy to thaw in the microwave, why not?—certainly not for the boy, who might not come. Neither were the green beans and potatoes and candied yams and sweet iced tea for the boy. If she made too much she could eat leftovers all weekend.

She had planned to take the bath she took. No reason not to put on a little makeup—

The doorbell frightened her. She had actually prepared herself to sit down to supper alone.

"Hi, Miss Walker."

"Come on in, Shang. Flowers! How sweet. Chocolates. Now ain't you something else. Come on in. Sit down."

For hours she had been worried—yes, worried— about what to say, what to do, what to expect. How to—He just kissed her. Full on the mouth. Without asking.

She enjoyed this boy Shang's company.

CANNONBALL'S THANG HAD BEEN fat and black and mean-looking; the doctors in the Marine Corps lopped off the foreskin so that it looked like a wicked, unstoppable black snake. This boy's thang was long and brown and smart-looking; he still had his skin and the tip peeked out slyly like a one-eyed secret behind a veil. Cannonball's thighs, she felt certain, had each been easily the size of her waist; powerful, hard things. This boy's thighs were slender like narrow trees, were the color of ginger. Cannonball's behind had been like his namesake, bunched-up black metal, solid as a train wheel. This boy's cheeks were round like dishes and soft to the touch, smooth. Cannonball had had ugly, horny feet with stubby little toes and evil split toenails and calluses; feet made to kick and stomp. This boy had feet like hands, long toes and rosy, gentle underbottoms; feet made to dance and sink into carpet. Cannonball had had a neck like a tree stump—some said he had no neck at all—on which his beloved, massive head perched, a cigar clenched between his teeth, a baseball cap on his head. This boy's neck seemed as long as a horse's, bent bow- like as he stretched to lick her ear or her neck. Cannon- ball's love had come running after you the way armies charge: it got what it came after: it laid siege: it ravaged;

like a compassionate general, he could be merciful, but to satisfy his troops he had to allow them to plunder now and again. This boy's love was rosemary leaves and coriander and thyme and clove and bay and cardamom, garlic, cinnamon, and fresh-ground black pepper.

HE STAYED THE ENTIRE weekend. Won't your mother be worried? No. She doesn't care. They did not leave the house all day and night on Saturday. Shouldn't you at least call or something to let her know? No. It doesn't matter to her where I am. On Sunday they stayed in bed throughout the daylight. Shang, I don't feel comfortable. Maybe you should go home. Do you want me to go? No. Okay then. On Monday morning, after she jolted him awake and he yelled and rubbed his behind and she kissed it for him and they laughed, he glanced at his watch and looked worried.

"I . . . I got to go."

"Work?"

"Yeah . . . right. Work."

"When will I see you?"

"Soon."

Not until he left did she think of the way he had said: "Soon." Back in the corners of her mind she remembered when she had first known a man she had not known and she had heard a "soon" like that . . . But no, she thought. He spent the *entire* weekend with you. Surely—

Going back to the bathroom to prepare for the day, she began to think about time. He's nineteen. I'm fifty-one. "Soon." As she pulled on her clothes and put on her shoes, the impossibility of it washed over her. She wanted to feel guilty but she could muster no shame whatsoever. Certainly, she had not seduced him; had not vamped him like some wicked Jezebel. He had come to her of his own accord. Unbidden. Unprovoked. Still he remained an enigma, even while he fondled her and whispered gently: Roll over. She had wanted to talk to him. Yet they had said little, really, for the entire weekend. He was gone now. Soon.

On her way out she glanced at the bed, the disheveled sheets, the quilt on the floor, and briefly considered making it up; she thought of the musk and the juices and the now-gone heat. She would wait. Perhaps the unmade bed was all she had left.

THAT SATURDAY NIGHT THEY had taken a bath together. His feet propped up on either side of her head; her feet on his shoulders. The suds making a quiet *sssssss* sound, the water a nice summer-warm. Air thickly humid. Mirrors steamed. Walls dripping moisture. Lena had not looked at a clock in what felt like days. She had no idea what time it was.

"Why did you come here last night?"

"Shussssh."

"Don't shush me in my own house, young man. And how old are you anyway?"

"Does it matter?"

"Shouldn't it?"

"No."

"Well?"

"Nineteen."

"Nineteen?"

"Does that bother you?"

"No. No, it doesn't."

"Good."

"But what—?"

"Shussssssssh."

She wanted to hit him, but she could not be sure if for his impertinence or his beauty. No one should look so good. So damn young. And she could not be sure if he truly looked good, or if it was just that: his youth. When Shang stared at her she felt ugly, old, unworthy. The way he stared made her think he did not see her, that he looked through her instead of at her. What did he see? A mother? An old teacher? It rankled her to consider that she might be fulfilling some unhealthy fantasy. That his unaltering gaze inwardly fell on someone else. But even if that were not so, how *could* he truly see her? Magdalena McElwaine Walker? How could he, a nineteen-year-old child, look at a fifty-one-year-old woman and see her? See her diminishing menstrual cramps, her sore feet, back pains, tired legs? How could he touch a fifty-one-year-old body and not shudder with fear? How could he, a young kid, know lust in the presence of someone surely as old as his mother? Or older? The thought made her quiver. So odd. Yet he stared right at her, still. She splashed him with water.

"Hey!"

"Quit staring at me."

"Why?"

"Why do you?"

"I like the way you look."

"Why?"

"Shussssssssh."

"Shang?"

"It doesn't matter."

Lena lay in the tub with a boy who told her what she wanted to know didn't matter. He continued to stare. He tickled her ear with his big toe. She splashed him again. Fine, she thought. Fine. It doesn't matter.

She grabbed a bar of soap and handed it to him.

"Do my back."

TWO WEEKS AND FIVE days. She tried to tell herself she was fine. That everything was all right. But she knew she was going mad. Had it been a dream? A hallucination? Had working with crazy people driven her mad? Had he been an angel sent from God? From Cannonball? From the Devil?

The guilt, so long delayed, came first. She had been irresponsible. He was a minor. She had no business taking a child into her bed. Let alone for an entire weekend. She could have said no. Surely, she had broken some law. If he told someone she'd be the laughingstock of Newark. Of New Jersey. She'd lose her job. She'd have to move.

Second came the pain.

Two weeks and five days. No sign of him. No word. He could have just as easily stepped out her door and onto the ocean floor. She made special trips to the bus stop, the Pathmark, the chicken place, the corner store. No Shang. She asked the boys on the corner. No one knew where he was. Had they seen him? Yesterday, maybe, day before. Where? Around.

She went to work. She shopped. She cleaned. She cooked. She waited.

Of course she tried to tell herself it didn't matter. This sort of thing happens. Happens to men and women every day of the earth's life. Especially with young men. Why did she think this would be different? But it felt different—Listen to you, Lena. *Listen.* So he spent the whole weekend with you. So what? Big deal. Some men spend half their lives with women and then up and leave.

On the twentieth day she decided it mattered. It mattered plenty. She had been sitting in the living room, now spotless from repeated cleaning cleaning cleaning from an energy she never knew she had, absently gazing at television. Without warning it came upon her, began seeping up like smoke under the door, through fissures and seams. One minute she had been a resigned widow; the next, capable of cold-blooded murder; pacing the room, clenching and unclenching her fists. The speed of the fury almost frightened her, but she was too angry to be scared.

She stalked from the room to the closet, grabbed her coat, and rushed out the door.

THAT DAMN RECORD. A single. He insisted on keeping it playing. At first it annoyed the hell out of her. Maybe we should put on some albums? No, I like the song. But—really, I like this one, just this one. Okay then.

An old forty-five she had forgotten she even had; but naked—so fine, so fine, like a juicy steak, come back to bed—he had gone to her records and picked it out in no time. Al Green. "Let's Stay Together." Her old Sears record player would go back to the beginning of the

record if you didn't lift the playing arm, and it did, over
and over, that entire weekend.

Panting, as she had never done before, even in
girlhood—what man would have taken the time, had
the patience in those days?—her hands clutching the
headboard, him atop her swimming swimming swimming in her, his head in her face smelling of cocoa,
sweat, of young man, she heard that damn song times
innumerable. Al Green's phrasing had been indelibly
seared across her brain, between her legs, on her breast:

> *I'm*
> *so in love with you*
> *Whatever*
> *you want to do*
> *Is all right with me*
> *Cause you*
> *make me*
> *feel*
> *brand new*
> *I*
> *want to spend my whole life with yoooouuuu*

The brass, that old organ music, Al's high tenor.
Damn. She couldn't think of one without the other.
Shang and the song. The slow groove, she was certain,
had affected the beat of her heart.

O baby leeet's . . . Let's stay togeth . . .

ON WEEKEND NIGHTS WHEN he was home, Cannonball would have a poker game. His cronies—some
fellow Marines, some truckers, some just fellows he

knew—would come and drink beer, smoke, cuss, and raise general hell. Lena would see to it that everyone got enough to eat and enough to drink, would put up with the smoke and the noise, and would often pray at three in the morning that they would call it quits and go the hell home.

Once she made the mistake of asking Cannonball to call last hand.

"Goddamn it, woman. Can't you see we in the middle of a game?"

"But, Cannon, I got to get to work tomorrow. I got to get some sleep."

"Well, sleep, goddamnit. I ain't stopping you."

"I can't with all this damn noise."

"Bitch, I work hard for my money to afford this house, and if—"

"I work hard too damnit and—"

"Don't tell me how hard you work, woman. I pay bills—"

"Like you didn't take money from me to fix that damn truck—"

"You want your goddamn money back? All right, I'll give it—"

"I just want to go to bed."

"Who the hell do you—?"

"Cannonball, I—"

"Bitch, just shut the fuck up. No, Stew, just sit yourself back down. We's gone finish this game if it takes to twelve noon. This is my house, goddamnit. My house."

In bed Lena tried to sleep but the noise, the guffaws, the loud cussing, kept jumping through the walls and chasing sleep away. At that moment she knew she hated Cannonball. Despised his might, his arrogance, his penis, his truck, his friends, his house, his behemoth rages, his hair, his teeth, the air he breathed, the very atoms of his being. At five he came to bed. She lay awake. He said nothing, hauling his half-drunk heft onto the mattress, which groaned with his weight. Part of her wanted him to hold her, to apologize, to reassure her that all these years and months and days and minutes had not been wasted, to reassure her that she was loved and wanted and not alone. But another part of her, the one that loved honesty, knew the truth, and that part sobbed silently with the knowledge that even if Cannonball had turned and kissed her tenderly and said, I'm sorry baby baby baby you know I'm so so sorry baby . . . even if they had made heart-stopping love and had basked in the warmth of the moment after and had slipped off into dreams of a splendid future, even then she would still be alone.

It doesn't matter, she had told herself.

EIGHTY-SEVEN GOODWIN AVENUE always had tenants moving in and out. People thought of it more as a hotel than as a home. Perhaps because the landlord, Mr. Washington, a city assemblyman, never really cared to keep the place up and folk left as soon as they got on their feet.

Lena rang the bell.

A girl, the color of Shang, came to the door.

"I'm Mrs. Walker. Is Shang at home?"

"Yeah." The girl couldn't have been more than eight.

"Who is it, Maria?" The voice of an older woman with a slight Spanish accent called out.

"Some woman looking for Shang."

"Ask her in. I'll be out in a minute."

At first Lena thought, I shouldn't. But walked in anyway.

The furniture, stained and ripped, looked like pieces Goodwill couldn't use. Two more children, a boy younger than Maria, and a girl who looked older, sat watching television, gnawing on potato chips and corn-puffs. Paint flaked from the ceiling and upper wall; one window was covered with cardboard.

"Can I help you?"

The woman who stood before Lena could have been no more than thirty-five, certainly not thirty-eight. Her face looked tired. She had a baby in her arms. Her long black hair was pulled back to reveal cheekbones Lena knew by touch. Lena smiled in spite of herself.

"I'm Lena Walker. Your son, Shang. He did some work for me. I wanted to thank him again. And pay him."

"Work? Shang? Get out a here. I'm amazed. Boy never worked a day in his life. What he do?"

"He moved furniture."

The woman harrumphed in cynical disbelief. "Well, I can't believe it. Can't get him to do a damn thing for me. Where is he? Luis? You know where your brother is?"

The boy didn't take his eyes off the television. "He out back."

"Well, go get him."

The boy stuffed more chips into his mouth, eyes wide, transfixed by the TV program.

"Luis!"

"What?"

"Get him!"

The boy slowly stood, his face one big frown, not losing sight of the screen until he actually left the room.

"Live here long?" The woman did not look at Lena.

"I've been here now on thirty years. Thirty-one this December."

"Jesus."

The boy came dashing into the room and plopped down in front of the set, reaching for the cornpuffs.

"Luisito? Where you brother?"

"Coming."

The woman jostled the baby a bit. "He'll be right here."

As if on cue a boy, no older than fifteen, looking an awful lot like the woman, the baby in her arms, and Luis, and—Lena quickly realized—nothing like Shang, came in. "Huh?"

"But this isn't—"

"Shang, this lady wants to pay you. You ain't told me you been helping people. That's good."

"Huh? Ain't helped nobody. Who you?" He regarded Lena with such suspicion she couldn't help feeling dirty.

"There must be some mistake. Do you have an older son?"

"No."

"About nineteen?"

"No."

"Eighteen?"

"No."

Lena stood there, ashamed to look into their faces, while they stared at her with benign puzzlement.

"Well—"

"Well, ain't you going to pay him?"

"But he's not the boy, you see. The boy who helped me is in his late teens. I thought he was your son. A much older child . . . man . . . boy."

"Shang? You help this woman move furniture?"

"Never seen her fore."

"I'm sorry. I'm sorry." Lena could not get out of the house fast enough. She almost knocked a lamp down on her way out.

Lena walked the October streets. Her mind pained her with the work, the bother, the anger, of this new riddle. What had happened? Had he just lied when he introduced himself? Did she get the facts wrong? But she had called him Shang. Shang. Shang. Shang as she moaned. Shang as she came. Shang when she called him to eat. Shang when he kissed her feet. Shang.

She walked without knowing where or to whom. Crossing an overpass, she paused. She could see as far as downtown Newark and knew that on a good day she could dimly make out the spires of Manhattan. She walked on.

There before her stood Phil. Have you seen Shang? No longer did she fear that he might get ideas, *the* idea that she had had a boy, a boy called Shang, a boy she had thought lived at 87 Goodwin Avenue, in her bed.

No, wait, did I see him at the pool hall?

Lena walked to the pool hall, only a few blocks away.

She stood outside and stopped there, looking at the door as if it were some portal to outer space. Inside, she was certain, she would see some of Cannon's old running buddies, who would be sitting at the bar and turn to see her and be bewildered at first and then remember themselves and say: Lena! How you been? Ain't seen you in a month of Sundays. Here, let me buy you a drink. How's things—? What would she say to them? Oh, I'm just looking for a nineteen-year-old gigolo whose throat I'm going to slit. How're you?

The door opened. Out walked a man and a woman; they appeared to be in their midtwenties. The man in jeans and a windbreaker, the woman in a long maroon coat.

"I mean it, Jay," the woman was saying. "If you lie to me again I'll kill you."

"Lie? Baby, I ain't lied to you."

"You lying now."

"Baby baby baby. Ain't nothing but a thing."

"Jay?"

"All right, baby. You the boss."

The man put his arm around the woman and they walked off into the night.

Lena made one step toward the door, turned, and headed home.

HE HAD STARED AT her, all of her, every naked inch of her, head to heel, and she had finally acquiesced. Feeling somehow changed.

Why
*   O tell me why*

Why do people break up
Then turn around and make up
I just can't . . .

He gave such attention to every part of her, and like
the Tin Man, she felt remade, bit by bit, bite by bite.
Her neck, which for so long she had thought too flabby
and too full of folds, he licked, his saliva coating it with
healing wet heat. She loved her new neck. Her breasts,
large, pendulous, melon-like (though she had never
borne children), he kneaded and caressed and sucked;
the nipples so large, pinched, nibbled. She adored her
new breasts. Her thighs, oh so fat, cellulite-covered, he
cuddled. Her new joy. Her ass, shapeless, ham-wide,
he returned to her, offered back to her as two powerful
mounds of lust and fire. Her torso, bulging unsightly
in clothing she no longer dared to wear, became an altar;
he made her a temple. Even the minor places—minor
up to that moment—he reclaimed for her, prayed over,
anointed with his precious spit, blessed the small of her
back, her toes, her heels, the back of her head, her elbows, her knees; and ultimately her loins—long given
over to mere voidance, holding no magic—cast holy
spells of liquid sparks, setting her entire person afire in
brilliance, asweat in voodoo cadences, her heart refur-
bished into a sacred drum. He gave her a new rhythm.
He came to worship. He came bringing frankincense,
myrrh, gold, diamonds, and a holy staff with which he
brought down the mighty mighty waters. Sweet Moses.
Sweet Jesus. Sweet Shang.

How, where, why had he learned such necromancy?
Or was it simple youthful desire? Holy in its unholy

lust; sacred in its profane want; divine in its sordid practice? Regardless, he had baptized her in fire. He had
raised the synagogue from the dust in three days.

Cause you make me feel brand neeeewwww . . .

Lena stood before the humble record player. Maybe,
just maybe, if I play it . . . She put the needle down,
turned the knob.

Let me say since
Since we been together . . .

She ran to the window and tried to force it up, realized the lock was on, unlocked it, threw up the sash,
ran back to the stereo, and grabbed it up, fully intending
to hurl it from the window; and on her way to the
window she tripped on the carpet and the old dusty
contraption made a loud and clumsy calamity on her
living-room floor: bouncing twice: the dust cover split-
ting in two so cleanly: the turntable detaching with a
snap and rolling around like an oversized penny: the arm
whipping off with an electric crack: a few of the knobs
shooting off, plump silver bullets.
    Unharmed, Lena stared at the mess on her floor with
a strange calm—as if she had forgotten the source of her
anger, so startled was she by this heap of broken plastic
and aluminum and diodes and the strange obsession that
had caused it to be there, now, before her on the floor.
    Surveying the curious wreck on the floor, Lena be-
gan to rise and she thought: Finally I can buy a new one.
    Lena began to laugh.

Laughing, she walked about the house regally. Laughing, she changed the funky bedsheets and cleaned up the shattered stereo. Laughing, she took a fat steak from the deep freeze to thaw for dinner, thinking how she would season it: coriander? thyme? bay? freshly ground pepper? Lena snickered at her old existence, sexless, joyless, barren—what she had allowed her life to become; and she watched the *idea* of Shang, like a bird released from captivity, unfold wings and take flight. Sweet Shang, or whoever the hell he was—archangel, dark demon, tramp; yet somehow liberator, prophet, friend. Take good care.

She sat down in Cannonball's mammoth recliner, kicked back, her feet up, and reached for a cigarette. O Lena, O Lena, O Lena . . .

RAGNARÖK!
THE DAY THE
GODS DIE

B ROTHERS AND SISTERS, I stand before
o o o you a shaken man, a man steeled in the
face of mortality. I knew Sister Tate as you all did, I
knew her vitality, I knew her strength, her dedication
to family, her generosity, her kind words in the time of
need. I am not sad to see her part company with us this
day. No, for as the Psalm-writer said: "The Lord giveth
and the Lord taketh away, blessed be—O blessed be—
the name of the Lord."

(I see her sitting on the bed that way with her back
arched like a cat and her titties just as pert and them
nipples just as hard as dimes, Sweet Jesus, you's a fine
gal, Louise. Well, I'm glad you appreciate it, Reverend.

How can a man *not* appreciate a sight as fine as you is, gal? and stop calling me Reverend. Now come here to me gal and let me give you some loving)

; and I am not aggrieved to eulogize her here today, for I know I will see her in that great getting-up morning where every day will be Sunday ever after on the Other Side; I am not in despair to see her body there still before me, for I know that all flesh is grass and that this flesh too shall melt away to the eternal dust from whence we all came. But I stand here this morning, Brothers and Sisters, moved by the idea of mortality, my mortality as well as your own. Moved to think on how I too shall one day follow this sweet sister, and how I must ask as everyone under the sound of my voice must ask: Will I be ready? Dearly Beloved,

(Sweet sweet beloved hot pussy—like those madams cried to the troops over in Seoul: Hot pussy, boys, hot-hot pussy, come and get it, and it was good, steamy and stanky, Daddy, is it good to ya? Oh baby baby baby Louise Louise, Sweet Mother of Jesus, is it as good to you, gal? Is Daddy sweet—? Ha-Glory! Sarah was never so sweet . . . Sarah)

In his mind he sees Sarah. Sarah Barden née Phillips. From the Piedmont. Statesville. Plump in middle age, in his vision destined to leave him a widower soon, at fifty-five. She died of leukemia at fifty-two. He sees her through the honey-toned and sepia-tinted memories of domesticity. He sees her grown too wide, too plain, too quiet; he sees her long-suffering; he sees her at her daily chores, mopping, cooking, weeding the garden; he sees her fast asleep, becalmed by dreams of her Lord. He feels jealousy at her relationship with her God, she knows some awesome peace that has eluded him since he picked up his calling, but that is why he married her in the first place, he thinks, a sanctified, simple girl, daughter of a poor farmer, bedazzled by this veteran of a foreign war, this Barden. In truth he had never been with a woman who gave herself, yet a virgin, with such tremulous fear. This thrilled him. This made her his wife. The wife of a newly ordained minister. He gave her a child—he sees her full, he sees her, his heart full of strange joy, with babe in arms, he sees her give suck and remembers twinges of shamed delight at that sight, unusually stirred. He gave her a home. He gave her heartache. He remembers her "female problems" at thirty-three and the end of the prospect for more children. He sees her now cooler, now resigned, now more a saint than a woman, less a wife than a helpmeet. Not that he felt an overwhelming desire for her in the beginning, just a thrill he mistook for lust; so unlike lust was his excitement that he mislabeled it love. But it matters little. Did he come to love her? He does not really know. He tells himself—flashing faded holy images of her in his memory—that he did. Yes. I loved her.

I want you all to look with me today to my text, Ezekiel, Chapter Thirty-seven, Verses One through Fourteen. "The hand of the Lord was upon me, and carried me out in the Spirit of the Lord, and set me down in the midst of the valley which was full of bones."

(The first time. Before we both were married, before

you knew ole Goose and I knew Sarah, yeah, before I
could smell my own musk good, and them there monster titties of yours were just little bumps. I had you
out there in the huckleberry patch, or more like you
had me, remember? They called you fast in them days.
I didn't know how fast till that day. Seems it was
better back then, don't it? Mosquitos biting your
rump; gnats going up your nose. Scared of getting
caught. Scared you might make a baby. Scared the
Lord might damn you then and there. Just scared. It
put a sweet edge to it, didn't it? Like putting hawk-
eyed gravy on your grits. I look at these youngins today,
they come to me pregnant and scared, boys come asking
what to do, you know: Reverend, what's the *right thing
to do?* And I look at them, young, in fine health, I can
see them getting that little taste of tail, their eyes wild
with it, cunt and cock crazy, and I see them in the act
of passion, skin and sweat and scent, and I try to be
stern and forgiving and tell them they should turn from
temptation and consecrate the act in Holy Matrimony,
of course I say that, what else can I say? Though deep
down I'm thinking, The Lord's army is in trouble cause
the Devil's arsenal is mighty, mighty sweet. I stand as
a witness)

Now witness with me, Brothers and Sisters. "And
he said unto me, Son of man, can these bones live? And
I answered, O Lord God, thou knowest.

"Again he said unto me, Prophesy upon these bones:
and say unto them, O ye dry bones, hear the word of
the Lord.

"So I prophesied as I was commanded. And as I

prophesied, there was a noise, and, behold, a shaking, and the bones came together, bone to its bone.''

(Carl. Bone of my bone. Flesh of my flesh. Son. Whither goest my son? My bone. You're a hypocrite, Papa. Son, don't talk like that, it hurts me. Papa, I can't sit here and watch you make a fool of my mama, a fool of the church, and a fool of me. Son, you just don't under— I understand plenty, you're a charlatan, a fake, a licentious old— Son, please, I beg of you. Beg? Did I truly beg? Maybe I should have begged, begged on my knees, bone of my bone. Where are you? You are my flesh, my flesh, full of the same weaknesses I suffer, that Jesus suffered, he turned away from temptation and I should have, but at least you should understand. Have mercy, son. I should have begged. You called and spoke to Sarah, hung up if I answered, I knew it was you, you knew I knew. Son, your spite is not godly . . . bone of my bone)

He worried about having a son, remembered, ruminated over all those whispered and snickered tales of preachers' boys. A preacher's son. Wild. Devilish. Hateful. He did not know how his own son would turn out and it worried him. It preoccupied him. It gave him sleepless nights. He'd go to the crib and peer into the child's face. Who will you be? Carl Henry Barden. A fine young man he became. Smart. A good student. First in his class. An athlete. A boy a father could be proud of, especially a preacher. Nothing like the nightmares Barden dreamed; worse. Too straight, too hard, too sure of himself, morally, mentally, physically. Barden loved and feared the boy; Carl hated Barden. Welling up for such a long time, it seemed, this young boy's hatred, as though from the womb he loathed his father. As a child he was secretive, and possessive of his mother. Barden knows he resented Louise—but how did he know? Barden ponders; so well-kept a secret, a preacher and a parishioner, of course they were careful. The boy left for college and rarely returned for a visit, and then, after strong words following his graduation, vanished up north, refusing to speak to his father again. Barden sometimes goes into Carl's room, left the way it had been when Carl was a boy, and tries to see the child. All he can conjure is the image of a young man's face twisted in anger.

"And when I beheld, lo, the sinews and the flesh came up upon them, and the skin covered them above: but there was no breath in them.

(Breathe strength into me, my Father. Though I have forsaken thee I long for the cleansing fire of your nostrils . . . This is the prayer I want to pray)

"Then said He unto me, Prophesy unto the wind, prophesy, son of man, and say to the wind, Thus saith the Lord God: Come from the four winds, O breath, and breathe upon these slain, that they may live.

(Fire. Nostrils. The four winds. Breath. Her breath. Some days stale, some days sweet, some days stinking of fish and onions, O but the breath, hot on my neck, in the middle of pumping, clawing, grunting. The young think they own loving, but we all need a little sometimes, O Father, O Son, O Holy Ghost, O Sarah, don't I have needs? Am I so wicked? So weak? So evil for having needs? I needed your breath, Louise, your touching, it wasn't about getting my rocks off, it was about rocking in my sweet baby's arms, ain't that the way Hank Williams sings it, Rolling in My Sweet Baby's Arms? Who will rock me now? Louise)

"So I prophesied as he commanded me, and the breath came into them, and they lived, and stood up upon their feet, an exceeding great army.

"Then he said unto me, son of man, these bones are the whole house of Israel; behold, they say, Our bones are dried, and our hope is lost: we are cut off from our parts.

(There were times we didn't do it, remember, Louise? We'd sit in the quiet and talk and just hold each other the way we couldn't with our own. I wonder why? Those were sweet sweet times, almost better than the loving. Just sitting quiet. Why didn't I have the sense to marry *you*, gal? But would it have been any different? In the end? Why couldn't)

"Therefore, prophesy and say unto them, Thus saith the Lord God: Behold, O my people, I will open your graves, and cause you to come up out of your graves, and bring you into the land of Israel.

"And ye shall know that I am the Lord, when I have opened your graves, O my people, and brought you up out of your graves."

(Stone-cold graves. Who will roll away the rock now? O my Jesus. O my people. O my family. O my Sarah. O my soul. I did love you, child. You knew that. Sarah. On your deathbed you forgave me, you wept. Don't cry, girl. I know I haven't been as good a wife— Don't say that, girl— as I should— Don't, Sarah— have been. Sarah, a man couldn't ask for a better— But Barden . . . She always called me by my last name, like in the military, "Barden," it put a kind of formal ring to it, together in the Army of the Lord . . . But, Barden, a wife should tend to *all* her husband's needs, I didn't, Barden, God forgive me, you understand, please say you forgive— There ain't nothing to forgive, baby girl, please hush your crying, please, Sarah, you ain't done nothing. Barden, I know you had to seek comfort in another woman's bed, I— That's not true, Sarah. And she just closed her eyes *tight* and clenched her fists and shook her head from side to side and I knew she knew I was lying. I know, Barden, ain't no use in denying it, but I don't blame you, it's my fault. Lord, I cried. Salty, hot, stinging tears, I can feel them on my face like I'm crying now. But I can't cry here. Such shame. I ran to the rock to hide my face and the rock cried out: No hiding place, Where do you turn to hide such shame, O Lord, I'm ashamed)

"And shall put my Spirit in you, and ye shall live, and I shall place you in your own land: then shall ye know that I, the Lord, have spoken it, and performed it, saith the Lord."

Listen to that again, Brothers and Sisters. These slain of Israel have been hitched together, bone to bone, flesh to flesh, and what do they say: "Our bones are dried, and our hope is lost; we are cut off from our parts." And the Lord says: *I shall put my Spirit in you, and ye shall live. Then shall ye know that I, the Lord, have spoken it, and performed it, saith the Lord. . . . Shall put my Spirit in you, and ye shall live.* What I want to talk about today, Beloved, is To Live Without Hope. To Live Without Hope. Now I say "live" but what kind of life can a man lead without hope? Oh, he can walk around, have a good job, drive a fancy car, wear fine, expensive clothes, eat steak every night, be full of form and fashion and outside show to the world. But without hope? He's like those dried bones full of wind and sound, cut off from his parts. He is not *alive*, he just *exists*. There is no life without hope. It is hope and only hope which gives his existence meaning and gives him life. Hope which moves upon the flesh and gives it meaning. Who among us can dwell without hope? How many of us do? None who live.

(Am I so bad to want to live, son? *Live*, Papa? You have to dishonor my mother, sleeping around, a god-damned minister, in order to *live?* Jesus, Papa— You don't understand, son, understand what it means to . . . ? Talk talk talk words weak vessels for carrying meaning, if only I could have made him understand. Live. Louise, I lived for those meetings, those quick moments of sweet breath, in motel rooms in Jacksonville and Wilmington and Goldsboro and wherever we could and did, in a car in the woods, in your sister's house far from the eyes of the Lord's flock, my flock, when we should have been at work, when I should have been tending my flock, and you your husband, me my wife, my son, O my son, lies, lies to cover sin, sin breeds like hogs to the litter, littering my life with shame. That's what I'd tell him now, Carl, I couldn't bear the shame of it, son, don't you see to bear the shame I needed strength, phys-ical strength, the spirit was willing but the flesh was so weak, son, you ought to know that, you're flesh and bone, my bone, strength Sarah wouldn't couldn't give, she wouldn't have me anymore, and once I fell I needed a hiding place, a place to hide my shame, and shame bred more shame, and then I was sinking in shame, sinking in my sweet baby's arms. I need a hiding place, O God, where will I hide now? Hide me away. I wish the Lord would hide me)

Ole Goose. Barden sees Goose as a boy (Richard Allen Tate, who they called Goose because of his long neck), hard-working, youngest of thirteen children. Fatherless. All in a house with broken Miss Luella Tate. Goose the runt of the litter. Sees Goose being chased by Haz Jones with a chicken snake. Goose hated snakes. Goose stuttered. Sees Goose as a man, thin and wiry, but a good worker still, a hard worker, a good man, selfless. He'd give you the shoes off his feet. Sees his family: his wife, Louise; his daughters, Marie, Phyllis, Corine. Sees the old house of Miss Luella's that Goose tries to keep up while holding two jobs and farming a little too. Sees him trying to keep ahead, especially after getting Louise Simpson to marry him, the apple of his heart. Sees him fighting bills, always behind, sees him fretting over his daughters, who will not work, and the one who is pregnant . . . again. Sees him help his brothers and sisters and anybody he knows in need, though they always seem to have more than he does. Funny, ain't it? He wouldn't deny a soul. Not Goose. Sees people laugh at him when his greying head is turned, calling him a fool. Sees them accept any and all help he will offer and tell him to his face what a good man he is. Barden thinks: Of all men to cuckold, why good ole Goose?

And where does hope come from? Ezekiel tells us. From one place. *I shall put my Spirit in you, and ye shall live. Ye shall live*, saith the Lord. With hope. Hope from the Spirit. Hope is a spirit. A spirit from the Lord. If you have breath, if you have muscles and guts, if you have bones and you have not hope, you are as dead twigs in the dust. But if you have the Spirit of God, then you shall live, as it says in Titus, Chapter One, Verse Two: "In hope of eternal life, which God, who cannot lie, promised before the world began." Hope, before the world began. Hope, Brothers and Sisters. Hope that we shall not die; hope that though our flesh decay, our breath rush out of us, our bones shatter asunder, we shall be free. We shall have eternal life. Hope.

(You lie here before me, baby girl, it's hard to believe. You're cold, child. I wish I could warm you. You're cold and I'm scared and feeling so alone up here, lying, lying, lying. Look at you. Just look. Who would have thought that to see you—thin in those days, your face all cheeks and dimples, your smiling lips painted bright red, and the way you kept yourself dressed so fine in your pumps and tight dresses— Oh, they whispered about you the way they always whisper, just jealous of your melons, gal—smelling sweet . . . Who would have thought to see you here now, cold and dead. Your face is chalky, Louise, and I am scared to look upon you. Cold. I'll be there soon and very soon, I can feel it in my joints when the weather changes, see the jowls hanging lower each year, and, Louise, I'm losing more hair, I'm growing balder and balder and)

That's what I'm talking about this morning, my children. Can I get an Amen? . . . Hope. Hope which springeth eternal and reneweth life. Hope which parts the Red Sea and makes a dry bed for your feet; hope which is a pillar of fire for us to see by night and a billowing cloud to guide us by day; hope which makes the blind to see, the deaf to hear, the halt to walk; hope which turns water to wine, O sweet Jesus, and feeds the multitude and calms the raging sea, peace, be still, peace, be still, for I have hope; hope, O my beloved, which comes to us as a dove bearing the olive branch, and which can cast out demons and raise the dead. Hope, O my Brother, O my Sister, hope which can raise dry bones, clothe them in meat, give them breath, and make them whole again. Hope to make *you* whole.

(Once I felt whole. But that was so long ago I can barely remember. Has it been twenty years? Years in which we'd mostly sit, of an evening, alone before the TV, at home, fruit of our labors, after a day of collecting insurance for the Mutual I'd come home to a meal of Sarah's neck bones and rice and cabbage and sit before the TV and nod, in our house of which we were both so proud, in our house, in my chair before the TV, nodding, not talking, not awake, not living, existing, Sarah knitting or doing the crosswords, neither one of us paying any attention to the TV, in our red brick house with the three bedrooms, the dining room, the living room we rarely used, the two bathrooms, all dustless and spotless from her constant attention, everything in its place, all full of nice polished furniture with the carpet and the plants and the pictures of family, and we'd just sit and I'd dream of nothing, just nod, not tired but weary, just like now, weary, Lord, weary of sin, weary of existence, you've taken them both and left me to find out what I've been preaching all these years, left me to come at it face to face. Maybe I'll call Carl tonight and say: Son, I've come face to face with shame, I can't run anymore, the Lord took away my hiding place, I can't run anymore, I'm too weary, son, of running, Lord, I want to hide, like Jonah in the belly of the whale, don't send me back to that house, full of shame)

The preacher tells us in Ecclesiastes: "For to him that is joined to all the living there is hope; for a living dog is better than a dead lion. For the living know that they shall die; but the dead know not anything." I stand as a witness today to tell you there's a lot of dead folk walking among us, children. Don't laugh. I ain't talking about them ghoulish movie pictures or what you see on TV. You all know what I'm talking about, they may *appear* to be lions in life, but there is no life to them. Why? Cause they have no hope. They are cut off from the one thing which could give their existence meaning, from the one port where they could seek safe harbor in the storm, from the place of comfort in times of sickness and despair, from that which steels us against the terror that flies by night and walks by day, from the eternal knowledge that the soul is safe in our Lord. Let the church say: Amen.

(Who shall hide me now? I have no place to go. I am the living dead denied the grave. No harbor. No nipple to suckle, no buttock to caress. I was a fool who lived by grace and I abused grace, I used grace like a whore. That's what I preach, that's how I lived: *Grace is sufficient*. But why doesn't grace comfort me? Have I murdered grace? Grace once had wings, but I rode it unto death)

For it is through hope that we attain grace, Dearly Beloved, and it is through God's grace that we attain salvation. Our sins are wiped clean and we are made pure again. Purified by the blood of the Lamb, who died so that we could be made whole.

(I shall never be purified. I cannot believe You will forgive me, Father, the prophets say your mercy is everlasting but in my heart I know I've run my course, so many many many sins. O my sins are thick and vile like working maggots. How can I approach the throne in prayer mottled as I am in filth and shame? I am a broken lyre, O Lord, beyond repair. Discard me, Yahweh, snuff me out. I deserve no hope)

Hope, my Brothers and Sisters, leads to faith and faith to prayer and prayer to forgiveness and forgiveness to salvation. Hope is the building block. Hope is the first gift on which all else is built. Hope, faith, and charity. And above all these three charity, love, gives us hope, which leads us to salvation.

(Seeing her on the hospital bed took my hope away, I could hear it flutter away on sooty wings, amid all that gurgling from the tubes up her nose and highfalutin machinery flashing, Louise, I wished I could die for you, gal, all those moments of lust, rolling in my sweet baby's arms, I didn't feel shame then, I felt safe, you were my hope, the God of Abraham, Isaac, and Moses, I worshiped your behind, your tender parts were the temple, even when I snuck into the hospital knowing ole Goose wouldn't be there, while I pretended to pray over you, all I could think of were those days of salvation between your legs. Why should I worry about your soul, my soul, when your spirit was upon me? And when you got sick and I should have returned to Jehovah, my hope remained in you, I never asked about your soul, child. Were you right with God, Louise?)

I knew Sister Tate as we all did, Beloved, I look on her husband and daughters before me and before God, and I offer you comfort in knowing she knew hope. How could we know her and not remember her kindness, her strength, her work for the Lord? Yes, she had hope, my children. Grieve not for her, for the Lord has claimed his own.

(One way or the other you were claimed, Louise, by damnation or divine heaven, claimed. What will you claim of me, sweet Louise, claim of us?)

Fear not, my blessed ones. If you have hope, true hope, ye shall live.

(Whither goeth Thy prophet, O Lord? Have You seen him of late? There he is, Lord! Lurking twixt the thighs of Babylon, the weak fool! Nuzzling at the teat of iniquity like a babe forlorn. What happened to him, Lord? Why did he claim false gods? Why does he lust to drink poison as though it were milk? How can he prophesy with the Devil's passion on his lips? How can he preach salvation while drooling lies? As for me and my house, there is no hope, I have no wings to veil my face, O Lord)

For salvation rests with those who against hope believe in hope.

("The fool hath said in his heart there is no God." What kind of fool am I who'd rather deny God than face Him? Do I hear wings? Do they come or do they go? Or is it just the sound of the wind?)

Trust in the Lord, for it is He who shall deliver you in this and all other hours of need, in your time of trouble, and in your moment of despair. Trust in the Lord, who cannot lie, who maketh the crooked edges straight and the rough road smooth. Blessed be the name of the Lord. Amen. Amen. Amen.

TELL ME,
TELL ME

HEL . . . HELLO?
——Bela? Oh God, Bela. He's back. He's *back*—

—Wha—? Ida, that you?

—He's here. I left him in—

—Ida, what— Girl, do you know it's three in the A.M.? What are you calling me at this—?

—That's what I'm trying to tell you! He's here. He's in my bedroom.

—He who?

—That same niggerboy we saw that night.

—Jesus. You mean *you* saw. Ida—

—Bela, I am not crazy. There is a pickaninny stand-

236

ing just as bold as daylight at the foot of my bed now—

—Well, honey, what you want me to do?

—Send somebody, for God's sake!

—*Who?*

—Can't you call your grandboy, Beau?

—At three in the A.M.? Because you thought you saw a colored boy in—?

—But I did, Bela. I did. I did.

—Okay, honey. Calm yourself down. Okay? Just calm yourself. Now did he say anything? Has he got a gun or a knife or something? How big is he?

—No, he didn't say anything. He's just a boy but he could have something on him for all I know.

—Do you see him now? Where're you standing?

—I ran to the kitchen.

—Is there a gun in the house?

—There's Butch's old gun but it's in the nightstand.

—Jesus. Well, get out of the house, then. Run.

—*Run?* Where am I supposed to run to at three in the morning in the middle of the summer? You know my car's still in the shop. There's not a house closer than five miles, you know that. I'll probably run up on a moccasin or something worse. Get me some help out here, Bela. Please. I don't know what he wants. Please. I—

—Ida, now calm yourself. Now you sure you saw him? You say he didn't say anything? He didn't touch you, did he?

—No.

—Was the light on?

—Not in the bedroom, in the bathroom. I got up to go and as I was walking back in I saw him.

—Uh-huh. 'Not in the bedroom.' See, Ida, it could have been a dream. You don't see him now?

—No, but—

—You can see the staircase from where you stand, can't you?

—Yes.

—And he hasn't come down?

—No.

—Okay. Now, honey, why don't you just go on up them stairs and investigate? I'll stay right here on the phone line. If you find him or something happens, I'll get help there in no time.

—But, Bela—

—Ida, you listen here to me, girl, and you listen good. Up to now you have been one of the sanest, most sensible people I know, and I'd hate to see that questioned. Now you smashed up your car and put my neck in a brace saying you saw some little colored boy in the middle of the road nobody saw but you. And now you want me to wake up half of Tims Creek cause you had a bad dream?

—It was not a dream! I—

—Okay, honey. You might have seen something, but don't you want to make sure, make double-sure, before you have me call somebody? Ida, folk will talk. You know they will. You want them saying you're crazy and have you sent to Dorothea Dix?

—No.

—Well then. Now you get you that broom you keep

behind the door and a knife and you go up there, turn
on a light, and see if it ain't nothing but a bad dream.
Probably those oysters you ate at the club. You had
oysters that other night too. Remember? Oysters must
don't agree with you. They didn't agree with my mama
either.

—Okay. I'll go.

—Good. Now I'll be right here, okay?

—Okay . . . Bela?

—Yeah, hon?

—What does he want?

—How the hell do I know what he wants? Money,
what else could he want? I know he wouldn't want to
rape no sixty-six-year-old, dried-up grandma, that's for
sure. I have heard of stranger things, though.

—Bela!

—You get yourself on up them stairs, woman. I
warrant you there's not a thing up there but shadows,
the wind, and a old widow's overactive imagination.
Maybe it's another stage of the change of life. You feeling hot?

—Bela, this is not a laughing matter. I—

—That's what you think. Now go on up them stairs,
Ida, so I can get some rest. *Please.*

THAT NIGHT—TWO WEEKS ago—was not the first
time she had seen him. But she had not dared tell
Bela—Bela, whose mouth flapped heedlessly like a flag
caught in a tempest. That was why she overreacted.

They had been coming back from the country club
in Crosstown—a banquet for old Dr. Henderson and

his retirement after fifty years of service. True, she had had oysters, but she had eaten oysters all her natural life without seeing black boys each time. Why now?

The car had just passed over the bridge, over the Chinquapin River, just outside town; Bela steadily going on, second-guessing the bride's choices for bridesmaids in a wedding to take place that Sunday, when—there he stood! Out of nowhere. In the middle of the road. Luckily, a small path leading down to the riverbank was there when she turned, but a big sweet gum tree came next and stopped her Buick cold. For the first time in a long while Bela sat simply stunned, quiet, grasping angrily at the seat belt that pinched her matronly girth.

Ida felt sick to her stomach. She knew she had hit the boy. In her mind's eye she could see him. See the placid look on his face, almost as if he could see her through the windshield, through the headlight beams; as if he recognized her. It was silly, she knew. Impossible. She refused to get out of the car.

After a while, she really didn't know how long, the state patrol—Phyllis Pickett's boy, Sam—the rescue squad, a wrecker, and about ten or twelve lookers-on, hoping maybe to glimpse a crushed skull or a severed limb, gathered about. She could hear Bela jabbering to the volunteer rescue workers in their pressed and decalled white shirts; one of them, a black woman named Sarah, who worked at the convenience store, finally coaxed Ida from the car, taking her vital signs, asking her a lot of seemingly pointless questions. The woods flashed with rhythmic lights: the swirling patrol blue, the pulsing ambulance red, the wobbling wrecker orange, and the angry stare of the many headlights.

"Is he dead?" Ida finally asked Sam. "Did I kill him?"

But Sam just looked at Sarah and then at Bela, who rolled her eyes and demanded to know what the hell Ida was talking about, then continued her litany to the medics about her back, her neck, and Look here, honey, my elbow feels kind of . . .

Ida gripped the sleeve of Sam's jacket. "You can tell me. Did I kill him?"

"Ma'am? Kill who?" Shadows obscured much of Sam's face and the medley of light distorted the rest, but she could see he was without a hint.

"That boy. That colored boy. There. In the road." She winced when she said "colored" and glanced sidewise to Sarah, who went about fussing over Bela. "He has to be there. I hit him. Head-on." Ida breathed deeply. "I heard it."

Sam walked her to the site. She saw the skid mark on the tarmac, the torn earth where the car had dug into the grass. But no blood. No torn clothing. No boy.

"But I saw him. I hit him. I—"

Sam searched around for traces of a boy crawling away from the road, his flashlight's shaft cleaving through the soft night, revealing bugs and beer cans and limbs and candy wrappers and wildflowers, but no boy. Into the woods a ways he cast his light but found no sign. He searched the gullies up and down; the rescue workers searched for a while as well, leaving Ida standing by the side of the road, feeling at the same time silly and certain: she had seen the boy. She had. She had.

She heard the metallic crunching of the car being hoisted from the tree.

"Ma'am? Mrs. Perry. I'm sorry, but—"

Ida declined to go to the hospital with Bela for X rays, declaring she was fine; Sam took her home. She climbed the stairs, walked into her bedroom, sat on the bed, and stared at the phone as if it might ring at any minute. She wanted to call her son, Tony, in Salt Lake, to tell him she had hit a boy and they couldn't find him. She focused on the phone but never touched it, nor did it sound once. Listening to the persistent hum of the air conditioner, she imagined the sounds of crickets and tree frogs outside that she would hear if she decided to turn off the central air and open the windows as she normally did in the cool of each night. But she didn't that night, finally lying back on the bed, not taking off her clothes, not turning off the light or turning back the covers. She kicked off her shoes and curled up, slightly. She thought she would dream of the boy over and over. Instead she dreamed of Butch.

Big, red-faced Irishman. Judge. Resolute. She dreamed of their wedding reception. 1943. The war. All her college friends. Sorority sisters. Tri-Delts. The Reverend Dobson. Her mother and father. His mother and father. At the Crosstown Country Club. Married in May. Butch in uniform. Done with warring. Accepted to law school. But no, he looks too old, stooped, his red hair greying, the fire in his eyes dimming, he looks— No, don't kiss my hand, you're not—

Ida's dream had absorbed her recollections of the dinner for Dr. Henderson, she realized upon waking with a start. Her Butch never lived for a retirement banquet: he died just before his election to the state superior bench at fifty-seven.

She woke before day, thinking she had not slept long. But it was five-thirty. She remained on the bed, fully clothed, in a well of loneliness and depression. Wanting to talk to someone. To anyone. Needing to tell someone she had killed a little colored boy. Hadn't she? What if I didn't? What if—? But I am Ida McTyre Perry, she reasoned, catching herself in midthought. Frank McTyre's girl. Frank McTyre, who had worked and scraped to build a drugstore from nothing, to send her to school and find her a good marriage; Frank McTyre, whom people called "a hard man," who taught her to be just as hard as, if not harder than he was. Ida McTyre Perry, widow of the late Honorable Judge Theodore "Butch" Perry, the gallows-eyed judge with the gavel of doom. A hard woman. She didn't *need* to talk to anybody.

That day Joe Abner Chasten, the Negro man who did her handyman work about the house, drove her to the mechanic and they stopped along the road near the bridge.

"Yes, ma'am. You gave that tree some aggravation."

Ida searched around on her own. In the daylight the bushes looked less thick, the undergrowth less forbidding "You see, Joe Abner? You see, he could have crawled away. He could have."

"But why would he, Miss Perry?"

"Scared, maybe. Scared he might get in trouble."

"I don't know, Miss Perry."

He had been there all right. He was there. Ida ran

her hand over her face, reassured of her sanity. Her certitude. Maybe she hadn't actually hit him. And if she did, he was alive; which did not concern her as much as manslaughter. Hit-and-run. She could remember Butch going on about what a heathenish and wicked lot hit-and-run drivers were, and she could rest easy that she was not among that reprobate crowd, exonerated in her own mind.

Joe Abner dropped her off at the front door and she walked up the steps of the plantation-style house. The nighttime and nagging doubt of her sanity safely banished, now she could concern herself with baking some pies with the fresh blueberries Joe Abner's wife had sent her, and finish going through the closets and maybe work a little on a suit she was making for Tony's boy, her new grandbaby. Yet at the threshold of the house it came to her; and she stopped, turning to look down past the lawn, which needed trimming, to the stand of trees blocking the view of the house from the highway and the highway from the house: she knew who that boy was: finally. Then she wiped the thought from her mind, like wiping mucus from her nose, and stepped inside and about her daily life.

IT WAS BUILT IN 1969, just before Judge Perry's first appointment to the bench—built from proceeds made through Jones, McPhee & Perry and their long-standing connections to Duke Power, Carolina Power & Light, and the Department of Transportation, among others. The house was designed in the Federalist style of orange-red brick, with tiles in the foyer, a bright, floral-patterned sun porch, a grand mahogany table in the

dining room; the decor an admixture of French Pro-
vincial and Early American and the popular neo-Deco
style of 1964, which Ida loves, all practically unchanged
in twenty years. The house contains five bedrooms, a
study, a well-stocked pantry. Yet there is a feeling of
emptiness, of long nights full of abandoned wishes for
hordes of grandchildren and great-grandchildren, for
festive Christmases and Thanksgivings and surprise
birthday parties. A weight of nothingness and past dis-
appointments tends to bear down in the kitchen over
meticulously prepared meals for one; and a bewildering
and unexpected and quickly suppressed happiness felt
from the foundation even unto the rafters when Joe Abner arrives for a day of work. Not a house of ghosts: a
house of loneliness.

THE HONORABLE JUDGE THEODORE Sturgis
Perry to the Reverend Howard Clemmons on the occasion of Thanksgiving dinner, 1979:

> *Now I don't claim to have dotted every i and crossed
> every t— any man who does is a damned liar, and How-
> ard, you know it to be true. In the end a man must look
> back on what he's accomplished and ask himself: Did I
> rise to 50% of the challenge? Did I make life easier for
> myself and others? Did I do right by my family and my
> God? And when all is said and done it is only between
> you and your Lord with whom you must reckon. And I
> tell you right now, Howard, I have no fear.*

SHE NOW KNEW SHE had seen him several times before the accident. The very idea unnerved her: How

many times did I see him face to face and not pay him one bit of attention? How many?

Once she was having lunch at the Old Plantation Inn, a restaurant oozing quaintness and doilied charm, with bright-red gladioli, and cross-stitched pillows on wicker chairs, under portraits of belles and horses posed beneath pines dripping with Spanish moss. A meeting of the Friends of the Crosstown County Library; Sarah Cross Burns, the state senator's wife, and the mayor's wife notable among those present. An unusual chill hung in the air; a fire crackled in the red-brick hearth. Ida remembered feeling so at peace in that setting: the warm, light conversation of the ladies in their soft Southern cadences: the civilized tinkle of ice cubes in crystal: the aroma of chicken in orange sauce, and new potatoes and green beans: the smart dresses and discreet glints here and there of pearl and gold and an occasional diamond. This is what we worked for, she thought, as a shower came up softly, lending its strumming rhythm to the ambience. This is what Butch and I strove to achieve. She sighed deeply with self-satisfaction and content-ment.

At one point in her mint tea basking she felt some-thing like a pinprick, nowhere on her person exactly but somewhere within: a bad feeling, a moment of disquiet in her hard-won quietude. She could feel eyes. She turned, for her back was to the French doors, and through the greenish-blue-tinted rainpour she could see across the street, beneath the ugly orange-and-blue phar-macy sign, gazing at her steadily, a little colored boy.

The boy wore faded blue dungarees, as well as she

could make out from where she sat, and a red-and-black shirt that could have been plaid for all she knew. His head had that African shape: too large for his thin frame and shaped like a peanut. His feet, oddly enough, were bare. She could hardly see his eyes, but she knew he was staring at her.

They peered at each other, over the distance, through the rain and glass, and Ida—warm, dry, richly fed, impressively dressed, and comfortable—became unaccountably angry with the boy—probably cold, definitely wet, unshod, black—staring at *her*. She flinched. Her right hand encountered Sarah Cross Burns's tea glass, which, luckily, missed that fine lady's new *white* dress and emptied onto the floor. In unison everyone at the table sharply sucked in air, then inquired after Mrs. Burns, and Ida, flabbergasted and embarrassed, repeatedly apologized while Sarah assured her that her dress was fine, just fine, dear, not a dram, really, see? just fine; and the waiter brought a fresh glass of sweet iced tea with a bright wedge of lemon, and Sarah Cross Burns resumed her gossip about a dinner with the First Lady of the State, and Ida stole a glance over her shoulder to see if she could see the boy, who was gone.

Of course Ida didn't think of the boy again after that. Why should she? The embarrassing moment lingered, but the reason, like a price tag, had been discarded without thought. Even the second and the third times—once she saw him staring at her at the Crosstown Shopping Mall as she got into her car; another time he stood at the entrance of the beauty parlor as she drove up—she paid him no mind. Afterward. At the time she felt annoyed, angered, invaded. But within moments of seeing him and reacting, something or someone would come between them and he would be instantly forgotten.

But the fourth time—or at least the fourth time she could recollect, and Lord knows it could have been the sixteenth as easily as the fourth—she had been alone in the garden, picking butterbeans from the latticed thicket of a vine, when she thought she heard footsteps, faintly, on the grass. She looked to the edge of the garden along the lawn, separated by a fence of treated posts and wire. She saw the boy walking the garden's width. He walked at an even pace, not exactly running but with large measured steps as if he had to get to church on time. Was it somebody she knew? No. At first she had been bemused; then annoyed; and again as always angered by the intrusion. "You have no business on this property!" she called to him. "Hey!" He kept walking. She called out again, louder, dropping her beans to the ground, missing the bucket. "Hey, you!" Ida called. The boy kept walking, and as he was near the end of the garden, where the woods began, he turned and looked at Ida, not slowing his gait one whit, and his look was full of accusation. Ida just stood, confused.

How could she have not recognized him then? How could she have not have identified the red-and-black shirt? The faded blue jeans? So obvious now that it was the same boy. But not then. Thinking back, it was hard to believe she had repeatedly tossed the memory aside: just an impertinent, trespassing Negro, she fumed. I'll have to get Joe Abner to put up some more fences and DO NOT TRESPASS: PRIVATE PROPERTY signs. It was not the first time she had seen strangers stomp across her property, hunting rabbits, deer, quail, trampling through the woods. So it was not particularly strange to her, just galling; and the phone rang in the house and she ran, taking off her Platex gloves, knocking off her straw hat, stopping to pick it up, and dashing through the gate of the fence and into the screened-in back porch to the phone on the table there, and it was Bela. "No. No, just picking beans . . . *Really?* She did? Well, I—" Banishing to the detritus of unpleasantness the episode with the little colored intruder.

—Bela?
—Well? Is he there?
—Well . . .
—Did you look?
—Well . . .
—You didn't?
—No.
—Why not? Don't you want this over, one way or the other? I mean—
—But, Bela, I'm . . . I'm too . . . I—
—Hon, I can understand that you're frightened—
—I'm not *frightened*, damnit! I'm just . . . just—
—Still and all, Ida, I know you don't want anybody to call you crazy, do you?
—Of course not, but. But he's here, Bela. I know it. Just go on ahead and call Beau, why don't you? Call him! If you don't I will.
—Now, Ida—
—Why don't I just call him anyway? Why didn't I call him or Joe Abner in the first place? You ain't good for nothing but—

—Ida—

—talk, talk, *talk*—

—Ida—

—I don't know—

—Ida—

—why I thought you would help me—

—Ida, now—

—All you're good for is—

—Ida! Ida! Plea—

—talking. A colored boy upstairs threatening me and—

—*Ida!* Ida, don't you hang up this phone! You hear me? Ida?

—What?

—What're you planning to do?

—I'm fixing to call Beau or Joe Abner or the state patrol, one.

—And if they come and don't find a boy upstairs or anywhere in the house . . . ?

—Well, I'll rest easy.

—Will you? Will you ever believe them? You need to go on up them stairs and see for yourself that there's nothing there but summer air, Ida. You're the best friend I've got living, hon . . . I sure don't want you declared senile. You're too young.

—*Senile?*

—You know that's what they'll say. And you know those children of yours will—

—Jesus, Bela. I—

—Ida. For me, please. Just go on up those stairs. Flip on the light and see if you see sign of that boy.

That's all. You can run. All you got to do is holler. Okay?

— . . .

—Okay?

—All right. But don't you go nowhere.

S O   M A N Y   T H I N G S   T O think about: and now this problem she could not avoid or ignore or put off. Doc Henderson had been her doctor for fifty-five years, and Ida did not trust that new doctor—too young a woman; not that she's a woman, mind you. Regardless of the fact that Dr. Henderson himself recommended her, Ida simply could not put all her faith in that woman. And it had nothing to do with her being Filipino. Nothing at all. It made perfect sense, her son being a doctor, that he could recommend someone with whom she could feel a bit more secure. That was all.

". . . really sorry we can't come home over the summer, Mama. You know we've got this share in Washington State and . . ."

It always took her a while to get around to the matter at hand, and sometimes she herself wondered why she buried the heart of the matter at the end of a conversation, like an afterthought. But he never seemed as surprised as she'd thought he would be.

". . . I'm glad to know the car is fixable. But most of all I'm glad you're . . ."

Ida thought a great deal of her son, Anthony. He had made her so proud, doing medical research now in Salt Lake City. With his wife, Rita, and the new grand-baby . . . what had they named it? Certainly, she would have been happier if he had become a general practitioner instead and stayed in North Carolina, but . . . It embarrassed her so to feel his embarrassment. After all there was no reason for such concern just yet. Just a spot.

"It's just a spot . . . No. No, of course you shouldn't come home. After all it's just a spot on the X ray. And this woman is new and everything and I just want a second opinion, that's all."

"Okay, Mama. I've got the address right here. It's . . ."

And despite what others might think, it was not that she didn't love and care for his sister, Carol, even though the little woman wouldn't think to call or drop a line. Not that Tony called or visited that often either; she had yet to see her new grandbaby more than once. But Tony was reliable. Sensible. She could trust him.

"If you want me to, I'll call her first. You know, just to make sure she pays attention . . ."

Just a spot on an X ray, now. Dr. Soh says it just may well be an infection, you know. Could be just the equipment. Don't . . . No. Tony, really. I hate to ask but—well, you can't be too careful, and that's the truth . . . No. No. No reason to come home . . . Yes, of course I'll be fine. Just fine . . . No. No, I had just gone in for a checkup . . . I know, I know I don't normally put much stock in modern medicine, as you call it. But I just, well, you know, Butch always used to quote Franklin: 'A stitch in time saves ni—' . . . Yes. Yes. Of course. Kiss everyone for me.

ONE DAY JOE ABNER walked in and found her sitting slumped in her armchair, her knitting tumbled to the floor in tangled disarray, her head tilted heavenward, her lips slightly parted, and Joe Abner had hollered, "Good Lord, Miss Ida, my Lord, don't tell me you done gone away from here to be with the Judge!" and Ida awoke with a start and peered slantwise at him, confused and annoyed by all his jubilation at her merely waking up—"Of course I'm not dead yet, Joe Abner"—and she ferociously brushed the sleep from her eyes, ignoring him, and went to see about supper, not daring for one moment to consider her own mortality.

While peeling potatoes, she came to think of Joe Abner's reaction to the thought that she had breathed her last; at first she felt amused by that silly black man's affection, and then she wondered if it were sincere; and she wondered what would become of Joe Abner and his wife and boy when she did indeed leave this vale of tears, and felt sad that he might go unemployed and then thought, No, he's a resourceful Negro and he has . . . character, yes, that's it, *character*. So many of them don't, these days. The way he brings me things from his wife's garden, the way he treats me respectfully, the way . . . Ida paused over skinning beets and thought, My God, I've known that man for twenty-five years—known him by name, by speech, by good work—but there are things . . . I don't know what his favorite meal is, for instance. I don't know what he likes to do when he's not working, or if he's truly religious. I don't . . . Suddenly Joe Abner reared up in her imagination as a grand and impenetrable mystery.

But she did not resolve to penetrate the enigma nor vow to know him better. She thought on it no more. She merely tipped the pan over in the sink, pouring the sanguine juice down the drain, and listened to the gurgle it made as it rushed down the pipes.

FROM THE HONORABLE Theodore S. Perry on the occasion of the ratification of the Fourteenth Amendment of 1964 to Joe Abner Chasten:

> *Well they've passed it, to be sure, but I warrant you, Joe Abner, with all due respect to those Martin Luther Kings and Roy Wilkinses and Whitney Youngs—and you know I met him once in Charlotte, don't you? A fine colored man, well spoken, good looking, a true credit to his race . . . Young, not that King fellow I mean— but I guarantee you it's done more harm than good, and that's the God's truth. Now you take a man like Booker T. Washington—he understood that your people need to establish yourself in this land before you try to compete with the white man. Higher education, participation in the federal and local government—it all boils down to responsibility. Now you look at your average black man—and I say your* average—*and you'll see a whole quorum of problems which need to be addressed before he can expect to assume that kind of responsibility and participate in what you might call* the mainstream. *It's just common sense. You know it. I was talking with Senator Ervin the other day and . . .*

. . . AND A DEER CAME up into the backyard, not ten feet from where she sat at the kitchen table, and munched and munched at grass and weeds for over twenty minutes, and Ida sat stock-still so as not to frighten it and wanted to go out to touch it but knew that would send it prancing away, so she sat, seemingly paralyzed, and watched its tail switch back and forth, its natural majesty making it appear larger than it actually was, until finally its marionette legs carried it into the never-never land of the woods, and she ached inside, filled up with so much beauty, so much tangible wonder, and the life-giving alarm of serendipity, and she alone in her great house, with not one soul for her to call out to and with child-like wonder say: Guess what I just saw?

THAT JUNE MORNING EVERYTHING seemed to glow and sparkle and radiate light from within. For a brief moment Ida allowed herself to feel a smarting of sadness, to consider: What if it is cancer? What if I have to leave all this? A brief moment in which she came to regret so much wasted time and energy and misplaced resentment and wished to have a chance to do it all over—but the arrival of Bela's grandchild, Beau, sent those silly thoughts scampering and she prepared for her journey.

It was so nice of Beau to volunteer to drive her to Wilmington, and she told him so. She admired his tall and slender good looks, but became more and more alarmed each time she saw how dark a tan he allowed himself. He had dropped out of the eleventh grade three years ago and now worked on his father's farm; his girlfriend was pregnant—something you wouldn't hear Bela flapping about. Of course it was true that Tony and Carol weren't here to see Ida to the doctor, but they did turn out better than Bela's brood. Still and all.

The trip to Wilmington took place in veritable

silence, though Beau turned on the radio midway, much to Ida's annoyance. The newly completed Interstate 40 took nearly twenty minutes off the drive, and Ida marveled at the way the terrain looked strangely like another state, like those stretches of lone timber and grass up and down from Bangor to Beaufort; not the landscape of soybean and cornfields and white houses and schools that she knew had been here before.

The gynecologist Tony had suggested worked out of an office in a village of clinics and specialists on the southeastern side of the town between the two main hospitals, a fast-growing medical community that looked like a group of pleasant suburban houses, bright, modern, professional, on newly paved cul-de-sacs. Dr. Harriet Bridge's office lay between the offices of a proctologist and an ophthalmologist.

Within the sky-blue building, as she announced herself to the young Negro girl who sat behind a desk at the end of the waiting room, Ida could feel her chest tighten. The weight of the air; the energy from the three other women in the room and the child playing with tiny toy men on the floor; the sweetly cheerful decor— one wall painted with a forest scene—all seemed to bear down upon her and make her wish and wish strongly that she were back on her sun porch reading *Southern Living*, sipping strong coffee, and not having to trouble with this foolishness. Beau sat down, crossed his legs, ankle atop knee, and began flipping through a copy of *Field and Stream*.

Tony had gone to Chapel Hill with Dr. Bridge, and Ida felt certain she could—would—dispel this aspersion cast on her unmistakably good health by the well-meaning Dr. Soh. Tony had said she was a brilliant woman who had studied in New York and done work all over. Even written a book. Ida used her memories of the admiration in Tony's voice to calm herself. She picked up a copy of *McCall's*.

"Mrs. Perry? Dr. Bridge will see you now."

Why do all doctors' offices have these narrow halls? They're all so frightening. As if you're going to your execution. I wonder how they could make them less frightful? Maybe—

"Mrs. Perry. It's a pleasure to meet you. Tony and I were good friends in school, and I can't believe we'd fallen out of touch. It was wonderful to hear from him. How are you feeling?"

"Just fine. Thank you."

She looked directly into the doctor's eyes only once. For the remainder of the consultation she peered at the diplomas; glanced at the curtains; fixed her gaze on an ashtray, the back of a desktop picture frame, a stone paperweight containing myriad graceful white fissures; stared absently at a painting on the wall of some distant city shrouded in mist and at a huge and ugly mask— maybe African?—but not at the exquisite cornrows that boldly arched up and slid down like two fat snakes be- hind the good doctor's smiling, autumn-leaf-toned face or her broad nostrils or her magenta-painted and full lips; Ida could look at her open white lab coat and the beige blouse underneath but could not look into her eyes.

Ida sat stunned, not listening really—though a word slipped through here and there since, at base, she did want to know the truth of her condition.

"We see this sort of thing a great deal. I don't want to mislead you, Mrs. Perry. There is always a possibility. But the chances . . ."

Marshaling an effort so great its effort could never be acknowledged even to herself, Ida smiled. She reached way, way down and dredged up those most lauded elements of character: humor and strength. Had she lost her sense of good humor about the world? So it was something of a shock? So it was like a God-played joke? So what, Ida? She chastened herself, smiling all the more broadly, though the grim nature of the possibilities Dr. Bridge was outlining called for a more somber countenance. The world is a strange place, Ida, and changing every day, every day, and you must change with it. To be sure.

And with every thought of how valiantly she had overcome her own mind—"Now if Tony says she's brilliant and good and to be trusted, I warrant you she is"—the more she smiled, the more affable she became; and after undressing and submitting to a number of peculiar and uncomfortable ministrations, and after getting dressed again and listening to the good, good doctor and asking some questions troubling the other half of her mind, Ida looked Dr. Harriet Bridge, M.D., straight in her brown eyes and felt an incomparable sense of goodwill, admiration, largesse, and confidence in both herself and the pretty colored doctor in front of her whom she had no choice but to trust either to save her life or to assure her, at least, that everything was going to be all right.

"You can expect to hear from me with the test results by the end of the week."

"Thank you, Doctor. Thank you and . . ."

Upon reemerging into the still incandescent morning, Ida felt her chest light and burdenless. So much so that she uncharacteristically regaled Beau with stories of the Judge and with stories the Judge used to tell and with stories of her mother and father and, when all else failed, stories of herself, to which Beau nodded and gave an occasional "Oh yeah."

As soon as she got home she went upstairs to take a nap, exhausted by the strain of talking, worry, and goodwill.

That Thursday Dr. Bridge called to say that Ida did in fact have only a bacterial infection and that she could prescribe the proper antibiotics over the phone, and gave her instructions about a special douche. Relieved to know she was going to be well—was well—Ida felt happier knowing she would not have to see Dr. Bridge again.

''NOW OF COURSE,'' BELA was saying—as they sat on Ida's sun porch snapping beans. Bela who seemed to care about nothing so much as other people's business. Ida strongly admired (envied?) Bela, wife of the late Henry Clay, longtime principal in York County—Bela, who had taught elementary school for thirty years and didn't have a third of the earthly possessions Ida laid claim to, yet seemed, unaccountably, to have more. She had five children to Ida's two, and a great-grandchild in the oven; people were in and out of her house year-round; and where Ida strained to keep herself busy, Bela seemed to have more to do than she possibly ever could. Bela—overweight, not particularly graceful, nosy—was saying: "Now of course" . . . Bela, full of good humor, prone to playful deceit masked by Christian generosity, troubled by a bad back. "Now of course, Ida, you're coming to the '34 class reunion. It doesn't matter when you graduated. Now you know what I heard? . . ."

For one fleeting moment, a fleeting second, Ida considered confiding in her about her realization that she was seeing the same boy again and again; she would let it slip out, she would unburden herself, and then ask:

—*Do you think I'm crazy, Bela?*

—*Oh, go on away from here, Ida. Of course not. You're as right in the head, if not righter, than anybody in Tims Creek, probably the rightest. You have got no cause to think yourself going off. Look at you. Look. At. You. No, girl, I'd tell you if you were going round the bend. I can tell. Yes I can. Besides, your mama, she lived to an old age without losing her wits, and you know that runs in families. How old was she when she died?*

—*Sixty-two.*

—*Oh. But your grandma, Miss Ida, she lived to eighty-seven, I know that for a fact. And there wasn't a more clear-headed woman going.*

—*What could it be?*

—*Well, hon, it might be, just, you know . . .*

—*What?*

—*I've heard tell—and you mustn't take this for law—that people have these episodes, you know.*

But Ida never did confide in Bela. Cocking her head to one side in steely resolve, sucking in air through her nostrils, setting her upper lip firmly, she told herself: There's no need, simply no need. Certainly, there's an explanation. And nodded to the tidbits of gossip Bela served up amidst the snapping and popping of the Kentucky Wonders.

"Oh, Ida, Frank Lanier told me . . ."

MᶜTYRES—OR PERRYS FOR that matter—aren't susceptible to such foolishness, she reasoned as she walked through the church parking lot. But as the Judge used to say, "What good is religion if a man can't find solace in it?" To be sure. So she had decided to talk to Reverend Clemmons about . . . about all the things on her mind. Would she mention the boy?

The door to the church study was open and she heard voices: one Reverend Clemmons, a voice she knew instantly from years of faithfully attended sermons; and the voice of a young man.

She tapped on the doorpost to announce herself and presented herself in the frame. She smiled, she applauded herself later, and her smile did not slacken, did not yield to gravity; her composure was maintained; her grace assured.

"Oh, Ida. How are you? Let me introduce the Reverend Peterson. He's just graduated from Trinity and is on his way to Edinburgh, isn't that something? He wanted to pick my mind about . . ."

Her handshake, she thought later, It's so good to meet you; her gentle inquiries, "Oh, the AME Zion in Wilmington, on Market, how nice"—had all been as if nothing were amiss. But of course nothing *had* been amiss. And after the good Reverend Peterson left— What an awfully nice gentleman—she did not once make note or mention of the fact that he was black. Nor did she discuss anything of import. She talked of arranging bake sales, of a fund-raiser for the new annex, of problems with the usher board, of the sanctuary needing painting; but not of the spot on the X ray, not of her empty house or her unending nights upon nights dawning into desolately cheerful mornings full of gossip and coffee and banter with Joe Abner. She did not mention the boy.

—Bela? Bela, you still there?
—Oh, course. Didn't I say I would hold on? Well? Did you see him?
—I think so.
—You "think so"? What do you mean, "think so"? Is he there or not?
—Well, I just peeked.
—Ida, you're beginning to sound like a child! I—
—Don't yell at me, Bela! You—
—don't believe you!
—stop yelling!
—I'm not yelling!
—Bela, will you call somebody?
—No. Not until you go up there and see there's nobody there.
—*I did see him!*
—Still there, where you left him?
—Yeah.
—Bull. Now think about this, honey. Think. If he were up there, don't you think he would at least go hide somewhere else, if not leave altogether?
—Bela, this conversation is pointless. Good-bye. I'm going to call the Law.

—Do and you'll never hear the end of it. Your children will have you locked up and all your money to boot. Just because you're scared of a bad dream.

—Scared of a dream? Woman, I—

—Fine. Call them then. Call anybody you want. You got Beau's number. Call him. Go on ahead. But let me tell you one thing: you would have called him in the first place if you were so convinced. Now wouldn't you?

—What are you—?

—What am I saying, Ida? That you know there's nothing up there as well as I do?

—But—

—And you're just tired of being alone and, honey, I can understand that. Lord knows I can. You've had a big scare and none of your children have come to see about you and—Jesus, Ida, just look at yourself. You haven't shown one sign of wear or worry. Think about it. Of course you're going to have bad dreams. I have them all the time, and I haven't got half the worries you have.

—You do? Have bad dreams?

—Of course! I'm always waking up, asking Tim or Ray to see about something I just *know* I saw or heard. Nothing. Not even the wind or the house settling. Just my head, child. And I know *I'm* not crazy.

—Well, I don't know about that. But you may be right.

—I know I am.

—Okay. I'm going to go look. But you stay right here.

—You know I will. And we'll have us a good laugh about this in the morning.

—Okay. I certainly hope so.

BUTCH PERRY TO IDA Perry: *"Why Ida, sugarpie, don't you worry. You know anything I've accomplished in this world I've accomplished because of, not in spite of you."*

THERE WERE MOMENTS THAT week when she came as close to calling Carol as dialing all eleven digits of her number and letting it ring once. She hung up.

I'll be damned if I'll call her. If I'll go to her. She must come to me. *She* must apologize. Not I. And she'll be the one hurt if I die and she'll be the one to regret not talking to me all these years.

But Ida vacillated like a metronome. One minute thinking of her child's once-sweet face and manner, the next remembering the fight over her marriage to that damned, good-for-nothing hippie looking to get her family money; one moment missing Carol with a pang that threatened to bring a tear, trying to recall her voice, but then hearing the venom in her tone when she called Butch a crooked old demagogue who should burn in hell for all his wicked doings—her own father!—Carol, how could you? But can't you see, Mama? Can't you see? All your life you've been bowing and scraping to that man and you don't even know where he got his money, the way the great potentate really did pay for this house, the hypocrite. Carol, I won't have you talk about your father—Mama, I'd rather not have a father than to have Theodore "Butch" Sturgis Perry for a father. Carol!

No. She wouldn't call. To be sure. Still and all.

RECLAMATION, DOUBT, SWIRLING AND opaque obfuscation, nagging presentiments, dread fear, deep-rooted arrogance, proprietary pride, all thick and treacherous and ever-present, had built this wall. A wall against what? What did she forget? Where had it been? On Emerald Isle. When? 1937. What?

A summer beach in late August and the odor of dead fish and salt in the Carolina air and the sight of footprints in the sand as the moon tugs and the tide rises. How many sets of footprints? Four. Who do they belong to? Clarise Williams, Rafe Terry, Butch Perry, and Ida McTyre. Yes, Clarise, her best friend; her father had a house on the then sparsely populated island; yes, Rafe was courting Clarise; yes, Butch was sparking Ida.

Perhaps under the luminous membrane of memory these images are stored away: Rafe chasing Clarise; Clarise giggling; Rafe thin as a bean pole, lanky, his arms moving like rubber bands; his face so innocent in the half-light; no thought of tomorrow; no thought of the Pacific front where he would lose an arm; Clarise, silly, spoiled, slow in the head but so unfairly pretty, her laughter lost in the lion call of the surf; Butch's hand on Ida's behind; yards away from Rafe and Clarise's romping; his hands hot on Ida; his face, red even then, freckled, his hair tousled like the phoenix's nest; Butch leers; Butch cusses; Butch always cusses; that's why Ida likes Butch; but Butch doesn't cuss in front of the grown-ups; no, Butch is going to be All-American, a football quarterback; Butch teaches Sunday school; Butch is a son of a bitch, she thinks, she thought, she does not now remember, but she knows, she knows, that is what he called himself, a son of a goddamned bitch, who drank and fought and was going to be the goddamned President one of these damn days, You just watch, Shug; he grabs her behind and says: Come on, Ida, I got the fever; Butch takes her into the tall grass and takes off her blouse; Butch bites her nipples, hard, and she almost cries; but no, Butch is her salvation, her future husband, a tall, big, red-headed demigod she wants to keep; submitting is not a question, only enduring; making it good for Butch, who is rough and makes strange animal noises as he gropes her in his adolescent passion; she hears a zipper and he places her hand on his tumescence and it feels foreign and hot and improbable and she fights back her fear and says in a cracking voice: Maybe we shouldn't; he says: Aw come on, and pulls down her—; Oh, shit; what? Who is that? Butch, what? Shit. Get out of here, goddamnit! What, Butch? What? She can see in the dwindling light the muscles of Butch's face clench, the color tone rise, What, Butch? she sits up; A nigger? a little pickanniny? Get on! Get out of here! But the little nigger just stands with his eyes wide and his mouth hung open, what a sorry sight, like a scared possum; Get on, I said! and Butch is up jerking on his pants and the boy turns to run and Butch chases after him and now Rafe, who has heard the hollering, comes; and Ida fixes her clothes, trembling, as though her very life has been snatched away from her, feeling naked and wicked and unclean; Butch,

Butch, Butch, don't! and in that particle of thought images flutter yet faster, like leaves in a vortex: Rafe and
Butch: Butch kicking: What you looking at, huh? See
something you like, huh? the boy between Butch and
Rafe: trying to get away: the boy darts left: Butch trips
him: the boy kicks Butch between the legs: Goddamnit!
I'll kill the little son of a bitch! Butch grabs the boy:
begins punching: kicking: kicking: Clarise screaming:
Shut up, Clarise, says Rafe: Rafe kicking: the boy crying:
Butch down on his knees: Butch pushing the boy's face
into the sand: Butch's face a wild boar's: punching: kicking: I'll fix you: Butch picks the boy up: Butch walking
toward the surf: Butch carrying the boy high over his
head: one hand on the neck, firm: one hand on the thigh:
the boy yelling: yelling: a wordless holler from the back
of his throat: Ida can feel the fear from the boy: Oh, my
Jesus: but can only say, in a voice like a soft breath:
Butch—: Let's see how far I can throw him: ain't as
heavy as a feed sack: foot-deep: ankle-deep: calf-deep:
waist deep: the boy no longer struggles; no longer yells:
his chest convulsing in sobs: the body makes a graceful
arc, a dark parabola: Ida cannot judge just how far: she
barely hears the sound the body makes as it enters the
water: a solid sound like a large stone: blurred half-
images of a child thrashing: splashing: calling caught up
in the thunder of the surf: Clarise stands crying: Rafe
yelling at her: yelling at her: yelling at her: Clarise shivers
and turns her back: Butch walks out of the water: Butch
with a peculiar grin on his face: like he has just made a
touchdown or shot a great buck: Ida forces herself to
smile: no, not forces: wills, creates, manufactures a
smile: it is real, her smile, not fake: he is just a bad boy,

her Butch: tsk, tsk: Butch, now you shouldn't have—:
Well, Ida, he shouldn't have: Just a nigger: Just a nigger:
Come on: Let's go get a drink of liquor: A drink? Yeah:
I know a bootlegger not far from here: You for it, Rafe?
Hell, yeah: Well, come on then: What the hell is she
crying about? You know Clarise, now: But what about
that coonboy? What coon? Hahaha. She ain't gone say
nothing is she, Rafe? Course not. She a good gal, she
got more sense than she look like, just excitable: Yeah,
but not like Ida here, she's a rock. Ain't you, Ida? Hot
damn, look at them titties on her, boy: I'll tell you—

But these images are locked away. Why should these
memories be disturbed? No body was found, or at least
no word of the incident intruded upon Ida's consciousness. And because she did not dare speak of it—or jeop-
ardize Butch, good, strong Butch, just following his
powerful nature—she did not think of it. And the memory took its place, shrinking, and drifted away, more
and more remote, amid the giga-fold angel-sized memory hordes stored over the 34,689,600 seconds contained
in sixty-six years of life on this planet.

Perhaps.

But some things you forget to remain innocent; some
things you forget to remain free; some things you forget
due to lassitude. Moral lassitude, intellectual lassitude,
human lassitude. However, Ida had not cared to remember; not to remain innocent, not to remain free,
not to spare herself worry, but because she simply did
not care. She did not care to remember.

HE IS A BOY, just a boy. He stands at the foot of the
bed as if waiting, and time within the room seems to

teeter, seems to shift as though time were a child's toy cocked at a capricious angle. What do you want from me? Why do you just stand there, looking, looking, looking? Do you want me to hit you? To yell at you to go away? Goddamnit! Leave me alone! Get away, you hear me? Get away. Leave me be!

This is what she said to herself over and over again as she stumbled out of the room, tripping on the carpet, looking back, thinking he'd be right behind her. No, good. So she ran, not stopping to tell Bela; Bela couldn't help her. Leave me be. Leave me be. She tumbled out the back door, no longer looking back, no longer able to, she lost one slipper but she did not stop, she caught a sandspur in her right foot but she did not stop. She ran as best she could on one foot and one tippy-toe, she could not stop, she would not stop, she would run, the bushes snagged her nightgown, but she would run, gasping, run till the sun came up, run till the boy was gone. All are guilty, none is free.

LET THE
DEAD
BURY THEIR
DEAD

*; Being the Annotated Oral History of the Former Maroon Society
called Snatchit and then Tearshirt and later the Town of Tims Creek,
North Carolina [circa 1854–1985]*

by the

RIGHT   REVEREND
JAMES   MALACHAI   GREEN

Abridged and Edited, with introduction by
REGINALD   GREGORY   KAIN

*The greatest part of a writer's time is spent in reading, in order
to write; a man will turn over half a library to make one book.*
Samuel Johnson, April 6, 1775

for
RANDY PAGE
and
NELL PAINTER

Besides these Soveraign Powers, Divine, *and* Humane, *of which
I have hitherto discoursed, there is mention in Scripture of another
Power, namely, that of the* Rulers of the Darknesse of this
world, the Kingdome of Satan, *and* the Principality of Beel-
zebub over Daemons, *that is to say, over Phantasmes that
appear in the Air: For which Satan is also called* the Prince of
the Power of the Air: *and (because he ruleth in the darkness of
this world)* The Prince of this world: *And in consequence here-
unto, they who are under his Dominion, in opposition to the
faithful (who are the* Children of the Light) *are called the
Children of Darknesse . . . a Confederacy of Deceivers, that to
obtain dominion over men in this present world, endeavour by
dark and erroneous Doctrines to extinguish in them the Light,
both by Nature, and of the Gospell; and so to dis-prepare them
for the Kingdome of God to come.*

Part IV, the Kingdom of Darknesse,
LEVIATHAN
Thomas Hobbes

Therefore, the fantastic in folklore is a realistic *fantastic: in no
way does it exceed the limits of the real, here-and-now material
world, and it does not stitch together rents in that world with
anything that is idealistic or other-worldly; it works with the
ordinary expanses of time and space, and experiences these expanses and utilizes them in great breadth and depth. Such a
fantastic relies on the real-life possibilities of human develop-
ment—possibilities not in the sense of a program for immediate*

practical action, but in the sense of the needs and possibilities of men, those eternal demands will remain forever, as long as there are men; they will not be suppressed, they are real, as real as human nature itself, and therefore sooner or later they will force their way to a full realization.

Forms of Time and Chronotope in the Novel
THE DIALOGIC IMAGINATION
M. M. Bakhtin

Now you are going to hear lies above suspicion.

Zora Neale Hurston

INTRODUCTION

O N MARCH 12, 1998, the Reverend James Malachai Greene died in a car accident on the way
home from a conference of ministers in Atlanta; he had
just entered the town limits of Tims Creek, North
Carolina.

Tims Creek, the town of his birth, held an unusual
fascination for the Baptist minister. For decades he had
acted as the town's self-appointed historian, quietly
chronicling the Tims Creek of past and present, of public
and private, of mythic and real, of virtue and vice. With
the exception of the nine years spent in Durham, North
Carolina, in school and teaching, Greene spent most of
his life in that small southeastern farm community ob-
serving, interpreting, compiling, researching, and writing. To say that he loved the town would be not only

a gross understatement but in many ways an indication of the shortcomings of the English language—James Malachai Greene seemed to exist for Tims Creek. The evidence is found in *Let the Dead Bury Their Dead*, the most compelling of all the works found in the Reverend Greene's home after his death.

James Malachai Greene was born in the town on March 12, 1951, to Rose Green [b. 1927]. Born out of wedlock—his father unknown—he grew up alongside his half-brother Franklin and his half-sister Isador, under the care of his grandmother Jonnie Mae Cross Greene [1904–1984], who inculcated in him not only his deep appreciation of religion (despite a period of apostasy as a young man) but also his obsession with Tims Creek. Mrs. Greene had been the oldest child of Thomas Cross, the patriarch of a prosperous farming family which had been in Tims Creek since the 1850s and in North Carolina for perhaps two centuries. Mrs. Greene enjoyed considerable status in the village as family head and as a community leader. Her telling of stories—as well as the stories of the other elders who surrounded young Jimmy—no doubt were an early source of Reverend Greene's fascination with the town.

After his undergraduate education at North Carolina Central [1969–1973], where he took a degree in education; divinity studies at Southeastern Theological Seminary [1973–1976]; and another master's degree at Duke University [1976–1978], Greene returned to Tims Creek with his wife, Anne Gazelle Dubois, a former civil-rights activist from Albany, New York. Tragically, Mrs. Greene died in 1983 of cancer.

Perhaps it was this void in the Reverend Greene's

life which led him to ensconce himself more firmly in the study of the town's history. He enrolled in the University of North Carolina graduate history program and over the years completed two semesters' course work toward his doctorate; but his duties as minister for the parish of the First Baptist Church of Tims Creek—of which he became associate pastor in 1982 and pastor in 1985 after the retirement of the Reverend Hezekiah Barden—and his appointment as principal of Tims Creek Elementary School, ultimately proved too demanding for him to continue his graduate studies.

Nonetheless, it is clear that he did manage to devote some time each day to writing about the town, and the result is an amazing trove of papers: essays, oral histories, diaries, poetry, and notes, none of which was published during his lifetime. At present the James Malachai Greene Papers, purchased by the DeNabone Foundation in 1999 and housed at the Southern Historical Collection in Chapel Hill, North Carolina, have not been fully catalogued, but the complete works are estimated to exceed 500,000 words.

It is fitting for *Let the Dead Bury Their Dead* to be the first work in this extraordinary oeuvre to see print. It is the record of a conversation with the Reverend's great-uncle, Ezekiel Thomas Cross [b. 1901], and great-aunt, Ruth Davis Cross [b. 1895], that took place on September 22, 1985, at the home of Mrs. Cross. It is in many ways emblematic of Greene's major preoccupations: the origins of Tims Creek; his family's slave past; the intermingling of the two Cross families, black and white; folklore and the supernatural; thanatology; issues of community leadership and decay. Greene also takes great liberties with the established patterns of oral history and documentation, often using autobiography to illuminate the text.

With the exception of three minor passages, which are largely repetitive, the following oral history is presented in its entirety. Extracts from letters, diaries, and discourses on natural history, though oddly positioned, were compiled in such a way by the Reverend Greene, and, after much reflection, are allowed to remain as he intended.

—RK, August 5, 2000
BROOKLYN, NY

I am particularly grateful for a sabbatical from the Department of Anthropology and Folklore of Sarah Lawrence College. Thanks also to the American Council of Learned Societies, the National Endowment for the Arts, the North Carolina Council for the Arts, the MacDowell Colony, and to the kind people of Tims Creek, North Carolina. And profound gratitude to the DeNabone Foundation of Zurich, whose administrators have given timely and generous support to the project of reorganizing and publishing the James Malachai Greene Papers.

—RK

LET THE
DEAD
BURY THEIR
DEAD

W ELL, THEY TELL ME that that mound you asked me about was the center of town, a long long time ago. You know, this here town used to be called Tearshirt, they tell me, and before that Snatchit. Won't see that in none of them textbooks they give you up in that University. No. See, this here place started as what they call a runaway, or a maroon society. Heard of them, have you? Slaves, run off from their masters, built up little towns and villages in the swamps so as the white folks couldn't find them. Live as free men.[1] These lived over in what we call Tims Creek now.

---

[1] Not enough has yet been written about maroon activity in the southern states. But evidence indicates that the number of such groups is significantly greater than originally held. Long before the

Long time ago. Well, before the War, you know, the war twixt the States.

—Tain't no such a lie—

—Hush, woman. Was my granddaddy told me, now. You's calling him a lie?

—Yeah.

—Well, I hope he come to get you tonight and whup

Underground Railroad, groups of blacks stole away into heavily wooded areas, swampy sections, and mountainous regions to avoid pursuit. See Herbert Aptheker, *American Negro Slave Revolts* (New York, 1943) and his "Maroons Within the Present Limits of the United States," *Journal of Negro History*, XXIV (April 1939). Also Nicholas Halasz, *Rattlin' Chains: Slave Unrest and Revolt in the Antebellum South* (New York, 1966), and Raymond and Alice Bauer, "Day to Day Resistance to Slavery," *Journal of Negro History*, XXVII (October 1942). It is now believed that maroon activity throughout North Carolina was very high, especially in the swampy regions of the Southeast, though these communities were never able to sustain high populations and were often found out and eradicated. Of course in other parts of the world maroons met with greater success. Consider the maroons of Jamaica, who were so powerful under their leader Cudgo that the British had to dispatch two regiments to quell their terrorist attacks; or, for example, the fierce struggles of the maroons in Haiti, dating back to 1620. Led by one Macandal, an African-born leader, they ultimately forced the colonial government to give them recognition in 1784. See Anthony P. Newton, *The European Nations in the West Indies, 1493–1688* (New York, 1943), and J. Ragatz, *The Fall of the Planter Class in the British Caribbean* (New York, 1928), among others. Perhaps the most successful maroon societies were the *quilombos* of Brazil. The blacks of Palmares waged war with the Dutch and Portuguese for more than fifty years. In its heyday Palmares was populated with close to twenty thousand blacks. See Eugene D. Genovese, *Roll, Jordan, Roll* (New York, 1976), p. 590.

up on your head. Anyhow, that there mound[2] you ask
me about. Some say ain't no earthly explanation. Just
is. Some folk say it was an Indian burial ground.[3] Won't
nothing grow on it cause it's a cursed people in the soil.
Say they killed a whole tribe of folk and the medicine

---

[2] This geological formation, located six miles east of Tims
Creek, North Carolina, has baffled scientists for well over one
hundred years. It is an elliptical crater approximately sixty meters
long and forty meters wide. Samples to date show minerals present
to be: sulfur, sodium chloride, potassium chloride, and balsite salts.
The most widely held explanation concurs with the study conducted
by Patrick Guilfoyle, "Field Studies in Geological Anomalies in
Southeastern North Carolina," *Earth Studies Journal*, XIII (May
1970), in which he puts forth the theory of a meteor composed
mostly of potassium sulfate; these are highly unusual but documented to exist. Many geologists, however, rebut this theory, questioning inconsistent indentation data, absence of thermodynamic
evidence, and lack of corroborating astronomical data. Another theory, put forward by Joseph A. Cincotti in his essay "Natural Sulfur
Deposits on the North American Continent," *Geology Today*, X
(June 1979), concludes that the area may be a natural formation of
deposits dating back to the Mesozoic age, similar to sites noted in
China, Greenland, Argentina, and Patagonia. Other theories suggest
meteorological-electromagnetic shift, thermochemical imbalance,
environmental/industrial trophism, etc. See David Fasio, *North Carolina Geology* (University of Nebraska, 1957), and Torbijon Reivant,
Great Geological Mysteries of the Planet Earth (Stockholm, 1963).
[3] This alternate belief is corroborated in Terrence Brayboy's *Native Americans of the Southeast* (New York, 1977). In this tale the
Mahuwama tribe of Duplin and Onslow counties is decimated by
the Yomahjo of Robeson County. Both tribes, known to have existed in the early nineteenth century, have disappeared (circa 1830–
1860). No explanation of their extinction is known. Most theories
cite smallpox, influenza, or execution by whites. See Brayboy, *Written in the Air: A History of the True North Carolinians* (New York,
1989).

man damned em all. They died and just rotted there. Some say was a church burned down with some run-away slave girls, girls running away from prostitution in New Orleans, burned up in spite by white folk. Say the earth is still mourning.[4] But my granddaddy told me—and I heard the same story from a whole lot of different people been round here longer than I have, so I'm inclined to believe it—told me it had to do with that runaway town, you know. And if my recollection serves proper, it had a lot to do with a preacher-man. Least, that's what they tell me.

—Old man, who told you this lie? Ain't no such a thing. I—

—Woman, I'm telling this. You wont raised in these parts. I was. I—

—I didn't grow up that far from here. I heard them lies you telling this boy. Boy, you wasting your time listening to this old fool. He—

—Woman, will you let me tell my story. I be danged. I declare you's got more mouth on you than any one woman I ever known. The boy asked me, and I'm gone tell him like it was told to me.

—Well, tell it then. Ain't one bit of truth in it.

---

[4] The only known documented case is from M. F. K. Hall's *Stories of New Orleans: Oral Histories* (University of California, 1966), in which a group of black women escape from a Bourbon Street bordello to an unspecified northern state with the aid of a Harriet Tubman–like character. The emancipator is then lynched in a small town, leaving the women—armed with munitions stolen from the town arsenal—to take refuge in a church. The town lays siege upon the church, which is ultimately destroyed. See also Randall Kenan, "Please Release Me," *Go Curse Your God, Boy, and Die: Stories* (New York, 1996).

—Anyhow, boy. See, it all started one night. In a graveyard over where them Batts people is buried. There was a grave there, you know, of the man who founded Snatchit. Old slave name of Pharaoh.[5]

—No such man ever existed.

—Let me *talk*, woman. They say that preacher-man sent them men to the graveyard. Four men. See, the old slave had been buried with a book. The preacher said the book was dangerous. Said man wont ready for it yet, but with it *he* could bring prosperity. Said if the white man got his hands on it it'd be the end of time.[6]

—My Lord Jesus!

—You telling the story?

---

[5] According to some accounts, the slave is named Menes, first king of the First Kingdom of Egypt. Other accounts call him: Sultan, King, Prince, Emperor, Lord, Caliph, Massa, Hero, Alexander, Caesar, William, Henry, and Montezuma. See Reginald G. Kain's monograph *Tims Creek Chronicles* (Oxford, 1999), and Peter L. Helm, *Oral Histories of the Rural South* (Boston, 1976).

[6] Many accounts suggest the book may have been an Arabic version of the Koran; those versions favoring Pharaoh having been a Muslim captive from Western Africa. Other accounts suggest a book in Carthaginian stolen from the library at Timbuktu, a text dating back to Zoroastrianism and containing creation myths, as well as an account of the origin of the "albino race"; most reports favor a book of spells, the Book of Life, the Book of the Dead, a time-travel device, and other lexicons of supernatural capabilities. Perhaps most resonant with our thesis (see note 9) is the possibility of a transliteration from one of the traditional Yoruba *oral* libraries, somehow transcribed—which most Yoruba would have considered dangerous and well-nigh heretical—into a book for North American posterity, either in English or an approximation of the Yoruba tongue. The likely purpose of which is uncertain. Most of these variations are discussed in Sheila E. Anderson's *The Fabled Book of Menes* (North Carolina Wesleyan, 1980). See also Kain and Helm.

—No, I don't tell such bad lies.

—Well, hush then. Seems Pharaoh he would guard it in death. But that preacher-man said he knew of Pharaoh. Said he had pulled the wool over the people's eyes. Said that book was in fact a map to a place where some riches was buried and they should go get that book, find the hiding place, and share the wealth, see. Ah, but that night. Old Pharaoh wont the first to be buried there, but he had marked his grave a long time before cause he thought like that. Now it was a big graveyard, scores of graves. Pharaoh's was far over, at the very head, in a corner next to the woods. Now they tell me the men got there late in the day cause they had been putting it off and putting it off. Seems they had a town meeting and folk fussed and argued about what to do, but most believed in the preacher and wanted to follow what he said and be rich. But a few remembered old Pharaoh, who had just died the year before, remembered what he said would befall folk if they dared look in the book. But the preacher-man was living and they feared him more than they feared dead Pharaoh, so they finally sent them boys off. Figured wont nothing to it one way or the other. Don't know why they didn't just put it off till morning. Well, they commenced to dig. Now, I have this on good word, cause what happened next prompted all four men to leave from round here permanent, that very night. I even know their names: Jake McNiece, Tom Ravenel, Pompey Johnston, and Zaceus Stokes.[7] You know about Zaceus Stokes, he

---

[7] Zaceus John Stokes [1850(?)–1917] lived in Fayetteville, North Carolina, from approximately 1892 until his death. Records of his

come to live over by Fayetteville way, is where he went to. His granddaughter married Pierce Franklin over in Deep Bottom. You know her, don't you? Well, he told me this part. Word for word. Near bout.

—He sure enough didn't.

—I said he did. Quiet now, woman. Ole Jake McNiece and Pompey Johnston dug first. Switched after a spell with Zaceus and Tom. And they dug and they dug. Didn't figure it was gone take so long. Seemed they had buried old Pharaoh deeper than most folk. Said it got darker and darker. Zaceus said that Pompey Johnston feller was scared to death, trembling in his boots. Kept saying, We ain't ought to be doing this, remember what Pharaoh said? But they kept on. Had to light lanterns. You know, didn't have no flashlights in them days. Said hoot owls beginned to hoot. Said bats come out flapping after bugs and such. They went on a-digging. By and by, they come to something hard. They thumped it. Hollow. They brung the lanterns down, seeing as it was pitch black now. It was the box they made special for old Pharaoh, made of persimmon wood. Hard wood, they say, shiny black, made for a

---

birth could not be found other than an 1892 census which listed his birthplace as York County. No record of his recounting the Tims Creek tale exists, nor do witnesses confirm his ever having discussed it. In interviews with two of his surviving twelve children, no stories of his days in Tims Creek surface. However, all held he did state the place of his birth to be "round bout Tims Creek."—RK

coffin like stone.[8] Should we haul him up? Hell, no. Just
open it. So they did. And brother: there wont nothing
in there.

   —Now why you want to go telling these haint stories to this boy? He ain't asked you bout—

   —Woman, this is how what he asked me bout come
to be. If you ain't got a mind to listen, you just get off
this porch and go on bout your business.

---

   [8] The recurring image of persimmons and persimmon wood in
the many accounts of this tale has led us to search for some added
significance. The persimmon tree can be found from southern Florida as far north as Connecticut, and as far west as Iowa and Kansas.
Though it is generally thought to have been named by the Lanape,
who called it pasimena, it was also called medlar along the colonial
Hudson, pilorum by the explorer LeMoyne in Florida, and pessim-
mers by the explorer Strachey on the James River. It also has been
called date plum, eastern persimmon, plaquiminier, possumwood,
seed plum, simmon, winter plum, ougoufle (Louisiana), piakmine,
pessimon, pessemin, pitchamin, puchamine, and parsemana. The
plant, *Diospyros virginiana linnaeus*, belongs to the ebony family
(*Diospyros* meaning "fruit of Zeus"). The trees, growing from 50
feet to 130 feet, have simple, untoothed leaves from 4 to 6 inches
long and 2 to 3 inches wide. It generally has unisexual flowers,
greenish-yellow and cream-white; though sometimes trees produce
male and female flowers on the same tree. The bark is thick, dark
brown or dark grey, tinged with red, and divided into multiple
plates. The tree has a deep taproot but sends out long stolons or
underground runners from which other trees grow; these run so
deep, it is often difficult to eradicate them when they have overrun
an area of land. Considered one of the most adaptable of plants, it
has great success in treacherous terrain such as strip mines and bot-
tomlands where water may stand for months. Though it may take
over a century for a tree to fully mature, it is then one of the hardest
of woods, which once fashioned will retain its shape to perfection
and gain higher and higher gloss with use. Since the wood can
endure great stress and does not crack under high impact, it is often

—*Tsk.*

—Like I said, wont nothing there. No corpse, no bones, no clothes. No nothing. They looked at one another not saying one word, not knowing what to say. After a while Pompey say, Well, maybe we got the wrongen? Zaceus asked, Whichen could it be? This the firsten. And I spect I ought to know since I helped to dig it in the first place. Somebody else say: Yeah, that's ole Pharaoh's grave, all right, yep. It took em all a while, they was concentrating so on that empty hole. Then that same somebody said: What y'all a-looking for anyhow? That's when they all turned round. They say that Pompey feller was the first to caterwaul, Good Lord, Good

---

used in textile looms, where it can be put through one thousand hours of mechanical weaving. However, due to the narrowness of the wood (trees seldom reach more than a foot in diameter) and its long maturation period, and because it glues poorly, it is impractical for wide commercial use; but it is often used in heads of golf clubs, billiard cues, and parquet floors. The North American persimmon is related to *Diospyros melanoxylon roxb*, the ebony persimmon, best known in Africa, Asia, and Europe as the source of ebony as well as of edible fruit and cigarette wrappers (the leaves). The wood from this tree was accorded magical properties and used for the procuring of obedient servants, dowsing the underground water level, and breaking exceptionally hard stones. The wood of the date plum (*Diospyros edenum koenig*), used today most commonly in piano keys, was beloved by the kings of Persia, Ethiopia, and India ("They brought thee for a present horns of ivory and ebony"—Ezekiel 27). The Egyptians used it to make carvings of the gods and goddesses of Darkness, Night, and Sorrow. See Donald Culross Peattie, *The Natural History of Trees of Eastern and Central North America* (Boston, 1966), Arnold and Connie Krochmal, *A Guide to the Medicinal Plants of the United States* (New York, 1973), U. P. Hedrick, ed., *Sturtevant's Notes on Edible Plants* (1919; 1972), and James A. Duke, *Medicinal Plants of the Bible* (New York, London, 1983).

Lord, he said. He took to running toward the woods, but then musta had a change of mind bout the direction he was heading in and turned round and ran right smack-dab into a tree. Knocked hisself clean out. Say ole Tom Ravenel couldn't say a word, just stood there trembling, pissed in his pants he did, with Jake saying: Come on, Tom! Come on! But that boy just stood there staring, staring at Mose Pickett, who stood there big as life itself. The reason they was all so scared, you see, is that they had just buried ole Mose a week afore. Said he stood there chewing a piece of sagebrush, contemplating that grave. Yep, that there's Pharaoh's grave all right, yep, he said. Zaceus said he held his wits bout him, figured there had to be an explanation, couldn't be ole Mose. Zaceus held that lantern up to Mose's face and said: Nigger, you ain't who they think you is, is you? We buried Mose Pickett last week. Mose winked at him, Yep, you sure did. It was Mose all right. That's when Zaceus said he dropped the lantern and took to running. And the damn thing sploded and that put that Ravenel boy in a mind to get in the wind too. Course he ran directly into the grave. Lord, what a mess. Zaceus and Jake had to pull him out. And as they commenced to run, tripping over graves and such in the dark, they heard ole Pompey holler. Seems he'd fell in the grave too. So they had to run back and get him. Cept for ole Tom Ravenel, who was halfway to Charleston by then, squalling worsen a cat afire. As they was hauling that Johnston boy out the grave, say ole Mose say: Want some help, and moved to help em. And well, say that was all Jake and Zaceus could stand. Say they dropped poor old Pompey, left him there in the grave, and took

off hollering to beat the band. Zaceus say he ain't stop
till he reached Wilmington.
—Now you know he's lying, boy.
—Hush, now, woman.

---

*She, here, is old. How old? Ask her and she laughs, a
hearty headthrownback chuckle, you see her pyorrheic
gums, her few remaining teeth, she takes the question
seriously: Oh yes, you want to know. Well, I was born
in 1895. Now how old does that make me? You tell her.
That's right. That's right. She cocks her head, regards
you almost with awe, you've lived such a pitiable fraction
of her life, know so little in comparison. She says: Never
figured. Never reckoned. She uses a walker of aluminum
with rubber soles. She disdains the air conditioner her
children have bought for her. She loves to sit on her porch
and listen to the wind. She loves to talk. She loves fatback
rind, collards, and neckbones. And dried apples. She
knows what she loves. You wish you did. Faithfully she
goes to church. Regularly. When she can. Tries not to
miss prayer meetings. She testifies: I don't dot every i
nor cross every t, but those of you who know the word
of prayer, pray much for me. She speaks of prayer often,
of God, the Lord, in the same breath as of her children,
the weather, sickness. She's been sick. She coughed up
blood two nights ago but wouldn't tell a soul, so ornery
is she. Finally she had a spell of coughing, blood, couldn't
seem to catch her breath. They had to take her to the
hospital. The next day, from the bed she looks up at
you, her wig is gone so you see her hair is sparse, a
winter field, only a few grey stalks left. She narrows her*

eyes and asks: What you doing home? Ain't you in school? You say, It's Thanksgiving, and she says, So it is. So it is. You remember you saw your first snake in her garden when you were three. She was babysitting you. You were playing in the cabbage row, and she kept calling to you to come here, boy, come here, from where she picked beans, putting them in her apron. You got on your knees and saw a long pretty shiny stick and you touched it, soft, and it moved, undulated beneath your touch, and then the head presented itself in anger and you ran ran ran. You didn't even know what to call it when she asked you what the matter was. You just cried. She laughed and pulled you to her: Silly child. She dipped snuff in those days and you could smell the stale sweetly sharp smell of the ground dust. And when you stopped crying she said: Now get on up from here, I got work to do. There was always work to do. Work to do. Work to do. Wasn't there?

—See, Zaceus knew he had to get out of Tearshirt. Cause of what ole Pharaoh had said. He said he ought to known before but that that devil-eyed preacher convinced them all different. See, Zaceus had seen Pharaoh walking and talking on the earth, and he knew the man's word was good. Now he knew it was good even beyond the grave. Sure enough did. Story bout ole Pharaoh is this, Zaceus told me. Seems he was brung here direct from Africa. Nobody know for sure cause he didn't say much bout it, but he was some kind of chief or witch doctor or medicine man or wizard or something over there and knew a whole hell of a lot. Could work magic,

they say. Had a hoop in one ear. Scars on his face. Say
the owner had him down in Mississippi, some say South
Carolina, some say Virginia.⁹ Say they couldn't do a

---

⁹ There has been much speculation and discussion of the possible
origins of the slave here called Pharaoh, more often referred to as
Menes or Caesar. The most convincing account comes from the
narrative of one Jõao Ubaldo Piñon of the pirate ship *Hell's Bane*.
The pirate ship was discovered and overtaken in New Orleans Harbor on December 17, 1848, and seized by one Captain Loomis in a
revenue cutter of its buccaneer captain, Sebastien Berri, and twenty-
one others of Portuguese, French, Brazilian, and African national-
ities. The whites were eventually set free as the ship flew the flag
of the independent Republic of Texas, but as they were charged
with piracy all the goods were confiscated by the Louisiana government, including the blacks who were now deemed property of
the State. Piñon eventually returned to Brazil by way of England,
France, and Macao, where he ultimately became a Jesuit priest.
Studying at Universidad da São Paulo and Escuela de St. Juan in
Argentina, he became a theologian and naturalist, publishing several
books before his death, including the influential *Natural Life of Southeastern Brazil* (Barcelona, 1863). In his memoirs, *Life of a Repented
Heretic* (Buenos Aires, 1883), he speaks of his days on the *Hell's
Bane* in great detail. In particular he recounts an exceptional African
who claimed to have been a Yoruba king or *oba* and also a shaman
(*babalawo*), an unusual confluence of power as the two offices were
normally kept separate, and even more unusual as he was extraor-
dinarily young to have been appointed to either position by a council
of elders. Further, according to Piñon, the African claimed to have
been the Oni of Ife, which is the "first among equals" among the
Yoruba chieftains. There are a number of different orders within
the Yoruba religion, but from what his autobiography states the
oba would have been from the *Orishi* (God) cult of either the *Oro*
(a secret all-male society known for their fearful bullroar and whose
traditional job it was to execute evil witches and other wrongdoers);
Ogun (worshipers of the god of iron and war); or the *Oshugho* society
who worship *Onile*, "owner of the earth." (For further exposition
on the sects see J. O. Awolalu's *Yoruba Beliefs and Sacrificial Rites*
[London, 1979].) Apparently it was in a battle between his people

damn thing with him, he'd fight and they'd whip him and he'd fight somemore and they'd beat him somemore and he'd run away and they'd catch him after

---

and the King of Dahomey (now Benin), in retaliation for a raid ordered by the King, that the oba in question was taken prisoner and ultimately sold to Dutch traders. In fact, according to Piñon's recollections, the oba had been seriously wounded in repeated attempts to escape from his white captors on the ship *Jesus* (which is documented to have sailed from Whydah or Ouidah, West Africa, to Jamaica in 1842). The ship encountered unusually rough seas and took an extra month to reach the West Indies, losing half its cargo (144 slaves) and two-thirds of its crew. Upon arriving at Kingston, during a hurricane, the ship was struck by lightning and as a result wrecked aflame. In the confusion the oba, now miraculously recovered, and a number of other captives escaped. This is when the oba encountered the infamous Captain Berri who rescued him and six other Africans and made an offer of an indenture of two years in exchange for return to the African Coast. The oba accepted. Unfortunately the Louisiana government prevented that eventual return. According to government documents the confiscated slaves were auctioned off in Baton Rouge on February 1, 1849. One slave—with markings corroborating those documented by Piñon in his description of the oba—was sold to Hanz Madison of Louisiana and the Texan Republic. The theory that this account describes the same Pharaoh/Menes is further corroborated by Madison's records that the slave he bought at auction in Baton Rouge was one of enormous recalcitrance and intractability, with the markings of a tribal chieftain now believed to be that of a Yoruba Oni of Ife, and that he was later either sold or given (the record is unclear) to one Owen Alexander Cross of Crosstown, North Carolina, in 1854. (See notes 11 and 12.) Of course there are other accounts of the slave Menes having been Muslim, Masai, Ibo, Hausa, and Zulu; of his coming from Boston or New York or Charleston. And one account speaks of his having made his way west up through Mexico and northeast through Texas whereupon he was captured at the Louisiana border. But none of these stories is supported by the persuasive amount of documentary evidence that underlies the New Orleans account.

awhile and he'd run away again. Each time it took them
longer and longer to catch him, cause he was learning
the land. Once he got in with some Waccamaw, I believe
it was. Indians round here somewhere in North Carolina. He stayed with them a long spell, over a year, learnt
they language and everything. That's where he come to
know so much about the land and the woods and
swamps in these parts. But them Waccamaw was round
up one day, most of them kilt, rest of em sent west.[10]
And ole Pharaoh sent back to his master; but he'd learnt
something powerful from the Waccamaw medicine man
they tell me though. And the man what owned him said
he was tired of trying to mess with that hateful nigger
so he sold him first chance he got. And the folks what
got hold of him were the Crosses. You know all about
the Crosses now, I know. They was *the* family in North
Carolina in them days. Come here when it was just
Carolina, see, no North nor no South to it. Said the
Duke of something or other give them damn near all

---

[10] Though no evidence exists regarding a massacre of Waccamaw
Indians, there is an account of a 1849 skirmish outside Burgaw,
North Carolina, in which a renegade group of Shakori (or Schoc-
coree) were subdued after reports of raids, looting, and terrorist
activity. They were said to number 37. (See Brayboy.) There is a
report of one "Negro" taken into custody and returned to his owner
in Louisiana. The name of the owner is not given but the "Negro"
is described as having "a Number of Vertical Marks about the
Cheeks." Several scholars have noted the assistance given to fugitive
slaves by Native Americans, particularly during the Seminole Indian
Wars of Florida (1816–18 and 1835–42), in which large numbers of
runaways participated. See Aptheker and Kenneth W. Porter's
"Florida Slaves and Free Negros in the Seminole War, 1835–1842,"
Journal of Negro History, XXVIII (October 1973).

the Southeast.[11] Owen Cross had just been elected to
the United States Senate, and his wife, Rebecca, they
tell me, bought Pharaoh as his election present—

---

[11] In April of 1690 the Duke of York ceded to one Phineas A.
Cross [1655–1709] land in the Carolinas roughly between what is
now Wilmington and New Bern on the coast, and extending inland
almost to Fayetteville; a prodigiously large triangle which now com-
prises parts of New Hanover, Sampson, Bladen, Lenoir, and Pam-
lico counties, and all of what is now Duplin, Pender, and York
counties. The Crosses (the family has held since the eighteenth century that Phineas was an illegitimate son of the Duke of York,
though they are usually considered to be of Scotch–Irish origin)
settled the land, duly rejected the crown in 1777, and through wiles
and ingenuity managed to maintain approximately two thirds of
what they were originally granted, though it was no longer a con-
tinuous expanse of land. The Crosses operated three plantations on
this territory growing primarily cotton, peanuts, sorghum, tobacco,
and sugar cane; and also engaged in a variety of other agricultural
enterprises. They also invested early in the burgeoning textile mills
of the Piedmont region and had interests in a Boston shipping company and a munitions works in Maine. So prodigious were their
holdings that after the War they were able to lay claim to at least
50 percent of their original wealth. To this day the family remains
one of the wealthiest in the country. [In the annual *Forbes* magazine
"400 Wealthiest People" list (October 1999, Vol. 327, No. 1), the
Crosses of Durham and Edgartown, Massachusetts, were estimated
to be collectively worth $975,000,000.—RK] The town which
sprang up around the main plantation, called *Canaan*, became Crosstown (pop. 5,000, circa 1985), now the seat of York County. Owen
Cross [1801–1870], the great-great-great grandson of Phineas Alexander Cross, was elected to the North Carolina State Senate in 1854,
having served as a federal magistrate from 1842 to 1852. The family
at one time owned well over 150 slaves. See Philip Owen Cross,
The Crosses of North Carolina (Chapel Hill, 1970); Rebecca Sarah
Cross, *Bury Me Whole* (University of Louisiana, 1980); and Ayesha
and Nakia Brown, *Robber Barons of the South* (New York, 1979).
Also the Cross *Canaan* Archives in Crosstown, North Carolina, and
the Southern Historical Collection, Chapel Hill.

—That ain't what they say. They say Owen Cross won him fair and square in a card game. You gone tell the story, fool, tell it right. See, the story goes, Owen and this man were playing poker in Richmond. They say Owen was beating the socks off that man. Say the man had give Owen all his money, all the gold and jewelery he was wearing and the man didn't have nothing else to wager. So he had the slick idea to put up Pharaoh. And if he lost, least he'd be shed of him, and he lost.[12]

—That ain't how I heard it, but anyway they took him and they took and named him Pharaoh, that's where he come to get that name. See, they use to do things like that, take a slave and name him after a king—Caesar, Napoleon, something like that. Thought it was funny, some kind a joke. But this time the joke was on them. They say ole Pharaoh had some plot cooking in his head from day one. See, them Crosses ain't know nothing bout his history of skipping off cause the man what sold him wont bout to run off at the mouth bout his always getting aloose and being so ornery. So ole Pharaoh played the good slave, Tomming it up, you know. Had

---

[12] Research reveals that Hanz Madison [1805–1869] (see note 9) originally of Galveston, Texas, was known to have been an inveterate gambler, legendary for reputedly having made and lost *five* fortunes. Of the losses, one was due to bad weather resulting in the destruction of a major crop and exacerbated by poor management; one was due to war; and three were due to gambling debts. See William V. Madison, *The True Giants of Texas* (Austin, 1990). Philip Owen Cross and other sources at the Cross Archives confirm that his great-grandfather was given one male slave of unknown age and in remarkable health in November of 1854. The slave was re-named Menes by the Cross Family. See Cross.

him out in the field first, cause he was so big and strong
and black. And from the way he worked and behaved
you couldn't a believed this had been the same man.
Ah, but he was a man of powerful magic. And somehow
or nother he got closer and closer to the house. Gradual-
like, they tell me. Them light-skinned niggers resented
him, you know, cause a field nigger ain't got no business
doing light work in the yard, nor driving a wagon like
they had him doing after a spell. Seemed ole Senator
Cross took more and more of a liking to Pharaoh. Impressed by his knowledge of things. Soon enough he
brought him in the house. Now I don't know what kind
of hoodoo Pharaoh used on him, but he witched the
sucker good-fashioned, they tell me. Nobody could figure it, but nobody was going to say anything to a man
like Owen Cross. If he wanted that big ole nigger waiting on him, so be it. And after a while Owen made him
his Number One nigger. The house niggers made a little
fuss about it, wouldn't talk to Pharaoh and such, but
they had to do like he said. Say he got so much power
over Cross he could give orders to the white overseers,
which didn't sit too well with them, you can magine.
But you hear tell of such things every now and then. I
even hear tell they had some black overseers. You wont
read about it in your history books, and that's for damn
sure. Anyhow, Pharaoh was in a prime spot, playing
that game for years, keeping that juju on Owen Cross,
but all the time plotting and plotting behind his back.
See, Owen trusted that boy with his whole estate, and
it was a biggen, biggest in the state, they say. He'd send
Pharaoh here and yonder, to check on this in Fayetteville, this in Wilmington. Send messages and such. Buy

things. After a while Pharaoh knew the area well, knew it better than the white man, knew all about the ins and outs of things, which roads went where, which rivers flowed where. He bided his time, learnt and learnt. And one day, by and by, like the Angel of Death coming, he up and went. Say a big storm come up that night, worsen a hurricane, uprooting trees, blowing the roofs off barns, lifting cows outen pastures. Say ole Pharaoh himself conjured it up. Seems Pharaoh had been picking, figuring, who he could trust. Who he couldn't. Who was strong. Who was weak. Who would betray him. Who would help him. They say he was a good judge of a man or a woman. Could tell you more things just by looking at you than by listening to you. And they took and kilt as many overseers as they could get they hands on and old man Cross's oldest son Owen, junior, and set fire to that house and up and went. Gone like that storm, leaving death and destruction behind.[13] Apparently, Pharaoh'd spirited away guns and supplies to last em years. Had been doing it for a long time. They say ole Owen Cross was heartbroke at first, then when the mojo wore off he was mad as hell. They brung out the dogs, you know, they use to find runaways like that. But ole Pharaoh had voodooed them too: they fount trails all right, but they led em in bout fifteen different directions. Had everybody in the state, the country, from Maine to Mississippi, looking for that treacherous

---

[13] On March 12, 1856, a fire did devastate a large portion of Canaan Plantation during a large thunderstorm. Eighteen slaves escaped; and Owen's oldest son, Owen Alexander, Jr., and five overseers were slain. None of the slaves was ever found. See Cross.

nigger. They say ole Owen spent a fortune looking for the darky who made a fool out a him, especially being a Senator and all. Said if he caught him he'd beat him personal, cut his private parts off, stuff em up his rear end, hack his limbs off, and let him bleed to death. Ain't nobody betrayed him so deceitful, he said. Talk like a great big reward was offered up. Make a man rich if he caught him. Dead or alive. For a while there Pharaoh Cross was the most wanted man in America.[14] But he died that-a-way. Ole Senator Owen Cross went to his grave still looking and mad. And they never fount Pha-

---

[14] The following notice was posted all over the United States by the agency McPherson & Lloyd:

$1000 REWARD. RUNAWAY from the Subscriber at Crosstown, NC, on the 12th of March, a NEGRO Male, named MENES, African-born, about 35 to 40 Years of Age, about Six-Feet-One Inches High, Square made, Left Ear pierced with Silver Metal Ring, Queer Markings about Face. Everything he took not known, but known to have taken two Oznaburg Shirts, and Pair of Tow-line Loafers and EIGHTEEN Other SLAVES! ONE THOUSAND DOL-LARS will be given for taking him up, if in any County bordering North Carolina, FIVE HUNDRED DOLLARS if taken up out of the State, and secured or returned to Me, and all Reasonable Charges paid by McPherson & Lloyd, Ltd., 1 Pineapple Street, Fayetteville, NC.

Other rewards of lesser amounts ($100, $40, $4, $3, etc.) were offered for the other eighteen slaves (Southern Historical Collection, Chapel Hill, and Crosstown *Canaan* Archives). The slaves remaining on the plantation were apparently very roughly handled, whipped, beaten, cropped, and branded—in order to discover the whereabouts of the runaways whom they were accused of abetting; but to no avail. On at least nine separate occasions over the next seven years, *Canaan* and the other two Cross plantations, *Charybdis* and *Chinquapin*, were mysteriously raided, losing an additional total of thirty-eight slaves. See Cross.

raoh. Oh no. Said it was some of his people took part in them little wars they had down in Bladen and Columbus counties . . . when did they say it was? '56? '55? '57? Well, before the war, you know. Uprisings, blacks come out of nowhere, raiding, killing.[15] Talk like when they caught some of em they killed themselves rather than talk. See, it was Pharaoh's dream to build a great big army in them woods. Take the state maybe. Seem farfetched, but I reckon with his knowledge and magic and enough people and time he could have pulled it off. Good God, could you magine? I heard it was tried before. That's what Nat Turner done.[16] But who's to say? Ole Pharaoh was a tough customer all right. If anybody was to do it, he'd a been the one. He figured here, in

---

[15] A series of 1856 terrorist uprisings in Robeson and Bladen counties, North Carolina, is documented. Runaway slaves were said to have gone on "the warpath." See Aptheker and John Hope Franklin, *From Slavery to Freedom*, sixth edition (New York, 1947, 1988).

[16] The first known slave revolt of significant proportions was the aborted insurrection led by Gabriel Prosser outside Richmond, Virginia, on August 30, 1800. Over one thousand blacks began to storm the city, but they had been betrayed by two slaves. For a full and detailed account see Arna Bontemps's award-winning novel, *Black Thunder*. Throughout the South, from Virginia to Louisiana to Mississippi, insurgences flared from the early 1800s until the War. Most famous perhaps is the revolt headed by Nat Turner, the self-proclaimed New Moses, on August 21, 1831. William Styron's controversial Pulitzer Prize–winning novel, *Confessions of Nat Turner*, evocatively details that event. In 1822 Denmark Vesey attempted to overthrow Charleston in a tremendously well-planned revolt involving approximately nine thousand blacks. Some twenty-five hundred revolted in New Orleans in 1853, only to be betrayed beforehand by one free black. Most large-scale revolts planned in the Antebellum South were thwarted in similar ways. See Franklin and others.

Tims Creek, to be the last place they'd find em. Pretty near jungle then, thick, snakey, water high, land mostly flooded, you know. Wont no white man coming out here. Even the Indians had let it be. Pharaoh's people hunted and fished to live, couldn't clear no land nor drain none; had to be careful with fire. But they survived out in them swamps somehow or nother. Multiplied. Had youngens. Raided plantations. Slaves disappeared. Dry goods disappeared. Livestock disappeared. And they thrived out there in them swamps. Growing, just a-growing strong. But you know the peculiar thing is this: talk like they use to have big big funerals in Snatchit, strange rituals with animals and smoke and mess. They say ole Pharaoh would preside, talk in his African tongue, you know, where nobody could understand him. Say he'd have his book with him. There'd be a procession, folk had to do this and that, you know, when somebody died. See, he claimed, ole Pharaoh did, when the time was right, he'd call all of them back, you know, back from the other side to join em in the fight.

—Lord, man, now—

—Swhat they say, now. But you know the time never did come. The war did though. Then freedom. It was a time, they tell me. Ole Snatchit a town of freedmen, yes sir. Called it Tearshirt.[17] Don't ask me why. Maybe something Pharaoh thought up. Well, I figure he didn't have no idea no mancipation was a-coming. Took him off guard, to be sure. White men from up North come down trying to get colored folk

---

[17] There is no documentation of a town or community named Tearshirt in any state or federal files or records.—RK

to vote and such, send colored folk to Congress and such. You know back in them days you had black congressmen and senators from Mississippi and South Carolina. Lord knows what done happened to us today. Folk commenced to build. They got a post office.[18] Cleared land. Drained parts of the swamp, started farming, cotton, corn, and indigo. Raised livestock. But Pharaoh was still the head of the community, you know, still looked up to, if somebody got sick or had a problem, they'd come to Pharaoh and he'd work roots and such on em, keep em healthy, talk to em in groups and tell em to keep themselves ready, to look out for one another, not to be like the white man, reaching and grabbing and trying to own everything, even people. Told em to remember that they come from a great land and a great people and such-like. Wont preaching he done, more like learning, learning em to love themselves and the world round em. Said a time gone come when they'd all reclaim their glory. And the town kept a-growing. Slaves with nowhere else to go, who didn't get their forty acres and a mule, or couldn't get on as sharecroppers, come to Tearshirt, town built by colored in a swamp. And you know the white folk left them alone mostly, for that very reason. Figured they couldn't give two bits bout some niggers in them there marshes. Long as they didn't bother nobody. See, they'd had enough of fighting. Most of the menfolk dead anyhow. Shiloh. Chancellorsville. Gettysburg. Vicksburg. Oh they were lynchings and such, the Klan was big round here, but they didn't mess with them Tims Creek folk.

---

[18] No such post office is on record.—RK

Might a just been scared to it. Bout ten years later, they tell me, ole Pharaoh up and died. First day of the New Year. At dusk dark, they say. Nobody knew how old he was, some say a hundred and twenty-four. Ain't no telling. He'd left instructions about not looking in the book. Don't know where it come from, and they was all too scared to look at it. So they buried him and it and went on about they business. And bout a year later, the preacher come.

The following excerpts are from *Bury Me Whole: The Diaries of Rebecca Cross*, edited by A. M. Homes (University of Louisiana, 1980). Rebecca Sarah Cross *née* Fish was born in New York in 1805 to an old and prominent banking family. Through visits to relatives in Charleston, she met Owen Alexander Cross. They were married in 1825. She bore him three sons: Owen Alexander [b. 1824], Alexander Fish [b. 1826], and Phineas Owen [b. 1830]. The diaries, which she kept sporadically, cover roughly the years 1840–1880. She died on May 3, 1881.

NOVEMBER 20, 1854
Owen again came Home drunk tonight. He almost fell from His Sulky. He came in bragging to Alexander about having won a Slave in a poker game. I reproached Him saying that Drunkenness & Gambling were Unseemly in a Member of the State Legislature. He lighted another cigar & Said I did not understand a Man's Needs. I

enquired *if indeed a Man's Needs are so different in fact
from a Woman's & would he in fact Abide Me to stay
Drunk 365 days a year & keep company with Whore-
mongers & Gamble away My Inheritance & Smoke
Filthy Cigars. He laughed & called Me a Foolish Woman
& went on bragging to Alexander.*

    *The Slave he calls Menes after some Egyptian, says
Owen. He is Huge & Black & has a Hoop in one Ear
& has Frightening Scars about his Face of a most disturbing Nature. He looks at Me with great Contempt.
I do not much like Him and Hope Owen will keep Him
far from the House.*

    *Recieved [sic] letter from Phineas today. He is to
arrive from England in a fortnight. It is good his father
will be mostly in Ralegh [sic] as I do not wish to hear
them Quarrel so. I pray my Lord Jesus that poor Phineas
has found Himself & will take to work & sense even as
his good brothers.*

    Owen did not come to my bed tonight.

    All is well.

OCTOBER 31, 1855

*Phoebe came running to Me this morning after Break-
fast. She was Full of Consternation & Pepper. Of
all the Negroes I have Always liked Phoebe best. Much
Brighter of countenance & Better than Black Clementine
with Her Bossy attempts to order Me about in what
She terms "Her Kitchen". Phoebe's Eyes were Huge
with Her Perturbation. She said: "Massa say dat
Nigga is ta be ober all usen Niggas in de Big House.*

Dat So, Maam?" I said: "Whatever Senator Cross says
is the Law, Phoebe." "But Misress," She says, "He
Big an Black an Hateful an der aint no cause fuh such
ta be ober usens in de Big House. It rit quar. Aint spose
ta be lak dat." "Phoebe," I said to Her, "You shall do
as The Senator says." "Yassum," She said & trotted on
off.

    I feel for them all. Even Clementine who muttered
[under] Her Breath to Me, "I aint laks it, dat Black
Nigger taken ober de House. Is de Judge sho nuff crazy
or sumpen?" "Hush," I said to Her, "You are not to
Question nor is it Your Place to Like or Dis-Like what
Transpires in this House, & My Husband is to be referred
to as The Senator, Clementine, not Judge, he has moved
on from the Bench to a Higher Calling." "Yessem,"
She said to me, but She indeed shot me a look which
from the Configuration of Her Countenance might surely
have curdled Blood.

    He is a Frightfull one, this Menes is. He has no
Place in a Fine House like Canaan & certainly not as a
major domo to a State Senator. I have tried to Talk
Sense into Owen but He just Snarls & Barks at Me &
says it is not My Business & calls this Blackamoor a
Genius & goes on about Him in a most Unseemly Fash-
ion. If I did not know My Husband's long History of
more Conventional Fleshly Perversions & Shameful
Self-Indulgences I might think He has taken this
Menes into Horrible Abomination, but My Husband,
the Father of My Children, the Former Magistrate &
now Senator is a Whole Man & despite his at times Un-
Gentlemanly & UnSeemly Behavior & Indulgences of
the Flesh, I Know him to be Sound & Good & I Praise

*Christ Jesus that is so. But this Negro Menes. He Alarms
Me. He Smiles at Me now & Behaves as He should.
But I Fear, I Fear Greatly. He is the Devil Himself
& I Fear what Evil He Might Reign Upon My
House. I Pray the Lord Jesus God will preserve and
Keep us . . .*

*Phineas continues in his little Room to dawdle [with]
his little Plants. I know not how to Lift this Boy from
his Strange Fascination with "Biology", nor can I see a
Way to Mend his Way with his Father. They do not
Speak now. I Shall Pray also For Mending Between
Father and Son . . .*

FEBRUARY 3, 1855

*Heavens, It is so very Hard to Keep at Journal some
Days. I lapse & I lapse . . . Owen tried to Throw
Phineas from the House Yesterday. I Pled & Begged
unto Christ God Almighty that He not do this Foul
Deed. I have not ever seen Him in such Bitter Humor.
He said to Phineas: "Both Your other Brothers are Get-
ting Along in the World, a Fine Lawyer and a Good
Business-man, but You My Shameful Son do Nothing
but walk about the Land as would some Johnny
AppleSeed and sit in that Room Reading and Di-secting
Flowers. I sent you Overseas," Owen said, "thinking
maybe England would knock some Sense into that Fancy
Brain you possess, but NO! LOOK AT YOU! LOOK
AT YOU! I AM ASHAMED TO NAME YOU
AMONG MY KINSMEN LET ALONE MY
SON. I will NO LONGER UnderWrit [sic] your
so-called 'Botanical Research'. You are a twenty-
seven year old CHILD. OUT of my House and*

Fend for YOURSELF. You are now Pennyless [sic] as Far as I am Concerned. Cut OFF. OUT!" But I prevailed, Praise God, and put Him Off my Youngest. But for How Long? Dear Lord, How Long? . . .

    I dreamt last night. I dreamt that Menes had come into my room. Naked but for a white cloth about His Loins & Forced Himself upon me, but He did not Disturb My Virtue. He shackled me instead and Forced me to do labor as Phoebe & as Clem laughed! Upon waking I was in Such a State of FRIGHT. The next morning He walked about as usual, Smiling & Devilish. I Begged Owen to Take him to Ralegh [sic] & Leave Him There. But Owen just Laughs at Me & Calls me a Silly Woman. He Claims Menes is needed to Help Run Canaan and Chinquapin and Charybdis. I Fear that Negro. I Do.

MARCH 19, 1856

I come back to this Diary after Days of Sobbing & much Supplication & Prayer. But my Tears have now dried yet my Heart remains Broken & My Soul is in Chaos, so perhaps here I shall Find some Solace. My Son dead. My House Destroyed, & that DEVIL—God SAVE US ALL. I tried to Warn Owen & Now He Sees, he SEES. But Too Late. Would that He have Seen Earlier. & it is Strange for Owen seems like a Man Returned, as though He has Taken-Up being that Man He Had Been Two Years before that ACURSED [sic] Nigger set Foot on Canaan. WON HIM IN A POKER

GAME. *Indeed. Satan sent HIM & He is SATAN & [to] think all this Time My CHILDREN & GRANDCHILDREN, MY HUSBAND & I [were under] the Same Roof with the Devil HIMSELF. That HORRID night will it ever be Expunged from My Memory The Howls of Agony? & afterwards the BLOOD. O! The Un-Grateful Thief. The MUR-DERER. Owen has offered $1000 for Him and Vow[s] to Have Him most thoroughly tortured and put to DEATH [and] cause Misery to Befall the Other Un-Grateful Fools who Followed after Him. But it will not Bring Back my most Beloved son, My First-Born & Beautiful Son. O why did not that Killer take me instead? Did He Mean to Pierce My HEART & kill 2 by Killing 1? For I am surely Dead, Dead, Dead. How could God let the Devil come into My House and Slay My Most Wonderful Son? What in His Most Infinite Wisdom can HE hope to Achieve by such a Barbarous Act? My Devotion? Well HE has ERRED. For I Renounce Him Now. I renounce such a Barbarous, Wicked God who would let inferior Blacks wreak such Terror on Good WHITE CHRISTIAN PEOPLE. And my Son. MY POOR SON. I have Cursed God, now just Let Me Die.*

MAY 1, 1859
They have come again. In the Night. Damnation will they not let us BE. We Know it is Him, the DEVIL. Three Slaves, a Picanninny, a Negress and a Buck. Gone. A Horse. Gone. He has hit Chinquapin

and _Charybdis_ within the last three months. Years
later, & he _continues to re-visit_ us. To remind Me
of My _Losses_. Will He take My _Two Remaining_
Sons? . . .

SEPTEMBER 3, 1862
Letter from Owen. A Miracle that it Arrived. Trapped
still in Richmond. No word from Alexander. I _fear_ the
worst. The last We Heard My Son was in Mississippi.
I try to run this Place, but so many have _Run-Off_. The
Ingrates. After all we have _done for Them_. O how it
Stings. Clementine stays, but Phoebe, that _Hussy_, was
one of the First to Run. It is so Hard to run this Place.
& I can feel My Age Creeping Up upon me. 58 in four
days, and only Mad Phineas to Help me Celebrate. Per-
haps I will not. Not with a _War_ & My One Good Son
& My Husband _in Peril_. My Other Son a _Cowardous_
Fool locked away and Scribbling and cutting Plants and
so forth.
    No. I will Pray. Pray to a Fickle God to Rain down
Power & Glory on the Confederacy like HE did upon
Solomon's Army so that They might _Crush the Wicked_
in Blue and Send My Family HOME. O I Pray Send
My Family HOME. It is Hard to Believe I was once
a _Daughter_ of the Very North which threatens to Tear
My Family and My Soul Asunder . . .

JULY 4, 1880
So Damnably Hot. So Damnably Old. Phineas writes
me that He has a New Book coming off press in London.
Contemptible & Bloody Fool. Who on Earth _cares_ about

these <u>Genuses</u> & <u>Phylums</u> that He is Forever Scribbling About. Me, alone, [trying] desperately to Hold-onto what is left of this Family & Him off in <u>God-Knows-Where</u> searching for Some WEED which will not change a thing on this damnable Earth. May the Lord Reach into His <u>Frivolous</u> Brain 1 Day and Shrink it to Normal Size and <u>Deliver Him</u> from this UN-Seemly Madness before it is Too Late. There is yet Time for him to Salvage his LIFE.

Now I must visit Wilmington. So much Business to conduct. I am glad to be rid of <u>Chinquapin</u> & <u>Charybdis</u>, & glad that at <u>Canaan</u> the corn crops thrive & the tobacco crops yield well & Bountiful. After I sell the holdings in Updike & Sons Shipping Co, I can sign the Contract for the Interest in the New Mill in Kanaopolis. Owen, God Rest His SOUL, always said the Work was <u>not Fun nor Easy</u> & I always dis-Believed Him in secret. I know now He was not <u>Prevaricating.</u> I Know Now the Pressure & Especially keeping up this House. Clementine remains though she now <u>wants more Money</u>, & Alex's widow and the children will come within a fortnight & for good this time, & this House will once again be <u>Filled with a Family</u> & an Old Woman will finally See the Seeds of the FUTURE & Know that Her work has not been in VAIN. & I am old, God grant me Good Rest. My Joints ache & my Digestion is not Good. But I am <u>Sound and Whole.</u> I Thank God who has SEEN FIT to Preserve this Clan on the Face of the Earth. <u>AMEN</u> . . .

—He had light eyes, they say. Light-green. That's
what most everybody remembers bout him, the ones
what seen him: Light skin like a mulatto and light eyes
clear as colored water. Say he fix you with them eyes,
you don't know what to do. Can't resist em. Them
eyes. Say he dressed all the time in white, all the time,
pretty, light-skinned man, they say, handsome enough
to make the girls just go pitty-pat in they hearts and
menfolk to do all kinda out of the way favors. And he
could preach, they say, Lord could he preach. Make you
fear the earth was gone split right open that very moment and suck down the wicked. Make you fear for
your soul, and everlasting damnation. Good hellfire
man. Say he knew the Bible backward, forward, and
backward again. Toted a white leather hand-tooled one
bout with him, made special for him, he say. First thing
he done, you know, come into town in big open daylight, and saw a man they called Rastus Fussell, blind
as the day is long, say he had been caught peeking in
on his master's daughter, Rastus had, and they blinded
him. Preacher come walking into town they say, out of
nowhere, toting that Bible, and seen Rastus sitting on
the steps of the General Store (bout the only steps they
had in them days) and walked up to him and say: My
brother, my brother, Jesus loves you, and spat on the
ground, and reached down in the mud, you know, and
scooped a little bit of it up and went to put it on Rastus's
face. And they say some other folk was there doing they
trading, and it was Zaceus say: Now hold on there,
feller, what you aiming to do with that spitty-mud. But
the Preacher-man he just ignore em and smear that mud

on ole Rastus who commenced to make a fuss. Oh he
whooped and hollered and cussed, and after while turned
to cuss the Preacher-man and lo and behold: he could see.

—Didn't I read that story somewhere el—?

—Hush, woman, course that what the Lord done,
but that's what the Preacher done too. And Rastus fell
down on his knees, you know, bawling like a baby.
And that Preacher-man he say he'd been sent by the
Lord thy God, said he heard tell of a bunch of Negroes
living way out in the backwoods like animals wallowing
in they heathen ways and he'd been sent, Praise Jesus,
to deliver they Souls, to make thee worthy vessels for
the Lord thy God, who will smote thee with his left
hand and pull darkness over thee with his right and look
no more upon ye lest ye repent and serve him. Come
into the temple, my brothers and sisters, he said. Come
into the Kingdom of Everlasting Life.

—Sound like that jack-legged preacher over by
Maple Hill. You know, he done just such a thing, and
they found out the blind feller had been—

—Yeah, yeah, we know. Anyway they took him in
and built him a church directly. The first in Tearshirt.
He told them to build one without windows so they
could concentrate on the Word of God. See, Pharaoh
hadn't been too big on the white man's God, they say,
told the people to love themselves and all things would
follow, said God's in everything, everything, everywhere, in the trees, in dogs and cats and birds, even in
them. Well that a lie, the Preacher say, God is high above
and looking low, to believe otherwise, well, Preacher-
man say, that's the sure way to hell and damnation. So

they took him in, they fed him, they clothed him (folk say he had them make only white clothes for him, no impure raiments for the Servant of the Lord, he'd say). He started a schoolhouse in that church. Taught the youngens himself. Suffer the little children to come unto me, he'd say. Had big revival meetings. Fairs. He'd baptize people in the creek. Had services three times a week. All day on Sunday. People loved that man, drawn to him, you know. Them eyes. By and by, he had folk damn near worshiping him. Had folk kissing his ring and such. He'd take what he wanted, walk into the little store, and just pick out what he wanted, and say: So a man giveth to the Son, he also giveth to the Father; God Bless you, my Brother. It was like the town had a new Pharaoh, though thisen was a bit different than the lasten. Cause come to find out there was some rumors floating round bout him, but people who heard were too scared to say much bout it. Seems one girl, named Iphigenia, I believe—pretty thing they say, pretty as the sun in the morning, young, sweet—went crazy as a woodpecker all of a sudden. Fount her, they did, out in a pasture trying to make love to a tree, would come into folk's houses naked as a hog singing them nasty chain gang songs a lady ought not to be singing. Say she finally hung herself on a persimmon tree.[19] Then it happened

---

[19] The dietary and medicinal uses of the persimmon plant and fruit are legendary. The fruit, which is technically a multiseeded berry, is plum-like, spherical or oblong, surrounded at the base by a hard and enlarged calyx. At first green, then amber, next orange, it is not ripe until the skin is wrinkled and the fruit mushy within; if eaten earlier its astringency can be most unpleasant. (Captain John Smith: "If it be not ripe it will draw a man's mouth awrie with

to two more girls at the same time. Just as crazy. Then it happened to a young boy, pretty boy, comeliest boy in town, went plumb crazy, trying to bite dogs, walking into somebody's house and pissing in they bed, with them in it, having his way with hogs and goats. They had to kill him. Then it happened to a boy no more than seven, they say, went wild, turned into a devil, couldn't do nothing with him. Run off into the swamp, come putting water moccasins in people's baskets, shit in they food jars, coming up on people in the night with a knife. They finally found him in the creek, his head turned all

---

much torment.") Often it is said the fruit should not be eaten until after the first frost. Nonetheless, especially in colonial and antebellum America, the plant found wide food uses: the seeds boiled for a coffee substitute; the fruit made into syrup, pudding, dried as prunes, fermented into beer. Many Native American groups made breadloaves with persimmons. The Osages of Missouri made a bread called stanica, described as tasting like gingerbread, which they are said to have given to DeSoto (Peattie). It may have been used even more widely as medicine: the Catawba used it to cure thrush; the Cherokee drank a boiled concoction to cure bloody stools; and from 1880 to 1882 it was listed as an astringent by the *U.S. Pharmacopoeia*. Further medicinal uses include infusion of the green fruit to treat diarrhea, dysentery, and uterial hemorrhages. The Hindus considered the fruit beneficial in the cure of ulcers and uterine and vaginal disorders; they also used the burnt bark of the ebony persimmon to treat smallpox, and the seeds, leaves, etc., for heart palpitations, mental disorders, nervous breakdowns, urinary, blood, and skin disorders, dyspepsia, corneal ulcers, burns, epistaria, ophthatalmia, scabies, tubercular glands, wens, night blindness, etc. The plant can be also used to "stupefy fish" (Duke). See Peattie, Duke, Hedrick, Krochmal. Also Michael A. Weiner, *Earth Medicine—Earth Food: Plant Remedies, Drugs, and Natural Foods of the North American Indians* (New York, London, 1972, 1980); and Phineas Owen Cross, *American Trees* (Harvard, 1900).

the way round and naked. Then a horse went berserk.
Had to shoot it. A hog. Had to butcher it, but no one
would eat it. And the Preacher-man steady preaching:
These things is come upon us cause the Adversary is
afeared of losing you. Come hither, Beloved. Clutch
tightly unto the Breast of the Most High. He will give
you suckle. He will deliver you from the Terror that
flies by night and walks by day. But you see, the rumors
were that these folk had had sexual congress with the
Preacher-man. Said that his seed or whatever it was
carried madness, and he had forced himself on them
innocent youngens and animals and drove em mad.
Then one night a woman come running, screaming. She
seen the Preacher, she said, naked in the pasture, mount-
ing a cow. Some men ran to the pasture and didn't see
nary a thing. That woman died a few days later and the
Preacher-man preached that she'd been o'ertaken by the
Evil One, who come to spread lies about the Handser-
vant of the Lord. Beware, Beloved, he'd say to them,
Beware; the Prince of Lies comes in divers shapes and
forms, bent on the Destruction of your Souls. Oh the
people were something scared, and they drew closer to
him. This shiny, pretty, light-skinned man, talking bout
the End of Time and the Salvation of the Saints and the
hundred forty-four thousand, dressed in white with
them light-green eyes, hypnotizing they were. And all
the time he was giving them signs and symbols and they
scared to give up believing on him. Said in one sitting
one Christmas Eve, he ate two whole chickens, an entire
mess of greens, corn, cabbage, a whole hog, and a cake
and a pie. He'd eat and they'd just keep bringing, wide-

eyed and plumb put out by the sight of it. Say somebody
mumbled something bout gluttony and the Preacher just
looked at him, mouth full of ham, just looked at him,
and that man never said another mumbling word for
the rest of his life. Said the Preacher kept a black snake
in his room and a big black bird. One woman say she
heard the Preacher talking to the snake and the snake
talked back. She went deaf. They said he been seen
walking on the creek once, the black snake bout his
shoulders, the bird on his hand; said he been seen once
taking food from a bear, once walking on the ceiling of
the church.

—Now this don't make no kind of sense. Boy, you
can listen to these lies all you want to, but—

—*Anyhow*. One day he preached a sermon about
Pharaoh. See, folk had been mentioning Pharaoh since
the Preacher come to Tearshirt, and he'd snorted and
spat, they say, he said Pharaoh wont nothing but a charlatan, a thief, a heathen, a ole faker. Said he was evil.
Sent from the Devil himself. Why otherwise would he
take the name of the King who held the Lord's people
in bondage for years upon years? And in that sermon
he said he had a dream, and in that dream the Lord said:
Get ye hence to the grave of the charlatan, for with him
he hath buried the keys to a great treasure more bountiful
than that of the white men of the North; seek it and
give it to my people, for they are pleasing in my sight
and worthy of my love; these riches are the proof of my
love. That's when he give the order. That's when the
Horror was let aloose.

—Horror my left tit.

Phineas Owen Cross [1830–1921] is considered one of the most eminent botanists of his day. He published a number of important works on carnivorous plants and Darwinian principles of adaptation. He is best known for his influential *Dangerous Lilies: Carnivorous Plants of North America* and *Leaf and Land: A Meditation on the Natural History of Botanical America.* His letters were published in 1952 (*Letters of P. O. Cross*, Harvard), but many of them were excluded, presumably due to their revealing nature on the subject of his sexuality. To this day the Cross family prefers not to discuss the matter. But Professor Cross himself (who taught at Cambridge, Cornell, and Harvard) was indifferent to rumors and reports concerning his homosexuality. The following heretofore unpublished letter is among his papers now housed at the University of Texas, Austin.

> *Canaan,*
> *Crosstown, NC*
> *April 13, 1859*

Dear Nigel,

Your last letter sent me into paroxysms of blithe delight. How I miss you, my Siegfried of the Isis . . .

I have gotten the appointment to Cambridge! I received the letter from the Don of Kings College yesterday and could not wait to tell you . . .

I have made a most startling discovery. Something of the most alarming and amazing implications—which I must not, at risk of peril, share with any other than innocent and far-away you, as it would lead to much death and horror, including unto myself.

As you know, my family, already rich beyond good taste, has grown wealthier through the exploitation of the fine and fertile soil most abundant in this area, not yet thoroughly exhausted, like the soil beneath your kiss-awaiting feet on the merry old, and by the growing and harvesting of Nicotiana tabacum [tobacco], Zea mayes [corn], Gossypium [cotton], Saccharum officinarum [sug-arcane], etc., etc. To aid them in this avaricious accu-mulation of Mammon, they, as so many on this continent, and as for a time even in your benighted Kingdom, enlist the labor of Blacks. Enlist has the wrong connotations, I should say force or coerce, as they are slaves, most pitiable, dark, glorious, and bound. I weep for these poor souls, Nigel, I truly do, for they are treated as animals, worked even harder, and their humanity is denied them. My father at present "owns" more than one hundred.

I know all this, you say, angelic, angevin, anglican Nigel, why recount this Phiny? I can hear you now.— Why? Well, last Tuesday I went off into some exceed-ingly forbidding woodlands in search of Dionaea mus-cipula [Venus's-flytrap], that most amazing of God's insectivorous creations, beguiling, beautiful, most deadly. I went very deep indeed. You can imagine the breadth and width of the territory to which my father most Cae-sarianly lays claim. Thousands upon thousands of acres it would seem. I went as far as I could on horseback, down trails between pine and oak and sycamore and per-simmon and sassafras (many thicker than two girthy Fal-staffs), dismounted, and trudged deeper yet. Oh, you would have been so proud of me, Nigel. This land

becomes as a tropical rainforest in its density and nigh-
unpassable brush. I travelled farther from my house than
I had ever been before. On my journey I disturbed a
multitude of creatures less frightened of seeing a white
man in their paradisio than I of them: snakes, some
poisonous I fear, opossum aslumber, squirrel, fox,
raccoon—O the Glory of it! I cannot begin to tell you,
after all those years in overly civilized Oxfordshire and
High Street, how exalted these timbers appeared, the
fallen needles so brown beneath my feet, the canopy vault-
ing above, and beyond that the beatific North Carolina
heavens. Keats would have trouble transcribing it. I
surely cannot come near.

But what, my sweet, has this to do with slaves, my
loving Anglo-Saxon cousin asks? I imagine you reading
this now, it atop the open Times of yesterday, not quite
finished, next to a piece of toast with quince marmalade
besmeared, your blond tresses tousled as it is probably
morning, Irish Breakfast tea hot, but growing tepid at
your side. What? What? What indeed. For as I crept
deeper and the bush grew denser and my heart sank lower
for my having seen nothing remotely like Dionaea mus-
cipula, I finally came upon a murky tributary of a trib-
utary. The light shone down upon it and it teemed with
such life—such life, Nigel—toads, snapping turtles, an
unprecedented array of fish. I frightened a herd of deer;
a heron stalked in the shallows and upon seeing me leapt
high, its seraphic wings bearing it over the water with
such grace my breath left me, O the ease with which it
glided through the air; and the air itself, fragrant with
the essences of waterlily, verbena, wisteria, and the
healthy decomposition of the peat moss beneath my feet.

*And I decided this place must be truly blessed, and I
blessed for witnessing such untrammelled beauty. Like
Adam I proposed to name it, and I could find no name
more suited than Thames, like the mighty river which
begins in Scotland and flows through our blessed Oxford—I cannot bear the wait to see you. Thames, as you
well know, meaning in Greek for senses, and surely this
place was made by God to manifest the glory of the sight,
the taste, the touch, the feel, and the smell of His grand
wonder. I trod along the bank of this sluggish body and
at length I happened upon, of all things, a girl, a Negro
girl, standing on the bank, dressed in a frock of the most
beguiling colors, not unlike cloth taken from that great
continent from which her forebears were stolen away.*

*She looked upon me with indescribable fright, just as
the deer and heron had, and fled; but I pursued, exactly
why I do not know, perhaps to question, perhaps to set
her mind at ease. If Providence had not placed an above-
ground stolon at her feet I might never have made my
discovery, for she tripped, interrupting her flight, and I
was able to o'ertake her. How come you to the majestic
Thames? I asked her in mock Arthurian, helping her to
her feet, but holding her small and swarthy hands firmly.
Hgh? she inquired. I mischievously asked: I say, my
Ebony Lass, how come you to the splendid Thames,
are you not far from home? Thames? she asked, not
fully comprehending my nomenclature for the God-made
wonder. The Thames, I said, pointing toward the placid
water. I had crouched beside her, holding her still, to
point, and while down I heard soft footsteps. I turned
quickly and stood and there about me stood six Negro
males, all tall, fine, healthy specimens of incandescent*

manhood, rippling mahogany and able-limbed, but their grim visages inspired within me, in truth, not so much lust as fear. The young girl ran to an older man and I instantly recognized him: the notorious slave Menes, the very one, who, 3 years past, had murdered my own brother and five white overseers and disappeared from the face of the earth along with eighteen other slaves, despite my father's tyrannical call to arms and pursuit and embarrassingly substantial bounty. At this point we believed them all either dead or in Canada. But here, and still on Imperial Owen's Land! The wonder of it! He is the most awesome of Negroes I have ever beheld; I had always looked on him with more than a little fondness, having found him so bewitching, virile, and more than anything mysterious in that way that only Africans can be. He said to me: Phineas Cross. You would have done well not to enter this place.

So noble is he. But I dare say Rousseau had never envisioned such as he who stood before me and commanded of me as would have Hannibal himself. I replied: My father owns this land.

He said without changing his stony glare: Only God owns land.

Well, I quipped, my father sometimes thinks himself God. How did you come to be here? How have you survived in these harsh woodlands so long?

Obviously, the duress which the encounter should have invoked within me did not occur, for I, ever the scientist, brimmed with questions upon questions, so full of fascination was I. The loss of my brother, I might add, did not trouble me in the least, as he was rude, unkind, and a cruel and crude whoremongering adulterer, *and I shall not repent from that hard view. The deaths of the overseers, even more beastly and subhuman white trash, were perhaps even deserved. And the loss of my father's $10,000 worth of human merchandise in fact delighted me.*

He said to me: It is not for you to know.

But, I began—but he then silenced me. I mean to say, he silenced me, not he raised his hand to silence me or he interrupted me. No. He merely raised his hand as if to silence me and I could not say one solitary word. It was perhaps the single most horrifying experience I have yet undergone. Paralysis it was. And he said to me:

If you were any other man you would be dead now, Phineas Cross. But your kindness to me and to others of my people has not been forgotten.—(And I transcribe as best I can remember and I am at a loss to explain how he can speak such polished English, unlike the other Blacks, who speak a sort of patois or pidgen. But he came to us thus and I also know, though he disguised it well, that he could read, which, as you know in these former colonial states, is quite illegal; that is to say, it is illegal to teach a Black to read.)—So I will let you go. But—and the conjunction seemed to ring into the very heavens above the piney canopy—but, be forewarned: If you utter one word, one word about what you have seen this day, you shall die. You shall die before you speak the second word, and you shall die in great agony. Do you understand?

I found that I could nod. And I did. He turned, motioning to the others, and they were gone, the little girl as well. And I could move. Quite miraculous all and all. It took me hours to return to Canaan. *And I went* immediately to sleep, hoping to find it all a terrible dream, which it might in fact have been. But I doubt, deep within me, that it was a mere phantasm. It reeked of reality.

I write these words—such a monstrously long letter, my love—half afraid of the perhaps-spell—and of course as a scientist I don't believe in that witchcraft nonsense. But what held me in paralysis? Dearest one? This naturalist cannot tell you, I fear. Hypnosis? (I once heard Burton lecture on being hypnotized by a Turkish fakir once, all very scientific I now think.) This African "witchery" may yet do its dirty work. But not only are these words not spoken, but they are not aimed to reveal those blessed runaways; yet further I feel that Menes— what a demented imagination my wicked and Croesus-like father has, to have named a slave after the founder of the world's second oldest dynasty—in truth knows that I have no desire to set the hounds upon them. Perhaps that threat of death was a mere formality. Or perhaps if I ever were to utter the words, which I never will, about the Thames and that transcendent creek, I should surely die and live no more.

But I shall endeavor not to die outside your arms, most beloved of men. For within them I intend to die a thousandfold sweet, resurrecting, and luscious deaths.

O, Nigel! I miss your eyes, your mouth, your lanky legs, your firm ——, the ever so British way you laugh, the way you make fun of my Southern diphthong. We will be together again soon, beloved. And I can stop worrying about your being seduced by some Christ Church peer, or worse, some weepy-eyed Magdalen poetaster. You always did have an eye for the young ones. But now that I'm soon to return you will not have to

brave coming to this war-torn Hell and slouch about the
primitive South. Though I could see us among the <u>Pinus</u>
<u>n</u>. [pine trees] or the lustrous and luxuriant <u>Magnolia</u>
<u>grandiflora</u>, intoxicated by its perfume, buggering like
mad . . .

   But anon. Anon.
   In love and anticipation . . .
                              Phineas

—Hush now. Said they all got up. Every last one
of them what died and been buried in Tearshirt or
Snatchit going back to the first who died when Pharaoh
first brung em out of bondage. Some of em dead twenty,
fifteen years. Clawing out of they graves. Like Lazarus.
Said folk didn't know what in hell happened. Knock
come at the door, middle of the night, and there stand
your mama, your daddy, your grandbaby, saying: I
missed you. Good Lord Jesus, can you magine? Some
wanted to sit and catch up on what all happened since
they been dead. Some wanted to eat their favorite eats,
pies or hamhocks or chitlens or chicken or beets or corn
and got mad when the people said they didn't have none
or it was out of season. Some killed hogs and smeared
blood on the doorposts of their loved ones' houses and
whispered through the windows: Beware, the Evil Ones
approach. These was the good ones, and they walked
out into the creek and was never to be seen again. But
the wicked they stayed, and well, how do you stop a
dead man? They ran into the houses of people they hated
most and beat the shit out of them. One man who was
killed by another went into that man's house, got his

best knife, and cut him wide open, and started gutting him before the man died. Oh it was a mess. One man, who'd been betrayed by his best friend over a woman, stomped into his friend's bedroom with a white-hot brand and stuck it to the man's privates and then to the woman's. Some raped. Others just tore up houses. Set fires. Killed livestock. People running and screaming. Would run into somebody they knew to be dead, and faint. Animals bellowing. And wont nowhere safe cause there was more dead than there was living. Some of the faithful ran into the church and barred the door. But when they lighted some lanterns they saw the pulpit and altar just crawling alive with snakes. Bunches and bunches of them. And all them black adders lifted up their heads and blew all together and made such a fuss. Boy, you heard a blow adder blow before, ain't you? Scare the fool out of you. Can you magine a church full of them things going *Fhurisisssss*, real loud? Said the people in the church run to leave, but they'd hear the dead and the live fighting outside, and the dead folks appeared to be whaling the tar out a them living folks. They heard all kind a heads bust and limbs crack. Oh they tell me the cries were something pitiful, Let us in, Please, Help, Let us in, you know. But the poor folk in the church wont about to open them doors for no-body. Then a voice come up outside, saying, Peace be still, Peace be still. It was that Preacher, they say, they could tell his voice. Peace be still. Why have you sealed us out, my brothers? he said through the door. Why do you quake with fear? The Lord is everywhere. The Lord will not forsake you, my children, if you have faith. Yea, if your faith is the size of a mustard seed you can move mountains, my Lord said. Is your faith so puny you cannot stand with me and pray to be delivered from this plague? Have you forsaken me, brothers and sisters? Fear not the dead any longer. Open the doors, come out, and we will kneel in prayer together that this scourge shall pass away. And they did. They opened the door. But lo and behold: Wont nobody there.

—Don't nobody believe this lie, old man.

I must tell Jesus! I must tell Jesus! Jesus can help me, Jesus alone, so much talk of Jesus, old man, so much supplication and piety, so much . . . Down at the cross where my Savior died, Down where for cleansing from sin I cried. So like a mask. Do I truly know you? Did I ever? Can I ever? Peer through this righteous mask? See a human being, alone, without the Lord Jesus Christ Almighty to shield you? There is a fountain filled with blood, Drawn from Immanuel's veins . . . Singing, always singing, as I remember, not always, but often a hum at your throat, a verse at your lips, as though casting spells to hold demons at bay. What demons? Temptation? Lust? Anger? When I came to know you those days were long behind you. You were old when I was born; you'd buried more children than I'll ever have. Remember the time you like to scared me to death, coming up to the window at night and poking your false teeth out at me, making a face, and I peed in my pants and you thought that was the funniest thing in the world, still do probably, will probably even bring it up today. I've seen the lightning flash, And heard the thunder roll. I've felt sin's breakers dashing, Trying to conquer my soul . . . But beneath the leathern skin, the halting, ever halting, walk, who dwells in your house? You tell stories of your youth, but who were you at my age? Was your hope to run a farm, as you do, raise a family, as you did, to slip off into old age with your good mind, as you have? I'm pressing on the upward way, New heights I'm gaining every day; Still praying as I onward bound, 'Lord, plant my feet on higher ground.' And do you dream now of death? dread it? I remember when your wife died and you, ever stalwart, Face to face I shall behold him, Far beyond the starry sky, did not break down until the casket lowered, and then you said nothing, a few tears just slipped down your cheek, Face to face in all his glory, I shall see him by and by. And I feel I must become you, but I don't know how. How did you learn? You've taught me: How to drive a tractor. How to tell when tobacco is ripe. How to tell when it will rain or snow. But these things about living, about life, do they just come with time, or did your Jesus teach you? And without your God am I doomed? You were so sad when I said I was not going to church again. You said: Boy, what foolishness you talking? This something you learnt up at that school? I said: No, it's something I decided on my own. Oh, you did, did you? Figure you're smarter than the Almighty? . . . No, sir, I just don't believe. Don't Believe? Don't Believe? Shall we gather at the river, where bright angel feet have trod; with its crystal tide forever flowing by the throne of God? So will I never be like you since I have turned my back on your Redeemer?

—Talk like the sky was boiling black and the wind
was coming up big. They took the lanterns out. Nothing. They all come out, slow-like, looking this way and
that, not knowing what to think. They huddled together. What we gone do? they asked. Get the devil out
of here, one somebody said. So they turned to run. But
there he stood, the Preacher, in white, all them dead
folk standing behind him like a army. Welcome, he said.
And well, that was it. They was all round em, had em
surrounded, and they come in at them poor folk with
axes and hatchets and hammers and knives. And they
weren't alone neither. Tell me they had all sort a evil
creatures with em: wolves walking on they hind legs,
buzzards eating people alive, red demons with bats'
wings put bits in women's mouths and rode em, beating
em with a thunderbush branch—you know, the kind
with them thick thorns—raced em against one another
like horses till they died. The dead folk shot at people's
feet, made em dance till they could dance no more. The
church was set afire. The general store. Three or four
dead men would jump on a girl or a boy and have their
way till the poor child could take no more. They said
the Preacher-man held a baby in his arms, didn't know
what he planned to do with it, and that's when ole
Pharaoh come riding through.

—Riding? I thought he come walking out of the fire?
Or was it the sky?

—Well, *I* heard he come riding in on a great black
bull with a shiny gold ring through its nose, snorting
flames. Said he had a big sword in one hand and his
book in the other. Said he rode right up to that Preacher
and lopped off his head in one whack, grabbed the baby

up in his arms, and declared: Damnation and ruin. What began as good has ended in evil. We are not ready. They tell me he reared his bull up on its hind legs and the bull let out a bellow that stopped all that ruckus, and Pharaoh plowed off into the night with that baby in his arms and then, they say, fire rained down from the sky just like the Lord sent to the cities of Sodom and Gomorrah and none of the wicked escaped. Said it burned for days like a furnace and didn't spread. Just scorched. Smoke filled the heavens, they say. When it died down, wont nothing left. Nothing. Just that mound you asked about, smoking hot. Took a year to cool off. Say it goes all the way down to hell. But—

—'But'? There's more?

—Yes, there *is* more. There were two people left, you know. An old woman and a boy named Elihu McElwaine.[20] That's where this story come from. He was a boy escaped from Mississippi during the war, had made his way up this far. They hung together and started over again over here where we is today, what become

---

[20] Some accounts identify the woman as Hannah Davis *née* Kenan [1850?–1938], who was born in Tims Creek, according to census records. She lived there all her life. Of her thirteen children, only one was ever questioned regarding the Tims Creek Menes Legend, Ruth Davis Cross, who vehemently denied any knowledge of "such nonsense"; though a grandson, Lucius Stone [b. 1917], vaguely recalls Hannah Kenan mentioning "the man with the book" and "a great fire" and "being a survivor." See Kain, *Tims Creek Chronicles.* Elihu McElwaine [1830?–1923] came to Tims Creek from Natchez, Mississippi, in 1865. The last McElwaine of Tims Creek, Elihu (VI) [b. 1946], disappeared after allegedly killing a white man while studying at the University of North Carolina at Chapel Hill in 1963.—RK

Tims Creek. They say the woman named it such, not wanting to remember the town before. Say they clung together and made it alone, and after the woman died the boy, now a man, took him a wife, started a family, and the town grew, but this time for both the black and the white. See, ole Elihu had laid claim to some land the Crosses figured they owned; but it was Malcolm Terrell finally swindled both of em out of that land. And it was Elihu McElwaine who kilt Malcolm Terrell. And his son Percy kilt Elihu in revenge. But that's another story.[21]

—Good Lord, man, ain't you told this boy enough foolishness. And as for Elihu McElwaine surviving it. *Tsk.* Elihu McElwaine come here from Mississippi in 1870 *with* his wife and twins, a boy and a girl, the boy named Elihu and the gal named Tabitha, cause I was a

---

[21] The Chinquapin Plantation site was originally sold to one Aloysius Goodman by Rebecca Fish Cross in 1880. Goodman died shortly thereafter, leaving his wife to run the large farm, a sizable portion of which was maintained by black tenant farmers. In 1918 Malcolm Terrell [1856–1923] purchased all the remaining property from Mrs. Goodman for $75. (Most accounts suggest that Terrell resorted to threats, extortion, and slander, among other tools of "persuasion," after Mrs. Goodman repeatedly refused to sell to him.) Apparently, Elihu McElwaine denied Terrell ownership of the tract of land of which he was in possession and refused either to pay rent or to surrender a portion of his crop; Terrell sought court action and, after a protracted legal battle, won and seized the land. It is rumored that the ninety-three-year-old Elihu McElwaine, who records show did indeed have rightful title to the land, was responsible for the murder of Malcolm Terrell on March 12, 1923; but McElwaine was never convicted as he was found murdered the very next day. No one was ever convicted of the crime. See Kain, *Tims Creek Chronicles.*

little girl when they was living and I remember it. Come here with a lot of money don't nobody know where come from and he ain't tell nobody and ain't nobody fool enough to ask him, cause he was a mean negro if ever there lived one. Bought some swampy back land from ole Thomas Cross, who got it from the white Cross family back in the 1860s. Drained it, made it workable. Then, come the Depression, he had to sell it to Malcolm Terrell. And you know, good as I do, that it was the ole man Malcolm Terrell they say got Tims Creek started way back when. And boy, all I heard about that mound was that it may have been some kind of cemetery for the Indians that they fixed so nothing would grow on it, you know. But some say it got something to do with . . . what you call it, the geo-ology of the land there. You know, some scientists and such from Duke and Chapel Hill and State come round every now and then to take samples and what-not. I even heard it might a been a meteor struck there, you know. One of them shooting stars, they tell me. But it sure as the devil wont the Lord destroying devils and dead folk and such-like. And you know it yourself, you old fool.

—I don't know no such a lie. And don't be calling me no fool. All I know is what my granddaddy told me, and boy, that was like I told you, word for word, near bout. Near bout.